DARK SECRET

DARK SECRET

EDWARD M. LERNER

an imprint of

ARC MANOR

Rockville, Maryland

ISBN: 978-1-61242-322-7

www.PhoenixPick.com

**Great Science Fiction & Fantasy
Free Ebook Every Month**

Author's website
http://www.edwardmlerner.com

Published by Phoenix Pick
an imprint of Arc Manor
P. O. Box 10339
Rockville, MD 20849-0339
www.ArcManor.com

Contents

DARK

(Landing Day)

1

The wind howled.

Blake Westford crouched to the lee of the shuttle, struggling to maintain his grip on the not-yet-inflated shelter. Plastic sheeting billowed in the squall off the inland sea, and one by one the stones with which he had weighted the shelter's corners rolled or bounced away. Every gust threatened to tear the flapping fabric from his hands. If it blew away, they would be sleeping in the cockpit.

"Almost there," Rikki Westford shouted, her breather mask and the shriek of the wind muffling her words. The gale had stirred her long ponytail into one massive snarl. Two steel pegs had bent rather than penetrate the rock-hard ground. She was tying a guy rope to her third peg—and cursed as the wind once more whipped the rope from her hands. Finally, she got the line knotted. "That's one."

He grunted acknowledgment, saving his breath. Grit pelted him and skittered across the barren ground. Standing here, playing windbreak, had exhausted him, not that he had kept much wind off Rikki. His whole body ached. And flight-suit electrical heater be damned, he *felt* cold.

They had cut things close, landing late in the day when the temperature dropped and the winds tended to pick up. Not that anyone had any business yet speaking of tendencies here....

"Got another tied," his wife shouted.

The sun was half-vanished beneath the sea by the time they finished anchoring the shelter. The compressor kicked on with a welcome roar.

Although the inflated structure jiggled in the wind like a bowl of Jell-O, by nightfall they, their hiking gear, and supplies for three days were settled inside. A portable heater had warmed the enclosed space almost to coziness. Their exertions done, they were able to shed their breather masks and eat a simple dinner.

He sidled across the shelter floor to put an arm around Rikki. Her face was drawn, her hair still a tangled mess. "A good day's work," he said.

She snuggled closer. "A long day's work," she answered.

He was tired, too. Exhausted, in fact. But they had not been alone together since…it seemed forever. Not since Mars.

Perhaps she had the same thought. With her free hand, she flicked off the shelter's glow strip. Starlight and moonlight streamed through the clear fabric of the shelter—

And the moment passed.

The sort-of crescent overhead rivaled *the* Moon, but there could be no confusing the two satellites. This body was lumpy, potato-shaped, and not massive enough to have collapsed into a sphere. Only its close orbit made it seem large. A second body, looking almost as big, hung beside the first. A brilliant dot, brighter than Venus, was this world's third, outermost moon. Nothing—not the constellations, or the spill of the Milky Way, or the splotches of dark nebulae—was familiar.

Remembered skies served as standards of reference, if nothing else.

Rikki was trembling. He said, "We don't know that everyone is gone."

"Don't we?" she whispered. "Why else are we here?"

To which there was no answer. And so, beneath an alien sky, as the wind screeched and moaned, they huddled together in shared melancholy.

✸

A dusting of snow had fallen while they slept, but the morning sun quickly burned it off. The wind had faded. After a quick breakfast they began prepping for their hike.

"Oh-two," Rikki read off her checklist. She looked better for having slept.

"Two full tanks each," he said, peering into the open knapsacks. One should be more than ample.

"Masks."

"Ditto," he said.

The shelter would be here waiting for them when they came back down the hill that afternoon; everything else they would carry. Water bottles, ration packets, radio headsets, smart specs, batteries, first-aid kits, cleats and collapsible hiking poles, rope, flashlights and flares, hats and gloves, emergency thermal blankets, hammers and pitons, folding shovels, cameras, sample bottles…the list seemed endless. Rikki caught him shifting a part of her gear to his knapsack and took everything back. "I carry my own weight," she snapped.

Only, unlike Blake, she was Martian born and bred. Merely standing here, she carried *four* times her accustomed weight. And he could do nothing about that. He tipped his head back to kiss her. "Sorry," he said.

Knapsacks on their backs, in sturdy boots, flight-suit thermostats at the ready, headsets on, breather masks dangling by elastic straps on their chests, they exited the shelter. The breeze off the water smelled vaguely of mold, citrus, and salt. It wasn't offensive, just strange.

Apart from scattered dirty snowdrifts, the landscape was all sepias and charcoal grays. The sky had a somber green tinge, except near the horizon where a haze of dust contributed hints of pink. The sun glowered a sullen orange-red, and the barren landscape drank up that feeble excuse for illumination. There was a reason they called this world Dark.

Blake wondered if they could learn to call it home.

Tidal pools dotted the beach. Except for things like algae mats, spongy bits, and fronds like kelp, the pools appeared lifeless. He saw nothing more animal-like than the spongy bits. They collected samples, from pools and the slow, rolling combers alike. Even if the local biota weren't edible (and why would they be?), maybe synth vats could do something with them.

"Comm check?" Rikki asked.

"Sure." He tapped his headset. "Comm check, *Endeavour*. We're ready to head out."

"*Endeavour*," a gravelly voice answered. The mother ship hung nearby in orbit and Blake hardly noticed the delay. "You're…up early."

According to shipboard time, perhaps. Here the sun had already climbed above the ridge he and Rikki would be climbing. Though basic astronomy said this was local spring, snowpack sparkled along the crest.

"Lots to do," Rikki said. "How are you today, Antonio?"

"Fine."

"How's our day going to be?" Blake asked.

"Cold."

That much Blake already knew. "Can you give me something more to go on?"

"When I…can…you'll be *the* first…to know." (Antonio's speech was like that, all unnatural pauses, rhythms, and emphases—unless he got lost in his thoughts. When that happened, all anyone got from him was monosyllables.) "I don't…understand…*the* weather here… yet."

For matters unrelated to astrophysics, that was a speech. Unless you happened upon one of Antonio's hot buttons….

Back when they still knew where they were, Rikki had inadvertently set their shipmate talking about food. A monologue on cooking or favorite breakfasts, Blake could have handled. Maybe, even, a monologue on pancake preferences. But fifteen minutes on the virtues of different blueberry types *in* pancakes? That was a bit much, because they had no blueberries.

But except for Antonio, they would all be dead.

"Okay," Blake said. "If you spot anything, let us know."

"All right."

"Who else is awake?" Rikki asked hopefully.

"No…one."

"We should get going," Blake said. "We'll call in when we reach the cave."

"Fine," Antonio said.

"Shall we?" Blake asked Rikki. He tapped off his headset.

She shrugged to reposition her knapsack. "Sure."

Long shadows spilled across the desolate terrain. Along the rock-strewn shore, wavy bands of jade-green sludge marked recent storm and tidal surges. Last night's gale had torn fissures in the algae mats, or whatever the drifting sludge was, that half-covered the inland sea. Their shuttle, looking tiny, perched five meters beyond the highest of the high-water marks.

The topo map on his specs showed a blinking dot scarcely two klicks away. An easy enough hike—if their way wasn't all uphill. If the oxygen even here, near sea level, wasn't already marginal and the carbon-dioxide concentration almost toxic. If gravity wasn't forty percent beyond standard, and the temperature just above freezing, and the rocky incline everywhere slick with melting hoarfrost.

If the fate of—everything—did not burden every decision they made, every step they took.

"If it had been safe to land closer," Rikki said, "I know you would have." She patted his arm before slipping on her breather mask. Leaning forward, she started up the hill.

Two klicks, Blake kept telling himself as he followed, ready to catch her if she fell. Nothing to it.

A thirty-degree average upslope was quite doable—on Mars. Here they were panting after fifty meters. Angling back and forth, improvising switchbacks, he guessed their two kilometers would end up closer to…six. They detoured around boulders and mounds of dust-speckled snow. Twice he feigned interest in stony outcroppings, giving Rikki a rest while he chipped away with his rock hammer. As the day warmed, they stepped across more and more trickles of snow-melt, the water-slicked rock shimmering like fresh tar. They seldom spoke, saving their energy for the climb.

He wasn't a hiker or a climber, but none of them was. No one on *Endeavour* was a spelunker, either. Or a geologist, or a meteorologist, or a….

Quit whining, he told himself. Keep walking.

"How about we break for lunch?" Rikki wheezed.

They had at least an hour until local noon. She must be beat. Still, they were almost to the cave entrance. They had done a good morning's work.

"Sounds good," he told her.

His mask dangling about his neck, Blake chugged most of a bottle of water. When he forgot to breathe deeply, even just sitting, he felt lightheaded. By virtue of their climb, the already low atmospheric pressure would have dropped by about a tenth.

No longer fixated on where next to set down his boots, the terrain seemed bleaker than ever. The shuttle looked puny, and the shelter beside it *very* inviting. There was nothing like a tree or a shrub to be seen, not as much as a scraggly weed. Life on Dark had yet to make the great leap to dry land.

"Are you cold?" he asked.

"Freezing, at the moment," Rikki said. "I'm okay when we're moving."

"Yeah. Me, too."

He had his back to the wind, but his bare face already tingled from the cold. The higher altitude alone could explain the temperature drop, or the weather might be changing on them.

He tapped his headset. "*Endeavour*, I see a line of clouds bearing down on us from the west. A weather front?"

"Yes," Antonio said, the connection crackling with static.

Almost certainly the hiss was in the low-power link between Blake's headset and the shuttle, not the shuttle's radio link to orbit. They were at the limits of the headsets' range; Blake had expected to set down much nearer to the caves.

"Rain?" Rikki wondered.

"I don't know," Antonio said.

Where Blake had grown up, a sky like this was ominous. On Dark, a green sky might be the norm. "Can you make a guess?"

Antonio finally answered, "Snow flurries, based on Earth and… Mars weather models."

"What good are those here?" Blake asked. Rikki gave him a dirty look.

Antonio took no offense. "Those models are…all we have. In time…*we'll* adapt them."

Shading his eyes with a hand, Blake looked uphill. He and Rikki were not far below the shadowed cave entrance. "Keep an eye on things. Let us know if conditions get worse."

"Will do."

Rikki was already stowing the remains and wrappings of their lunches. "Best not dawdle."

"Right," he told her. "I don't like that sky, so only a quick look around today. If the caves show promise, we'll come back up."

He pretended not to notice her wince.

An uninterrupted thirty-minute climb delivered them, both panting, to the cave mouth. A warm, steady draft poured from the opening. He heard water trickling.

The orbital radar survey had revealed a system of caves beneath this ridge. Even a short distance underground, the temperature would be moderate. They would be safe inside from the elements, no matter the weather. They would have room to deploy *Endeavour*'s irreplaceable biological cargo. The nearby sea would supply their fusion reactors with deuterium. Used up close, the ship's anti-space-junk laser could carve out a landing zone near the cave mouth, perhaps even etch a road between the caves and the shore.

He would have liked a forest they could harvest for lumber, but that wasn't going to happen. Not for a *long* time. Never, unless they managed to start a forest from seeds, for which, first, they needed to turn rock into soil, for which first—

Big picture here, he lectured himself. This cave system could be the first step toward a viable colony.

"We've reached the cave mouth and are about to go inside," Blake radioed. "Keep watching the weather for us."

"Copy...that," he made out over the hiss.

"Let's see what we have," Rikki said.

Flashlight in hand, barely having to duck, she strode into the cave. Without ducking, Blake followed.

The beam of her flashlight, sweeping deep into the cave, paused on a rock formation. "I've never seen anything like this," she said. "Rock icicles?"

Mars had been geologically dead for *so* long. Did that world even have caves? "Those are called stalactites. They form from"—he needed a moment to retrieve an old memory—"calcium carbonate dissolved in dripping water."

"They're beautiful," she said.

He tried to send images to *Endeavour*, but his connection to the shuttle kept dropping. His voice link was unintelligible static.

The radar survey from orbit had suggested the entrance opened into a large space, and the echoes of their footsteps agreed. By flashlight beams alone, he couldn't prove it. He reached into a pocket of his flight suit.

"Flare," he warned Rikki. With a yank on the cord, the flare ignited. That quickly, his hopes died.

Rubble piles littered the chamber floor. Looking up, he saw where part of the roof had collapsed. Handing Rikki the flare, he focused his flashlight on the stump of a massive stalactite. Though wet with dripping water, the fracture surface looked flat. The break could not have happened very long ago. Certainly not geological time ago.

An inky something meandered along the cave floor. Stepping close, he saw the zigzag was a rift, not a shadow. When he removed a glove, the rim felt knife-edged and new.

"There's been a…seismic event." That he hadn't called it an earthquake had nothing to do with precision. In subjective time, at least, the loss was too fresh. "Not long ago, either. We can't live in these caves."

She sighed. "It would have been nice."

"Yeah. Well, there are other cave systems." Ignoring sore muscles, certain that Rikki ached more, he said, "We'd best start back down."

Lips pressed thin, she nodded.

Maybe it was just the contrast with the warm air underground, but Blake shivered as they returned to the surface. He retrieved hat and gloves from his knapsack, then radioed, "This cave is a nonstarter. We're on our way back to base camp."

"Walk fast," Antonio said. "The temperature is…dropping over… that inland sea. It could…snow…more than flurries."

"We weren't out of touch that long," Blake protested.

"Never…the less."

Blake could picture the shrug.

Dark was…Dark. No world like it had ever been imagined, much less modeled. And if, by fluke, an existing weather model somehow applied? Model predictions were no better than the information that fed them. They had no sensors on the ground, and scant hours of observational data from their few weather microsats. Sudden storms might be normal here. Or not.

"How bad?" Rikki asked. She had put on hat and gloves, too.

"I can't...tell."

"Let's get moving," Blake said. With luck they could break camp, pack everything onto the shuttle, and move on to the next landing zone before the cold front ran them over.

Halfway down the hill an icy blast struck, and Blake knew they weren't going to have that sort of luck.

The temperature plummeted. Wind howled. The snowfall, when it hit, changed in minutes from flurries to a blizzard, like the worst nor'easter he had ever seen. Beneath the snow, where the ground temperature remained above freezing, snowmelt made every footfall treacherous.

With rope and clips from his knapsack he linked Rikki and himself together. They got out their collapsible poles and cleats.

What they needed, and didn't have, was snowshoes.

First he caught a boot tip on something hidden by snow, falling to his hands and knees, almost pulling down Rikki. He got back to his feet, and three steps later her feet flew out from under her. She went splat, flat on her back, but the snow and the knapsack cushioned the blow and she got up unharmed. Every few paces one of them went down. But for wrist loops, the hiking poles would have been long gone.

The temperature kept dropping. His electric heater was on max, for all the good that did. The distant shelter sagged under the weight of the snowfall.

"W-wait," Rikki said, her teeth chattering. "B-blankets."

They wrapped themselves in emergency thermal blankets, as best they could and still keep moving.

He reached under his mask to tap his headset. "*Endeavour.*"

No response.

"*Endeavour,*" he tried again, louder.

Perhaps the crackle in his earpiece intensified for a second. More likely, that was wishful thinking.

"It's the storm. There's too much static for the headset link." Rikki leaned against him, her eyes wide. "We're in trouble here, aren't we?"

"Things could be worse," he said. "Let's keep going."

Two steps later, his feet flew out from under him. He crashed to the ground with the wind knocked out of him.

And started to toboggan downhill.

And felt a yank as the safety rope went taut.

And heard Rikki's gasp of shock and the *poof!* of snow as she fell.

Flapping arms and legs, he brought himself to a halt. Rikki tumbled into him; his mask flew off and he choked on snow. Together they slid another few meters before stopping. Coughing, laboring to breathe the thin air, the sky was dimmer than he remembered, or the snowfall thicker. Maybe both.

From uphill, louder and louder and louder, there came a rumble....

DOOMED

(About seventy years earlier)

2

A swarm of uniformed police met *Clermont* on the tarmac. "If you will come with us," one of the cops said. Her nametag read *Petty*. Over the whoosh of her breather mask, she sounded tense. "With the governor's compliments."

It did not strike Blake as a request, and he waited to see how Dana would play this. Captain's prerogative, and all that.

Dana McElwain brushed off the hand that had presumed to urge her forward. "What's this about, Officer?"

"I don't know, sir," Petty said. "You'll have to ask the governor."

"Who is waiting," another cop said, gesturing to the first parked cruiser in a long row.

Petty glared at the man.

"Are we under arrest?" Blake asked.

"No, sir," Petty answered, "but I was told that the matter is time sensitive."

That much Blake could guess from the urgent recall from the Belt and their diversion halfway around the world from *Clermont's* home spaceport. But the message Dana had shared with him, authenticated but short on details, came from the university. Why the cops?

He waited again for Dana's cue.

"All right," she said.

He joined Dana in the backseat of a police cruiser, while *Clermont's* lone passenger was directed to the next car in the row. With lightbars strobing and sirens wailing, both vehicles sped from the spaceport. Out the rear window, craning his neck, Blake glimpsed the other cruisers redeploying around *Clermont*. The cop cars looked tiny beside the ship.

Westbound toward the New Houston dome, bumps in the road twice sent them airborne. Cursing under her breath, Petty slowed down just a bit.

The sky, pink and all but cloudless, revealed nothing. Phobos in full phase hung low over the horizon.

With a soft trill the cruiser finished pressurizing, and Dana slipped off her breather. Mask straps had matted her hair, short and ash blond, to her head. Her eyes blazed, and even more than usual she reminded Blake of a coiled spring.

"Any thoughts?" she asked him.

They had speculated about the recall throughout the flight home, any distraction being welcome at two gees. All their conjecturing had accomplished nothing, but to judge from the uniforms left to guard *Clermont*, the ship was involved.

In every way but one *Clermont* was ordinary.

"Something to do with the DED," Blake decided, enunciating each letter of the acronym.

Ordinarily he pronounced it "dead," if only to pull Jumoke's chain, but she rode in the trailing cruiser. And inside a careening cop car, he wasn't about to call *anything* dead.

"My guess, too," Dana said. "What hasn't the good Dr. Boro shared with us?"

"I wish I knew." Blake got the datasheet from a pocket of his flight suit, half expecting Petty or her partner to commandeer the device, or that the cruiser would jam his comm link.

Neither happened.

Blake pulled up a news summary; the headlines looked commonplace enough. His message queue likewise had no insights to offer.

At home this would be the dark of night. He left Rikki a voice message that *Clermont* had landed, he'd be in the capital for a while, and he'd call her later. It wasn't as though he knew anything, so why wake—and worry—her?

He lingered over Rikki's holo. With delicate features on a perfect oval face, her eyes hazel and slightly slanted, she was exotically beautiful. Her gaze was poised and intelligent. Flowing black hair framed that gorgeous face. And that dazzling smile....

"Newlyweds." Dana rolled her eyes.

He laughed. If he wasn't supposed to still feel this way after four years, too bad. "More or less," he told Dana, before folding and pocketing the datasheet.

The red-and-pink plain gave way to startling splashes of blue, green, yellow, and orange: gengineered lichens patiently breaking stone into soil. Next came long, low greenhouses filled with crops of corn, wheat, and soy. Beyond a kidney-shaped lake, the wind roiling its surface, the road widened to two lanes each way. Traffic began to build, robotrucks from the farms and passenger vehicles alike hastily pulling off the road at the cruisers' approach. Blake began to distinguish individual buildings inside the Capital dome.

Half off the road, the two cruisers bounced past the orderly queue at the dome's main vehicular air lock. They sped straight for City Center with sirens wailing. Cars and trucks scattered at their charge.

With brakes squealing, they pulled up outside Crimson House, the governor's office and residence. "You're wanted inside," Petty said, throwing open her door. Without her breather, she had a sallow face with unfortunate bushy black eyebrows.

He and Dana got out. Two meters away, the second cop car was emptying.

"What the *hell* did you do, Boro?" Blake demanded.

The three from *Clermont* were all Earth expats, but Jumoke Boro was half Tutsi and stood as tall as many Martians. She had a Brit accent Blake found delightful.

Ordinarily.

"What do you mean?" Jumoke asked, looking bewildered.

Dana glowered. "Apart from the DED, *Clermont* is as mundane as ships come. If not the DED, why the sudden government interest in her?"

"I don't *know*," Jumoke said. "Look, this wasn't our first flight. I see no reason for the DED to interest anyone now."

Petty cleared her throat. "Come with me, please."

"I don't *know*," Jumoke repeated.

Petty led them up broad stairs to the Crimson House's public entrance, past the Security checkpoint, and down a long, noisy corridor. No one paid them any attention, not even after they went through a second checkpoint into the residence wing.

Maybe Jumoke *doesn't* know, Blake thought. If the DED were the cause of their summons, would they have been allowed to bicker about it in public?

At the end of the hallway, Petty shepherded them onto a restricted express elevator. The four of them filled the elevator car.

The elevator doors opened with a soft chime. "Come this way," Petty said, pointing.

"Look," Jumoke said, "I can't conceive of a dark-energy emergency, but suppose one is possible. We wouldn't have been summoned as we were, 'With maximum dispatch.' We would have been ordered home using the standard drive."

"Taking weeks to get home," she didn't bother to add.

Because while fusion drives could out-accelerate the dark-energy drive, that was true only for as long as the fuel and reaction mass lasted. The DED—when it worked—just kept pulling energy out of, well, Blake didn't know where.

As best he could judge, Jumoke didn't know that, either.

"Then why the government seizure of our ship?" Blake countered.

Jumoke shook her head.

Rounding a corner they came to a door marked PRIVATE. Petty knocked.

The man who opened the door was all but bald, with vulpine features, ice-blue eyes, and a trim salt-and-pepper goatee. It was a face you wouldn't forget even if its owner weren't so often in the news: one of the planetary governor's most senior advisers, and her liaison to the Civil Defense Authority.

Blake did his best to ignore politics and doubly so politicians, but having grown up in Massachusetts, Hawthorne wasn't a name Blake could forget. This was Neil Hawthorne, not Nathaniel, but that was close enough.

"Dr. Boro, the governor is eager to speak with you," Hawthorne said. "Please come in."

Huh? "Aren't we all wanted?" Blake asked.

"Officer?" Hawthorne said.

Petty motioned toward a sofa along the corridor wall. "Why don't you two wait here?"

Once again, her words did not strike Blake as a request.

3

Dana McElwain sat tall at her end of the sofa, tuning out Blake's fidgeting, weighing the possibilities. She didn't like mysteries, and she *really* disliked deceit, but an important part of leadership was thinking before speaking.

Across the hallway, long, slow combers rolled up a digital beach and ran out again. Scraps of seaweed swirled in tidal pools. A crab scuttled across the wet sand. Seagulls soared in the virtual sky. The susurrus of the waves and the faint cries of the birds masked whatever Jumoke and the others discussed in the private office.

"Jumoke is involved," Dana finally admitted, "at least in what she chose not to tell us."

"Then this *is* about the DED."

"It's hard to see things any other way," Dana said, "but there must be more to it. If our recall were only about Jumoke or the DED, why bring in the two of us? We fly the ship, we don't own it."

Blake had no answer for that.

He had a square face, all planes and angles, more wholesome than handsome. His sandy hair stood up in fashionable spikes; his eyes, blue and deep-set, sat beneath wispy blond eyebrows. He went in and out of wearing a pencil-thin mustache, just as wispy. This month the fuzz was out.

Blake could be charming, and with Dana he usually was. He could also have a temper. Just then he looked ready to deck someone.

"Whatever the reason for our summons," Dana cautioned him, "hear them out."

At last, the anonymous door opened. "Captain McElwain," Hawthorne said. "If you would please join us."

Blake had the good sense to keep quiet.

"And Mr. Westford...?" Dana hinted.

"Will wait here," Hawthorne completed.

She brushed past Hawthorne, prepared to demand answers and, perhaps, an apology.

Until Jumoke's deer-in-the-headlights expression stopped Dana cold.

✳

Dana paused in the doorway, taking in the scene.

The utilitarian office held a massive oaken desk faced by a shallow arc of padded armchairs. Behind the desk, a floor-to-ceiling clear wall overlooked the city. Sheer white curtains softened the view. Three sides of the room were data walls, all dark.

A silver-haired woman, native-Martian lanky, dressed in a tailored black suit, sat at the desk: Governor Luella Dennison. The governor came across as flinty in person as on the net, but something unexpected peeked out from behind her eyes. Grim determination.

To do what? Dana wondered.

Jumoke, in the leftmost chair of the arc, had turned toward the door. She managed a nod of greeting.

A man sat beside Jumoke, studying the floor, and Dana recognized him, too. He was short, even by her Earth standards, and stocky, with dark, curly hair, a strong jaw, apple cheeks, and a jagged scar across his chin. Apart from his Mediterranean complexion, he could have passed for a leprechaun.

Dr. Antonio Valenti had flown on *Clermont*, maybe four outings earlier, deploying probes for some kind of distributed, deep-space observatory. Dana had learned in one try never to call him Tony. It had been a long flight, in more ways than one. On topics other than gravitational waves, condiments, extinction patterns of marine invertebrates, Paris subway schedules (why Paris, she had no idea), and nineteenth-century Pacific island commemorative stamps, Antonio was a clam.

It had been a two-for-the-price-of-one excursion, combining deployment of the Einstein Gravitational Wave Observatory for Antonio with another long-range test flight of the DED. So: Jumoke had been aboard, too. Not a coincidence, Dana guessed.

"If you'll take a seat, Captain McElwain," the governor said.

Dana sat next to Antonio. She tried to catch his eye, hoping for some hint there about the purpose of this gathering, but his gaze kept sliding away from her.

Hawthorne closed the door before settling into the chair at the opposite end of the arc. He retrieved a folded datasheet from a corner of the governor's desk.

"Captain, thank you for coming."

"Yes, Governor." The words had almost come out *Yes, sir*: old habits coming to the fore.

Dennison glanced down at her desktop. "Please confirm that I have this right. Born into a military family, 2093, in London. Twenty-five years in the UW military as a pilot, mustered out with the rank of commander. Several commendations for meritorious service and bravery."

"Space Guard," Dana clarified. Dad had raised her on heroic tales of the evac after the Tycho City dome collapse. Absent an interplanetary conflict, the Space Guard operated apart from the United Worlds armed forces. "Customs enforcement. Asteroid tagging and deflection. Mainly I flew search and rescue."

"Most notably, rescuing fifteen survivors from the cruise ship *Logan*."

From what had remained of the *Logan*. Dana still sometimes bolted awake in a cold sweat, trembling with the memories of threading a path through the debris field, of the flotsam—and vacuum-bloated corpses—caroming off her hull, of matching course with the tumbling, wobbling stub of a ship left after the drive explosion.

She had worse nightmares of the derelicts she hadn't gotten to in time.

"Yes, Governor," Dana said.

"You emigrated to Mars in 2140. Why?"

"No profound reason, just good opportunities here." And after so many years off Earth, no way did she want to retire to *that* gravity.

"For the twelve years since relocating here you've done lots of work as a pilot. For the past seven years, you've been a test pilot for Percival Lowell University."

Clermont was a typical inner-system runabout, suitable only for short-range jaunts, and that's what the university bought her for. The university operated field stations around the world, most often under contract to the Terraforming Authority, facilities to and from which she and Blake carried supplies and people. They also provisioned bases on Phobos and Deimos and, now and again, outposts in the Inner Belt.

Basically, *Clermont* was a delivery truck.

When the Astronautical Engineering Department requisitioned a ship on which to test fusion-drive enhancements, some green-eye-shade type in the provost's office determined that a ship the university already owned averaged only three days a week in use. Why buy a ship for occasional engine trials, when another ship more often than not sat idle?

Five flights later, it was the DED that came up for trial. And from that series of tests, without a clue why, Dana found herself *here*.

"Close enough," she said.

"Has anyone ever had to rescue you?" the governor asked.

"No, Governor. Nothing has ever come up that my engineer couldn't fix. He's good."

"Hawthorne, what do you think?" the governor asked.

"I'm sold," he said. "But as for Westford…"

Dana squared her shoulders. "Do you have a problem with my colleague?"

"Something of a Don Juan, don't you think?" Hawthorne said. "A bit immature?"

Shipmates, especially aboard a vessel as small as *Clermont*, don't keep secrets. Dana knew all about Blake's shipboard affairs and the girl on every world, but those days were past.

To Dana's way of thinking, her friend had met the right woman and grown up. By the time Rikki's ship had landed on Mars, she a passenger in steerage returning home from a graduate program on the Moon, the two were engaged. He had quit his job for the cruise line, filed to immigrate, and taken a position with Dana, set for happily ever after.

Nothing about this situation had the feel of happily ever after.

Dana had kept her tone neutral. Now she put an edge in her voice. "Even if that were true, how is that relevant?"

Governor and adviser exchanged a look. "Perhaps it's not," Dennison said. "Neil, bring in Westford."

Blake started at seeing Antonio, but sat beside Dana without commenting.

"I appreciate your patience, Mr. Westford," Dennison said. "If you wouldn't mind reviewing a few details for me?"

"If I can," Blake said.

"Born in Boston, 2120. Spacecraft engineer by training. Five years as ship's engineer aboard commercial space liners, servicing—"

"Is this a job interview?" Blake interrupted. "Respectfully, what's this about?"

"It's about deciding whether to tell you what this is about," Hawthorne shot back.

"If *everyone* will be patient just a little longer," Dennison said. "Commercial flights among Earth, Earth's moon, the L4 and L5 habitats, and Mars. Certified to maintain life-support systems and fusion drives. Promoted to senior engineer in 2145. Demoted 'for a poor attitude' within the year. Reinstated in 2147 just in time to resign."

"And we're done here." Blake stood.

Dana almost went with him. Instead, wondering if it was curiosity or deference to authority that held her, she ordered, "Hear them out."

"Do you trust this man, Captain?" Dennison asked.

"With my life," Dana said. "Every time we launch."

"Then he'll do," Hawthorne said.

"Gee, thanks," Blake said.

"I respect the captain's opinion," the governor said. "Sit, Mr. Westford."

He sat.

"If you hadn't guessed," the governor said, "what you're about to hear is classified. You can't discuss this with *anyone*. Not with your loved ones or your closest friend. Not with your doctor, psychiatrist, or priest. Not with your goddamned cat. Am I clear?"

"Yes," Dana said, experiencing Space Guard déjà vu. The longer superior officers put off the bad news, the iffier the mission would be.

This mission would be *bad*.

"Understood," Blake said.

"Dr. Valenti?" the governor prompted. "Will you bring everyone up to date?"

Antonio had shrunken in on himself. He mumbled something Dana couldn't make out.

"A bit louder," the governor encouraged.

"I can't," Antonio said, barely above a whisper, fingering the scar on his chin. "Not…again. I'm…*tired*."

Dennison sighed. "I know how you feel."

"An imminent GRB," Jumoke said. Her face had gone slack, and her shoulders slumped. "*That's* what Antonio found, after he deployed his new observatory. I swear, I first heard about it today."

Blake translated. "Gamma-ray burst. Cousin to a supernova."

(He had once told Dana that the cruise line insisted its officers chat up the passengers, even the quiet ones. And laughed: most shipboard hook-ups began that way. The schmoozing must have become habit, because she'd seen him chatting up Antonio on their flight. She guessed the two had talked astronomy.)

"But the sky is full of GRB's," Blake went on, turning toward Antonio. "Astronomers see them across billions of light-years. That's what you said when we deployed your probes. Is this particular GRB somehow special?"

Antonio's head bobbed jerkily.

"Christ, yes," Jumoke said.

"If I may summarize, Governor?" Hawthorne said. "I've done research since Dr. Valenti first came to us. He can correct me if I misspeak."

Dennison nodded.

"Picture it," Hawthorne said. "As though someone threw a celestial switch, a star blazes in the sky. It's too bright to look at directly. Even at high noon, if that's when this happens, the star casts its own crisp shadows. But the light fades after only a minute or two.

"As intense as that visible light was, what you couldn't see was fiercer. The atmosphere blocked the event's gammas and X-rays—and in the process emitted an electromagnetic pulse that fried every computer, electric motor, power grid, and satellite on that side of the world. Only the collapse of civilization is the least of your worries."

As Antonio rocked in his chair and Jumoke slumped in hers, as the governor, grim-faced, watched Blake and Dana, Dana understood that—somehow—this was the future foretold.

Hawthorne had not finished. "Hours later, moving at a hair under the speed of light, the deluge of subatomic particles hits. Think cosmic rays, though by comparison the hardest cosmic rays are a gentle rain shower. As the particle storm slams into the atmosphere, it throws off cascades of many more subatomic particles—"

"Muons," Antonio interjected.

"Muons," Hawthorne acknowledged. "Billions per square centimeter. Many times the lethal dose, down to two kilometers deep in the oceans, down to a kilometer deep in solid rock. Everyone on that side of the world soon dies."

Two kilometers deep? Only one world had such oceans. Horror and relief—and shame at her relief—washed over Dana. "You're saying the GRB will strike Earth. *Not* Mars."

"Both," Jumoke said hopelessly. "More. It'll blanket the solar system."

Blake broke a lengthening silence. "You said a minute or two. That leaves half of each world untouched. What about people, animals, all life on that hemisphere?"

"Ordo...*vic*ian," Antonio intoned, his face expressionless. "They're dead. Everyone is dead. Every*thing* is dead, only...more slowly."

Dana couldn't not ask. "How?"

Hawthorne finger-swiped his datasheet several times, skimming. "From the ozone layer half-blasted away. The solar UV pouring through has become withering, lethal. Much of the oxygen from dissociated ozone recombines with atmospheric nitrogen. I'm hazy on the chemistry, but it means extreme acid rain, with widespread slaughter at the bottom of the food chain."

"And also a haze of...reddish-brown nitrogen...dioxide reflecting the sunlight. It starts an...ice age."

Blake shivered. "What's this Ordovician thing?"

"The Ordovician Extinction." Antonio straightened in his seat, stroking his scar faster than ever. His voice strengthened, taking on the tone of a lecture. "Four hundred fifty…million years ago. Before anything lived…*on* land. The second largest extinction ever…of marine life. Animals not native to the…ocean depths soon…died off." His voice faded and cracked. "Paleo…climatologists…have reasons to *be*lieve…a gamma-ray burst did that."

"When?" Blake asked. "When will it happen?"

"It *has* happened," Antonio said. "More than seven thousand… years ago. In three…years at most…the blast…hits us."

At Dana's side, Blake trembled. He said, "Respectfully, Governor, people should be told. They deserve the opportunity to make peace with what's coming, to spend time with their loved ones. Why fritter away their last days in meaningless toil? Why bring babies into the world only to die before they've had the opportunity to live?"

"Meaningless toil?" the governor said. "That attitude, Mr. Westford, is why you *will* keep quiet. Why everyone in the know *must* keep quiet. The universe has declared war on humanity, and war demands secrecy and sacrifice.

"Without a functioning economy, we have no options. Let the people suspect that the end is near, that we're all about to die, and society *will* implode, whether from neglect, looting, or panic. On this world, and the Moon, and countless asteroids, everyone will die for the lack of oh-two or food or water long before the GRB strikes."

Was ignorance bliss? Or was withholding the truth immoral? Dana didn't know, couldn't guess, could not begin to confront the questions. She couldn't get past the death of everything and everyone she knew, written in the stars.

It was too much, too fast. Her thoughts skittered. Her head spun.

But what was that about options?

Dana asked, "Where are you sending us, Governor? What is our mission?"

4

The only conceivable "mission" was spending time with loved ones before the end. And digging very deep holes, for all the good that would do. Mission? Blake saw nowhere *to* go. Dana was in denial, hoping that duty could fill her remaining time.

They'd see about *that*. Dana was family, too, damn it.

In a fog, Blake heard Governor Dennison answer. Her words took a moment to register.

"Scouting the way to a new home."

Some deep recess of his mind latched onto the governor's words. Now *you're* in denial, Blake told himself, even as the dispassionate, problem-solving facet of him stirred.

Dennison continued, "To survive, humanity must send out starships. Colony ships. *Clermont* will lead the way."

Because with its DED, *Clermont* wasn't limited in its range by the fuel it could carry. It could, in theory, accelerate till it reached relativistic speeds, could get clear of the solar system before the GRB struck. *Clermont* could reach the stars.

No matter that their test program had them still two flights away from first attempting a trip to Jupiter, humanity's farthest outpost. Their longest flight to date had gone a few millionths of the distance to the nearest star—with the DED breaking down once both coming and going.

And no matter that "dark energy" was less an explanation than a label for astrophysical ignorance. *Something* made the universe expand faster and faster, and Jumoke had found a way to move a vehicle with that something. No one could say what dark energy *was*. Not in any nuts and bolts, or gluons and quarks, terms a lowly ship's engineer could understand.

Suppose they made the DED reliable. At relativistic speeds, the ineffably thin gas and dust between the stars would become a hailstorm of radiation—lethal, if still nowhere near as intense as a GRB.

And if they overcame the radiation problem? They could never carry enough supplies for a years-long flight. And no one had a clue what they might encounter between the stars. And no one had ever tried to navigate across such vast distances.

The practical problems seemed limitless, but Blake couldn't help but consider each as it occurred to him. Maybe he didn't dare let his thoughts run any other way.

"How many?" he asked.

"People?" Dennison said. "A few thousand, just don't ask me how. Without at least that much genetic diversity, any colony will eventually fail anyway."

"Which star?" Dana asked calmly.

"One second, Dana," Blake said. He could not move past one fundamental problem. "Do I remember this correctly, Antonio? The beam from a GRB is many light-years across. In three years, how can any ship get us to safety?"

Antonio gave one of his awkward, forced smiles, the kind that never got as far as his eyes. "No, you're right. But I think...*this* one will just...graze us. The gravitational waves are polarized, and that... suggests the...direction of the beam."

"Which star?" Dana asked again.

"We don't know that yet, either," Hawthorne said. "Dr. Valenti will be working on that."

That's how it would be, Blake realized: lurching from one hasty decision to the next, wondering at every turn if it was already too late.

Jumoke flinched when Blake touched her sleeve. He said, "Tell me what you'll need."

She frowned. "What do you mean?"

"*Clermont* couldn't make it to Jupiter, much less to another solar system. What'll you need to failsafe the DED?"

"You don't understand," she said. "I've got to focus on getting people up to speed, here and on Earth. That's the only way we'll ever scale up the drive to accommodate colony-sized ships. It's the only way we'll go from a handcrafted prototype—a kludge, you once called it—to mass production."

"Because it *is* a kludge," he snapped back. "And a poorly understood kludge, which is why it drops offline every few days and why you cluttered my main engine room with sensors and lab gear. Face it, you're needed aboard *Clermont*."

"You're right," Jumoke said, almost in tears. "You're right about all that. But I'm needed more *here*. So, you…"

"Me?"

Dennison smiled. "Do you begin, Mr. Westford, to understand the interview you just had?"

"*I'm* the backup DED expert?"

"Aren't you?" Hawthorne asked. "You only need to keep the drive running, accumulate more flight time with it, do some fine-tuning. No one expects you to explain it. Dr. Boro assured us you are familiar with her prototype, that without you she could never have integrated it into *Clermont*'s systems."

"You and Jumoke worked side by side for three months," Dana said. "You can do this, Blake, if anyone can."

"More to the point," Hawthorne said, "*you* can do it *now*. Anyone else would need training. You'll have access to Dr. Boro by comm."

"Time *is* of the essence," Dennison added, keeping up the full-court press.

Better to die trying than die waiting, Blake knew. But nothing was ever that simple.

"As the tests continue," he said, "we make longer flights. Correct? 'Scout out the path to another solar system,' I believe those were the governor's words."

Dennison nodded. "That's what I said."

"So at some point, we don't come back."

"You wouldn't want to," Dennison said. "Not if you plan to live. Quit dithering, Westford. Are you in?"

"You tell me." Blake took a deep breath. "I'll not desert my wife. If you want me, Rikki comes, too."

5

"Surprise!"

Rikki Westford jerked to a halt in the doorway. Family and friends packed all she could see of her and Blake's apartment. Mom wriggled through the living-room crowd to give her a hug. Dad, tending bar in the dining room, raised a beer stein in salute. Her three surviving grandparents grinned from the living-room sofa. Two nieces bounced and giggled on the loveseat. Even her ex was there in a corner.

It was all Rikki could do not to sob.

"Smile and go in," Blake whispered from behind her. "For their sakes."

Fighting back tears, she did her best. "Umm, hello, everyone."

"Wow, we *did* surprise you," Aunt Lucy said. "You're not that good an actress."

I'm not any kind of an actress, Rikki thought, but I need to be one now.

With a hand on the small of her back Blake guided her through the door. He slipped past her into the crowd. "Hi, everyone. How about a hint? Whose birthday or anniversary did I forget?"

The quip got a hearty chuckle, leaving Rikki to marvel how he did it. The ready charm she understood. That was just…Blake. But how did he keep on the brave face?

Aunt Lucy gave Blake a peck on the cheek. Like all Rikki's relatives, she towered over him. "You two didn't expect to sneak away to Titan without saying goodbye, did you?"

More like, sneak away to another star. But they couldn't say that. The cover story, of a short-notice mission departing for Titan, already strained credulity.

More like, leave everyone behind to die.

"I suppose not," Blake said. In a stage voice, he added, "Someone tell me. What does a guy have to do to get a drink in his own house?"

"I estimate about four meters this way," Dad answered, laughing.

And another piece of Rikki's heart died.

Her kid sister pressed through the crowd, towing by the hand a skinny, tattooed guy Rikki guessed was the latest boyfriend. Whoever he was, an apartment filled with Janna's relatives seemed not to faze him. A serious BF, then.

You're all doomed! Somehow, Rikki held the shriek inside.

"My, you're quiet, Sis," Janna said. "What's up?"

"What's up with you?" Rikki countered. "As in, who's your... friend?"

"This is Glenn." Janna slipped an arm around his waist and snuggled close. "As you would know if you hadn't been holed up for the past three weeks. Glenn, meet my sister Rikki and her husband Blake."

"Hi, guys," Glenn said. "I've heard a lot about you."

Blake offered his hand. "Glenn, I'm pleased to meet you. And though it pains me to admit it, you could do worse than Janna. You'd have to search high and low, but you could."

"Good to know," Glenn said as Janna mock-scowled at both men.

"I still need a beer," Blake announced. "Can I bring anyone anything? No?" He headed to the other room.

Rikki left her greeting at "Hi." She wanted to say, grab life while you can. She wanted to say, enjoy every day to the fullest, because so few days remain. She wanted to say—

"Here you go, hon." When Blake returned, offering the beer she had not wanted, she shook her head. Alcohol would only make her sadder.

Glenn, with a grin, accepted her bottle. "Titan? Man, that's far."

"And cold," Blake said. "But if Saturn is half as beautiful as Jupiter was, wow." He and Glenn clinked bottles.

"So tell me, Sis. What's a science historian do on Titan?"

"Are you kidding?" Rikki said. "The first crewed mission to Titan is history *and* science."

"She's a natural," Blake said.

No, I'm an imposter, Rikki thought. Whether on the scouting mission or the colony ships to follow, science historian might be the last specialty anyone needed. But humanity needed scouts and the scouting mission needed Blake—she believed that, whether or not he did—and so she must go. So, she had trained her *ass* off.

Every day comparing herself with the experts—scientists and engineers, prospectors and explorers—who'd been selected for what *they* knew and had accomplished. Every day, finding herself wanting.

At least she wasn't an Earthworm. She'd lived her entire life under pressurized domes. She reacted instinctively to leak alarms and recognized the tell-tale signs of hypoxia. She'd been in space, if no farther than to the Moon. Breathing gear and pressure suits were familiar.

To pull her own weight, that left her with only a million *other* subjects to master. When Blake and Dana were off-world, stress-testing the DED, Rikki studied everything she could find about standard shipboard systems, and the half-dozen nearby solar systems any of which might be chosen as their destination, and about terraforming. With *Clermont* undergoing its final overhaul and provisioning, she haunted the shipyard, asking questions, tagging along behind Blake and Dana for whatever insights she could absorb without getting in their way. And in any time left, she pored over the latest life sciences. Astrobiology had changed a lot since her undergrad days, no matter that the very existence of its subject matter remained in dispute.

Not that with any of these topics she could do more than skim the surface. Mostly she hunted down libraries and knowledge bases that might be useful, adding them to the near-endless list of digital resources the still-to-be-integrated shipboard AI would continue to ingest for as long as the ship remained within comm range of Mars. And fretted about what else she could be doing, or should be doing, or might have done.

Till Hawthorne, of all unlikely people, had ordered her home for a day of R & R.

"Rikki, sweetie, are you all right?" Janna asked. "You look exhausted."

"Maybe a little tired," Rikki admitted. "The mission trainers work us hard."

"Good talking to you guys," Blake said. "I'm going to get this little lady"—said looking up at Rikki, and with a self-deprecating grin—"to a chair."

She found a seat on the sofa, between Mom and Grandma Betty. Grandma had a crochet hook in hand and a half-made doily on her lap. Knitting, tatting, crocheting: Grandma did them all. She kept her hands busy with needlecraft at all times. When time permitted, Rikki had always intended to have Grandma teach her the ancient arts. Only time would never permit….

There on the sofa, people kept seeking out Rikki. Whatever she saw or heard or said, she knew could be her last memory of that friend, that neighbor, that relative.

Never able to say goodbye.

And poor Blake? *His* family was on Earth, with just about everyone he'd known before meeting her. There wasn't time, not even by DED, for sentimental journeys. Which of them had it worse?

Her eyes brimmed, and her cheeks quivered with the struggle not to weep.

Mom tugged on Rikki's sleeve. "How should I say this? You seem very emotional today. Are you and Blake all right? The truth, now."

The truth? The truth was that untold eons ago, two neutron stars fell into a deadly embrace. That the longer their mutual orbit decayed, the more they warped space-time itself. That shortly before the stars smashed together—before they collapsed into a black hole, in that cataclysmic process spewing gamma rays and subatomic debris—the gravitational waves cast off by the inspiraling stars had become so intense that even across 7500 light-years they were detectable—

To herald the doom that followed close behind. Day by day, as the gravitational waves intensified and measurements accumulated, Antonio revised his estimate downward.

The truth was that within days she must leave. The truth was that in a few years everyone here to see her off would die a horrible death.

"You're scaring me, sweetie," Mom said.

The truth, even if Rikki weren't sworn to secrecy, could not help. But a lie might. She knew the news Mom and Dad and her grandparents had been hoping to hear, words that beyond excusing her moodiness and exhaustion would create a bit of joy.

"Blake and I are pregnant," Rikki whispered. "It's early. We're not talking about it yet."

"That's terrific!" Mom whispered back. "You two will make great parents."

"Hold on," Grandma Betty said. "You're pregnant and you're going to *Titan*? For two *years*?"

"Titan's not far, not using the new drive." Rikki's guts clenched with the evasion. "Besides, we'll have a doctor and infirmary onboard."

"You don't look so well." Grandma patted Rikki's hand. "Take it from a pro, dear. The morning sickness goes away."

Later Rikki saw Mom take Dad aside to whisper in his ear, and Dad breaking into an ear-to-ear grin. As they were leaving, Dad picked up Rikki and spun them both around as though she were a toddler.

"See," Dad said, beaming, "I still have it in me."

After the last guest finally departed, Rikki sobbed for hours.

6

Dana imagined herself as an island of stability amid a sea of chaos. In smart specs and a headset, she figured she looked like a cyborg.

She stood on *Clermont*'s bridge, where mechanics had unbolted an arc of consoles—for nav, comm, flight, and sensors—to accommodate extra radiation shielding in the bow. Simulations drawing on the ship's design and maintenance files predicted that, with a handful of exceptions, the existing wiring harnesses would accommodate repositioning everything twenty centimeters aft. With the consoles moved, she and Blake, without a lot of knee room, would still manage to sit here. Most others among the crew, when they drew watch duty, would want to stand.

Flick.

Her specs cut to an external security camera. Beyond the thirty-meter ellipsoid that was *Clermont*, like some giant North American football perched on fore-and-aft landing legs, stretched the gentle curve of the temporary dome that by nautical tradition was called a dry dock. White mist rose from the LOX and liquid-deuterium tanker trucks waiting to offload. Stevedores bounded up the ramp into *Clermont*'s aft air lock toting crated chunks of a short-range shuttle and up the ramp into the fore air lock with starter-culture tanks for the newly installed food-synth vats.

Flick.

In the already cramped crew quarters, under the deck beneath her feet, sparks flew as welders attached a closet-sized bio lab and infirmary. Other workers stocked the galley with basic rations, and yet more laborers bolted a multipurpose exercise machine to a bulkhead.

Flick.

Astern, in engine room one, several of Jumoke's acolytes were replacing the rat's nest of sensors and cables accumulated over the many DED test flights with a tidy array of permanent instruments.

Flick.

Stacked and heaped halfway around the dome, packaged in assorted crates, cases, canisters, satchels, cabinets, racks, and tied bundles, an exterior camera showed her yet more supplies remaining to be loaded. Geometry and simulations be damned, it seemed impossible that all this stuff could fit aboard.

Flick.

Mid-ship, in cargo hold two, workers had removed several deck plates to run cable bundles and liquid helium lines to the cold-sleep pods. Dana tried to forget that cold-sleep pods were meant for medical emergencies, and for intervals measured in hours, not years. She tried and failed.

Across the hold, out an interior hatch, at an oblique angle down the central corridor, and into an open equipment closet, she glimpsed mechanics at work doubling life-support capacity.

Flick.

At Dana's elbow, someone cleared his throat. She turned. "What?"

"Captain, we've got an anomaly," the mechanic said. Jerry Tanaka, she thought his name was.

Blake should be directing this three-ring circus—only he had done just that nonstop for three days running. She had had to order him to get some sleep, and still not gotten him farther than a borrowed cot in the foreman's shed, still inside the dome. That he could nap amid this din, even wearing earplugs....

"Captain?" Tanaka pointed at a many-colored cable bundle stretched taut between the bulkhead and the back of the unbolted copilot's flight console.

"Hold on," Dana told Tanaka. In a crouch, Dana got a better view behind the console. "Specs, display mode off. Camera mode on. Ten X zoom. Marvin, what do you know about this?"

Marvin was among the first of the mission retrofits, networked into every sensor and control across the ship. Marvin's program resided in an anachronism: entire freaking deck-to-overhead, two meters wide, racks of computing equipment. That much circuitry allowed for massive redundancy, and so, in theory, resilience against even multiple failures. Its storage capacity was into the zettabyte range.

Unlike Dana, Marvin could handle many camera feeds at once, even while sifting through huge databases. Marvin didn't think, not in the human sense, or show initiative. It did follow directions, match patterns, find correlations, draw inferences, and, with reasonable accuracy, speak and interpret spoken language.

"I see it," Marvin said. "That cable bundle is nowhere in my files. The logo and string of digits I see pressed into the insulation of the yellow wire suggest a manufacturing batch from eighteen years ago."

If the undocumented *whatever* had been installed new, that meant two owners prior to the university's purchase of the ship. At a word from Dana, Hawthorne would doubtless sic half the government on hunting down both prior owners. She was tempted for perhaps a nanosecond, but what was the point? She would never trust the ancient memories of anyone sloppy enough to mod his ship without updating its records.

"Tanaka, figure out what that is before you touch it," Dana directed. "Open the console if you must. Trace signals through the ship. Marvin can help. If you need other resources, tell me."

Because once they started to snip mystery wires, the checkout time for this latest overhaul would expand to....

Dana had no idea, beyond way longer than she could afford.

"Yesterday, Mr. Tanaka," she ordered. He got back to work.

"Specs, resume security-camera scan."

Flick...flick...flick....

"Specs, pause." Dana pressed the intercom button. "Cargo hold one, I'm seeing crates for both shuttles stowed all over." And inter-mixed, which was worse. "Keep the crate sets together, one shuttle to each side of the exterior hatch."

"We're arranging things to get the snuggest fit," a worker answered, sweat soaking his tunic and trickling down his face and neck. "Your way would reduce packing density."

"Understood, but at the other end"—an eventuality Dana didn't dare to find fantastical—"when we're ready to assemble a shuttle, it won't do to first have to rearrange half the contents of the hold."

And with every nook and cranny of the ship to be filled, shift the contents to where? The memory flashed of a fifteen-piece sliding number puzzle she had played with as a little girl—only this puzzle involved hundreds of pieces, in an endless array of shapes and sizes.

"Marvin, what do you think?" Dana asked.

"There is an enormous number of ways to pack and unpack so many items. Are the shuttle crates the only cargo to which you will want optimized access, or are there others? I have ideas about staging items through the crew quarters, but I will need your confirmation."

While she and Marvin talked, another crate of shuttle parts got stowed in the deep recesses of the cargo hold. Dana hit the intercom again. "Cargo hold one, am I not making myself clear?"

The worker said, "To accommodate your suggestion, I'd have to unload and repack most of—"

"It wasn't a suggestion," Dana snapped. "Do it."

Flick...flick...flick....

Blake shuffled onto the bridge, yawning. Dark, puffy skin pouched below his specs. "What'd I miss, Dana?"

"The opportunity to sleep," she told him. "Blake, go back to bed. I'll handle things for another...few hours..."

"What?" Blake asked.

An exterior camera showed her a cloud of red dust. "Specs, freeze on camera twenty-six."

"Specs, camera twenty-six," Blake repeated. "Got it."

"Too localized for a dust storm," Dana said, tapping her headset. "Security officer. Do you see incoming vehicles?"

"Yes, Captain. It's nothing."

"And you are?"

"Lieutenant Anderson, Captain, ma'am."

Anderson: a freckle-faced militia officer fresh out of OCS, little more than a boy. Any conspicuous security presence would have undermined the cover story of a university-sponsored Titan mission.

Dana asked, "Who's coming, Lieutenant?"

"Supply trucks. Nothing to be concerned about."

"No trucks are due for hours," she reminded him. Because more trucks inside the dome could only get in the way.

"They radioed ahead with the proper codes," Anderson insisted.

Blake had zoomed the outside camera. "Is it just me, or do most of those vehicles look military?"

Within this dome alone, fifty-plus people might have inferred that *Clermont* was headed for somewhere not Titan. Hundreds more constructing the three new "space habitats" and the scaled-up DEDs to propel them must have their suspicions. How many diggers were questioning the sudden massive "ice mining" projects? How many legislators had the governor taken into her confidence to get these mega-projects approved? How many people were involved in the urgent, long-range consultations with governments on Earth and elsewhere?

The nightmare-within-a-nightmare, the disclosure of the GRB secret, had been all but inevitable. And if, in a panic, people had decided to flee?

Dana said, "Lieutenant, you may need to defend this ship."

A familiar voice came onto the command channel: Hawthorne. "That won't be necessary, Captain McElwain. I'll be at the dome within five minutes to explain."

As she and Blake waited outside the ship, three stevedores toting crated microsats went up the aft ramp. In a sane universe, they would take aboard cargo *after* the final shakedown cruise. Still….

Another few days and we *will* be ready to go, Dana thought. Unless Hawthorne screws things up.

A convoy of cars and trucks braked to a halt outside the dome's primary entrance. A sleek limo, its tinted windows concealing those inside, was the first vehicle to emerge from the air lock.

Dana and Blake strode after the car as it parked. From the corner of an eye she saw a truck pull close to the ship's aft ramp. More cargo? Cargo she had not reviewed and approved? What the *hell* was going on?

"Change in plan, Captain," Hawthorne said, getting out of his car.

"What do you mean?" Dana asked. "Who are the people going into my ship, and what are they doing?"

Hawthorne said, "The short answer to *all* your questions is that this ship leaves as soon as the new cargo is loaded."

"Leaves for where?" Blake asked.

Dana said, "Specs, translucent mode, cycle among shipboard cameras only, two-second loiter per view." The madness had only grown since she'd walked off her ship. And Tanaka, his forehead furrowed, had removed the back panel from a bridge console and was peering inside. "Hawthorne, the ship is still torn apart. Half the systems need to be checked out again."

"Do checkout on your way," Hawthorne said. "Use fusion drive at first, if you must."

"Our way *where?*" Blake tried again.

Dana said, "At the moment, the bridge consoles aren't even bolted to the deck. We're still making room to cram lead shielding into the bow."

"Put the consoles back where they were, if that gets you away faster," Hawthorne said.

Two troops stomped down a ramp carrying *out* a cold-sleep pod. Wiring harnesses and cryogenic lines looked like they had been sheared off! Then another pod came out, and a third.

"*Hawthorne!*" Dana said. "Without cold-sleep pods, we don't have a mission. We can't carry enough food and water, or maintain life support long enough, to reach a safe distance from the GRB. If we could, it wouldn't matter. Before we get anywhere near light speed, the interstellar muck turned to radiation will have killed us."

"You'll have pods in hold three for a crew of six," Hawthorne said. "I need hold two for more important things."

Blake said, "This is insane. Explain yourself."

"Or what, Westford? Or you won't go?" Hawthorne thumped the top of his car. "Everyone out."

First Antonio appeared, then two people Dana didn't recognize. All were ashen. And then—

"Rikki!" Blake said. "What's going on?"

"Quiet!" Hawthorne gestured at a squad of troops. "Westford, you *will* go. If necessary, you'll be carried aboard bound and gagged. If that's how things play out, one of these marines takes your wife's berth."

Troops emerged from the ship carrying three additional cold-sleep pods.

Swallowing hard, Rikki said, "I go where Blake goes."

Antonio shuffled toward Dana. "The ship leaves right…away… or…it's the end."

The longer superior officers put off the bad news, the iffier the mission would be. "So what's the new mission, Neil?" Dana asked softly.

Hawthorne said, "Walk with me, Captain. Everyone else, get back to work."

7

Two hours after tight-lipped soldiers had hustled Rikki from an astrobiology drill, she was buckling herself into one of the jump seats that folded down from the aft wall of *Clermont*'s crew quarters. To her left sat Antonio, already strapped in, wringing his hands. To her right, fumbling with their five-point harnesses, were the woman and man Rikki had met in Hawthorne's limo.

They were dazed.

The end of the world. Rikki remembered when she'd first heard: the shock and pain. The days of denial. The survivors' guilt at being included in the scouting mission. The crushing depression at the futility of it all.

Compared to Li and Carlos, learning of the apocalypse as the limo jolted and swayed, Rikki had had an easy time of it.

The cabin's forward wall awakened, to display the scene off the ship's bow. Jettisoned equipment, mostly cold-sleep pods, lay in a jumble to their right. (To starboard, she chided herself inanely, remembering one of her many lessons. Yeah, that's important.) Outside the clear plastic dome, cars and trucks trailing clouds of dust sped away. Virtual ship's instruments shone through the exterior view.

Rikki thought, I'm seeing what Blake is seeing. The thought calmed her.

"Attention, all hands," Dana announced over the intercom. "This is the captain speaking. We are about to launch. Prepare for immediate acceleration."

Not an hour earlier, Rikki had heard Dana declare this ship a shambles, unfit to fly. And now....

On-screen, a dazzling red light sprang from the bow. The laser beam swept up and aft, and as it did the fabric of the dome sagged. Knowing it was her imagination, Rikki heard pressure alarms keening through the hull.

"Comm laser," Antonio muttered. "Faster than...deflating *and* removing...the dome."

Dana came back on the intercom. "Launch in ten seconds. Nine. Eight..."

On zero, to the eerily silent workings of the DED, the bulkhead at Rikki's back became the floor. Her weight surged. She'd only seen elephants in holos, but now the invisible, metaphorical kind dropped onto her. In the hold aft of the crew quarters, hastily stowed cargo thudded and crashed.

In an instant, *Clermont* burst through the slit in the still settling dome.

Within seconds, Rikki lost sight of the ground convoy. The drydock area shrank into the landscape and the horizon began to curve. As they climbed, the night side of the world came into view, and only the occasional brave glimmer of a domed city relieved the darkness. Cargo in the holds must have fallen as far as it could, because the clamor from aft began trailing off.

But the acceleration went on and on and on....

In a corner of the display, the mission timer reached five minutes.

Dana announced, "Everything continues to look good. We've cleared the orbits of the innermost satellites."

To Rikki's right, the woman grunted, "How long?"

"Will we be accelerating?" Rikki guessed. "I have no idea."

There must have been an open mike in the crew quarters, because Dana answered. "Better get used to it."

"I *was* used to it," the woman said, her voice a soft, airy contralto. "Then I moved to Mars."

Rikki had guessed as much. Li was petite, even by Earthworm standards.

"And *where* are we going?" Li's companion demanded.

"Another few minutes," Dana said, "and we'll be clear of most traffic. Then we'll talk."

✳

The bulkhead display at which Rikki stared flipped to the interior of the bridge. Blake and Dana, in the gimbaled pilot and copilot chairs, hardly seemed inconvenienced by the acceleration. Earth-normal, Rikki supposed, struggling to see how "normal" could describe any aspect of this situation.

Certainly the stoical expression on Blake's face wasn't normal. The mask might fool the others, but *she* knew. He was terrified.

Dana said, "I'd join you if I could. The conversation we must have should be done face to face. That's not practical."

Because under acceleration, with the four of them splayed across the aft-bulkhead-become-deck, Dana would have had to hang like a bat from the forward-bulkhead-become-ceiling. Rikki swallowed the laughter that ached to burst from her. If she allowed it to start, it might never stop.

Dana said, "For what it's worth, Neil Hawthorne asked me to extend his deepest apologies."

"His goons *abducted* me," Carlos said. "For what it's worth, apology rejected."

"He saved your life." Dana waved off Carlos's protest. Her eyes darted. Below the view of the camera, her hands did—something.

Rikki gasped as the ship slewed. Safety-harness straps cut into her left side. Their acceleration surged.

"Sorry about that," Dana said. "As for Neil Hawthorne, hear me out before you condemn him. I don't believe any of us knows everyone, so introductions first. I'm—"

"The pleasantries can wait," Carlos interrupted. "I want to know—"

"You'll know soon enough," Dana said, with undertones of *careful what you wish for.* "I'm Dana McElwain, formerly of the Space Guard, and the captain of this vessel. *Clermont* is, was, owned by Percival Lowell University, which is to say, by the state."

"I'm Blake Westford, ship's engineer."

"Captain, why was I shanghaied?" Carlos demanded. "Why did Hawthorne's goons ransack my lab? Why—"

"Do you have a name?" Dana asked icily.

"As if you don't know," he huffed. "I am Dr. Carlos Patel. I hold the Francis Crick Chair in microbiology and nanotechnology at Bradbury University."

Despite the brutal acceleration, Rikki risked turning and raising her head. Patel was taller than she. A native Martian, too, most likely. And he was *hairy*, with a shaggy mop of black hair, a bold, drooping mustache, and tufts sprouting from the collar of his jumpsuit. Hairy, haughty, and hawk-nosed.

"And you, Miz?" Dana's voice changed. "Hold on, everyone."

As the ship veered, this time the safety harness mashed Rikki's right side.

"Can you not fly in a straight line?" Carlos snapped.

"Not today," Dana said cryptically. "Miz?"

"I'm Li Yeo," said the petite woman beside Rikki. Li was fine-boned, with expressive brown eyes, flawless complexion, and long, straight, raven hair—in a word, lovely. She might have been any age from forty to sixty. Something about her level gaze impressed Rikki as shrewd. "I'm a psychiatrist, specializing in family issues. Couples counseling, problem children, that sort of thing."

"A medical doctor, then, too," Dana said.

"Of course, by training. It's been a while."

"Why don't we finish the introductions?" Dana said. "Antonio?"

"Antonio Valenti. Astrophysicist. Lowell…University."

Leaving Rikki. She said, "Rikki Westford. Science historian." Of late unemployed, or self-employed, take your pick, working on a book. Readership at most six, if she finished it.

A cackle tried once more to escape from her.

"Science *generalist*," Dana said, "and I predict we'll make use of that big-picture perspective. A biologist before that."

Who here would a B.S. in biology impress? Having her qualifications defended only made Rikki feel more insecure. And why had *Dana* defended her?

"And that's everyone," Dana said. "Thank you.

"You now know, even if you first learned of it on the drive from New Houston, that a gamma-ray burst is aimed at us. The likely outcome is mass extinctions across the solar system. Governments on Earth, Mars, and elsewhere have been working frantically to construct new 'habitats' that are, in fact, colony ships. That's why a few of us had been prepping to take this ship on a scouting mission."

"A colony *where?*" Carlos said. "You said the whole solar system was at risk."

Dana said, "Alpha Centauri, precise destination to be chosen on the scene, because from this distance none of the planets looks all that hospitable. Unfortunately, the most recent data shows that we have only months until the GRB hits."

Months? They had been told *years*! As Rikki turned toward Antonio for confirmation, the ship again zigged. Her stomach lurched.

"It's true." Antonio's chin sank to his chest. "The closer the neutron…stars inspiral, the stronger…the gravitational *waves* they emit and…the shorter the…wavelength. The less…ambiguity in the signal. Older gravitational…wave observatories can now…detect the stronger, faster signal so…we can better triangulate *to*…the source. The GRB…hits Sol system in about eight…*months*.

"Put it all…together and…it now looks like Sol system *will*…be about…one-*fourth* light-year…from the beam edge. It will take us almost…eight months…just to *get* clear."

"So what's the *point*?" Rikki raged. "There'll be no one for us to scout for. The new colony ships won't, can't, be completed in that time, much less get clear. Suppose we few do escape the burst. It will only prolong the mourning."

"I don't...know."

"Then what are we doing?" Rikki asked.

"I don't know," Antonio whispered. "Hawthorne...he heard my news this morning, and...." The words faded to unintelligibility.

"Hawthorne heard you, and *what*?" Carlos demanded.

"And...so, we're *here*." Antonio rubbed his chin. "I suspect Hawthorne or...the governor...worried this *might*...happen. That our preparations would...be cut short."

"There *is* a plan," Dana said. "Thanks to Neil Hawthorne."

A plan for the six of them? That was nonsense, Rikki thought. Only Blake's steady gaze kept back her insane cackle.

Dana said, "Everyone, *listen*. Hawthorne had troops break into a fertility clinic. They stole several freezers of frozen embryos, and the artificial wombs to bring them to term. And with no time to explain himself, or ask anyone's permission, he brought together the right people, with the right skills, for us to complete the mission.

"Li, to help us raise and nurture a new generation. Carlos and his nanotech gear, to help us fabricate the tools we forgot or lack the space to carry. Antonio, to guide us on our way and plumb the secrets of new worlds. Blake, to keep our ship humming. Rikki, to fill in the gaps between specialties."

Then we're screwed, Rikki thought.

Blake leaned toward the camera. "And Captain McElwain to make it work. To make *us* work. We all follow her orders."

Dana flashed Blake a glance that was *thanks* and *don't interrupt* all in one. "Humanity still has hope—if we rise to the occasion, if we pull together to complete this trip."

Carlos said, "You believe this can work? Honestly?"

"Yes, I believe it." Dana's eyes blazed. "You will, too. You *all* will. There is no alternative. There are no do-overs. Failure is not an option."

"And Hawthorne?" Rikki had to ask. "This is his plan. He chose the people. Why isn't *he* aboard?"

For the first time in the years Rikki had known Dana, she was speechless.

At last Dana said, "Government representatives today stole thousands of people's dreams, their *babies*. People will demand explanations, to know who is responsible, and to see justice done."

"The embryos have no more future than anyone else," Li protested. "Not left on Mars."

Dana said, "Ignorance of the coming disaster is an act of mercy, and keeping that secret means there is no justification for the theft. Hawthorne stayed behind because he wouldn't let anyone take the blame for actions he had ordered."

"Then we…?" Rikki choked, unable to put the implication into words.

Dana nodded. "As far as the public is concerned, we six are among Hawthorne's fellow cultists. We hijacked the Titan ship, plotting to create a utopian society from the stolen embryos." The ship swerved and decelerated. Seconds after, it reaccelerated. "That's why we have every Mars-based Space Guard cutter chasing us, and doubtless Belt-based cutters yet to come into our radar range. That's why I keep taking evasive maneuvers. For what it's worth, the Guard ships can't maintain a pursuit for long. Without a DED, they don't have the range."

Li asked softly, "What happens next?"

Dana said, "Neil stayed behind to do his duty as he saw it. He expects us to do ours. We will not fail him."

8

"This isn't like you, Dana," said the familiar voice. "You *help* people. Don't ask me to believe otherwise."

The words pierced like a knife.

Dana's final four years in the Space Guard, she had served under Fred Torrance. On the comm display, seated amid the familiar hushed bustle of the bridge crew, Fred looked older and wearier than she remembered him.

Dana felt old and weary, too. She reached to toggle the transmitter to ON—

And pulled back. What did she have to say?

Hours ago, Mars had fallen off her situational display. One by one, the ships in pursuit had turned back. Low on fuel? Recalled on some pretext?

But one ship remained in the chase. The blip, not even three light-seconds behind, showed the transponder code for *Reliance*. Fred's ship. Dana's old ship.

The governor, if she was interceding, had waited too long. At this distance, at these speeds, the odds of tracking a ship, much less of getting a message through to it, were slim to none.

And if Hawthorne's self-sacrifice had failed to contain the scandal? Then Governor Dennison was embroiled, too. Best not expect relief from that source.

"Talk to me," Blake said. "What are you thinking?"

"That's my old ship, and my old captain," Dana said.

"He doesn't understand," Blake answered gently. "He can't."

"I'm listening, Dana," Torrance urged.

She opened a two-way channel. "I won't permit you to dock, Captain."

Apart from the light-speed lag, Torrance's response was immediate. "I'm no longer your superior officer, Dana. We're two old friends, just talking. Tell me what's going on."

"Hawthorne can explain when you get back to Mars." He'll have to be the one to explain, she thought. I don't know enough not to contradict his cover story.

"Stealing a ship? Stealing unborn *children*? Messianic cults? That's not you, Dana. I refuse to believe any of it."

"Believe all of it." Because this was how she would be remembered—for the few months anyone had left.

Blake laid a hand on hers. "Break the link," he mouthed.

She shook her head.

Torrance said, "Do you remember rescuing the survivors on *Logan*?"

He was appealing to her better nature, and she chose to misunderstand. "Did you imagine docking with *Logan* was hard? This isn't a derelict, inanimate. If you do catch up, this ship will be bobbing and weaving, spinning and tumbling. I won't let you dock."

"Nor do smugglers," Torrance said. "You know the drill, Dana. Don't force me."

"We've distributed embryo banks throughout *Clermont*," Dana lied. "Do anything to disable this ship, and it's almost certain you'll destroy hundreds of embryos."

Silence stretched. Had she gotten through to him? Disgusted him?

"If I have to stop *Clermont*, the consequences are on your head," he said coldly. "We *will* catch up. We almost have. *Reliance* began this chase with full tanks."

Dana froze the link, audio and vid. "They can sustain three gees. If they set out with full tanks, they *will* overtake us."

Blake hesitated. "What if…?"

"If what?"

"What if *we* stepped it up to three gees? Maybe a touch more? Would they give up the chase?"

"They would have no choice, but aren't we topped out?" Dana hated to think about how their passengers were faring after a day at a sustained *two* gees. But Blake knew about them, too.

"Yeah, a hair above two gees is the DED's limit. But suppose we also fire up our fusion drive?"

They had never tried running both drives in tandem. With good reason: the bridge controls and sensors weren't configured or calibrated for that. And what if they needed all their deuterium on the other side?

Because she had to believe they would make it to the other side.

"Let's try another way first," Dana said. "Do you trust me?"

"With my life." Blake grinned. "Every time we launch."

She reopened the comm channel. "Are you sure you want to know what this is about, Fred?"

"That I am."

"Only you," she told him. "No recording, either."

"Hold on."

Fred's image froze. When the display returned to life, minutes later, the backdrop had changed.

In Dana's years aboard *Reliance*, she had been to the captain's cabin maybe a half-dozen times: sometimes to give her candid opinion, twice to get chewed out. She recognized the cabin's tidy compactness. The holos on the bulkhead behind Fred were new to Dana, but without question were of his wife and sons.

At three gees his trek from the bridge would have been brutal.

Fred had put on earphones. He asked, "Is this private enough?"

"If what we're seeing is real," Blake whispered.

"Yes, sir," Dana said. And she explained.

When she had finished, Torrance asked, "That's the truth?"

"Every word," she said. "I'm sorry beyond words that I had to tell you."

"From you, I believe it." Torrance saluted. "It has been an honor, Commander. Godspeed."

The comm display went dark.

"Godspeed to us all," Dana said.

Ten minutes later, the radar blip that stood for *Reliance* began to fall back.

9

Dana checked the console chronometer yet again. They had been boosting at two gees uninterrupted for almost six hours. It was past time to give her passengers another respite—That must soon become a session at hard labor.

"Throttling back to one-third gee," she announced, "in three… two…one…now."

Over the intercom she heard a ragged chorus of cheers.

Blake unbuckled from his acceleration chair. "Damn, that feels good."

"Don't get too comfortable," Dana advised him. She went on the intercom again. "Forty-five minutes of free time." That meant taking turns with the bathroom and sonic shower, and grabbing a snack from the galley. "After that, we have work to do."

"Go ahead," Blake suggested. "I'll hold the fort."

"In good time." Because passengers came first. Her eyes closed, Dana said, "Marvin, you have the conn. If we come within two minutes of hitting anything, tell me. If we're within thirty seconds, sound the collision alarm and dodge. Other than that, maintain this course and acceleration. Understood?"

"Understood, Captain."

"And Marvin, tell me when ten minutes are up. Wake me if necessary." Not hearing the rustle of Blake getting out of his seat, without opening her eyes, Dana said, "Go see your wife." And still not hearing him move, she added, "That's an order, sailor."

The chair beside her finally creaked. Blake said, "If I don't see you in the galley in fifteen minutes, I'm mutinying."

She faked a snore, and he left, chuckling.

Marvin *did* have to wake her. Yawning, she went through the hatch to the crew quarters.

The little fold-down table had been deployed, and Li and Carlos sat across from each other. Carlos had a cigar in his hand. He sniffed and stroked it before, with a sigh, tucking it away into his shirt pocket. (The last cigar you'll ever have, Dana thought. And also: *I* wouldn't fondle a cigar in front of a shrink.) Antonio stood in the narrow galley, rubbing his chin, intent on the disordered contents of the pantry. Blake and Rikki stood together in a corner, whispering.

After hitting the head and a quick sonic cleansing, after polishing off the sandwich and both juice bulbs Li had given her, Dana felt almost human.

"What's next, Dana?" Carlos asked.

"Captain," she corrected. A ship isn't a democracy.

"Fine," Carlos said. "What's the plan, *Captain*?"

This one will be trouble, Dana decided. "You accompany Blake to the engine rooms. He's going to start showing you maintenance procedures."

"I meant longer term than twenty minutes from now, but all right." Carlos glanced toward the Westfords. "What's the purpose of me tagging along? You have an engineer."

"I believe you said you hold 'the Francis Crick Chair in nanotech?'"

He actually preened. "Microbiology and nanotechnology."

"I heard 'tech,'" Dana said. "No one else aboard can say that. If it makes you feel better, I expect you to train Blake to back *you* up."

"I really don't think—"

"Try it," Dana said, and Carlos's face reddened. "Suppose anything happens to any one of us."

"I agree, Captain. We all need understudies," Li said. "I, for one, would welcome the help."

"Rikki seems like the logical choice for you," Dana said.

Li smiled. "Very good."

Li's intervention only made Carlos scowl.

Doesn't he get it? Dana wondered. However incredible and unfair, the six of them were humanity's last, best hope. They had to pull together. They had to be a team.

All too soon, the break period ended. Dana said, "Enough lolling about, everyone. Blake, show Carlos what's what in the engine rooms. Li, Rikki, check out supplies in life support and the infirmary. When that's done, survey the file servers we took aboard at the last minute."

Because as one defunct hope among many, forget about anyone beaming data after us as we recede. Whatever archive Hawthorne's men pilfered on that last, chaotic day is all the knowledge we bring.

Dana went on, "Antonio, you and I have shielding to install. We have the literal heavy lifting."

Antonio looked away from the pantry bins, though not quite at Dana. "All right," he finally conceded.

"Let's go to work, Carlos," Blake said, getting people in motion.

Dana retrieved emergency toolkits from drawers on the bridge. When she returned to crew quarters, Antonio had not budged from the pantry.

She lobbed a toolkit at him, and he bobbled the catch. "Okay," she said, tapping the deck with a foot where the jump seats were folded and recessed. "First we remove the jump seats."

"Why?"

"We're going to plate the deck, here and in the bridge"—likewise forward in the ship—"with lead. Aft of this level, everything will be shielded."

In cargo hold three: the cold-sleep pods in which the six of them would sleep away the long trip. In cargo hold two: the embryo freezers, artificial wombs, and seed banks they would need at their destination. And in a corner of cargo hold one, Marvin's computing complex.

The prospect of years on autopilot made Dana's skin crawl.

"What about the...other *end* of the...holds? For when we... decel*erate*?"

"After we flip, the main fusion reactor will be between us and the oncoming radiation. The reactor's shielding should suffice."

"How *will* we fasten...the lead?"

"A dab of glue," Dana told him. It struck her that she had all but ceased to notice Antonio's halting speech and odd emphases. So were his verbal tics worse today? Maybe. He struck her as even edgier than usual. "Acceleration will pin down the sheets anyway. Once we have the shielding in position, we'll mount the jump seats to the raised floor with nail guns."

"The seats...will have nowhere to...stow anymore. This cabin is... going to be crowded."

"One more reason to finish prepping and get into the pods," Dana said.

"You remind me...a little...of her. Very focused."

You think *I'm* focused? But Antonio had never before volunteered anything personal about himself, so Dana chose not to quibble. "Who is that?"

"Tabitha. My wife." He took hold of his wrench by its socket, spinning the handle round and round, the ratchet clicks as arrhythmic as his speech. "I miss her."

Dana began loosening the bolts of the first jump-seat assembly. "What happened? But only if you feel like talking about it."

"A tornado." With his free hand, he began stroking his chin scar. "My fault."

"How can you blame yourself for a tornado?"

"I taught at Cambridge. We were…happy there, but…I chose to take a sabbatical at…Purdue." In a flurry of ratchet clicks, he started unbolting another jump seat. "North Americans talk about a tornado alley. Indiana is…in the middle of it. A tornado hit our…house. It collapsed. Tabitha…Tabitha…"

"I'm so sorry, Antonio." That's how he got that scar, Dana supposed, and why he never had it removed. She guessed the accident was also why he had left Earth twenty years earlier. "But it's no one's fault."

"Isn't it?"

All she could come up with was, once more, "I'm so sorry."

"Let's…get these seats out."

"Sure."

In silence, they finished unbolting the four jump-seat assemblies and lifted them from the deck. They leaned the seats, still folded flat, against the curved, exterior bulkhead. Then their task moved to cargo hold one, restacking cargo to get at the bundles of lead sheets.

They had seemingly unending cargo to shift. Vitamins and nutritional supplements. Freeze-dried emergency rations. Grain seeds: wheat, corn, rice, and crops she had never heard of. Vegetable seeds, fruit-tree seeds, and seeds for trees to provide lumber. Guns and ammo, for whatever wild animals they might encounter on the new world. (At least Dana didn't think anyone expected them to find aliens at their destination, or that the six of them would wage war if there were.) Spare parts for ship, shuttles, and spacesuits. Grab bags of hardware, from electronic and photonic integrated circuits to literal nuts and bolts.

If only there had been time in dry dock to retrofit shielding into the bow, where it belonged.

If only she had the luxury of time for "if only."

Antonio kept bumping into and dropping things. Even at one-third gee most of the crates were heavy, and at any acceleration (or with none, for that matter) their inertia was substantial. Twice Dana lunged to grab something he had fumbled.

Under acceleration, the ship's central corridor had become a ten-meter-deep shaft. If he should drop a lead sheet in or down that shaft....

Dana made the command decision: Antonio was too clumsy for this job. Maybe he had realized that going in. Maybe that was why he had been so anxious.

She said, "No offense, this isn't the task for you."

"I'm sorry. I do want to contribute."

"I know you do. And you have, or none of us would even be here."

"If it's okay, I'll scan *ahead* of the ship."

"That's a good idea." Dana brushed sweat-slicked hair off her forehead. "We've got new long-range sensors. It would be a big help if you could confirm the calibrations. Call on Marvin if you need help. But don't touch any other console."

"I promise not to break anything." Antonio managed an awkward smile before leaving for the bridge.

She pressed the intercom button. "Blake, Li, I need you in cargo hold one. Earth muscles, and all that."

"Be there in a minute," Blake responded. Li just showed up.

Blake finally arrived. "What do you need?"

"First, you can help me tote this stuff forward." Dana rapped the stack of lead sheets. Li hefted one—and winced as it wanted to keep going. "Sorry, Li. This won't be easy."

"Don't worry about it."

Dana said, "Li, stand near the top of the ladder. Blake will take the middle and we'll get a bucket-brigade thing going between here and crew quarters."

"Lead buckets filled with lead," Blake said. "Good times."

"What did you leave Carlos doing?" Dana asked him.

"I told him to inventory spare parts in both engine rooms."

"And how did that go over?"

"Inventorying is a task beneath the dignity of the Francis Crick Chair," Blake said as he grabbed a lead sheet from the stack. "I can live with that."

Li paused in the hatchway. "May I offer an observation, Captain?"

"Of course."

"Carlos is scared," Li said. "I don't mind admitting it: I'm scared, too. It's the literal end of the world, Captain. You have your military training to fall back on. Stiff upper lip, and all that. Carlos doesn't have that. When he falls back on academic snobbery, or any other familiar behaviors, it's no surprise."

"I see your point," Dana said. "But you heard the bad news when Carlos did. You aren't"—a pain in the ass—"reacting like him. Is that because you're a shrink?"

"Oh, no," Li said. "Psychiatrists are nuttier than most people you'll meet. I suppose it comes of listening all day to complaints and traumas. Doubtless I'm still in denial. Give me time and I'll get insufferable."

"Something to look forward to," Blake said.

Dana asked, "Any more professional advice?"

"We're confronting a terrible ending. It would do us all good to refocus on new beginnings." Li tipped her head, considering. "Just a crazy idea, but suppose we rename the ship? Suppose that as a crew we come together on a new name?"

"Interesting," Dana said. And at worst, harmless. "Why don't you make the proposal?"

"Very well." Li flipped on the intercom. "Everyone, this is Li. Despite the tragic events that have set us on our course, a part of me can't help but be excited at the prospect of exploring a new world. We'll be building a new home, establishing a new civilization, beginning new lives. What better way to mark this rebirth than with a new name for our ship?"

"I propose...*Santa Maria*." As Antonio turned off his intercom pick-up, Marvin was saying something cryptic about string.

"Excellent," Li said. "Other suggestions?"

"*Mayflower*," Blake offered. "Of course that's just the Bostonian in me talking."

"Isn't renaming a ship considered bad luck?" Carlos called. "Not that I believe in luck."

"From the Department of Every Silver Lining Has a Cloud," Blake whispered.

Dana went on the intercom. "If so, Carlos, that ship has sailed. So to speak. When the university bought this vessel, it was named *Beaumont*. That was fine for a delivery truck, but then Blake and I started flying around with experimental drives. At Blake's suggestion we renamed the ship *Clermont*, after the first commercial steamship."

Because I can pilot a ship knowing as little about its experimental drive as Robert Fulton knew about thermodynamics.

"As it happens, the name *Clermont* was Rikki's suggestion," Blake said. "I just passed it along. She's the science historian."

The intercom offered the clatter of things plastic and metallic, and then Carlos said, "Whatever. It doesn't matter."

"And you, Rikki?" Li asked. "What are your thoughts? How do you feel about a change from *Clermont*?"

"I'm for calling it *Endurance*," Rikki said. "After the Antarctic exploration ship."

Blake's eyes flicked forward toward life support, where Rikki remained at work.

Dana toggled OFF the cargo hold's intercom mike. "Blake, is something wrong?"

He shook his head, and she reactivated the control.

"How about you, Captain?" Li asked. "What name appeals to you?"

Dana said, "How about *Endeavour*? HMS *Endeavour* was a ship that James Cook sailed around the world, on the trip in which he discovered Australia and New Zealand. And by the way, he had renamed his ship; *Endeavour* wasn't the original name. NASA called one of its Apollo command modules *Endeavour*; and also one of its early space shuttles. And the ship that Johansson first flew to Ceres was likewise an *Endeavour*. It's an honored name, but I believe our aspirations are worthy of it."

"I withdraw my suggestion," Antonio said from the bridge. "I like *Endeavour*. That's what we're…doing: embarking on a great endeavor. And as unscientific as luck…is, we can use some. *Endeavour* sounds like an…auspicious name."

A judgmental-sounding sniff came over the intercom. Carlos?

"I also like *Endeavour*," Li said.

"Me, too," Blake said.

"Carlos?" Li asked. "What's your opinion?"

"I don't care," Carlos said. "*Endeavour* is as good a name as any."

"I'll make it unanimous," Rikki said.

"Can I get back now to my skilled labor of counting?" Carlos asked.

Li mouthed, "Give him time."

So much for the benefits of psychiatry, Dana thought. Picking up a lead sheet, she said, "Let's all return to work."

10

The hardest part was the not knowing.

Would *Endeavour* get clear in time? If not, its crew would die unaware. Without a planetary atmosphere to cushion the blow, the blast of the GRB would kill them in an instant. They could only keep running and hope for the best.

While they waited, they dug through the cargo, including things thrown aboard at the last minute. They sorted and stowed it all. They installed shielding. They ran full diagnostics on every ship's system and cold-sleep pod, every cryostat and liquid-helium backup loop. They tweaked and tuned, calibrated and recalibrated everything.

Marvin assessed it all, assessed itself, and declared itself ready to take charge of the vessel—

Only to have its offer rebuffed.

As difficult as it was not to know, for as long as familiar planets shone brightly to stern no one wanted to withdraw into cold, dark oblivion.

The days since departure had become a blur.

Blake climbed up and down the ladder in *Endeavour*'s central corridor, his muscles aching. If he caught anyone but Dana doing this, he would read them the riot act. A tumble down the shaft under acceleration guaranteed broken bones, if not worse.

If anyone caught him, he'd assert his Earth-grown skeleton, med nanites that maintained it, and lots of shipboard experience—knowing that he was rationalizing. With Dana pounding away on the ship's one piece of exercise gear, he had nowhere else to work out the stress.

If only he could *sleep*.

At two gees, no one slept well. At two gees, the usually comfortable knotted-rope hammocks became torture devices, determined to slice a person into stew meat. He had tried sacking out in one of the jump seats. He might have dozed in fits and starts.

Rikki somehow managed. When he had last peeked into the crew cabin, she'd been softly snoring.

Farther from home than Pluto was from the sun, they had gone farther than any human *ever*. Their speed, still climbing, verged on nineteen thousand klicks per second.

And yet they had gone only a small fraction of one percent of their way.

"Marvin," Blake whispered. "What time is it?"

"Twenty minutes before eight," the AI said.

Twenty minutes then until Blake was due for another cross-training session with Carlos. Today's lessons: more on DED diagnostic modes in exchange for more tricks of nanotech-fabricator programming.

Twenty minutes was more than ample for a homeward look. No one had ever before seen Sol system from so far beneath the ecliptic. And though Blake tried not to dwell on it, his parents and sister, nephew and nieces, aunts and uncles and cousins lived on that pale blue dot.

Where, a few months hence, along with many old friends, all would die.

The next time his vertical excursion brought him to the top of the shaft, he went through the open hatch onto the bridge deck.

From the copilot's seat Antonio stared at the main bridge display, toward an amorphous black cloud that all but vanquished a big chunk of the star field.

The Coalsack Dark Nebula. This was the view ahead, not the view toward home.

Blake did not see any centaur among the stars, but even had their target not been straight ahead, there could be no overlooking Alpha Centauri. It was the fourth-brightest star in the sky.

"You know what just struck me?" Blake said, and Antonio turned. "Our old sun will be as bright in our new night sky."

"Bright enough. Not as bright as we see Alpha Centauri. It's a triple star."

"Is Alpha Cen what you're looking at?" Blake asked.

"Watch." Antonio pointed into the scene.

"I see stars."

"No, *watch*." Antonio pointed again.

Nothing happened. "What am I looking for?"

"You'll know." Antonio leaned closer, poking a finger into the holo. "*Here*. Now watch."

Nothing happened. As Blake pondered what he would have for breakfast—a star flashed.

"Did you see?" Antonio demanded.

"The flash? Yes. What *was* that?"

"Microlensing."

Blake had a vague notion of a massive object bending light, gravity functioning as a lens. But what massive object could be between a star and *Endeavour*? "A rogue planet?" he guessed.

"Marvin, did you register…it, too?"

"I did," the AI said.

"Show me the current data set."

Red, blinking dots appeared in the holo, in a cluster of three.

Blake said, "You can't make me believe you found *three* rogue planets."

"I didn't." Antonio stretched to engage the intercom. "Captain to the bridge."

Blake sidled to his left for another perspective on the data. Though the blinking dots did not quite fall into a line, together they suggested a direction only a few degrees off *Endeavour*'s course. "How long have you been watching?"

"Five days." Antonio yawned. "I think."

Dana appeared in the hatchway. "What's up, guys?"

"You're seeing…ancient history."

Rikki, her hair sleep-tousled, opened the hatch from the crew cabin. "The blinking dots are?"

"Microlensing events," Blake told her, sorry that their chattering had wakened her.

Rikki's eyes went round. "A cosmic string?"

"I believe…so."

Dana said, "Less mystery, more explanation please."

"You'll…explain quicker, Rikki."

"It has to do with the very early universe," Rikki said. "Here's the twitter version. Big Bang fireball. Everything's super-hot and expanding. Expansion cools things, like expanding water vapor can condense to liquid water."

Blake thought, I love you dearly, but this is the *quick* version?

"Vapor to water is a phase transition," Rikki continued. "Cool further, and the next big change is from water to ice. Ever see an ice patch form on the inside surface of a dome when the outside temperature plummets?"

Or the inside of a windowpane during a Boston cold snap. On the glass in Blake's mind's eye, random lines and curves crisscrossed the icy coating. But what did window frost have to do with anything?

"Picture the fracture lines in the ice," Rikki said. "Each line is where expanding regions of spontaneous phase change, water turning to ice, collided. Where matters get hand-wavy"—and she gesticulated, illustrating—"is in likening the collisions between cooling space-time regions with ice fracture lines." She hesitated. "Help me out here, Antonio."

Antonio said, "Energy got trapped…in the interstices. Lots of energy. Theorists call these objects…cosmic strings."

"Because cosmic strings remain theoretical," Rikki said. "No one has ever seen one."

Dana turned to study the star-field holo. "But you have, Antonio? The red dots?"

"Right."

Rikki said, "Well, we can't *see* a cosmic string, not directly. But they're massive, so they bend light. That's why we're seeing microlensing events, when on our fast-changing line of sight a star drops behind the string."

"And you're the first person to spot one?" Dana said skeptically.

"This string points more or less straight at Sol system. The backdrop is…the Coalsack. Few stars are visible through that to be lensed. Both factors…would make this…string hard to spot."

Rikki said, "And remember where we are: far beneath the ecliptic, about thirty times Pluto's distance from the sun. No one has ever had this perspective."

"You said trapped energy," Blake said. "Isn't it the presence of mass that bends light?"

"Energy. Mass. Same thing," Antonio said.

Because $E=mc^2$, Blake thought. I know that. And I need to sleep.

"This is all quite educational," Dana said, "but how does it matter?"

Antonio shrugged. "Some things are just interesting."

11

Angry voices roused Dana from restless slumber. A man and a woman, Dana noticed. She couldn't make out any words.

Antonio, his mouth agape, was fast asleep across the crew cabin. He didn't stir as Dana left her jump seat. Blake and Rikki had the bridge and with it what passed aboard for privacy. Feeling like a voyeur, Dana pressed an ear to the hatch onto the bridge. The yelling was not coming from inside.

Antonio stirred at the hinge squeak when Dana opened the deck hatch. "Go back to sleep," she whispered and he settled down. She went into the central shaft. With one hand, she kept a grip on the ladder; with the other, she slowly let down the hatch, trying to avoid the customary *clang*. Her arm trembled with the effort.

From within the shaft, she recognized the quarreling voices: Li and Carlos. They were inside cargo hold three.

"…could be our last chance…you can't tell me you don't…," Carlos said.

Dana let herself down closer.

"I *am* telling you," Li said. "You're better than this."

"Don't be such a tease. You came when I asked."

"Not knowing the kind of 'help' you had in mind," Li said. "I won't say this again. Get away from the hatch."

Shit! Dana thought.

She had allowed herself to believe people would act like adults. Aboard *Reliance*, no matter the mixed crew, people did. But those were trained professionals who expected, someday, to go home.

Li was *tiny*, almost a meter shorter than Carlos. Dana grabbed for the hatch latch—

And jerked her hand back as the hatch shuddered. From inside came a surprised basso grunt, then a thud.

As the hold's hatch opened, Dana scuttled a few rungs down the ladder. Let it appear she was coming from an engine room.

Li grabbed the ladder, swung into the shaft, and slammed the hatch behind her. She was breathing heavily, all but panting. "Oh, Captain. I didn't know you were up and about."

"Just making rounds," Dana said. "What's going on?"

"Oh, nothing."

"I thought I heard voices in the hold," Dana hinted.

"Carlos asked about my help with something, and I advised him to handle it himself."

"And everyone is all right?"

Li sighed. "Okay, so you overheard. I believe Carlos has acquired an appreciation for my point of view."

"Which is?"

"That if he's Adam, I'm AWOL. And that a scrawny Martian beanpole shouldn't cross Earth girls who know tae kwon do."

"Applied psychology?" Dana asked.

"Self-defense."

A soft moan drifted through the hatch.

Dana said, "From what I overheard, he deserved what he got. That said, I hope you didn't inflict any permanent damage."

"He'll be fine, and perhaps wiser. I could have planted my foot much deeper."

Carlos didn't seem the type to admit that his advances had been spurned, or that a woman had decked him—especially to another woman. Dana said, "Assuming that he doesn't bring the matter up to me, do I know what happened? It's your call."

"I don't think that will be necessary, Captain. Not that I noticed a brig on this ship."

"It's your call," Dana repeated.

Her hands shaking, Li started up the shaft toward the crew cabin. "Damn Hawthorne!" she burst out.

Huh? "What do you mean?"

Li paused on the ladder. "Rikki and Blake, dotingly married. You and Antonio, of similar ages. Carlos and me, the same. Don't you imagine Hawthorne had more than professional skills in mind when he picked this crew? Or that Carlos also sees the obvious pairing?"

In encrypted files Dana would never admit to having aboard, Hawthorne had revealed Antonio as a widower, Carlos as three times divorced, and Li as between serious relationships. Of Dana herself, the same data field had delicately declared: *career-oriented*.

Dana said, "It's understandable that you don't care for the apparent matchmaking."

"You *do*?"

Antonio was *so* focused, the marvel was that he had ever gotten together with someone. All Tabitha's doing, Dana had to believe. There would be no unwelcome advances from that direction. That made Li's situation all the more unique.

"Regardless," Dana said, "Carlos has no right to act as he did. Forget him *and* Hawthorne. Are you all right?"

"Fine, Captain."

"Dana. One woman talking with another."

"In that case, I've been better."

"What do you say you and I check out the supply of medicinal alcohol?"

Li tipped her head, considering. "That, Dana, is an excellent idea."

✸

Under the ongoing, relentless acceleration, the pilot and copilot seats were the closest things to comfortable on the ship. Blake and Rikki's turn had come around again on the rotation and he dozed fitfully, listening to her gentle snoring and wishing *he* could sleep. But since he couldn't, he took turns watching Rikki and, in the main bridge display, the unblinking, brilliant spark that was Sol.

Someone rapped on the hatch set in the deck.

"Go away," Blake said.

"It's Dana."

"Sorry," he said. "Come in."

Cautiously, the hatch swung open. Dana climbed onto the bridge and squeezed into the space beside his seat. Antonio followed, to stand beside Rikki. Despite the crowding, Antonio latched the deck hatch while Dana secured the already closed hatch to the crew cabin.

Blake started to stand. With a hand on his shoulder, Dana nudged him back into the acceleration chair.

All the rustling or the whispering woke Rikki. "What's going on?" she asked.

Blake shrugged.

Dana turned to Antonio. "*Now* will you tell me what we all must hear?"

"One of the big issues with Big…Bang theory is that…"

After—could it have been a month?—cooped up together, Blake recognized the enthusiasm in Antonio's voice. More astronomical esoterica?

"Stop," Dana said. "Before you get going on the Big Bang, tell me why I wouldn't be better off sleeping."

"Because maybe we don't have to…die."

Rikki twitched.

"Maybe start at the end," Dana said.

"Our odds of getting clear," Antonio said. "Maybe two percent."

"You've said we had *days* of margin," Rikki said.

"There are uncertainties. I gave you the best-case scenario."

Perilously close to a lie, Blake thought. He noticed that Dana didn't look surprised. "You knew?"

"Hawthorne told me. The more realistic, longer odds didn't change what needed doing, so why deny you some hope?" Dana turned to Antonio. "All right, you have my *complete* attention. But can we start a few billion years after the Big Bang?"

"I'm afraid not." Antonio began fingering the scar on his chin. "Many observations about the universe make sense only if everything…had enormously rapid expansion *right* after the Big Bang."

"Cosmic inflation," Rikki said. "Space-time expanding at many times faster than the speed of light."

Dana frowned. "I thought nothing went faster than light."

"Right," Rikki said, "but space-time isn't a thing. And if space-time did once expand at super-luminal speeds—faster than light—otherwise counterintuitive observations make sense."

"Like the uniform distribution of galaxies across the…universe."

"About not dying?" Dana prompted.

"Cosmic inflation is a *mathematical* fix," Antonio said. "It fits what astronomers see so well we've come *to* accept…it as what must…*have* happened. The particular details don't matter."

"Then why are we talking about it?" Dana asked.

"Because there's an alternative mathematical fix. If certain universal constants *aren't* constant. Maybe only their ratio must be.

"I only vaguely…remembered this old theory. None of the files aboard mention…it. I had to derive enough to reconstruct the hypothesis."

"And that hypothesis *is*?" Dana tried again.

"Under early universe conditions, *light* went faster than light. Than light does…today."

Blake saw the struggle on Antonio's face, the words refusing to come out. "Take your time," he told Antonio.

Even though time is the commodity we most lack.

"May I try?" Rikki asked. "I think I see."

Eyes cast downward, Antonio nodded.

Rikki said, "Suppose light speed *was* much higher under early-universe conditions. Cosmic strings, like the one we see ahead, froze bits of the early universe. Near a string, the speed of light may be faster than what we now know."

"Near the string?" Blake asked. "Not inside the string?"

Rikki shook her head. "You can't get inside. The string itself is very thin."

"Like a…proton."

"How does this *help*?" Dana asked.

71

"Antonio?" Rikki said. "I know this is important, so be sure I get this right. The faster our ship goes, the more relativistic effects we experience. Before the DED, unable to keep accelerating as this ship can, these effects never mattered."

She leaned forward to read numbers off a console. "We've reached about fifty thousand klicks per second, about one-sixth light speed. Marvin, what is our relativistic mass effect?"

"About a percent and a half," the AI answered.

"Not yet dramatic," Rikki said. "But it will be."

"The faster we go, the more massive we get. Pushing more and more…mass, the DED is…less effective. But maybe close to a cosmic string…"

At last, Blake saw their point. "If light speed is much faster along a cosmic string, we won't experience relativistic effects. So our mass won't increase, and *that* means we'll accelerate faster than otherwise."

"Indeed," Antonio said.

Dana said, "The string you found points toward the Coalsack, somewhat off our course. Maybe that's okay. Drawing upon dark energy, we don't spend fuel to detour. But will we gain enough extra speed to get clear of the GRB?"

Antonio murmured something.

"What's that?" Dana said.

"Yes," Antonio said. "Unless we don't."

"Meaning *what*?" Dana pressed. "We're talking in circles."

"Case A," Rikki said. "Cosmic inflation happened. The speed of light along the string is exactly what we are accustomed to. Case B. Inflation never happened, and as we approach the string, light goes faster and faster."

"And we can't know…which…till we get there."

Dana asked, "Suppose we detour and find that the speed of light hasn't changed?"

"Then…we die."

Dana frowned. "What are the chances either way?"

Rubbing his chin more briskly than ever, Antonio shrugged.

"So either fifty-to-one against us or we just don't know at all?" Dana asked. "Do I have my scenarios right, Antonio?"

"Yes, Captain."

Blake turned toward Dana. "It's your call, Captain."

"Life or death for the human race?" Dana said. "That's everyone's call, Li and Carlos included."

When they found the other two, Carlos uncharacteristically subdued, and Dana put the ship's course up for a vote, the decision was unanimous to steer for the cosmic string.

12

Six long, tapered tubes with their piano-hinged lids tipped back—the cold-sleep pods gaped like open coffins.

Though no one commented, Blake would have bet anything that everyone saw the resemblance.

He stood with Rikki, among the passengers, along the cargo hold's curved, exterior wall. Rikki's hand in his felt clammy. Dana stood opposite, at the feet of the pods.

There should be a speech, Blake thought, but after six weeks living like sardines in a can what could possibly remain to be said? Regardless, Dana was about the last person he knew to make a speech.

Death stalked the worlds of man. Billions must die. Civilization *would* die. Maybe, against all odds, the six of them would escape. Maybe they would survive to add a chapter to humanity's story. Far more likely the GRB would blast this ship, too, and their riddled corpses would hurtle forever through the interstellar darkness.

In any case, *I* shouldn't give a speech.

Then Dana surprised him.

"The time has come, my friends," she said. "I know the situation is dire. I know that our prospects look bleak. But consider: we are on a mission grander and more important than anything we might ever have dared to dream of. Good people believed in us; good people gave their all to hasten us on our way. Already we have gone where no human has gone before. *Endeavour* is a fine ship, a proven ship, and Marvin knows what to do while we sleep."

But *did* Marvin know? Blake wondered.

How complete could their modified nav software be? No one had ever approached a cosmic string. And how meaningful were the AI's assurances that its hastily coded program extensions had not broken it?

"I'll see you all on the other side," Dana concluded firmly.

Antonio shuffled toward the first pod in the line. He sat, lifted his legs over the platform edge, and lay down. "On the other…side."

Li followed, offering a brave smile, then Carlos.

In Blake's grasp, Rikki's hand trembled. "It'll be all right," he told her.

She nodded.

"Let's do this together," he said.

They took the few steps to two pods at the end of the row. He helped Rikki settle inside hers, trying *not* to think of coffins. Leaning over, he gave her a kiss. "Sweet dreams."

She forced a smile. "Sweet dreams."

As Blake lay down, he saw Dana had taken her place in the final pod.

"You have the conn, Marvin," Dana called. "Close the pods."

"I have the conn," Marvin acknowledged. "Commencing cold sleep."

The transparent lid pivoted down. As freezing mist billowed, Blake turned his head for a last glimpse of Rikki.

Never had he seen her so despondent.

Did her hopelessness evoke the memory, or was the sudden chill to blame? Maybe both. In proposing a ship's name, surely Rikki had not intended to reveal the depths of her despair. After all, how likely was he to recall one particular conversation from three years ago?

Only he did.

She had once, her eyes shining, told him about the Heroic Age of Antarctic Exploration and the race to explore Earth's last frontier. One adventurer, too late to discover the South Pole, had set out to be the first to make a land journey across Antarctica. He had run an advertisement in the London newspapers:

"MEN WANTED: For hazardous journey. Small wages, bitter cold, long months of complete darkness, constant danger, safe return doubtful. Honour and recognition in case of success. Sir Ernest Shackleton."

On the way to Antarctica, Shackleton's ship *Endurance* became trapped in pack ice. After almost a year in the grip of the ice floes, with its hull crushed, the vessel foundered. Its crew was cast adrift, far from any land.

And *Endurance* was the name Rikki had proposed for this ship.

But in search of rescue, in one epic feat after another, Shackleton had conquered ice, ocean, and mountains. Everyone on the expedition survived.

As frigid vapor filled Blake's lungs and the cold permeated his body, as consciousness failed and thought congealed, Blake found hope in Shackleton's ultimate triumph.

This crew, too, would endure.

DETOUR

(About forty-five years later)

13

Indistinct, out of reach, *something* beckoned.

Light? Through closed eyelids, she sensed brightness. Space to move about? That, too. But most of all—and most enticing of all—warmth.

But how to enter the warmth? That mystery eluded her.

From the depths of an abyss, she sensed movement. Shaking? Convulsing? No, something between. Coughing. *She* was coughing.

And there was sound. Speech.

"Time to get up. Time to get up. Time to get up..."

Whose voice was that? How long had it been speaking? "Yes," she said, only the word came out as an inarticulate croak.

"Good, you are awake," the voice responded. The words had a flatness that belied the sentiment.

An AI. Marvin, she recalled. What else did she remember? A racking cough vanquished that thought. And did she hear someone else coughing?

Her eyes, like rusted hinges, resisted opening. Opening them anyway, she glimpsed through tendrils of white mist a frost-speckled clear dome. The dome canted at a steep angle.

So that I can get out. Laughing at the absurdity of even sitting, the first, sharp intake of breath set her chain-coughing again.

The spasm finally subsided.

"Mar...vin," she rasped.

"You might want to take it slowly," the AI said. "My readouts indicate that you may need a minute."

I'll need hours. As glacially as her thoughts churned, she had an insight. "I'm not heavy."

"We are decelerating at one-third gee," it said. "*Endeavour* is safe."

Safe? Safe from what?

The whole panic/horror/insanity crashed down on her. Along with whom she was. And who was with her. And the billions who were gone, dead, fried.

"Blake!" The shout tore at Rikki's throat, set her coughing again.

"Yea-ugh," someone sputtered. It might have been him.

She remembered where his pod was, and turned her head. Even in Mars-like gravity, her neck muscles screamed with the effort. She found Blake looking back at her.

She said, "You look..." Wheezing preempted the description.

"Yeah, but we're *alive*." He attempted a smile. "I'll grant it...doesn't feel that way."

Beyond Blake's pod, Rikki saw the others stirring. There was Dana, blinking as though to clear her eyes. And Li, groggily turning her head from side to side. At the end of the row, Antonio had managed to sit up. With a hand raised to his face, he was stroking his chin scar. And in the middle—

"Carlos's pod is still closed!" Rikki said.

Marvin said, "His readouts had drifted beyond the desired parameters. I thought Li should make the decision whether to interrupt his cold sleep, and be here to monitor the process."

Dana struggled into a sitting position. "Marvin, report," she whispered hoarsely.

"We avoided the GRB, and all major shipboard systems continue to operate within acceptable limits. As expected, radiation degraded external sensors as the ship's speed increased. I kept sensors powered off and shuttered as much as practical to extend their lifetimes. The bridge also sustained radiation damage. I cannot quantify the impairment, beyond severe enough that diagnostic programs fail to run to completion. I believe we have the spare parts to repair everything."

"What about life support?" Dana prompted. "Propulsion?"

"Both systems are operating within acceptable parameters," Marvin said.

Rikki sat up and swiveled, dropping her legs over the side of the pod. The change in position made her head spin and she did not dare to stand. Her arms and legs trembled. The taste in her mouth was like old cardboard.

All from the cold-sleep process?

Once before, Rikki had been in a pod. She'd been researching the history of the ice industry. Getting miners at one of the oldest still-producing tunnel complexes to agree to meet with her had been a struggle. When the appointed time came, despite having felt queasy for days, she'd gone anyway. The queasiness became abdominal discomfort; having flown halfway around the world, she ignored the feeling as best she could to continue with the interviews.

But discomfort became soreness became pain. Stomach upset turned to nausea. When the vomiting began, there was no ignoring it.

Acute appendicitis, the miners' medical AI had diagnosed. The miners popped her into a cold-sleep pod for transport to the nearest hospital.

Awakening from that pod in the OR, she had been in agony. But that had been a localized pain. Now she hurt—everywhere. And though she had felt feeble that time, she didn't remember being so bone-weary, or confused about who and where she was. But that incident had involved only a few hours in the pod.

Rikki asked, "Marvin, how long have we been in cold sleep?"

"According to the ship's clock," Marvin said, "it has been almost forty-five years."

14

Logic, thermostat readouts, and gushers of warm air from the bridge air vents be damned, Dana was *freezing*. The sensation was all in her head, surely, but she felt chilled to the marrow of her bones. She gulped from a drink bulb, burning her mouth and throat, but the scalding black coffee could not melt the cold fear.

Forty-five *years*? Something had gone horribly wrong.

She sat in the pilot's acceleration seat, dying to rub her arms with her hands, and resisting. A captain did not hug herself for warmth.

No matter how shaken she was.

She had ordered Blake and Antonio forward to check out the bridge. In the minutes spent strapping Carlos into a stretcher and helping carry him to the infirmary—he limp and delirious, she and the other women lightheaded and wobbly—Blake had already begun repairs. Antonio perched on the outside armrest of the copilot's seat, scrolling through data on the sensor console, uploading numbers from the ship's files to the datasheet draped across his lap.

Blake squirmed, muttering, flat on his back on the sliver of deck between the acceleration couches. His head and both hands were deep inside the nav console. After years flying together, Dana had calibrated his cursing. She interpreted: he had found plenty out of kilter, the ship's overall integrity was satisfactory, and he trusted his ability to make the necessary repairs.

She wouldn't worry until that mumble morphed into something louder.

"Eighth time's the charm, maybe." Blake wriggled out of the console, clutching a scorched electronics module. He set the ruined part with the rejects already littering the deck. "Oh, hi, Dana. How's Carlos doing?"

"Stable, is all I can tell you. Still out of it. How are things here?"

Squeezing past Antonio, Blake settled into the copilot's seat. He shut the access panel with a shoe tip. "A good question. Marvin, try the main displays again, fore and aft views."

The infirmary, where Li and Rikki continued to monitor Carlos's condition, must be even more crowded. But the women's voices—when they rose above the drone of the ventilation fans—were calm. The tone struck Dana as positive.

Unlike what came from the repaired holo projector. Ahead: countless unfamiliar stars. Aft: formless, foreboding darkness.

So much for her deduction upon hearing they had overslept. That *Endeavour*'s velocity had peaked early, for reasons unknown. That the ship had crawled, comparatively speaking, making the trek to Alpha Centauri at "only" a few percent of light speed. That if nothing else had gone according to plan, at least they knew where they were and where they were headed.

Wishful thinking, it seemed.

"All right, Marvin," Dana said. "Explain what happened, why you kept us in cold sleep for so long, and where we are."

"I cannot say where," Marvin said. "Somewhere beyond my chart files."

Dana frowned. "You must have *some* idea."

"The cloud may be the Coalsack: that is the closest dark nebula to Sol system. If so, still relative to Sol system, we are on the nebula's far side."

"Past the *Coalsack?*" Blake said. "That'd be more than six hundred light-years!"

"That's about right," Antonio said. "I have bearings on several beacons."

Who could have put beacons out here? Dana pinched the bridge of her nose. Behind her eyes, a killer headache waited to pounce. "What are you talking about, beacons?"

"Natural beacons. Pulsars." Antonio kept prodding his datasheet as he spoke. "Some neutron stars emit regular RF...pulses. Each star pulses at a unique rate, related to...its rotation. With bearings on a few known RF sources, it's just geometry to *find* our location." He did something to the datasheet, then handed it to Dana. "Our coordinates."

She felt like Marvin: off the charts. The coordinates were mere numbers, meaningless. They might just as well have read, like the periphery of some medieval chart, *Beyond this point be monsters.* "Why did you bring us here, Marvin?"

"The cosmic string brought us here," Marvin said. "I did not have sensors to characterize it. I only know that it pulled us in. It required the DED *and* the fusion drive to achieve orbit."

And what an odd orbit it must have been! Thin as a proton, Antonio had called it. The cosmic string was like a line in space, a line along which they had spiraled to exploit the locally faster light speed.

She downed another swig of the hot coffee. It once more refused to warm her.

"But why remain along the string?" Dana asked. For forty-five *years*!

Antonio was only too happy to theorize.

The stuttering, hesitant torrent of words went over her head, and Dana realized she had let curiosity get the better of her. *How* they had gotten here, so far from home, no longer mattered. Because home was gone. What mattered was that they *were* here, escaped from the GRB.

And that having survived, she had a job to do. They all did.

She said, "Antonio, excuse me for a moment." Because lost or not, dangers might lurk nearby. "Marvin, how fast are we traveling?"

"Relative to the interstellar medium, we have slowed to about one-tenth light speed. That is estimated from measured radiation levels. I waited to wake everyone until you could move about the ship in complete safety."

The interstellar medium was as close as the galaxy came to a perfect vacuum. Dana asked, "Other than that, what's our speed?"

"Relative to what?"

A damned good question, for which she had no answer. "What's nearby?"

"Nothing is within radar range."

Peering into the holos, she saw not a single star with a visible disk. Thermal readings from the hull confirmed that the ship was deep in the interstellar deep freeze.

"How far to the closest stars?" she asked.

"I don't know which stars are closest," the AI said.

"So where are we headed? Why are we under acceleration?"

Marvin said, "We came off the string at near-light speed. We are not so much going somewhere as we are slowing down. I don't know where *to* go."

And she did? "Antonio? Suggestions?"

"I'll look into it." Antonio straightened on the armrest. "About our flight along the string. I have some thoughts…what may have happened."

"Good," Dana said. "You and Marvin carry on while I check on Carlos."

Blake nodded. "I'll get you caught up later."

His recap would be simpler and more succinct than anything she could hear by staying. "Great," she said.

A few steps returned her to the infirmary.

Carlos was lying on the fold-down cot, beneath a thin white sheet. He had sensor patches on his forehead, wrists, and, to judge from wrinkles in the sheet, on his chest. A saline bag hung nearby, the IV tube coiling and swooping to his arm. To Dana's untutored eye Carlos appeared jaundiced, but on the nearby scanner the EEG/EKG traces were steady and only scattered amber entries interrupted the many readouts in green. He was awake.

Dana asked, "How are you feeling?"

Carlos patted the sheet. "This wasn't how I pictured first getting naked with you women."

It was empty bravado, the bluster of a man terrified by a close call—and too macho to admit it. Behind Carlos, Li rolled her eyes.

Dana let the effrontery pass with, "It's good that you're well enough to make jokes."

"Jokes?"

Dana turned to Li. "What can you tell me?"

Li shrugged. "Not much. Metabolites, neurotransmitters, platelet counts, a hundred proteins and trace-metal concentrations are off-kilter. But so are mine, if not as dramatically. So are Rikki's. When I test the rest of you, and I will, I expect I'll find much the same. To the best of my knowledge, no one has ever spent this long in cold sleep. The marvel is that we came out of it at all."

"I'm loaded with med nanites," Carlos said. "Top-of-the-line, cutting-edge, full-spectrum health maintenance bots. Why am *I* the one whose biochemistry is out of whack?"

Because you're a jerk? As capable as some nanites were, Dana supposed the tiny bots weren't that perceptive. "Li, any thoughts on that?"

"My guess? It's *because* of the nanites. I doubt they were programmed for prolonged cold-sleep conditions. Why would they be?

"With his metabolism slowed way down, bodily functions wouldn't behave as the nanites expected. His biochemistry being slow to respond to treatment, the nanites would try bigger and bigger dosages.

Eventually, at cold sleep's glacial rate, as his body did react, he'd have way too many nano-synthed meds in circulation. His system would overshoot, and the nanites would have new problems to address—still without proper programming for cold-sleep responses. I'll have to filter some bots from his blood sample and download the memory files to know for certain."

Carlos propped himself up on an elbow. "And until then, Doctor?"

"You stay here, under observation."

With his free hand, Carlos stroked his sheet. "As you wish."

Dana guessed he would be discharged as soon as humanly possible. Or that he would get a sedative in his IV.

Rikki said, "Any word as to where we are? Why we slept so long?"

"We're not sure yet," Dana said. "Blake and Antonio are reviewing the data. In a little while, I'll check on their progress."

"Send the men here for a quick eval," Li said. "And you, too, when you can spare a minute."

Not till Carlos is gone from the infirmary, Dana resolved. "As soon as it's practical."

15

Dana decompressed with a snack and a fresh bulb of coffee before going to look for Blake. By then he had left the bridge. With Antonio and Marvin still babbling in tongues, she headed for the opposite end of the ship.

She found Blake in engine room two, frowning at the fuel readout. An access door had been removed, and instrument cables had been clipped to the paraphernalia within. A signal analyzer sat on the deck.

He followed her gaze. "Half the systems aboard need recalibration. Component properties will drift a lot in forty-five freaking years."

"I suppose so." One more thing that might have killed them.

"Is Carlos doing any better?"

"He's well enough to kid around." Dana saw no reason to volunteer that the supposed wit encompassed getting naked with Rikki. "How are *we* doing?"

"We almost didn't make it," Blake said.

"How's that?"

"Our deuterium tanks are about dry."

"We were supposed to be flying on the DED this whole while," Dana said. "And I thought the DED drew enough power, from wherever, to also supply shipboard systems."

"That's the point." Blake took a deep breath, then exhaled sharply. "You ready to hear what happened to us?"

"Sure."

"If you ask me, the core issue is that no one had ever before seen a cosmic string. From a sufficient distance maybe it's fair to consider it one-dimensional. Antonio and I made that assumption when we modded the nav program."

"I gather that on approach to the string we got within that magic distance. Marvin mentioned needing the fusion drive to achieve orbit."

"I *wish* the problem had only been on approach." Blake grimaced. "Back to that one-dimensional-line simplification. Time and again Marvin needed both drives to maintain a safe distance."

"The line isn't so simple?"

"Back at the university, did you ever catch astrophysicists telling jokes?" Blake asked.

Huh? "Not funny?"

"Funny enough, just odd," Blake said. "A bunch of their jokes begin something like, 'Assuming a spherical cow…'"

"I don't get it."

"When a real calculation would be too complicated, they assume away the complexity. Imagine a galaxy with billions of stars, all of them in motion, within clouds of dust and gas, within an invisible halo of dark matter. You can't very well calculate the exact mass distribution. So someone interested in, say, how a particular star will move within the galaxy might begin by assuming the stars and clouds form symmetric disks embedded in a symmetric sphere of dark matter. Just as he might consider that a cosmic string is a one-dimensional thread of uniform density."

It felt good to laugh. "Got it. So mocking themselves, knowing that they sometimes oversimplify, a cow becomes a perfect sphere."

"Right."

Dana liberated a sturdy-looking crate from behind cargo netting, set it on the deck, and sat. "How did our cosmic string differ from a uniform line?"

"How didn't it differ? Knotted and snarled, maybe. Or the density varies along the string's length. Or there are overlapping pieces, or a dashed line of pieces, the primordial strings having long ago fragmented."

Dana shivered. "They *fragment*?"

"They must have, and repeatedly. The very early universe was very much smaller. Any cosmic strings still intact from that era would have become stretched to millions of light-years, maybe longer. They would have dictated the structure of entire galactic clusters."

"Okay, then," she said. "Knotted and snarled and whatever. With none of that complexity in the nav program."

"Uh-huh. And if we had crashed into the string..."

As thin as a proton, Dana remembered. "We'd have been sliced in two?"

"According to Antonio, each klick of length along the cosmic string has a mass comparable to Earth's." Blake paused. "So, yeah. Picture a dandelion puff meeting a chainsaw."

After the fact, Dana saw that she had taken a lot on faith. Forty-five years after the fact. Such as trusting Marvin to navigate the ship along a cosmic string. How does one follow something too thin to see?

Cut yourself some slack, she chided herself. It's not like you had the time to think about it, or decent options. And remember: we survived.

She said, "I still want to know what happened to us, and where we are. Did you coax either from Marvin?"

"More Antonio's doing than mine, but yes. You remember how he first found the cosmic string?"

"Microlensing. There were enough background stars microlensing to navigate by?"

"Nothing so straightforward." Blake hunted around the engine room until he located a plate with a half sandwich. "Back on Earth, did you ever swim underwater? Snorkel or scuba?"

"Snorkel. Why?"

"Did you ever happen to look up while you did, and see something unusual?"

One January after term finals, she'd been among a bunch of cadets from the Academy who'd flown down to the Virgin Islands. What a week they'd had! Wind surfing. Paragliding. Beach volleyball. A day trip to a Mayan ruin on the mainland. And one day they had all gone snorkeling above a reef, the coral vibrant with sparkling whites, warm pastels, and shocking pinks. She remembered the fish, hundreds, sometimes thousands of them, darting and weaving in formation like flocks of birds.

And one giant sea turtle.

She remembered Liam, her boyfriend at the time, pointing upward when Dana looked to see who had grabbed her ankle. The turtle, blue with white speckles, longer nose to tail than she was tall, gliding majestically overhead. The *top* of the turtle—it was covered in overlapping leather plates rather than by a hard shell—seen as clearly as its underside. The turtle's back was reflecting off the smooth boundary between sea and sky.

"Total internal reflection." She thought the startling effect had something to do with the indices of refraction of the neighboring media. Beyond some critical angle dependent on the ratio (if she remembered that correctly), all light striking the boundary bounced off. "Sure, I've encountered it. What's that have to do with our situation?"

"You would be surprised. Whatever you saw while snorkeling involved light in the water unable to cross into the air, never light in the air kept from penetrating into the water. That's one example of the rule: total internal reflection happens within the medium having the higher index of refraction. That's the medium with the slower speed of light."

Dana flexed her drink bulb, almost empty, as she pondered. "Near the string, where light is uncharacteristically fast, starlight bounces off?"

Blake nodded. "Except for incoming light that is all but perpendicular to the string, that's the case. The closer *Endeavour* approached the string, the faster the local light speed and the less starlight would reach us."

So much for a turtle's back, crystal clear in reflection. Marvin's challenge had been more like a nighttime plunge into the ocean depths. She tried to imagine following the distant, unseen surface with nothing to guide her but occasional faint glimmers of starlight.

The tepid dregs in her drink bulb couldn't touch her resurgent chill. She hoped Blake hadn't noticed her trembling.

Dana said, "Leaving Marvin to infer the location of the cosmic string from the level of incident starlight." She shifted her empty bulb from hand to hand. "Still, when the string twisted or curved or got denser unexpectedly, when the starlight went away, how did he know which way to veer? The distribution of stars isn't all that constant."

"Know? A cynic would say, 'guess.'" With a sour expression, Blake set down his plate, the food untouched. "Marvin *didn't* always know which way to turn, especially as external sensors degraded. Whenever it guessed wrong, whenever by accident it veered the ship toward the string, it needed both drives to back away to safety."

No *wonder* they had all but exhausted their supply of deuterium!

Dana said, "I'd call Marvin a freaking genius, except for one thing. We aren't supposed to *be* here. Why didn't we break free from the string after a couple of light-years?" Like we told Marvin to do.

"We were trapped," Blake said. "Breaking free would have involved prolonged thrusting at right angles to the string. We'd have been broadside to the oncoming radiation all the while. It was bad enough that we got short blasts of radiation with every orbit-maintenance maneuver."

Dana considered. *Endeavour*'s only meaningful shielding was fore and aft: what they had retrofitted near the bow, plated over the decks of the bridge and crew quarters, and around the fusion reactor. Perhaps more than the long years of cold sleep were behind how crappy she felt, and Carlos's deterioration. "So breaking away would have given us a lethal dose."

"Other than by flying off an end of the cosmic string, yeah. And the attempt would have fried Marvin, too. Its circuits aren't much happier with radiation than our cells are."

"So we flew to the end," she said.

"As fast as the ship could deliver us there."

"What if the string had been a lot longer?"

"Antonio says this string couldn't have been *too* much longer," Blake said. "Much more mass would have had a visible effect on the local distribution of stars. A longer cosmic string would have been detected centuries ago."

Dana preferred that answer to the notion that once *Endeavour* exhausted its deuterium, they would have been done for.

Blake yawned, and Dana followed. It was ridiculous that after forty-five years asleep, her body cried out for a nap. Ridiculous but not to be denied for much longer.

She said, "Bottom-line it for me. Where the hell *are* we?"

Blake yawned again. "As the interstellar-capable crow flies, about one hundred light-years beyond the Coalsack. Call it seven hundred forty light-years from Sol system. But we took the scenic route: sweeping around the nebula, not through it. If the string had run through the cloud, gravity would have collapsed a big clear channel through the Coalsack long ago."

"Any idea how far we actually came? As the ship actually flew?"

"Marvin knows how long we accelerated and how hard. It knows how long we coasted. From that, at least a thousand light-years. Jumoke would have been proud of her DED: we peaked out a little above thirty-nine times normal light speed."

Thirty-nine times? Fuzzy-brained from exhaustion, or radiation, or years in cold sleep, stifling yet another yawn, Dana had to ask, "At *least* a thousand light-years?"

"Will you quit that, please," Blake yawned back. "Yeah, at least. The estimates rely on elapsed time as measured by the ship's clock, and in our own frame of reference, by definition, our clock ticks normally. Did we experience time dilation relative to home? We don't know.

"So: the estimates are in the ballpark if the local light speed was *way* faster than forty times normal. Otherwise not. We have no way to know. And do you remember the pulsars Antonio is using as beacons? Like any star, pulsars drift. Our locational fix is as iffy as our time fix."

If we can't know where we are, I'll waste no more energy thinking about it. Because I have quite enough to worry about.

Dana said, "So we're on the wrong side of a dark nebula, in galactica incognita. No astronomer has ever seen this region of space. I suppose that means no one knows where we might find a planet suitable for establishing a colony."

Blake arched on eyebrow. "You thought this was going to be *easy?*"

16

With a decent telescope and a spectrograph, a ship could analyze asteroids from a distance. Most asteroids were mere rock, worthless—but a few were treasure troves of precious metals and rare-earth elements. Spot an asteroid like that and stake a claim, and your fortune was made.

Clermont, become *Endeavour*, carried a decent telescope. Emphasis on the past tense. Decades of pounding by cosmic rays had degraded that telescope into something at which Galileo would have sneered.

At least that was what Antonio had to say on the subject.

"We don't *have* replacement mirrors," Blake reminded. He was as tired of repeating himself as he was of stacking-room-only meetings on the bridge. Though he did not mind Rikki sitting on his lap. Forty-five years was a lot of abstinence, even asleep and frozen solid. "And before you ask, I can't polish and replate these mirrors, either. I'd have to make the tools to make the tools to make the tools, with maybe a few more iterations. Don't even ask how long that'd take. A while."

"We can't afford rations for 'a while,'" Dana said. "We need to *get* somewhere."

"Look, Antonio," Rikki said. "I'll never know half the astronomy that you do, but I know something of the history of the subject. The Galileo crack is an exaggeration, don't you think? And not just because his telescope didn't use mirrors.

"By two centuries ago astronomers had approximated the distance to nearby stars. They did it without any computers worth mentioning. They did it, being earthbound, despite atmospheric shimmer blurring every observation. *We* have a modern telescope, even if it is a bit dinged up, and Marvin to handle all our calculations, and no atmosphere to distort our viewing. I refuse to believe we can't match twentieth-century science."

"I suppose," Antonio conceded.

"Walk me through the process," Dana said. "How would we measure the distances?"

"Sure," Rikki said. "By way of an analogy, hold a finger in front of your nose. With one eye closed, look at the finger. Notice where the finger appears against the background of the bulkhead behind it. Now switch eyes."

"The finger seemed to jump," Dana said.

"Right. And knowing the two viewing angles and the distance between your eyes, you could calculate the location of your finger relative to your face."

"My finger represents a star," Dana said. "And my two eyes?"

"Two separate sightings on the star. For old-time astronomers, that meant observations made six months apart. Earth's orbit is about one thousand light-seconds wide. The parallax technique located stars as remote as a few hundred light-years."

"We're not orbiting...," Dana began. "Scratch that. We're moving."

Blake did rough math in his head. "Every three hours or so, we're crossing a distance like the width of Earth's orbit. In a day, even with our scarred-up mirror, we should have lots of good readings."

"Can we focus on individual stars?" Dana asked.

"Focus?" Antonio stroked his chin scar. "Not to my satisfaction. But yes, we can locate and take bearings on individual stars."

"Good," Dana said. "You and Rikki, get to work."

✳

Blake gazed around the machine shop, waiting for something to happen. Nothing did. He rearranged the tool cabinet. He buffed a streak of grease off a bulkhead. There wasn't room to pace, so he shifted his weight from one leg to the other.

He did *not* want to be here. But the only meaningful activity aboard was on the bridge, and he could contribute nothing to star hunts.

"It's just milk," he said.

"And you're a pile of common elements, worth pocket change." Carlos sighed without looking up, intent on the scrolling readout from a portable synth vat. He stood, hunched over the workbench. The shop stools and workbenches fit Blake.

"Well?" Blake finally prompted. "Did I make milk, or not?"

"Milk is a complex suspension of proteins, fats, sugars, vitamins, and minerals, and you're trying to synthesize all those. Give me a minute to sanity-check what we have here."

"A cow does it faster," Blake said.

"Do you *see* a cow on this ship?"

"No, alas. I would enjoy a good steak."

The words just popped out. A moment after, Blake realized that someone named Patel might be Hindu. No one ate beef on Mars— raising cattle took too much water and feed. Grain *or* grass, Mars didn't have enough of either.

Only now Mars had nothing.

Wistful, embarrassed, and sad: all in an instant. "Please excuse my obliviousness, Carlos. If I offended you, I apologize."

"My father would have taken offense. He grew up in Bangalore, didn't emigrate till he was twenty-eight. That you would eat beef doesn't matter to me in the slightest."

"It's hard," Blake said. "Losing our families, and not even getting to say goodbye."

"It was different for me." Carlos turned away from the synth vat. "My parents and a brother died in the Blue Plague when I was a child. My adoptive parents, from my mother's family, weren't religious. Had they been, it would have been Catholicism."

"I'm sorry," Blake said. Blue Plague had swept Mars in 2120, when Carlos would have been about ten. Hell of a nasty way to lose anyone. Hell of an age for a child to lose his parents. "But you had other brothers or sisters?"

"I was the fourth of five children. Sanjiv, the brother taken by the Plague, was the oldest. He was in university, studying nanotech. I always looked up to him; my involvement with nanotech maintains the connection. The rest of us? After the Plague, we were close. We had to be, coming into a household that already had six children."

A middle child and an orphan. It explained a lot about Carlos.

The synth vat beeped.

Carlos checked the readout again. "Ready for a drink? That's the final test."

The fluid Blake decanted looked like milk, if with the blue tinge of the skimmed variety. It smelled like milk. It tasted like milk. So why was Carlos watching him expectantly?

Then Blake's stomach lurched.

Carlos leapt back off his stool, although nothing had come up. Not quite.

There wasn't a rag or towel in sight, and Blake wiped his mouth on his sleeve. "Where did I go wrong?"

"It'll be faster to say what you did right."

Ignoring the ominous gurgle in his stomach, Blake said, "You may as well give me the complete version. It's something to do while we wait."

17

Antonio flopped in his hammock like a fish out of water, exhausted but unable to sleep.

How long had he worked without a break? Rikki had proposed they take a breather, then Dana had. Somewhere along the line Rikki must have left on her own, because when she had returned to the bridge with food trays he realized he hadn't seen her for a while.

Not until he had nodded off in his seat and startled himself awake with a loud snort had he conceded to reality.

On the bridge or here in the crew cabin, eyes open or shut, it made no difference. His mind churned with vectors and parallax measurements and error bars. For star after star, there were estimates of mass, and age, and metal concentrations. About half the stars were binaries, and those added orbital parameters to the numeric stew.

And planets discovered? That also was a number. Zero.

Numbers had always been his friends. Unlike people, numbers were precise, trustworthy, and unambiguous. Numbers made *sense*. And then—

From an adjacent hammock, a shadowy presence in the dark, Li said, "Once you find our new home, we become parents to twelve thousand children. Imagine that."

"I…can't," he'd stammered.

She laughed. "Soon you won't have to imagine it. You might want to sleep while you have the chance."

"Point taken. Goodnight."

Twelve thousand. That single, chilling number all but drove the rest from his head.

I'm one sixth of humanity, Antonio thought. Sixteen and two-thirds percent. Zero point one six six six six….

He could recite sixes to himself without end, and never reach peace of mind. Against all odds, he had saved a few people. That he could believe. But that he should have a role in raising twelve *thou-*

sand children, and then the offspring *they* would bear? These were numbers beyond logic, beyond sense, beyond comprehension.

Yet here you are, the memory of Tabitha reminded. She was smiling. In his mind's eye, she always smiled.

Of course his mind's eye did a better job than his physical eyes of looking *at* people.

With an even warmer smile: You'll do fine, honey. Somehow, you always do.

From the next hammock: even breathing. Had Li fallen asleep?

Six of them to raise thousands, if not in person then by setting the example. The longer he spent with his shipmates, the more impressed he was with Hawthorne's selections—

Except for one glaring lapse: not one of them had ever raised a child. Carlos had *fathered* a child, in his second marriage, but from everything Antonio had heard, Carlos's contribution to rearing his daughter had been limited to sending money and keeping his distance.

Neither was an option here.

Quit worrying, Tabitha gently scolded, still smiling. I *know* you. You'll be a great dad.

Soon after meeting Tabitha, he'd deemed her as trustworthy as numbers. With a grin, she had called the comparison high praise— and it was like he'd been struck by lightning. Another person *could* understand him. In that instant he had known she was the one.

He would have believed the affirmation coming from Tabitha. He had believed everything she said. But believe his own wishful thinking, words put into Tabitha's mouth? That his subconscious would undertake such a pitiful ruse only terrified him further.

Twelve thousand young minds to educate. Even sooner, twelve thousand mouths to feed, cribs to build, and bottoms to wipe. Twelve thousand eager gazes to avoid.

"You're restless," Li murmured. "Something I can help with?"

You've helped enough. "Twelve thousand diapers to change. It seems like a lot."

"Isn't that the truth," she said. "You can take comfort that we have far fewer artificial wombs. Though once we have a world into which to spread, I expect our techies will find a way to construct more. And of course there is the old-fashioned way to make babies."

Shelter for thousands. And food. Clean water. Sanitation. Power. Healthcare. Clothing. A city's worth of people—and a city—all somehow to be provided on an unknown planet.

Antonio did not understand people. He *knew* that. Just the attempt—seldom successful—to parse facial expressions could exhaust him. He had barely managed to give lectures at the university.

His right hand, unbidden, rose to his chin. He began stroking the long, jagged scar that connected him still with Tabitha. How could *he* be father to thousands?

("Short words, honey," she would counsel when he couldn't get out of giving a lecture or a public talk. "Simple, direct sentences. You'll do fine.")

"Build a society. From…scratch. Do we know how?" he asked Li.

"We'll figure it out," Li said confidently.

How had he ever imagined the worst would be over once they escaped Mars?

"It's quite fascinating," she continued. "I expect that the first children we raise will help tend to their younger cohorts. Some of them, anyway. Others of the firstborn will contribute to supplying the material needs of the settlement. And in time the children will have opinions, too, as to what our priorities should be. Nor will they always be children. Fascinating."

"I'm still overwhelmed by all the dirty diapers." And scared shitless myself.

"Then get some sleep." Li rolled onto her back. "Goodnight again."

"Good advice and good…night."

Only Antonio never did fall asleep. Twelve thousand. The number echoed in his brain.

When he quit trying, when he got up to contend with the more tractable, somehow friendlier, number of nearby stars, he could not shake the oddest impression.

That Li had been awake the entire time, observing him. And that their conversation was not at all as casual as it had seemed.

✸

Li studied her datasheet, stylus in hand, surreptitiously studying Dana. You could not be a therapist without the ability to read and take notes while observing a subject.

Not that Dana was formally a subject. In fact, *Dana* was studying *Li*. They had the galley/commons to themselves—and by the way Carlos had scuttled off at Dana's entrance, the coming tête-à-tête was no mere happenstance.

"What have you got there?" Dana asked.

Li looked up and smiled. "Earth history." She went back to her reading.

Dana filled a drink bulb. "Would you mind if I join you?"

"Please do." Li folded her datasheet.

Dana sat across the table from Li. "Earth history. A very broad subject."

Dana doubtless imagined herself being subtle. She had never admitted to having personnel files, but of course she did. Neil Hawthorne had had his reasons for kidnapping this particular crew; he would not have left his surrogate uninformed.

Let's show you something about subtlety, Li thought. Not that I expect you to notice. "Yes, a long history. Many accomplishments. Many lessons learned. It's hard to take in that so much has come to an end."

"Aren't we continuing that history?"

"In the sense of biological continuity, I can't argue. Assuming we're successful, of course. But in any deeper way? I have yet to see that."

"We survived. Survival had to come first."

"You caught me in an introspective mood, Dana. I didn't mean to imply any criticism. What you have accomplished is little short of miraculous."

Compliments discomfited Dana's type; Li let her squirm. You have something to ask me, Dana? Then ask.

"You and I are very different people, aren't we?" Dana finally said.

"How is that?"

"I don't answer questions with questions."

"Touché," Li said, laughing.

"We talk. I enjoy your company well enough. I respect you. Still, I know nothing about you. After so much time together, that strikes me as, well, not an accident."

"How does that make you feel?"

"*Damn* it, Li, I'm not on your couch."

"Habit. It slipped out," Li lied. She'd intended the clichéd question as a goad, and it had worked.

"I'm sure I lapse into habit, too." Dana sighed. "Let's try this. You and I are two of the last six human beings in the universe. We'll need all our strengths to start a colony. As we've seen: without you, I think we would have lost Carlos."

"Circling back to the two of us being quite different."

"I come from a military background. No secret there, but maybe there's more to it than I've volunteered. Dad was Space Guard, too. Dad's mother flew in the ASE Force. I guess Dad and Gram were made of sterner stuff than I. When I left the Guard, no *way* was I going to retire to Earth's gravity."

A self-deprecating admission, to encourage Li to share. How adorably amateurish. How patently *obvious*.

Li said, "You wanted to know why I came to Mars? Let's just say I chose to put some distance between me and a messy break-up."

Messy enough to put her practice, even her med license, at risk. Messy enough to invoke Mother's influence in smoothing things over. And Li had gotten that help, too. For a price. She had been ordered far enough away that Mother would never face such "embarrassment" again.

Well, Mother, I was just as disappointed, learning the hard way that the Famous Radical Free Thinker could be so conventional. So… Victorian. I mean, who was hurt, really?

None of which Li had any intention of sharing.

She went on, "And if you're curious about my family tree, you *could* just ask."

Anger flared in Dana's eyes. "I'm frustrated that I *have* to ask."

"To my knowledge, I've followed your every order, Captain. Now I'm supposed to anticipate your curiosity?"

"That's ridiculous," Dana snapped.

And Li had Dana where she wanted her.

"Yes, we *are* different," Li said.

Hawthorne's files would have reported that Li's mother was political. That Li had made a few unsuccessful runs for municipal office, back on Earth. That while she had not run for office on Mars, she had become influential behind the scenes in the Social Justice Party.

What Dana truly wondered? Whether Li meant to compete *here* for authority.

Li continued, "Here we are, the sole survivors. The last, best hope of humankind. Here's what strikes me. That we've not had *one* conversation about what it means to be human, or civilized, or how the colony-to-be can best preserve our heritage. It saddens me."

"You never said anything."

"Could I, without undermining your authority? Your priorities aren't a big secret."

Dana frowned. "I'm doing my damnedest to keep us alive. To bring us somewhere safe, no matter that we have yet to find a haven. If on occasion I overlook longer-term goals, people need to remind me. *You* need to remind me."

"That's good to hear." But not *quite* where I want your mind to go. Li waited.

"So tell me, what *does* it mean to be human?" Dana glanced at her wrist. "In ten minutes or less."

"I never claimed to be a philosopher." Li patted her folded datasheet. "I find comfort in reading them, though."

Dana said, "I haven't had a lot of time to read. But maybe, while Antonio and Rikki go on about their survey…"

"'Had we but world enough, or time.'"

"What's that?" Dana asked.

"A classical lament." From a poem about sex and seduction, not study, but none of Li's shipmates were of a type to know that. Take the hint, Dana.

"Enough time," Dana said wistfully, and stood. "I'm glad we had this talk. We few have endured all this for a purpose. I appreciate the reminder. But me reading philosophy? I wouldn't know where to begin. Can you offer some suggestions?"

"Of course."

Dana walked away, then hesitated in the hatchway. "You proposed soon after we left Mars that the crew rename this ship. That turned out to be an excellent idea."

"I'm happy I could help." You're *almost* where I want you, Dana. Now take the final step.

"World enough, or time," Dana mused aloud.

"So it goes," Li said.

"What if...?"

"If what, Dana?"

"Suppose we all begin discussing candidate names. Planets and moons. Continents and oceans. Mountains and rivers and reefs. Everything will need a place name once we find our new home. Suppose we let those names remind us, and instruct us, about our past accomplishments. Maybe, great thinkers. Maybe, philosophers. Or poets. Or scientists."

Li grinned. "I *like* it. If your proposal doesn't get everyone thinking about humanity's great accomplishments, and whom from our history we should honor, and whom we should strive to emulate, I can't imagine what will."

"Thanks again, Li. Net me that reading list." And then Dana was gone.

No, thank *you*, Captain.

Because you are about to set off a tidal wave of independent thinking.

18

Carlos had avoided cargo hold three since the day he'd been carried out strapped to a stretcher. The other two holds were crammed; apart from the central corridor, no place else aboard would have accommodated all of them.

He would rather have stood on the ladder. Instead, grinding his teeth, making himself stand tall, he followed the others into the hold. He took a spot beside Li, between two cold-sleep pods.

"Is everyone comfortable?" Dana began.

Yeah, right. He'd gengineered a virus to mod the software in his nanites, but it remained mere theory that addled med bots had all but killed him in cold sleep.

Li said, "I believe I can speak for everyone in answering, 'No.'"

"Fair enough," Dana said amid chuckles. "We have something important to talk about. Just maybe, Antonio and Rikki have found our new home."

That brought a smile to Carlos's face.

Antonio said, "Marvin. Image…one."

Someone had magneted a datasheet to the hold's forward bulkhead. At Antonio's halting request, the display came to life.

The parallel black lines, irregularly spaced, reminded Carlos of something he had once seen in a museum. Some kind of ancient product identifier.

"Absorption lines," Antonio explained. "A glimpse of atmospheric composition. The constituent gases…gases…"

"Would you like me to explain?" Rikki asked.

"No thanks." Antonio added something under his breath.

Carlos thought the mumble might have been, "Short words." And could there have been something about twelve?

Antonio went on, "We've been surveying nearby stars. The lines are *spectro*graphic data about a planet we observed crossing *in* front… of its star. The planet's atmosphere absorbs…some of the starlight. Each gas absorbs at *its* own characteristic…wavelengths."

"And these gases are?" Li asked.

Rikki beamed. "Oxygen, nitrogen, and hints of water vapor."

Like Earth's atmosphere, then. Only Dana had started off this session with a *just maybe*. What was the bad news? Carlos asked, "What does the planet look like?"

Antonio choked on at least three answers, or justifications, or excuses, before sputtering to a halt. After a deep breath, he got out, "We can't see it."

"It doesn't matter," Rikki said. "This does: the planet has an oxygen-rich atmosphere. Without replenishment, an atmosphere doesn't retain oh-two. As happened on Mars, the oxygen gets trapped as oxide in the rocks. So we know *this* world has oxygen-producing life. The water vapor suggests oceans, too."

Carlos reserved judgment on whether distant gases mattered. "Where is this world?"

Antonio said, "About fourteen light-years...from here. Toward the Coalsack."

Li shivered.

Dana said, "I remember as well as anyone that we set out to go *four* light-years. But consider the experience we've gained. We know *Endeavour* is good for the distance. We know that the cold-sleep pods are good for the distance. And we—"

Opinions differ about how well the pods work, Carlos thought. "How long do you anticipate it would take to get there?"

"Twenty to thirty years," Dana said, "which allows for decelerating on the other side. Without a cosmic string to follow, we'll experience relativistic effects. We don't know how the DED performs in those circumstances. I'm not inclined to stress the drive."

Blake said, "In my opinion, we should get moving sooner rather than later."

"Not so fast," Carlos said. "We've only been surveying for a few days. Might there be something better, closer?" Someplace we could reach *without* the cold-sleep pods?

"A fair question." Dana said. "Antonio?"

"The nearest star is five light-years *from* us. That star is a red *dwarf*. It could be a flare star, as many...red dwarfs are. Regardless, very cool. Its liquid-water zone will *be* very narrow. Almost surely it has no habitable planets."

"Does it *have* planets?" Carlos asked.

Antonio shrugged.

"Do any nearby stars have planets?" Li asked. She laughed uncertainly, as if at the absurdity of applying *nearby* to objects light-years-distant.

"Statistically, several…should," Antonio said. "That's based on what we know about solar systems. With our instruments, the challenge is…spotting them."

Because we need more challenge, Carlos thought. The universe has taken it so easy on us thus far. "Maybe you could explain that."

Antonio looked pleadingly at Rikki. She nodded.

"We can't *see* planets," Rikki said. "Not with this telescope. Not at anything near these distances. That brings us to an indirect method, the way astronomers found the first extrasolar worlds. We look for stars that wobble back and forth from the tug of their orbiting planets.

"We won't know what we have, though, until we see the full cycle of a wobble. If a planet takes, as an example, a standard year to orbit its star, we'd need half that time to deduce its orbit. And till we understand a planet's orbit, until we compare that orbit to the luminance of the star, we can't begin to guess whether the planet is in the habitable zone."

"Six months cooped up in this tin can?" Blake said. "We don't have the supplies for that."

"You're right, we don't," Dana said.

"Then how *did* you two spot the oxygen planet?" Carlos asked.

"There's another method for spotting planets." Rikki tipped her head, furrowed her forehead, choosing her words. "Imagine a planet that's crossing between its star and our ship. We can't see the planet— it's too small *and* it's lost in the glare—but from our vantage point it covers a bit of the star. The starlight we see dips just a little. The duration of the dimming implies how fast the planet is moving, from which the full orbital period is estimated. And sometimes, as in this case, we capture the faint absorption lines of starlight viewed through a planetary atmosphere."

Carlos said, "A planet that happens to cross in front of its star? It sounds like we'd have to be lucky to find *anything* that way."

"You're right," Blake said. "We *were* lucky. If we had the supplies, we could sit here for years without finding a better possible home. And maybe not find any."

Five light-years to the nearest star, Carlos thought. Fourteen to the nearest candidate habitable planet. He could die in the pod the next time. But for certain, he'd starve to death if he refused.

When push came to shove, what choice did he have?

"Oxygen and water," Li said. "Do we have anything more to go on?"

"By inference," Antonio said. "The star is…K class. Orange, like Alpha Centauri B would have been. By quite straightforward math we—"

"Skip the math," Carlos snapped.

Skipping the math rendered Antonio speechless. He turned again to Rikki for help.

She said, "The planet orbits maybe a tenth closer to its primary than Earth does to the sun. But this star is only half as luminous as Sol, so the planet we glimpsed may be cold. But maybe not. Even trace amounts of some greenhouse gases will warm a planet substantially—and water vapor is a greenhouse gas. Oh, and the planet may be a tad larger than Earth.

"That's where the data run out. Does the planet have moons? What's its land-to-sea ratio? Are there other planets in the system? We have no idea."

"'The planet,'" Li echoed. "'Its primary.' I thought we had agreed on some names."

Carlos said, "Me, too. For certain, I thought we'd converged on Plato as the name for whatever star we end up at."

Li turned, looking surprised. She patted his hand. "Thank you, Carlos."

After that misunderstanding back in Sol system, he must be the last person she would have expected to support her. But that was light-years and decades ago. Since then, she had saved his life.

Plato, Pluto, Plutarch, or Pippi Longstocking—what the hell did he care what anyone called the star? If calling it Plato fixed things up with Li—

And if he made it out of the pod alive—

There weren't enough women left in the universe.

"Let's hold off on names," Dana said. "Antonio and Rikki recommend that we set a course for this planet. You've heard what they've learned. You've heard why we're unlikely to find somewhere better, or closer, even if we keep searching. Does anyone disagree?"

No one did.

"Excellent," Dana said. "As there is nothing to be gained by delay, as soon as Marvin has navigational guidance for the trip we'll—"

"Excuse me, Captain," Carlos said. "There *is* something to be gained. Before I go under, it would be prudent for Blake to take more training on programming nanites and using the synth vats." *Because next time, I may not come out alive. And because Blake can't make a glass of milk that will stay down, much less do gengineering or other precision work.*

Dana nodded. "I'm confident you'll be fine, Carlos, but to be extra safe we can afford a few days. Barring equipment emergencies, Blake's top priority will be to take more training from you. Will three days suffice?"

You're confident of my safety, are you? I still plan to enjoy my last cigar before *we go.* "Yes, Captain," Carlos said. "I can promise that by then he'll know a lot more about using the synthesis equipment."

And that I'll have synthed enough tequila to get me back into a pod.

DISCORD

(About twenty-four years later)

19

Her head throbbing, hollow with hunger, aching from head to toe as though she had been pounded on by experts, Dana gazed without insight at the nav graphic on the main bridge display. "Only" twenty-four years, but she felt more wretched than she had waking from cold sleep the first time. She would not have believed that possible. Maybe the pods were wearing out. She knew *she* was.

None of that mattered. Not on this mission.

Dana had the pilot's chair. Antonio stood behind her, leaning, the weight of his forearms squashing her headrest. Blake, looking pale and a bit queasy, had the copilot's seat. Carlos, coughing tubercularly, but having reached the infirmary under his own power this time, was getting examined by Li. A clatter of plates and cutlery located Rikki in the galley.

Dana wished Rikki would move faster, at least with some coffee.

"Okay, Marvin," Dana said. "I see a star field. The very bright star straight ahead must be our target. What else should I be seeing?"

"That some of those 'stars' move," the AI said. "There are planets."

"We came because of a planet," Dana said. "Extras aren't a surprise, are they?"

"No," Marvin agreed. "Still, we did not know."

"Any signs of life?" Dana asked. "Of intelligence?"

"Life, to be sure," Marvin said. "As you know, a planet doesn't keep free oxygen otherwise. Intelligence, indeterminate. The only detectable RF is noise from the star and one of the gas-giant planets. We remain too distant to see any surface details."

"Show us all the orbits," Antonio said.

The star field disappeared, displaced by a graphic with six nested bright loops. From innermost to outermost, the colors ran the gamut from purple to red. At this scale the orbits looked like perfect circles, and their differing tilts scarcely registered. A white-orange spark shone at the center.

"The star first," Marvin began. "It is about what we expected. Compared to our former sun, this star has ninety-one percent of the mass. It is about nine percent cooler and its radius is about fourteen percent smaller. The star is fifty-one percent as luminous as the sun.

"As for the planetary system, we now know much more. While decelerating I identified six planets. The orbital determinations are most precise for the innermost planets, but they all should be accurate to within two percent.

"Closest to the star, its orbit shown in purple, is a world somewhat like Mars before planetary engineering. This world orbits about half an AU from the star."

An astronomical unit: the average separation between the Earth and the sun. As a measure of length, the AU was destined for the obscurity of furlongs and cubits. The realization saddened Dana.

"Not habitable, then, without extensive terraforming," she said.

"Quite right," Marvin said. "Bringing us to the second planet, its orbit shown in blue, at about ninety-one percent of an AU. *It* has water oceans and an atmosphere with oxygen. This is the world we came for."

Blake had shipboard diagnostics running on his console. He looked up from the scrolling text. "Earth-like, then?"

"So it seems," Antonio said. "But water...oceans, Marvin? You're sure? That far from *the* star, it seems like the water would be...frozen."

"I am certain," Marvin said. "Water vapor would not be this prevalent in the atmosphere without significant liquid water on the surface."

"Can we have a look?" Blake asked.

A tiny disk appeared alongside the blue loop. The only features Dana could make out were white specks at opposite ends. Polar ice-caps, she presumed.

"I cannot yet provide much detail," Marvin said. It managed to sound apologetic. "When we get closer, we will see better."

"It's dim," Antonio said. "Apart from the icecaps."

Blake nodded. "I suspect that's a good thing. That means it's soaking up sunlight."

Where was Rikki with some damn food? "Big picture, here," Dana said. "Is this world habitable, or not?"

"Habitable, yes," Marvin said. "It may not be hospitable."

"What does *that* mean?" Rikki called.

She stood in the hatchway bearing a tray piled high with snacks. With a grin, Blake got up and began handing around plates and drink bulbs.

Marvin said, "It will be colder on average than on Earth. The air will be dryer than on Earth and thinner than at Earth's sea level. Still, parts of this world will be friendlier to life than, say, Earth's deserts and high plateaus."

The Earth of some dusty database. Earth *now* was a charnel house gripped in an ice age.

Dana turned her attention to coffee. Habitable: that was damned good news.

"What else do we know about this world?" Rikki asked.

There was that circumlocution again.

Their new home needed a name, no matter how uninspired Dana found some of the suggestions. In hindsight, though, setting everyone to talking—arguing—about names hadn't been her smartest decision.

She set down the coffee bulb. "Blake can catch you up later. Marvin, go on with the grand tour."

"The next world, at a bit over two AU is…"

Green, yellow, orange, and red: all the outermost worlds were gas giants, the one nearest to the star Saturn-sized and the rest much smaller. Green and yellow showed prominent ring structures; orange and red offered hints of rings. Green and red, at least, had substantial moons. The outer planets ranged from about two AU to about thirteen AU from the star.

EDWARD M. LERNER

Her headache easing, Dana tried her sandwich. She chewed, oblivious to whatever was between the bread slices, reviewing. An almost sun-like star. Six worlds, one habitable.

She should be ecstatic. And yet—

"The separation between blue and green worlds looks wrong to me," she said. "Too big a gap. Could there be a planet you haven't spotted?"

"Possibly," Marvin said. "Based on the other interplanetary gaps, theory suggests there should be a planet orbiting at about 1.3 AU. But if there were one, I should have spotted it."

"An asteroid belt?" Rikki guessed. "Maybe that big gas giant prevented a planet from forming, just as Jupiter seems to have done back home."

Marvin said, "If there are asteroids, I could not spot them from this distance."

"Not *just* asteroids. 1.3 AU will be right by...the ice line. There might be very short-period...comets, too."

Blake squinted at the graphic. "Comets or asteroids, they would be too damned close. Lots of rock and ice will orbit nearer to our new home than Earth does to Mars. I have to wonder, how often does our future home get slammed?"

"*Is* there a significant bombardment risk?" Dana asked Marvin.

"Insufficient information, Captain. Sorry."

Rikki said, "Maybe the planet looks dark because of a recent impact. An asteroid strike would put dust and smoke in the atmosphere."

"Same answer," Marvin said. "I cannot know more until we get closer."

Her head once more throbbing, Dana wondered if the human race had a cosmic bull's-eye on its metaphorical back.

Not that they had a viable alternative to continuing on their course.

Dana said, "Let's get closer and find out."

20

Antonio took refuge on the bridge, relinquishing the copilot's seat only for food, the toilet, and twice to splash water on his face. He needed order and routine, and as the ship swooped toward the new planetary system, the scurrying of his shipmates denied him both.

For once, he was not the only one obsessing. *Everyone* labored till they dropped. Not that there was a reason to rush about, or any suspected harm that might come of a few days' delay before a closer look—

There was only the longing to declare their odyssey at an end.

Most intercom mikes were active across the ship, the better to coordinate, and some half-heard *thud* brought Antonio shuddering awake. He had no memory of having closed his eyes. Trying to orient himself, he heard grunts and terse directions as Blake and Rikki continued rearranging crates, still digging for a full set of parts for at least one short-range shuttle. He heard tuneless humming and staccato bursts of keystrokes as Carlos reconfigured some of their synth vats. He heard the squeaks and squeals of hinges unused for decades, the captain inspecting her ship. From the central corridor, not via the intercom, he heard a rustle of clothing: by process of elimination, Li. She moved about the ship more than anyone, ostensibly to lend a hand wherever she could be most useful, in practice lobbying for her scheme of planet names.

He was too clumsy to handle irreplaceable cargo, too impractical to touch the synthesis equipment or to program nanites.

That left studying the worlds toward which they hurtled. He had terabytes of data, and every few hours, interrupting their deceleration to turn the ship forward, Marvin collected additional close-ups. There was beyond enough information to occupy him for a lifetime.

He had scans from across the spectrum and plenty of old-fashioned optical imagery. With it he had refined orbital parameters, approximated each planet's period of rotation, identified several moons, broadened the spectrographic analyses of atmospheres, and even counted sunspots. Numbers, numbers, numbers....

Alas, numbers had again lost their customary ability to sooth. Perhaps there could be too many numbers.

Which left him what?

In college, eons ago, a deep dive into psychology archives had uncovered the diagnosis once made of people like him. Asperger's Syndrome was a grab bag of eccentricities with no known cause and no treatment, a label that explained nothing and contributed nothing. The term had fallen into disuse.

He just didn't behave like most other people, and that was that.

As activities across the ship became ever more frantic, Antonio set aside numbers for some other security blanket.

But which? Beyond salt and pepper, salsa and curry, the galley was without condiments. And never again would he encounter a postage stamp: Pacific island, commemorative, nineteenth century, or any other. The daily precipitation for cities across Europe—and he could recite decades of such data—no longer held meaning. And although deep within Earth's oceans some life would have survived, the GRB would have rendered extinct whole families, orders, classes, maybe entire *phyla*, of invertebrate animals. He would never know which.

What remained to count and compare, to categorize and arrange?

The chatter over the intercom offered inspiration.

The captain had begun the discussion of place names, but his shipmates had been quick to join in. Not Antonio. He didn't see the value. Still: many names were being championed, and many naming systems. There were numerous pros and cons that one might consider....

And so—meandering through an archive about philosophy, one more prescient gift from Neil Hawthorne—Antonio encountered a disquieting pattern.

✱

Revived by a quick shower and fresh clothes, it hit Rikki: she was *starving*. Before getting snacks for Blake and herself, before the two of them resumed an uneven contest with the overstuffed cargo hold, she decided to see who else might want a bite to eat. She began with Li and Carlos in the infirmary.

Rikki would have bet large sums, had money retained any value, that nothing in the new planetary system could infect them. People had more in common with paramecia than with whatever life forms they might encounter here. But no one was willing to bet the human race, and that had left Li dreaming up novel infectious agents against which Carlos might preprogram nanites ahead of time. Just in case.

The low voices she heard in the infirmary were discussing neither biology nor nanotech.

Something awkward had transpired between Li and Carlos early in the voyage; for a while, things had been tense. Rikki was certain Dana knew about it, too. But though she and Dana had long been friends, Dana had gone all captain-y on that topic and refused to admit anything.

Whatever the conflict had been, Li and Carlos must have gotten past it. *Way* past it.

Neither saw Rikki standing in the infirmary hatchway.

"Family and loyalty," Li said. "That's what Confucius stood for. His ethical system became the underpinnings of the most populous society on Earth. How can you *not* like Confucius as a name for our new home world?"

Li's words were serious; her body language was a whole other matter. Standing close to Carlos. Leaning in. Touching him lightly on the arm.

"I think I could be convinced," Carlos smirked.

Next: the casual hair toss. Li knew exactly what she was doing. All to enlist Carlos's support for a planet name?

Li said, "Isn't loyalty something to cling to?"

"I have a suggestion, while grasping something is on your mind." Carlos did a double-take. "Ah, the fair Mrs. Westford. Do not fear. There's plenty for two to hold."

Eww. And if Blake ever hears you hitting on me, you'll be holding your own head.

Rikki couldn't understand how Carlos had succeeded in marrying once. But three times? It spoke ill of her gender.

She said, "I'm getting snacks for Blake and me. I dropped by to ask if either of you wanted anything."

"No, thanks," Li said.

"Another time, perhaps," Carlos said, with an eyebrow arched.

"I'll leave you two to work," Rikki said. Hint, hint.

It wasn't only Carlos whom Li was lobbying. Rikki hadn't yet gotten a turn, but she knew Li had bent Dana's ear: that fostering respect for humanity's accomplishments and preserving the past were as fundamental to their mission as preserving genes.

Rikki wondered who else had been pitched on Li's favored planet names. And whether Li would try that flirtatious crap on Blake. And how he would react if Li did.

Maybe it was time to reclaim the bridge and what passed aboard ship for privacy....

Rikki found Antonio asleep in the copilot's seat, head tipped at an awkward angle, his mouth sagging open. Displays scrolled, oblivious to his stupor. Okay, no snack for him. No alone time for her and Blake. She grabbed a blanket from the crew quarters and spread it over Antonio.

And woke him up.

"Sorry," Rikki said. Settling into the pilot's seat, she got a glimpse of the scrolling text: very dry philosophy. It was not at all what she had expected. "How are you?"

"All right," he said, looking guarded. Because he couldn't distinguish when *how are you* was or wasn't meant literally? "I'm taking a break from astronomy."

"Fair enough. I'm getting a bite to eat. I came to ask if I could bring you anything."

"Not for...me, thanks."

She asked, "Any updates about where we're headed?"

"Our destination has at least two...moons. Small, maybe four hundred klicks across."

"Two moons," she repeated. "A touch of home. Anything else?"

"I've determined those moons' orbits."

By basic orbital mechanics, knowing those orbits would serve to establish the mass of the planet. Mass plus the planet's size determined its surface gravity. He could have just volunteered the gravity.

"Unpleasant, I take it," she said. "How heavy?"

"Almost one point four times…standard."

Approaching four times the gravity to which she had been born. "Ugh."

"Nanites might help build up bone mass."

"Yeah. Yet another task for Carlos to take on." When Li has finished leading him on. "Anything else?"

"The local day will be about twenty…five hours, fourteen minutes, in standard units. The year is 421.6 local days or…443.3 standard days. We could be traditional and divide the year into twelve months, each of thirty-five local days. In that…case, I'd suggest five- or seven-day weeks. Or we could use fifteen months, each *with* four…seven-day weeks. Or twenty-eight months of fifteen days. I guess those would be less months than fortnights."

Fortnights? As Antonio rambled on, she guessed that obscure units of measure were yet another of his fixations. And to keep months the same length, there was something about a New Year holiday not falling within a month at all, whether the year had fourteen, fifteen, or twenty-eight of them. And about extending that annual holiday by a leap day in three years out of five. And preserving standard seconds, rather than recalibrate their records and instruments. And….

Rikki abandoned hope he would ever wind down. "Okay, I'll be off for my snack."

"One other thing. I have a planetary temperature. Call it five degrees…Celsius."

And *that* was the afterthought? Not, whatever they were, fortnights? She said, "Above freezing, if just a little. As you had predicted."

"A planetary average. Marvin, does any Earth city have a similar average temperature?"

"Fargo, North Dakota."

"Never heard of Fargo," Rikki said. Or North Dakota, for that matter. "But that there is a city in such a climate is another data point to say we can settle here."

"Marvin has been busy…too. With all the images we've collected, I had it assemble a…composite. Cloud cover is averaged out. Marvin, show Rikki the second planet."

A mottled, spectral globe appeared between them. Large icecaps surrounded the poles. Gray and brown predominated, with splashes of dark green.

Leaning closer, she could just make out indistinct threads on the land surface. The twisty features, whatever they were, had to be *huge*. Mountain ranges? Fault lines to shame the Valles Marineris? Rivers to dwarf the Amazon? The Great Wall of—what did Li propose to call this world? Confucius?

Rikki resigned herself to more days without answers.

With a flick of the wrist she signaled for Marvin to spin the image.

"Not much water," she commented. By Earth standards, she meant. Compared to home this world brimmed with water.

"All in how you look at things," Antonio said. "Here, land is seventy percent of the surface, the rest water. Earth is the…opposite. But the total area here surpasses Earth's. As dry as it…looks, this world offers more *water* surface than the Pacific Ocean."

"And desert everywhere else, it appears," she said. "Still no radio signals?"

"None."

Rikki stood and smiled. "Thanks for the update. I'll give Carlos a heads up that we'll need skeletal nanites." And hope I don't interrupt anything. "What the hell," she added to herself, reminded of Li and her campaigning. "We have to call these worlds *something*."

"One through six?" Antonio asked. "Purple through…red?"

"Wouldn't those be nice and easy?" With a chuckle, Rikki turned to leave.

"Wait," Antonio said.

She turned back. "Uh-huh?"

"Li's name suggestions," he said. "So far, I've studied up on three. Plato. Confucius. Thomas…Hobbes. I'm concerned about the… pattern."

"Hold that thought." Rikki shut and dogged the hatches, and made sure the intercom mike was OFF. "Concerned in what way?"

"These names are…important…to Li." It was a struggle, but for a few seconds Antonio managed to look straight at Rikki. "I wonder why."

An astute question. Because Li *was* pushing hard for her choices.

Li was a psychiatrist. She would know what buttons to push with each of them. Flirting with Carlos. Logic with Antonio. Duty with Dana.

When Blake's and my turns come, what will Li try? Or *has* she tried with Blake?

"I don't know that I could tell Thomas Hobbes from Tom Thumb," Rikki said. "But Plato? Confucius? Even *I* know those names. They were among humanity's great thinkers."

"I didn't know *much* either," Antonio said. "And yet…"

"Out with it. What's on your mind?"

"Philosopher kings," Antonio murmured. "That's who Plato thought should run society. His so-called republic…had an unelected ruling class."

"Did it?" Rikki shrugged. "I half remember some Plato text getting assigned in a poly-sci class. At best I skimmed it. Regardless, his republic is theoretical. I mean, no one ever created such a society."

Maybe Li hopes to be the first. And to be its philosopher queen. "Until…now?"

Rikki shook her head. "One famous philosopher. It doesn't need to mean anything."

Except to judge from the distasteful scene she had walked in on, it was more than one. She asked, "Do you know anything about Confucius?"

"Now, I do." Antonio gestured at an open text display. "He spoke for family loyalty…respect for elders and ancestor worship. About rites and ritual. He saw that kind of family as the model for…government. Confucianism developed into a centralized state with a…bureaucratic class and the king as moral example. The system of ethics evolved into a rationale for political elites."

"And you mentioned Thomas Hobbes?" Rikki said.

"Without government, he said, life would be 'solitary, poor, nasty, brutish, and…short.' He was defending sovereign absolutism."

"Okay," Rikki said, "Maybe I know *one* difference between Thomas Hobbes and Tom Thumb. Didn't Hobbes talk about the social contract? That people consented to government to avoid all that nasty brutishness? A social contract seems progressive."

"A contract of submission to the monarch," Antonio said.

Once is random. Twice is coincidence. Three times is a trend. Maybe Li *was* predisposed toward certain forms of government. So what? She was only one among six.

Rikki said, "Does it matter what we call the star and the worlds? Mars was named for a mythical war god, but growing up on Mars didn't make me warlike."

Fingering his scar, gaze downcast, Antonio said, "It's the pattern. Maybe to choose these individuals, to make their ideas prominent, will sway the children. They're bound to get curious *about* the names."

If anyone aboard understood the shaping of children's minds, Li would. It was why Hawthorne had drafted her.

That and having her office minutes from the dry dock.

Rikki wondered just how one phrased the question. So, Li, are you setting up the six of us as an aristocracy? How about yourself as the queen?

Even the questions were too weird, too…freaking *medieval*, to take seriously.

She gestured at the spinning globe and its all-but-featureless expanses. "I'll be interested in what else you learn about our new home."

Looking hurt, Antonio banished philosophy from his displays.

Not smooth, Rikki chided herself. She had not meant to offend. "Okay, I'll talk to you later."

She undogged the hatches and started aft, her appetite gone, keen to lose herself in the mindless slinging about of crates.

Parenting and mentoring: they would all have those responsibilities, of course. But anything more? Conditioning the children for deference? Fostering ancestor worship? That was beyond crazy.

Nonetheless, as Rikki clambered down the central-shaft ladder, planets one through six sounded better and better to her.

21

After much shuffling of cargo and many EVAs, they had assembled what, in theory, was a functioning short-range shuttle. So far it had passed all diagnostics. Its deuterium tank had been filled from *Endeavour*'s depleted reserves and its reaction-mass tank with melt-water from an ice body intercepted on approach to this new planetary system. For more than a day the shuttle had maintained a shirtsleeves environment. Still, the limit to Carlos's faith in the spacecraft-from-a-kit was removing his pressure-suit helmet.

While keeping that helmet within arm's length.

The narrow cockpit permitted only two crew. Carlos occupied the back seat, his legs spread wide and his knees wedged.

Out the canopy the vista was humbling. A short docking tunnel removed: the scorched and pitted exterior of *Endeavour*, the toll of the light-years all too evident. Beyond that abused hull hung the world they meant to settle. Scattered seas, clouds, and snow fields interrupted his view of its bleak surface. A colossal mountain range, ridge after ridge after ridge, revealed the slow-motion collision of two tectonic plates.

From the cockpit's forward seat, Blake asked, "How are you holding up?"

"Fine. Just taking in the scenery," Carlos said. The truth was, he had yet to regain his customary vigor. Merely assisting with checkout—toggling switches, tapping in short commands, and reading out displays—had exhausted him. In free fall, no less.

"Station-keeping maneuver coming up," Marvin advised by radio.

"You still secured?" Blake asked.

"Uh-huh." Not that, shoehorned in as Carlos was, a seat harness added much.

"All right, Marvin," Blake radioed. "Do what you must."

For a few seconds Carlos felt pressure against his back and a hint of weight, and then zero gee returned. He said, "It's quite the view, don't you think?"

"No argument here, though I'm more interested in how things look on the surface. When you're ready, we'll move on to sensor diagnostics. Passive instruments first."

As boring as checkout was, the work needed doing. "Starting with infrared. IR sensors: self-test passes. Temperature readout across the surface looks plausible." And freaking cold. "Moving on to visual." Sweeping the shuttle's modest telescope along the mountains, he homed in on a gray blur. "Directional controls are fine. The focus could be better."

"Try it with the adaptive optics."

"Adaptive optics: self-test pass." The image sharpened; the blur resolved into a roiling ash plume. Carlos said, "That did the trick."

They exercised the shuttle's short- and long-range radars, confirming distances against *Endeavour*'s measurements. The very precise laser altimeter—wasn't. Reading records aloud from the runtime log, Carlos began wheezing.

"Let's take five," Blake said.

"Thanks."

Within two minutes the fidgeting began. Carlos ignored the pop-popping noises and the finger-tapping. He could use the full five.

"So, you and Li," Blake said.

"Me and Li," Carlos agreed.

"You two seem to be getting along."

Having something she wants may have something to do with that, Carlos thought.

"So I wondered…," Blake went on.

"What?"

"Is Li lobbying you, too, for specific planet and moon names?"

"Some," Carlos admitted. Nonstop. But she hadn't yet made his endorsement worthwhile.

"Do you find some of her ideas are, well, a touch reactionary?"

"As if I know who any of those dead Earthworms are."

Except Carlos did understand the question. *Let* Li be a social engineer. Let her instill respect for authority and deference to elders.

Half of the submissive young colonists would be women.

"Still," Blake said, "don't you find Li is rather...impassioned... about this?"

Let's hope so. "What's in a name?" Carlos laughed. "That planet out there can be Gertrude, for all I care." Or even *Li*, if she's passionate enough.

"You scratch my back, and I'll scratch yours?"

"Something like that."

In the canopy, Blake's reflection disapproved.

Blake said, "Back to work. Let's finish checking out the sensors, and then move on to backup power distribution."

"Fine by me," Carlos said.

Because the sooner the shuttle scouted out candidate landing sites, the closer he was to those thousands of cooperative young women.

✳

It's time, Li thought.

She was the last one to float into the cargo hold. Smiling, making eye contact with everyone, she allowed her gaze to linger on Blake and her smile to broaden. On cue, Blake smiled back. Reflexes, if you understood them, were useful tools.

Rikki flinched.

So did Carlos. Then he motioned Li over to a spot beside him.

Dana shoved off a bulkhead to drift toward the forward end of the hold, grabbed a handhold, and turned to face Li and the others. "If you haven't already guessed, I called this get-together to confirm our readiness for a scouting mission. Blake, how's the shuttle?"

"All set to fly," Blake said.

"And make a landing?" Dana followed up.

"That, too," Blake said. "And even return to orbit."

"I've picked out candidate landing sites," Antonio said.

"I'll play devil's advocate," Dana said. "What will we encounter down there? Marvin, give us a rundown."

"Full detail or a qualitative overview, Captain?"

"Just the highlights, please," Dana said.

"It will be cold," the AI summarized, "not far above freezing even at the equator. The air is thin and dry but breathable near sea level. Be wary of exertion, both because of the low partial pressure of oxygen and the near-toxic level of carbon dioxide. The ozone layer, although thin, will block most of the UV. The magnetic field seems sufficient to keep out cosmic rays. The sunlight is redder and dimmer than you're accustomed to, but still quite adequate. Instruments will notice the color-balance shift, but I doubt your eyes will.

"Because the candidate landing sites are near coasts, be aware that the tidal situation is complex. The innermost moon raises tides comparable in height to *the* Moon's. Because this moon orbits so close to the planet, these tides last most of a day. The middle moon adds tides about a third as high, but with different timing. The tidal pattern shifts day to day because the moons do not orbit in synch."

"And it's a *rock*," Carlos said. "On land, there isn't a scintilla of life."

Perhaps he meant to give full value for his side of their...transaction, but this was no time for him to improvise. Li thought daggers at him without looking. If she had, someone might have noticed.

"Continue, *Marvin*," Dana said.

"Gravity is about forty percent above standard. Humidity varies more than across Earth, likely attributable to the reversal of the land/sea ratio. Not a factor for this initial exploration, but worth a comment: I have detected few traces of surface metals. Because of the higher gravity, whatever metals there are will have tended to sink before the planet cooled. And—"

That's *enough*," Rikki snapped. "Earthworms are so damned spoiled. Apart from the gravity, this planet is a damned paradise. Breathable air. An ozone layer. A bit more sunlight than Mars gets. Plenty of water for agriculture."

So *Marvin* was an Earthworm? Li thought. Well, maybe his programmers were.

Only the Earthworms about whom Rikki truly worried were her husband and Li.

Rikki was on a tear. "...so there's a lot of cee-oh-two? Be glad, because the greenhouse effect is what keeps the average temperature above freezing.

"And if metals are scarce on the planet? We're starfarers! All the metal we could ever want is waiting for us in the local asteroid belt—and *it* is more convenient than the old belt was to Mars.

"Can you imagine what the early settlers on Mars would have given to have had *this* world as their starting point?"

And then Rikki stopped, gone red in the face.

A bit embarrassed at our outburst, are we? Li toyed with ways to put that reaction to use.

Blake gave his wife's hand a reassuring pat.

How touching, Li thought. Especially the way Rikki yanked away her hand.

"Anything else, Marvin?" Dana asked.

"No."

"Anyone else?" Dana pressed.

"Dress warm," Antonio said.

Dana said, "To recap, a shuttle is prepared. The world is habitable. We're all due for a change of scenery. Are we ready to review landing sites and protocol?"

That discussion was more businesslike. They reviewed the camping supplies a shuttle would carry. They agreed upon an initial four areas to inspect. Each region was in a mid-temperate zone or lower latitudes. Each offered a cave system for shelter, a lake or sea to filter for deuterium, and a broad river delta for farming. On a world devoid of land life, silt would be the closest thing to soil.

"Then that's it," Dana said. "I'll pilot the shuttle and—"

"No way," Blake said.

Dana blinked. "What's that?"

"My job was to get *Endeavour* here. Done. Your job isn't finished till you land this ship."

Dana's eyes narrowed. "I don't like your logic...but I accept it. And I concede you're qualified to fly the shuttle. So, okay. Blake pilots this time. Any other volunteers?"

"I'll go," Carlos offered. Trying to impress Li, of course.

"Absolutely not, and that's doctor's orders. You're not ready yet. I'll go." Smiling at Blake, Li added, "We'll have fun."

Steam seemed to rise from Rikki's ears. She said, "That's okay, I'll fly down with Blake. My job was to get *him* here."

"The gravity won't be fun," Li said. "For this first outing, at least, we should leave it to"—let's push Rikki's buttons again—"the Earthworms. We have more stamina."

And she winked at Blake.

Dana jumped in. "No way, Li. If there are infectious agents on the surface, I can't have our only doctor exposed. Those are captain's orders."

Antonio fingered his chin. "I think I'll be…more useful *up*…here."

"Then it's settled," Dana said. "Blake and Rikki will make this first flight. That's it."

Rikki was seething, a Vesuvius about to blow. Blake was conflicted: flattered by the come-on, and even mildly intrigued; upset at Rikki's anger; eager to explore. Carlos was jealous, Dana annoyed, and Antonio—as always—oblivious to the undercurrents.

All Li's pieces were in place.

She cleared her throat. "First, we have some unfinished business."

"Not names again," Blake stage-whispered.

Li pretended not to hear. "Surely, Captain, we're not about to set foot on our new home world still calling it 'the planet.'"

"You've made some interesting suggestions," Dana said. (*Interesting* carried more than a hint of disapproval. The pawns had been comparing notes.) "The problem is, we're nowhere near a consensus on planet names."

"Symbolism matters," Li said. "Never mind how like Earth or Mars this planet may be. We're keeping it at a psychological distance. It's 'this planet,' and 'this world.' We need to make it *home*."

"Then *call* it Home, with a capital h," Blake said.

Li feigned considering the suggestion. "Alas, no. There's none of our heritage in that name. It is my professional opinion that—"

"Oh, just give it a rest," Rikki barked.

"That's one opinion," Li said. "However, this affects us all. I propose that we put it to a vote whether to decide on names, at the very least on picking this world's name, before the initial landing. Surely we can manage *that*."

A subtler barb, but this time Dana stiffened. To manage things was the captain's job.

By now Blake, Rikki, and Dana would reject anything Li proposed. She couldn't win—and that was as she intended. Li said, "Well?"

And then Rikki surprised her. "We've gone *on* and *on* about naming conventions. Philosophers. Playwrights. Composers. Poets. Artists. Explorers and castaways. What we haven't done is agree.

"So here's *my* suggestion. There are six planets and six of us. We draw lots, and each of us names one world."

"That sounds fair," Antonio said.

"Hurrah," Blake said. "The Gordian knot, nuked."

Dana seemed to consider. "In this scheme," she asked, "how would we address moons and geographical features? With this world, for example, it's three moons and six of us."

Rikki stammered, "I…I'm in favor of deciding that later."

Ad libbing are we?

"Fair enough," Dana said. "I'm game."

"*Think* about this," Li said. "We need to be serious. For the sake of the children and their heritage. Blake? *You* understand, I'm sure."

Rikki's eyes smoldered.

"I'm with Li," Carlos said.

At least his hormones were.

Dana said, "Four out of six, or captain's prerogative: take your pick. We'll go with Rikki's suggestion. And Li, we're following your lead by choosing names before the landing."

Li bowed her head in defeat—exultant inside. After this finely crafted debacle, none would think of her as subtle.

May they never learn the error of their ways.

Soon enough, on a dozen folded sheets of paper, two sets of six numbers waited to be drawn from opaque bags. One set related to the planets, the other to the crew.

If luck came to Li's aid, she might even get to name the world below. That would be a pleasant bonus. But no. In the lottery for planets she drew *four*, one of the gas giants.

In the second round, Li did get the consolation prize of naming "her" world first. She picked Hobbes, just in case Carlos had drawn the second planet. He had, alas, only drawn the innermost planet, the Mars-like world. Glancing to Li for approval, or maybe to claim a favor, he declared his world Confucius.

Antonio, going next, had drawn *three*: the biggest, nearest, gas giant. He dubbed it Ayn Rand. He didn't meet Li's gaze. If his selection weren't defiant, he wouldn't have anyway.

For the outermost world, when her turn came, Dana chose Kierkegaard. An interesting choice: a philosopher who had not made it onto Li's recommended reading list. Existentialism. Christian ethics. Blah, blah, blah. Better, though, than the biblical nonsense to which Li had expected Dana might turn—not that Li would deny that the old myths resonated with people. Quite the opposite, in fact. She admired the old stories' cultural tenacity, just not anyone gulled by them.

Rikki, dithering *still* when her turn came, settled on Newton for planet five.

But it was Blake who had won the sweepstakes: the privilege of naming humanity's new home. When at last the moment came to exercise his right, he didn't, as he had intimated, opt to call the planet Home.

The world they would settle would be known, forever after, as Dark.

22

"R eady back there?" Blake asked. On his cockpit instruments everything showed green. "This will be fun."

"Ready," Rikki called from behind him. She sounded dubious about the fun.

He toggled on the radio. "*Endeavour*, this is the shuttle *Discovery*. We're go for launch."

"Safe journey, *Discovery*," Dana radioed back. "Keep in touch."

"Will do," he said.

With mountains and valleys, lakes and rivers and seas, icecaps and glaciers and boundless plains, Dark beckoned. Here and there, a whorl of cloud obscured his view. The planet was in all-but-full phase, and even the slender visible rim of night side glimmered in double moonlight.

"Releasing docking clamps," Blake announced. "Engaging thrusters."

With puffs of compressed nitrogen, he edged the dart-like shuttle away from the much larger ovoid that was *Endeavour*. "I'm off to deploy our cargo," he reported.

Endeavour could have delivered the weather microsats as easily as the shuttle, but he wanted to get a feel for his controls before attempting entry and landing.

He had his doubts this exercise would buy them more than flight practice. None of these satellites would stay parked. Not with three close-in natural moons to perturb their orbits. Not with the innermost moon dipping daily below the altitude of synchronous orbits.

Five or six microsats, even drifting, might keep the entire planet under observation and maintain a line-of-sight comm ring. They had three.

Synchronous orbits? Above Dark, the notion was ludicrous. Out of necessity, they would learn to live with sporadic downlinks when one of their few satellites happened to wander overhead.

The scarcity of on-orbit sensors was emblematic of everything they lacked. Automated landers. Robotic swarms to make the initial explorations. Construction equipment. A real med lab. Months of food in reserve. Portable reactors and enough deuterium to—

Stop it, Blake ordered himself. You're *alive*. It's time to earn your place among the lucky few.

"Copy that," Dana said. "When you're done with your deliveries, how about you find us a nice homestead."

"Beachfront property," he promised. "*Discovery*, out."

"Copy."

Blake flipped off the ship-to-ship radio. "Main drive in ten seconds."

"Okay," Rikki said.

No one had commented on his spontaneous christening of the shuttle.

Carlos and Antonio were probably sick of picking names. Dana, traditionalist that she was, might even approve of Blake's choice. *Discovery* had been among the ships bringing the original settlers to the Jamestown colony. Another *Discovery* had accompanied James Cook's third expedition around the world. Robert Scott had taken yet a different *Discovery* to Antarctica.

And Li? Blake supposed she was off licking her wounds after the name-the-worlds fiasco. Unless she had found a reason to like the name. When the Jamestown colonists sent their *Discovery* seeking a Northwest Passage, its crew mutinied. They abandoned the captain, Henry Hudson, in a small boat. He was never seen again.

And Rikki? She was all but monosyllabic. She was mad about something, and he had no idea what.

He asked, "Do you want to talk about it?"

"About what?"

He guessed. "We'll find a place for the colony. We *will* succeed."

"I know," she said, but her voice was sad.

"Your family would be proud."

"And yours," she said.

He found no more solace in the reassurance than she had.

Discovery's trajectory plunged them into darkness. As his eyes adapted, more and more stars appeared—except where the Coalsack took a huge chunk out of the sky.

"Coming up on the drop point," Rikki called.

"Copy that." He kept watch on his own displays. "On my mark, make the drop. Three, two, one, mark."

"First satellite dropped." There was a pause. "Telemetry received. It's online."

He went on the radio. "*Endeavour*, that's one satellite on station." While its onboard fuel lasts. "We're on our way to the next drop point."

"We have it," Dana said.

On the way to the third deployment, Rikki said, "Li is beautiful, don't you think?"

That was one hell of a non sequitur.

Yes wasn't what Rikki wanted to hear. *No* was hardly credible. Ignoring the question wasn't an option. Blake settled on, "Carlos certainly thinks so."

A sniff said he had taken too long to answer. So was Rikki's funk about Li?

After the third microsat was deployed, returned to the world's day side, Blake called, "*Endeavour*, this is *Discovery*. We're ready to go in."

"Copy that." In a softer voice, Dana added, "Take care, *Discovery*."

"Always," Blake said. "*Discovery*, out."

With a blast of their main drive he shed velocity. The shuttle trembled at the first wisps of atmosphere. He swung left, then right, getting a feel for the bite of the shuttle's control surfaces. Lower and lower they plunged, and the tremor became a quiver became a bone-rattling shudder. The leading edge of their wings glowed a dull orange.

Nothing about their descent was *quite* what he expected. The atmosphere was shallower than over any world where he had ever flown, because of Dark's high gravity. The pressure varied more rapidly with altitude, for the same reason. His laser altimeter started talking nonsense again. His backup altimeter was useless, still calibrated for atmospheric pressure above Mars.

He had radar and eyeballs. They would suffice.

His controls kept refusing to act as his instincts expected: pressure-gradient differences again. He put the craft into a steeper dive, pulled out of it, banked left, then jinked back right. Tearing through experimental banks and turns, he began to get the feel of his craft and this world.

"If you do a barrel roll," Rikki said, "I'll divorce you."

Blake had to laugh. This *was* fun. "No rolls," he agreed.

The world became flat. Plains as colorless as charcoal stretched in every direction. To the west he glimpsed a great crevasse. From the topo map compiled on orbit, that was a river canyon.

The gravity wore at him, just sitting—and it was worse for Rikki.

At about eight thousand meters, the shuttle broke through a thin, uniform layer of white. Ice crystals spattered off the canopy. Cirrostratus, he wanted to call the formation, too ignorant of weather processes to even guess if Dark and Earth would share cloud types. Maybe Antonio would know.

They had slowed enough to be out of comm blackout. (Under Earth conditions, he reminded himself.) He gave radio a try. "*Endeavour*, this is *Discovery*. Do you read?"

"Good to hear from you, *Discovery*," Dana said. "Though to judge from the ionization trail behind you, someone enjoyed the ride too much."

"Negative," Blake said. "Just the proper amount."

"No, Dana, you were right," Rikki said.

A blue-and-green dappled expanse was straight ahead of them. The inland sea was long and skinny, with a slight bend at its midsection. Except for the color it reminded Blake of a summer squash.

But the sea was a lot bigger than a summer squash. If his mental arithmetic was correct, the sea covered an expanse bigger than Lake Superior. Two of the many bays that dimpled the seacoast had to be bigger than cities. Radar indicated depths to eighty meters. Most of the lake bottom failed to return an echo; the center must be far deeper.

Blake said, "*Endeavour*, we have a beautiful afternoon. We'll do a quick flyover, then set down at our first landing zone."

"Copy that," Dana said.

Exploring the area they crossed a great chasm. They soared along a mountain chain that must rival the Andes. Dark was…magnificent. Reveling in the stark beauty and the freedom of flight, swooping through the empty skies, time got away from him.

By the time he circled back to the sea, the sun, about to set, almost kissed the waters. ("It's Plato," Li's astral projection scolded.) The star, by whatever name, sent its rays almost parallel to the ground. The light cast the weathered, snow-capped mountains east of the waters into stark relief. Broken ground and boulder fields extended almost to the toffee-colored beach.

"I have to set us down near the shore," he said.

"Is that a problem?"

"Only for the morning. We'll have a long walk to the caves."

She said, "A walk by sunlight, in fresh air. I'll take it."

He brought them in low and slow, paralleling the coastline. As near to the cave mouth as he dared to land, he engaged drive deflectors and—gingerly, still getting the feel of this gravity—set down. The faint rattle of pebbles against the shuttle's underbelly was his imagination, of course; the drive exhaust had fused sand and loose rocks into place.

"*Endeavour*, he reported, "*Discovery* has landed."

"Copy that," Dana said. "And it's about time you finished joyriding."

"You'll have your turn," Blake said.

"Yeah, yeah. Enjoy your evening. *Endeavour*, out."

"*Discovery*, out," he responded.

He read the ground temps with IR sensors. Still hot. He got out Mars-style breather masks and lobbed one over his shoulder to Rikki. He checked the IR sensors. He and Rikki admired the fiery sunset sparkling off the waters. He checked the IR sensors. They marveled as the apple-green sky faded to something closer to olive. He checked the IR sensors. He reached overhead with both arms, tap-tapping on the canopy till Rikki kicked the back of his seat. *She* checked the IR sensors.

When, at last, sensors showed they could safely exit the shuttle, the wind had kicked up. The sun had half-vanished beneath the sea. Two moons hung overhead, and the waves lapped to within several meters of their landing skids.

"Are you ready to make camp?" he asked.

"Sure," she said. "Ready, in any event, for an air mattress."

"Mask on?" he asked.

"Mask on."

"Releasing the canopy," he advised her, and then did. To the wailing of the wind, louder with each centimeter that the gap widened, the canopy receded into its stowage in the hull.

Grit pelted him. The air was *cold*, and it refused to fill his lungs. He slipped on his breather mask, then gloves. He shouted over the wind, "Stay put."

He hung the boarding ladder outside, hooked over the rim of the cockpit. Leg muscles screaming, he stepped down the three rungs and onto the ground. Sand and salt spray stung any bit of exposed flesh.

He slid the ladder aft, to Rikki's end of the cockpit, leaving his hands on the rails. "*Carefully*, climb over the side. I'll steady you."

Her boot slipped off the bottom rung, and they tumbled together to the ground.

Blake was pissed at himself for not setting down earlier, when they had had better weather. He was pissed at Li for goading Rikki into volunteering, never mind that he'd intended all along to invite her. And, to be honest, he was pissed at Rikki herself. What the *hell* was her problem? Li? Why wouldn't Rikki talk to him about it?

Rikki unhooked the ladder and closed the canopy with its remote while he stewed.

Unloading their gear from the shuttle's cargo locker, he asked, "Are you ready for dinner and some sleep?"

And if you get over your foul mood, and I over mine, maybe putting an air mattress to a more communal use?

"Sounds like a plan," Rikki said.

But not his only plan. As they ate, the staked-and-inflated shelter shimmying in the wind, he mentally reviewed the next plan's few, simple stages:

—A leisurely morning stroll.

—Reconnoitering and approval of the nearby caves.

—*Endeavour* on the ground.

—Some honest labor, specifics to be determined.

And everyone lives happily ever after.

But as Rikki slept fitfully and Blake not at all, beneath the pitiless stare of an alien sky, the Coalsack—vast, inchoate, stygian—scoffed at the effrontery of mere human aspiration.

DECISIONS

(Landing Day, plus one)

23

"Avalanche!" Blake screamed.

Or tried, anyway. Snow down his throat choked off the warning and set him to coughing.

Rikki didn't answer.

"Rikki!" he managed to wheeze, scarcely audible above the roar of the onrushing snow. She had come to rest, bent double against one of the jumble of boulders he had just missed. Blood dribbled from a gash on her forehead. "Rikki! Avalanche! We have to *move!*"

She didn't stir as he struggled back to his feet. He shoved her, hard. Nothing.

The roar of the avalanche was palpable. The churning mass racing at them looked perhaps a minute away.

On skis—maybe—he could outrun the avalanche. Not on foot. Not carrying Rikki.

Her breather mask, like his, had been knocked off. The mask dangled by its flimsy elastic strap around her neck. He slipped Rikki's mask up over her mouth and nose. His chest heaving, he dragged her in among the clustered boulders and leaned her up against the tallest of the stones.

Because he had to leave her! Abandon her! If the snow should bury them both—they both died.

After the avalanche blasted through, he would be lucky to see the tops of the rocks. Would he recognize this spot? Rikki's hiking pole was nowhere in sight; he started slipping off the wristband of his pole, to wedge it as a marker among the rocks.

And paused. If the avalanche carried away the pole, he'd have nothing with which to probe for her beneath the snow.

("We have maybe fifteen minutes to save an avalanche victim," a ski instructor had once cautioned Blake and a half-dozen other beginners. Blake had been more attentive to the ski bunnies than to the lecture. "Do *not* lose your beacon. Even with a beacon, the odds of rescue are about fifty-fifty.")

Fifteen minutes. With an organized effort and a radio beacon to guide the rescuers.

The wall of snow was no more than thirty seconds away.

In anguish, Blake unclipped from their safety line. He began running/sliding/falling *across* the slippery slope. He couldn't outrun an avalanche, but maybe he could get to the side of it. With each glance over his shoulder, the chaos drew nearer.

The tide of snow crashed over the cluster of boulders. He tried to sear into his brain the configuration of the boulders.

If the snow completely buried them, he'd *never* find Rikki.

Seconds later, with an earsplitting growl, the edge of the snow torrent swept him off his feet. Downhill he went, tumbling like dice in a cup.

Stones and clumps of ice pounded him. The snow ripped off his hat and gloves, breather mask and headset. The hiking pole vanished, its wrist strap snapped or torn from his arm.

At least he couldn't slam into a tree.

Snow was *everywhere*: down his back, filling his boots, up his sleeves. His breather mask was gone, its thin elastic strap unequal to this abuse. Snow plugged his nostrils. Each breath began by spitting out snow, and ended with another mouthful.

But the avalanche was petering out. He had stopped tumbling. Bobbing along on the surface, he dared to hope the worst was past.

Until, being denser than loose snow, he began to sink.

Lungs burning from exertion and the thin air, Blake started to swim. A knapsack strap had snapped, or in his flailing the strap had slipped off one arm. The bag, hanging like an anchor from one shoulder, dragged him into the snow. Shrugging off the remaining strap, still swimming hard, he managed to stay on top.

He came to rest somewhat vertical, leaning forward, in snow up to his diaphragm. Already, he felt the snow settling and compacting around him like concrete. He could not move his legs, not so much as wiggle a foot.

("Fifteen minutes," that long-ago instructor's voice echoed in Blake's mind.)

A rock slab, leaning, protruded nearby from the snow. The slab might have served as an impromptu shovel.

Instead, just beyond his reach, it looked to serve as a gravestone.

With his bare hands—soaking wet, his teeth chattering—Blake began to dig.

✳

His hands numb with cold, Blake finally dug himself free. He'd lost his wristwatch, too, but fifteen minutes must already have passed.

He had left Rikki in the shelter of the rocks. Maybe *her* breather mask had stayed put.

Part of the avalanche had crashed its way to the inland sea, but to the north of their camp. A good kilometer distant, through the diminishing blizzard, both shuttle and inflated shelter looked untouched.

Half a kilometer in another direction was the boulder field in which—he was *almost* certain—he had left Rikki. He tugged the stone slab free of the snow, and set off. Gasping for air, slipping and falling, hands and feet like blocks of ice, he slogged through the snow.

His suit heater wasn't working. Controls smashed? Heating circuits broken? Battery knocked loose? He did not bother to look. Whatever the problem, without tools and spare parts he could do nothing about it. If he'd still had a knapsack, he couldn't have afforded the time.

A few meters downhill from that group of rocks, a silvery glint caught his eye. A rope clip!

His hands had frozen to the rock slab; when he released it, it took skin with it. A sharp tug drew a few centimeters of red nylon line up out of the snow—and the frigid clip from his grasp. More palm skin went with the clip. Here, too, the snow was firmly packed.

He stared for a while, stymied, at the brightly colored nylon line. Then he studied the raw, red, angry flesh of an injured hand. As painful as the wound looked, he couldn't feel it. Of course he couldn't feel anything in either hand. Now what was he doing here…?

He was looking for Rikki! How could he have forgotten that?

As through a fog, he *did* know: hypothermia from the cold. Hypoxia from the thin air, the altitude, and the exertion. Maybe shock from the pummeling of the avalanche.

Clutching the rock slab with numb fingers, Blake pushed in among the boulders. Rikki would be at the base of the tallest rock. *If* the rush of snow hadn't swept her down slope. He began digging frantically.

Digging, digging, digging.…

Confusion overtook him again; he lost sight of what he was doing until—with a jolt—his improvised shovel hit something. Something that *twitched*.

He threw aside the rock slab to burrow doglike with his hands. He found—a leg. Why had he dug so far from the boulder? "Rikki," he called.

If she had heard him, he couldn't hear her answer.

The bit of pant leg he'd exposed looked to be just below her knee. If she still leaned against the boulder, then her head would be…he struggled to puzzle it out…here.

Minutes later, his hands—stiff and blue—rammed the hard plastic of a breather mask.

And she moaned! She was alive! Ten interminable minutes later, he had uncovered her to the waist. He unclipped her from the safety line, meters of which remained buried deep in snow.

Only then did he raid her knapsack for her spare mask, oxygen tank, and gloves. The oh-two jolt cleared his muddled thoughts enough to slam one of her spare battery packs into the empty, lid-torn-off compartment of his flight suit. Blessed warmth began to flow, except in one sleeve, in which the heating elements must have broken.

"Blake?"

Her eyes were open! He said, "I thought I'd lost you."

"I did, too."

"I'll have you out of there soon," he promised. With the folding shovel from her knapsack, finishing the job was a matter of minutes.

An hour later, bone-weary, they stumbled into their snow-covered shelter.

✸

They took off before nightfall for *Endeavour*.

"For replacement equipment," Blake radioed to Dana: a partial truth. The absolute truth, if hands counted as equipment. Under the gloves he hoped Rikki didn't notice he continued to wear, knuckles screamed at every motion, and the skin was pale and blistered. He suspected severe frostbite on his feet, too.

Soon enough, Li confirmed his fears—extending the diagnosis to nose, ears, and random patches on his legs. The thawed areas hurt like hell, sometimes also managing to itch, until Li pumped him full of painkillers.

As nanite swarms labored to repair the damage, Blake focused on an ever-growing supplies list. They still needed to find a home for the colony.

On his next flight to Dark, he would be better prepared.

24

Dana floated at the forward end of cargo hold three, beside a datasheet magneted to the bulkhead. The comp projected an orbital view of Dark. "Whenever they're ready," she told Marvin.

"It should be only another few minutes," the AI said.

Three of the crew waited among the cold-sleep pods. Antonio poked at something on his own datasheet. Carlos whispered unintelligibly at Li, who silenced him with a hard stare. She looked…distracted? No, preoccupied.

Please, God, Dana thought. Not more squabbling about names.

"Blake says he and Rikki are ready," Marvin announced.

The orbital view vanished, displaced by a close-up of Blake and Rikki—both grinning from ear to ear. Behind them, seen through the clear wall of their shelter, extending to the horizon, was an inland sea.

"You two look so disappointed," Dana deadpanned.

"Well, we didn't find the Fountain of Youth," Blake said. "Is everyone there?"

"As you requested," Dana said. "Okay, it's your show."

Blake nodded. "Hi, everyone. We surveyed three candidate sites this trip. Any of them would meet our specs. This one is damn near optimal."

Rikki added, "We're at landing zone three."

"Tell us about it," Dana said.

Rikki nodded. "It's located at about twenty-five degrees north latitude, almost within the tropics. The seasons won't be extreme. This near the equator cyclonic storms won't be common and shouldn't be severe. It's local spring, so we can try farming without a long wait. Caves, sea, river delta, the works. Bottom line, it satisfies all our requirements."

"To provide an overview, we made a vid," Blake said. "Marvin, if you'll project it up there."

On the hold bulkhead, the display switched to a wide-angle, outdoor shot of the sea. The camera panned along the shoreline, paused to admire gentle waves lapping at a white sand beach, then swept up a rock-strewn and furrowed slope to a range of low, rounded hills. A crescent moon, daylight ghostly, hovered over the hills.

Nowhere, apart from slimy green film on the undulating waters, did Dana see any color.

Their perspective returned to the shore, where Rikki, her breathing mask dangling on her chest, mugged for the camera. The shuttle and an inflatable shelter stood nearby.

"Pause," Blake said. "Our campsite, of course. The sea offers more than ample water as a deuterium source, and something like algae mats as feedstock for our synth vats."

"If this is so perfect," Carlos muttered, "why didn't you land there first?"

Antonio looked up from his datasheet. "The local *caves* run deep. I couldn't determine the extent of this cave system…with ground-penetrating radar."

"Salt water or fresh?" Carlos asked.

"The sea?" Blake said. "Brackish. Nothing we couldn't purify, if needed. Any other questions?" He paused for a few seconds. "Moving on, then. The hike up to the caves takes forty-five minutes. Marvin, can you fast-forward, say fifty to one, and debounce the vid while you're at it?"

"Done," the AI said.

The vid zigzagged up the slope, dodging boulders and gullies. Every few seconds, at this accelerated pace, the camera turned to gaze back. From these higher elevations Dana saw that two rivers emptied into the sea. One river entered in a spectacular waterfall. The second river reached the sea through a sinuous gorge and a broad delta.

They "arrived" in less than a minute at a high cliff face. In the vid, Rikki paused in a cave mouth that was more or less triangular. With her height as a reference the opening measured about four meters wide at ground level, and three meters high.

"Marvin, resume real time," Blake said.

"The front door," Rikki-in-the-vid narrated. "And a mere hundred or so meters away"—the camera following as she pointed—"once we clear away the boulders, a ready-made landing field for *Endeavour*."

Dana almost missed Carlos glancing at Li from the corner of his eye.

What's she up to? Dana wondered.

At a walking pace, the vid went inside. Marvin adjusted the apparent illumination so smoothly that Dana almost didn't notice the sputtering of one flare and the igniting of the next. They moved from one grotto to another. Twice, a soaring ceiling opened through a great shaft to the blue-green sky. Sinkholes, she guessed. One shaft looked at least a hundred meters deep!

It all reminded her of…what? Mammoth Cave. Now *there* was an ancient memory: she had been eight or nine when her family passed through Kentucky on holiday in North America. And just as in Mammoth Cave, moving deeper and deeper underground brought them to a rushing subterranean river. Sub-Darkian. Whatever.

"In-home running water," Blake said. "Fresh, by the way."

"What's the inside temperature?" Antonio asked.

Blake said, "Away from the entrance and the air shafts? Call it twelve degrees Celsius. Often, that'll be warmer than the surface."

Twelve? Balmy by Martian standards, too.

"How about flooding?" Dana asked. "Any data?"

Blake grimaced. "My guess is it won't be a problem, but that's *so* outside my area of expertise. Here's what I can say. The terrain outside slopes away from the entrance. The cliff overhangs the cave mouth, so rain runoff and snowmelt should hit downhill and keep heading away. Inside the entrance—"

"The one we've found thus far," Rikki interrupted.

"Fair enough," Blake said. "Inside *this* entrance, the cave floor trends downward. Its slope should carry away whatever rain and snowmelt does get inside. Supposing the cave has other, flood-prone entrances, there is a huge volume to fill before water can reach the upper chambers. And because the caves are dry now, we know the river drains somewhere. That's also encouraging."

As much as Dana wanted to believe, she wasn't convinced. "How about rain coming through those sinkholes?"

Rikki said, "There are big chambers upslope of where the sinkholes empty. I'd think we'd want to keep to those upper reaches, at least till we've experienced a couple rainstorms."

Antonio, his brow furrowed, was flipping holo frames on his datasheet.

Dana asked, "Antonio? If you have something to add?"

"I've been examining *the* vid up close. A violent torrent would sweep up big rocks and scar the cave walls. I haven't seen grooves like...that. There aren't many puddles. There's little dried mud and none of *it* is high on the walls."

"Then there's *no* flooding risk?" Dana asked.

Antonio shrugged.

"And seismically?" Carlos asked. "Is the area stable?"

Blake said, "On our flyover, I didn't notice any faults or indications of volcanism. And nothing inside these caves suggests otherwise."

"Is that definitive?" Carlos persisted.

"You want *definitive?*" Blake glowered. "We don't have seismometers. I doubt they'd be hard to build, but even on quake-prone territory they might give no indication for years. And minor shocks, if we did detect any, could be the norm everywhere on the planet."

"Look at these…stalactites." Rikki glanced at Blake for confirmation of the word. "They're *old*, aren't they?"

From what Dana remembered, stalactites grew maybe a few millimeters per year. Blake's vid showed stalactites at least three meters long. A thousand years old, then, without a major temblor? In a few years, surely, they would learn to build here and would vacate the caves.

She liked those odds.

"That whole area must be old," Antonio said. "Consider those sinkholes. There wasn't much rubble beneath them. All that rock dissolved. Imagine how…long that process took."

"It's a new world," Carlos retorted. "Can we really know?"

"But not new physics. I…think."

The longer they analyzed and weighed, mulled and debated, the more Dana wondered, why is Li so quiet?

✳

Li would never forget the night Mei Yeo won her seat in the California state assembly. Campaign aides and well-wishers thronging the tiny apartment. Anxious chatter and too loud laughter. The sudden hush whenever some volunteer observer texted an update from a polling place. Excitement mounting as the early returns broke Mother's way. Exuberant cheering—and Mother's tears of joy—when, long after midnight, her opponent called to concede.

Li had never seen her mother so happy.

And never did again. Anyone electable from the People's Republic of Berkeley was too extreme to advance her agenda in Sacramento.

And so Li learned at a young age that the purpose of politics is power, not popularity. Mother never did get that lesson. She ran and won and was miserable, stymied, one dreary term after another, rather than admit to the futility of it all. Even after, in her bitterness, she drove Li's father first to sluts and then to divorce.

Li had goals for the colony soon to be. And unlike Mother, *she* would see them come to fruition.

※

Would Dana *never* come to the point? Li wondered.

Finally, Dana did. "What do you say, folks? Have we found a home?"

"I'm ready for elbow room," Carlos said.

"This site looks good," Antonio said.

"Rikki, Blake," Dana said, "I think I know how you feel. How about—"

Li cleared her throat, reminding everyone how unsubtle she was. And that something more than site selection was on her mind. "The caves seem adequate, Captain, and my compliments to our intrepid explorers. But I have a question."

"Of course." Dana nodded agreeably, relieved to have consensus about a major decision. Clueless, Li hoped, about the issue at hand.

Li said, "As I understand it, we'll land near the beach, hike uphill and clear the boulder field on the flat expanse near the cave entrance, then hop *Endeavour* to its permanent landing spot. Right?"

"Right," Dana said. "Um, wait. What do you mean, permanent?"

"That that's where the ship will stay. Over a power cable, *Endeavour* is our power source. When something surprises us, she's our emergency shelter and, worst case, our way to evacuate. She's a secure place to stow some reserve portion of our cargo, for safekeeping."

"And the only place within light-years with a shower or a galley," Carlos threw in.

Dana frowned, uncertainly. "The DED as a power supply for six of us? That's like swatting flies with tactical nukes."

"It won't always be just the six of us," Li said mildly. "The larger point is, we're settling a barren wilderness. For that we need tech. Unless we conserve the little tech we have, it will wear out before we can replace it."

Dana's eyes narrowed.

Sensing deeper meanings, finally, are we? Li pressed on. "Without this vessel, we have nothing. No way to power the synth vats, maintain cooling for the embryos, or run the artificial wombs. No way ever to develop the tech to get us *out* of caves. No way—"

"I take your point," Dana said coldly.

"Do you?" Li shot back. Get really pissed off, Captain. "Wear out this ship through unnecessary use, and to what energy source do we revert? Campfires of our dried shit?"

"Ethanol distilled…from algae mats. Maybe a hydroelectric… power plant."

As he spoke, Antonio squirmed. He did not fare well with conflict and, moreover, was an innocent bystander. Li regretted putting him through this, but it was for the greater good.

She did everything for the greater good.

"Alcohol lamps," she sneered.

With nostrils flaring, Dana said, "And after the settlement becomes dependent for power on *Endeavour*? She's unavailable then for the unanticipated."

"So: alcohol lamps," Li scoffed again.

She heard Dana's teeth grinding.

Work it through, Captain. I'm defying you. Why? Is it because with the ship grounded your claim to any special authority over the rest of us is grounded with it?

"If I may, Captain," Blake said. "Li poses an engineering problem, and it has an engineering solution."

"Go on, Blake," Dana said.

"The second shuttle is still in crates. Run the colony off its reactor. Scavenge that shuttle, as needed, for high-tech parts."

"While you joyride around the solar system?" Li challenged. "*Endeavour* has served us well, but it's old. Tired. When our one long-range ship breaks down far out in the solar system—and it will—then what?"

"She's *my* ship," Dana forced the words between clenched jaws. "That hasn't changed. She isn't grounded till *I* say she's grounded, and *if* that happens, it'll be on an engineer's recommendation, not a shrink's."

"It's all very well to—"

"*Enough*, Li," Dana growled. "We'll offload the spare shuttle's fusion reactor. It'll give more than ample power to start our colony. We'll offload most parts and supplies from this ship. Hell, we'll disconnect and offload Marvin's servers, so that no matter where *Endeavour* goes, if it goes, the colony always has the use of Marvin's archives. All right?"

"Yes, Captain," Li said meekly.

With a parting glower at Li, Dana turned the conversation to scheduling the landing.

"That was brutal," Carlos whispered to Li.

No, she thought, that was reverse psychology. I have Dana *just* where I want her.

25

Dead tired, Dana swung her pickaxe up over her head. It came down, *clang*, on the unyielding ground. A few sparks flew, and bits of gravel.

From starship captain to manual laborer in one week and one easy lesson.

Despite morning chill and a stiff breeze off the newly dubbed Darwin Sea, sweat ran down her face and neck and plastered her shirt to her back. Knees, hips, shoulders…was any joint in her body *not* in agony from the extra weight hung on her by Dark's gravity? Certainly the damned pickaxe weighed a tonne. Taking a rest break every ten minutes and whenever she felt lightheaded, she had managed, so far, to forgo a breather mask.

Headache, dizziness, insomnia, and lack of appetite: she could be the poster child for altitude sickness. Tough. She told herself they had higher oh-two pressure than any Tibetan.

Trying to forget that Tibetans were no more.

Once again, the world spun around her. Dana laid down her pickaxe, carefully, before she hurt anyone with it. She sat on a boulder to wait out the vertigo. The blue-green sky made her queasy, too. She wished she could remember how long Mars's red sky had taken to come to seem normal. Years, she guessed.

Blake, nearby, wielded his own pickaxe. The result so far—as in her case—was more dimple than hole. But pickaxes were easier to fabricate than jackhammers.

Among untold gaps in Marvin's knowledge, rock blasting was the first to bite them. How much explosive would they need? How deep should they plant the explosives? How far apart?

Dropping his pickaxe, Blake wiped his forehead with a sleeve. His beard (all three men had started one, for warmth) remained scruffy. "This is a lot of work on an empty stomach."

"Nonsense," she said, shuddering. "We had gruel."

He stooped to reclaim his tool. "You always could motivate me."

Dana wished he hadn't reminded her of breakfast. Pond scum à là Carlos. According to every test Carlos and Li had devised, the reformulated slop was safe—

And with each mouthful Dana channeled old mystery novels. Arsenic poisoning was *not* how she wanted to go.

Dark's biology, what there was of it, in many ways resembled Earth's. So, anyway, her experts told her. Both biochemistries relied on DNA and proteins. Both used twenty-two amino acids, most of them in common. And when they differed? Dana didn't know one amino acid from another, anyway.

But she could not get past arsenic taking the role of phosphorus in terrestrial biochemistry.

With every swallow, she wondered how complete was the process of removing arsenic and inserting phosphorus in its place. Maybe only the merest trace of arsenic stayed behind. A little poison with every morsel....

With renewed vigor, she attacked the rocky ground. These excavations were the first baby step toward farming.

✷

"Fire in the hole!" Dana called.

Two meters distant, behind his own hulking granite boulder, Blake covered his ears.

She flipped the toggle on the detonator.

The sharp *blam!* was a satisfying conclusion to a morning at hard labor. Or would be, if they'd done it right.

The patter of gravel slowed, then stopped. "Let's have a look," Dana said.

The synthed charges had blasted six birdbath-sized depressions in the rocky ground. Three pits showed hairline fractures; to play safe, she decided to seal all six.

While the sprayed-on glue cured, they ate an early lunch: more gruel. What little regular food remained was being kept for emergencies. After choking down a few spoonfuls, Dana stretched out on the hard ground. The midday sun was warm on her face. She closed her eyes....

✱

Between feather-light nudges from her attitude jets, Dana was in free fall. No gravity? No acceleration? No matter.

Duty weighed her down.

Her hands had not left the flight controls or her eyes the console instruments for…she had no idea. Too long. Surreally long.

Shedding debris and spurting gases, spinning and weaving like a toy top about to fall over, the dying ship had her stymied. Only this gyration would never stop. And faster than she could infer any underlying pattern to the hulk's erratic wobble, another of its compartments would rupture, spewing atmosphere, or an attitude jet would misfire.

Across the bridge, the mayday call looped endlessly. As though she needed a reminder.

She could end the madness at any time. No one would question her pronouncement that docking was impossible.

No one except her.

On the dying vessel, desperate passengers and crew awaited rescue. In *Reliance*'s main air lock, suited up, the rescue party stood by awaiting their chance to board.

Everyone waited for her to dock. Without crashing. Without dooming everyone aboard both ships.

Again the wreck lunged. Faster than conscious thought, Dana fired her forward thrusters. Flotsam caromed off her hull even as, by a terrifyingly small margin, the ships slid past one another without colliding.

Slowly spinning, a vacuum-bloated corpse floated past the bridge view port.

A warm, firm hand squeezed Dana's shoulder. Captain Torrance. Though he must have felt her trembling, he did not say a word.

And so, once more, she edged toward the careening, floundering, bobbing wreck.

There was no denying duty.

*

Dana jerked awake.

"Are you okay?" Blake asked.

She shrugged. What could he do?

Pursed lips said he knew she was holding out. After a while, changing the subject, he said, "The aggravating thing is that Li's right, in part."

"Which part?"

"We *don't* have enough supplies." He gestured down the beach, to the plumbing monstrosity on which Carlos and Rikki had spent days fussing. Their construction had tied up a major portion of the colony's metal reserves. "Beginning with deuterium."

Because every workaround to their many shortages—when someone came up with a workaround—seemed to take energy. Getting more *energy* took energy.

In Dark's seas, as in Earth's, heavy water could be found as one molecule among about sixty-five hundred. To become energy self-sufficient, they had only to separate out the heavy water. And split the deuterium atoms from the heavy water. And capture the deuterium. And freeze it, near absolute zero, into fuel pellets for the fusion reactor. Simple in concept; not so simple in execution.

Witness Carlos and Rikki shouting. Again.

Peering down the beach, Dana still could not make out what they said. Not a triumphant declaration of success.

Atop the tallest distillation column, a dish antenna pointed uphill. On a mast outside the cave mouth a second dish pointed downhill. Between, invisible to the eye, blazed an intense beam of microwaves: yet another workaround. They lacked the copper to run power cable from the reactor in the cave to the distillery on the shore. They lacked enough, well, *anything* to build pipes to pump water from the shore up to the cave. Or a big enough pump.

And so, while Carlos tinkered, trying to master the process, their scant deuterium reserves dipped lower and lower. The not-yet-operational distillery was a power hog, made more so by the inherent inefficiency of beamed power.

Grunts wielding pickaxes didn't use deuterium. Apart from the power to synth their daily gruel....

Blake tried again. "I'm worried about supplies."

Et tu, Blake? "You want the ship grounded?"

"Hardly," he said. "A tech civilization takes natural resources. It defies belief that we'll find everything we'll need within walking distance. That doesn't mean I'm not worried."

"Needing the ship to scout for and recover resources. Too bad I didn't think to give that as a reason when Li made her pitch. It would have sounded so much better than 'Because it's *my* ship, and I say so.'"

"Yeah. And too bad I lost my samples in the snow on the first scouting trip."

Because if they had had biological samples earlier, they would have known Dark's biota relied on arsenic, not its periodic-table cousin, phosphorus.

Who knew phosphorus was the sixth most important element in terrestrial biology?

Copper. Deuterium. Phosphorus. How many other critical resources did they lack? Bringing Dana to wonder how their homemade glue fared. She said, "Back to work, sailor."

"In a minute," Blake said. "Answer me this. I don't believe for a minute Li's proposal to ground the ship was spontaneous. She claimed to be worried our tech will wear out. Then wouldn't she also have worried about raw materials for that tech?"

"You'd think." Dana stood. "Come." Because the basins, once the glue set, should be waterproof. A theory that could be validated only by filling the basins with water lugged from the shore in buckets, like cavemen.

She giggled. They *were* cavemen.

Blake raised an eyebrow at her.

Retrieving an oh-two tank and mask from a tote bag, she breathed deeply. "It sneaks up on a person," she said.

"And that's why you, in your wisdom, decreed a buddy system." Grinning, he pointed across the beach. "Though those two don't sound all that buddy-buddy."

Dana and Blake took turns, one toting pails, and the other dribbling seawater through a molecular sieve. What passed into the pools, in theory, was pure water. They had built the test ponds near the beach, but hauling water was still exhausting. With each bucketful, the way uphill to the cave looked steeper.

They rested while waiting to see if the ponds held water. All but one did. Dana hoped the sealant also meant no arsenic would leach from the ground into the ponds.

She added to the water-tight ponds, in precise ratios, sulfur, phosphorus and other trace elements from their limited stores. Nutrients whose inventory became more depleted each day they relied upon, and had to alter chemically, the native biomass....

In Petri dishes, beneath sunlamps, Carlos and Li had proven they could grow photosynthetic earthly bacteria. To feed themselves until crops came in—and no one had a theory yet how long before they could even plant crops—they needed biomass in much larger quantities. Once they got bacteria to prosper in these test ponds, they would scale up the process.

And she and Blake would fly off, to no one yet had a clue where, in search of phosphates and other nutrients. Take *that*, Li.

Dana was exhausted well before they finished. The sun hung low in the sky, the wind off the sea had picked up, and the temperature had plummeted. That morning, she had sweated from exertion; now, she shivered.

Pond by pond, she distributed bacterial samples. "Eat hearty," she commanded her fellow Earthlings. You do your duty and I'll do mine.

26

Rikki traced circles with her spoon in an otherwise untouched bowl of gummy stew: lunch, such as it was. Her back was to Blake, but she sensed his worried look. Between her foul mood and her broken arm, he hadn't gotten much of a homecoming.

She tried to care.

"Are you all right, hon?" Blake asked.

"I'm fine," she said, setting down the spoon. In the glow of lighting strips, the glop clinging to the utensil looked as insipid as it tasted.

"Yeah, right."

"I'm a bit tired," she admitted. Dog tired. Drained. Exhausted. Whereas Blake had fallen asleep last night within minutes, oblivious to her tossing and turning.

"Uh-huh," he said doubtfully. He gestured at the curtained opening of their little private alcove. "It's almost time. If you're done with lunch, maybe we should wander over."

The last place she wanted to be was in another meeting, particularly a mysterious one. But if she stayed behind it would only bring attention, from Blake most of all. She didn't want the attention. And so, she nodded.

He led the way, their footsteps echoing, to the soaring, stone-columned chamber that everyone called the cathedral. The two of them were the first to arrive. As they sat waiting, Rikki wished, or wished it mattered enough to her to wish, her sadness would go away.

Either way, the despair ignored her. As always.

From the corner of an eye Rikki caught Blake chewing on his lip, brow furrowed, debating with himself. *No, Blake, I do not want to talk about it.* She said, before he made up his mind, "At least here"—unlike aboard ship, crammed in among the coffin-like cold-sleep pods—"we have room to spread out."

It wasn't that she wanted to be far from Blake, returned the night before from a prospecting run. She just didn't want to *talk* with him.

And that was problematical because he had not let her out of his sight, annoyingly solicitous of her mood and her arm.

The latter was nothing: a clean break. Over the space of two days, industrious nanites already had the bone half knit. Also, it was her own stupid fault. A Martian weakling on Dark had no business levering boulders to help clear a more convenient landing field. Not, at least, till she'd given exercise and a whole different batch of nanites enough time to bulk her up.

The despair was different, whatever the hell had brought *it* on. Besides…everything.

Inside the cast her arm itched like mad. She almost welcomed the distraction.

"Seriously, are you *sure* you're okay?" Blake asked her again as she scratched beneath the plaster cast with the tip of a pen.

"Suspense aside, yeah," Rikki lied.

Li had requested the meeting. There was never any predicting what that woman had on her mind. Other than trouble.

"Just rest and enjoy the moment," Blake told Rikki.

She tried. The soft breeze that ever sighed through the caves. The air that, if a bit thin, was eminently breathable. The sunlight that streamed through the sinkhole high overhead.

It only made her mourn for the generations who had labored in vain to make such a world of Mars. Survivor's guilt and depression, Marvin surmised, when she had consulted the AI. She was not about to open up to Li.

Antonio and Carlos arrived and took seats on separate concrete benches. Local concrete, mixed from local materials. As time and more urgent projects allowed, the men planned to experiment with concrete construction on a larger scale.

Huh. Maybe the six of them *were* making progress. Rikki still couldn't imagine ever calling this place home.

At last Dana and Li emerged from a side tunnel to join the rest. Somewhere down that twisty passage was the cavern's most recently discovered entrance, this doorway opening onto the backside of the ridge. A view onto an endless, barren, rocky plain? Rikki hadn't seen any point in checking it out.

Dana looked relaxed. No, happy.

It was hard to fault Dana. She and Blake had brought *Endeavour* home with its holds filled. They had mined enough asteroid ores, rich in sulfates and phosphates, to expand the bacterial farms a hundred times over. They could jaunt back anytime for more.

The mineral lode assured the six of them all the arsenic-free biomass they could eat. No matter that the slime-coated birdbath-sized test ponds reminded Rikki of aquaria gone very, very bad. At every single meal....

And while Dana and Blake had been away prospecting, Carlos had tweaked his seaside deuterium distillery past breakeven. They had begun filling their tanks, not depleting them.

Yes, it was hard to fault Dana's good spirits.

Rikki still managed.

Dana sauntered toward the unoccupied end of Antonio's bench. At the soft pad of her footsteps, Antonio, rather than avert his gaze, looked *up*. Rikki, from where she sat, couldn't be certain, but just maybe Antonio had made fleeting eye contact with Dana. Was something happening between those two? If so, it was long overdue. *Someone* should be happy.

In principle, anyway.

Li had noticed their silent exchange, too, and her smile broadened.

That smirk made Rikki's jaws clench and her teeth grate. Almost nonstop since landing day, Li had flitted about, blathering, full of vacuous good cheer. Blake called it Li playing cruise director. To judge by the funk Rikki tried to care that she couldn't shake, Li was terrible at cruise directing.

Rikki slipped her good arm around Blake's waist, shrugging when he looked at her questioningly. She *knew* a shoe was about to drop. Why?

Still smirking, Li went to stand in a shaft of brilliant sunlight.

Li was why. Rikki bent down and whispered, "A bit theatrical?"

"I'd say political," Blake whispered back. And he detested politics.

"If I could have everyone's attention, please." Li, beaming, one by one caught the eye of everyone but Antonio. (And in the process, didn't her gaze linger on Blake?) Li said, "I asked Dana to call us together, to give us the opportunity to celebrate our achievements."

"Let's all raise a glass of slime," Antonio said.

For *Antonio* to joke, this was a special moment.

Li chuckled. "I have it on good authority, as it happens, that our farmed biomass is fermentable."

"It's true," Carlos called out, grinning. "And Tuesday's vintage is not undrinkable."

"Then we have even more to celebrate," Li said, again laughing. "Seriously, who could have imagined it? Who among us would even have dared to hope it? No one, I'm sure, and yet see what we have accomplished. A month after we first reached an unknown planet, we have not only survived, we've made a home for ourselves. We've…"

A month. Set at thirty days, after yet another inane discussion. A measure of time carried over from a world on which Rikki had never set foot. On which she never would. Billions, surely, had died on Earth. On Mars, everyone would have died. Recoiling from sudden gaping emptiness, Rikki tried to concentrate on Li's words.

"…even feeding ourselves with locally grown food. I am *so* proud of us. We all should be proud of ourselves. Above all, I—and I believe I can speak for everyone—am grateful to our esteemed captain." Li began clapping, and after a moment everyone joined in.

Rikki glanced over her shoulder. More than surprised, Dana looked…pleased. Maybe this get-together was mere cruise directing—

And maybe Li meant to blind-side Dana.

Li helped everyone with their tasks, but except for cruise director—and seeing to the occasional broken bone—she had no responsibility to call her own. Nothing to distract her from scheming.

But that could be changed.

"Since we're doing so well," Rikki blurted out, "maybe it's time to take the next step. Maybe it's time we begin raising some children."

✳

Dance, my marionettes. Dance.

Li kept her expression blandly cheerful. How subtly she had conditioned her companions to believe her unsubtle. With such understated skill had she primed them to speak their lines!

As pathetic, pliable, oblivious Rikki had just taken her cue.

"Children," Dana repeated. Getting out the single word seemed to be a struggle. Beside her, Antonio twitched in surprise. Carlos nodded agreement, and Li had no difficulty reading *his* thoughts. But he was manageable; she had years before those perv tendencies would matter.

Li struck a contemplative pose, silent, waiting. Blake owned the next important line in this melodrama—as clueless as he, too, was of his role. She studied his pursed lips, his furrowed brow, the nuances of his posture....

He would take a while to get there.

"Can we?" Dana asked. "I mean, could we manage children? Li, what do you think?"

Li took a moment, hands clasped behind her back, pretending to consider. The point of the exercise was to make the decision seem anyone else's idea. "The artificial wombs do the work. But are *we* ready? That's harder."

"Wrong," Rikki snapped, rising out of her apathy to take the bait. "If we started today, we'd have nine months to prepare."

How sprightly the puppets leapt as Li tugged their strings.

"Is anyone ever prepared?" Antonio murmured something more Li couldn't quite make out. Something, maybe, about diapers.

Dana managed a wistful smile. "I remember my brother and his wife finding out they were expecting. They spent the entire pregnancy in a panic. And when the baby came, they did fine."

Carlos offered, "And we have Marvin to keep an eye on them round the clock. It'll take only a few cameras strategically placed."

"True, children won't be mobile right away...." Li allowed them to think that they were swaying her.

Dana tipped her head, looking unhappy. *She* wasn't ready to take on parenting.

Blake looked close to a decision. When he next looked in Li's direction, she, with an all but imperceptible nod, answered the question he still wasn't quite certain how to articulate: would mothering raise Rikki's spirits?

And at last—

"*I* think we should," Blake said firmly. He gave Rikki's hand a squeeze. "Sooner rather than later. Why are we even here, if not to restore the human race?"

Quite right. No matter that, at the moment, humankind's future was merely Blake's means to a very personal end.

Deep down, a part of Li regretted the pain she had caused. *First, do no harm*, the ancient dictum went, and she agreed. But in the face of extinction, her priority was the greater good. Of the six of them, who better than she to orchestrate a new society?

She had tried her hand at politics, at Mother's urging, two worlds ago. And gone nowhere, not even as far as Mother. But unlike Mother, Li had learned from their mistakes.

Hence, today's puppet theater.

Many people stumbled from grief into depression. It hadn't taken much—the occasional "ill-chosen" remark evoking memories of home and family—to nudge Rikki over the precipice. Thereafter, it was all about waiting for the right moment.

Which Rikki, snapping one of those chicken-wing arms of hers, had obligingly delivered. Sidetracked, feeling useless—she had fallen *hard*.

Li ignored the stirrings of guilt. When the cast came off, the "nutritional supplements" she would provide would rebalance Rikki's neurotransmitters.

"Well?" Blake demanded.

Head canted, Li gazed off into space. "What I said about the artificial wombs? Let me rephrase it. Of course they'll nurture the unborn—but I'll have to monitor the process at all times. We don't dare put our trust in software that never had our circumstances in mind.

"What harm did decades of radiation do to the frozen embryos? Without a doubt, some, and those effects will be random. Ditto for the biotech of the wombs themselves. And though we understand fetal and early childhood development on the Moon and Mars and piddly little asteroids, we know nothing about the process in *more* than a standard gravity. We don't know what sensitivities or allergies a fetus might develop to amniotic fluid synthed from Dark biomass, or infants to formula synthed locally. We'll need major reserves of every possible trace element, nutritional supplement, and medicine. We'll need—"

"We'll do what it takes," Blake said. Turning, he focused his gaze on Dana. "Won't we?"

Would Dana deny her old friends? Li doubted it.

Dana asked, "Does any of this become easier if we wait?"

"Who *cares* about easier?" Li said. "I love children. Why do you suppose I did what I did, back home?" Dramatic pause. She would have preferred a dramatic, heartfelt sob, only she couldn't carry that off. Not, in any event, with Mother's sarcastic laughter ringing in her memories. "This needs to work. *I* need this to work."

"We all do," Dana said. "Tell us everything you will need and how we can help."

And so, centimeter by centimeter, Li allowed them to coax her into starting the first cohort of babies. Whatever that took. With everyone standing ready: to test, tweak, and fine-tune the artificial wombs, under her guidance. To come running whenever her medical training—or, so much on Dark being uncertain, her instincts—insisted human eyes and brains were needed to observe. To synth or, whenever templates weren't available, to improvise, everything they would need on hand: from diapers and hypoallergenic cleaning supplies, to blankets and bassinets, to bottles and nipples and a stockpile of formula, to specialty tiny surgical gear just in case....

Everyone at Li's beck and call.

Dana, throughout, would be scouring the solar system for every obscure trace element imaginable—certain all the while that her being anywhere *but* the colony was wise and responsible, and vindication of her insistence on keeping the ship flying, and her very own idea. Leaving a complete leadership vacuum on Dark.

Dance, my marionettes. Dance.

This, Mother, is how one exercises power. With finesse.

DYSTOPIA

(Spring, Year Four)

27

Beneath a sullen teal sky, under the pitiless glare of an alien sun, Blake plodded forward. No matter the ceaseless wind, despite the remnants, all around, of the spring's latest unseasonable snowfall, he dripped with sweat. He was as tanned as a walnut, as filthy as mud, as exhausted as...as....

Words failed him.

Somewhere beyond the too distant horizon his destination beckoned. If only he could reach it. If only he could see his goal. If only he could spare a moment to rest. If only he—

To a flourish of trumpets, he shuddered awake.

Bach? McCartney? Copeland? Some centuries-ago composer. A way to keep alive a bit of the culture they had left behind, that Li insisted it was important for them to cherish. Most mornings, the random selection was okay.

This was just a discordant bleat.

"I'm up," Blake croaked, so Marvin would kill the noise. "Lights on dim."

At Blake's side, Rikki tugged the blankets over her head.

"Time to get up, hon," he said softly, sitting up.

She burrowed deeper.

"We have things to do."

"Yeah." She threw aside her covers, but required a minute to summon the energy to stir further.

Blake understood. He hadn't felt rested since....

Since Eve arrived.

After willing themselves from bed, he and Rikki quickly showered and dressed. Outside their concrete cabin, the dawn air had a chill to it. At the height of summer, mornings would have a chill to them.

The sun had yet to clear the horizon. Almost as baleful as in his dream, the dawn light, blood-red, blazed down the settlement's lone street.

Red sky in the morning, sailor take warning, the ditty bubbled up from his subconscious. What about a sun that ever verged on red? What about a greenish sky?

Blake turned toward the dining hall. Rikki, a wistful look in her eye, faced the other way, toward the much larger, but no less utilitarian, squat concrete box that was the childcare center.

What the hell, they could gobble breakfast. It was only fuel, best not noticed.

"We can spare a few minutes," he told her, offering his hand.

Rikki led them down Main Street, the rutted path there was never the time or the resources to pave, into the childcare center. A broad corridor, its inner wall entirely one-way glass, enclosed the facility on all four sides. They paused first outside the gestation room, its glow panels still night-dim. On forty-eight empty wombs, READY lights shone a steady green. Carlos expected to have another ten or more units finished soon.

On a rear-wall display, above and behind the wombs, counters ticked down toward Family Day. Forty-five days....

Around the corner, in the gallery outside the nursery, he and Rikki tarried longer. In twenty-seven glass-enclosed cribs, eerily hushed, babies slept, or stirred, or fussed. The little ones only seemed silent; so that they would not disturb each other, noise cancellers in each enclosure masked most sounds. Though the babies varied in size, they were almost identical in age: about four months.

Through sensors wired into the cribs, Marvin watched, listened, and sniffed ceaselessly for any hints of distress. From displays at the foot of each crib the AI's smiling animation would be beaming down, crooning or speaking soothingly to each infant as it (or, rather, Li's verbal generalities turned by Carlos into updated programming) deemed appropriate.

Antonio, passed out on the room's rumpled cot, an out-flung arm trailing on the floor, remained on duty for whenever the AI needed hands or suspected a problem. To judge by the line-up of empty formula bottles on the table along the wall, and the overflowing diaper pails, Antonio had had a long night.

As Rikki reached for the doorknob, Blake said, "Don't. You'll wake Antonio." Who, like Dana, was old enough to be a grandparent. In a fairer world, neither would be expected to pull all-nighters like this.

Rikki jerked back her hand, looking sad *and* relieved. "It's so… cold."

Impersonal, she meant. "I know," he told her.

And yet inescapable. He nudged her around another corner and they peeked in on the toddlers. Marvin kept watch here, too.

Most here were awake, playing and babbling in their cribs. By accident or with insight, a few had opened the refrigerated compartments in their cribs and helped themselves to formula bottles. Antonio would be along soon—roused by Marvin, if need be—to help those who hadn't managed to feed themselves.

And to change diapers. Lots of diapers.

Rikki reached for the knob of this door, too. Once inside, she wouldn't leave without first rocking, cuddling, and cooing over each of the twenty-six.

If any child would let her. A haunted expression told Blake she, too, feared their recoiling.

"We need to get a move on," he said, not meeting her eyes.

Around the final corner they looked in on the oldest children. This room had no cribs; mattresses resting directly on thickly padded carpet hid much of the floor.

Eleven of these children were just shy of three standard years. Some played, as often side by side as with one another. A few rammed around, bouncing off padded walls and each other. Three sat in a corner staring at an animation with images of colored toys. When Blake pressed an intercom button, Marvin was teaching numbers. From other wall displays, Marvin's avatars praised, cajoled, and chided its charges.

Then there was the oldest cohort. The guinea-pig generation.

Blond, blue-eyed Eve, by almost a day the grande dame of the Dark-born, was loading a tray with snacks. Castor, burly and intense, was piling plastic blocks. Pollux, his black hair a tousled mess, frowning, sat hunched on one of the room's tiny toilets.

The trio struck Blake as wise—or was it wizened?—beyond their five standard years.

He tried to remember when he had seen any of them smile. And he pretended not to notice Rikki brushing a tear from her cheek.

This...*factory* was no way to raise children, but how else could six adults cope? And duty demanded they bring yet more children into the world, while growing food for everyone.

"Let's get some breakfast," he said gently.

Rikki nodded, too choked up to speak.

When they retraced their steps through the gallery, Antonio was up, yawning, a red-faced, bawling baby in his arms. From another room, furtive scrabbling sounds announced that at least some of the lab mice had awakened, too. But not Li: they found her in the ICU, dozing in a chair, her mouth fallen open. Her patient, asleep in the room's single occupied isolette, was sticklike, its joints misshapen. Li had not had any explanation beyond, "It happens."

She works harder than all of us, Blake thought. And *she* can't leave the settlement, can't ever stray more than a few steps from the children.

The moment of empathy almost kept Blake from not dreading the remainder of his day.

✳

Breakfast was as best-ignored as usual. He and Rikki scarcely overlapped with Carlos and Dana, heading out that morning on a quick flight to gather more phosphates. Carlos swigged from a tall glass; Blake guessed that the synthed orange juice was laced with vodka.

"We can't have too much phosphate," Li had said again and again, when she wasn't pushing them to stockpile other minerals and trace elements. "If *Endeavour* ever breaks down..."

And she was right, although phosphates half-filled their largest storehouse.

Until recently it had been a full warehouse. The crush of snow from the winter's final storm had buckled the roof; three days of torrential rain only the week before had washed away half their reserves.

Blake missed robins as the first sign of spring.

He and Rikki packed lunches, grabbed a tractor from the garage, and trundled down Main Street. Past storehouses and workshops. Past a massive, deeply buried bunker, showing only its roof and slanted double doors. It safeguarded their most precious treasures: embryo banks, both human and animal, and seed bags, and Marvin's servers. Past their other bunker, housing a fusion reactor. Past the ethanol-fueled, steam-powered generator that backstopped the reactor, and the ethanol refinery. Past the chemical fertilizer plant and its noxious odor. Past the chicken coop, with its clacking, clamoring occupants and their worse than noxious stench. Past the glass-walled hydroponics conservatory and its touches of terrestrial greenery. Past the foundry in which he had fabricated, among many things, parts for this tractor.

Past twelve headstones and twelve heartbreakingly tiny graves.

Gravity's effects on gestation? Local toxins? Radiation damage from the long voyage? Li couldn't always tell, and that meant they could expect to lose more children.

They drove in silence down to the silt plains.

To the roar of the tractor engine, Blake began tilling. The throbbing of the motor ran up the steering column, out the steering wheel, into sore hands, aching arms, and tense shoulders. Despite gloves and bandages, he kept popping blisters faster than med nanites could heal them. He felt about a hundred years old.

The stiff morning breeze off the Darwin Sea whipped across the Spencer River Delta, pelting him with grit and roiling the dust plume that trailed behind the tractor for a good fifty meters. Should he plow the lifeless silt with or across the prevailing wind? Follow the contours of the landscape? He had no idea, and Marvin's databases, though rife with esoteric botanical theory, offered little practical how-to to enlighten him. Last year's trials with silt and fertilizer in a few pots and planters, as encouraging as they had been, suggested nothing about plowing techniques. So Blake changed course every few rows, putting in furrows every which way. When the crops came in—*if* the crops came in—he would have a better idea for next year.

Not that Marvin's knowledge wasn't useful: it showed they had dodged a bullet. Their seeds, all varieties gengineered for Mars, fixed nitrogen directly from the atmosphere. Blake hadn't taken biology since high school, so maybe he'd forgotten that unmodded crops often depended upon nitrogen-fixing bacteria in the soil. More likely, he had never known it in the first place. Inner-city curricula didn't dwell much on farming.

Rikki plodded along behind the tractor, hand-planting the field row by row and labeling test plots. When she had tired of stooping and he of the shuddering of the tractor, they swapped places. The windborne silt by then had turned them both a dusky gray.

Except by shouting, they couldn't make themselves understood over the roar of the tractor. He resented the noise and fumes, but the ridiculous internal-combustion engine was dependable and easy to maintain. There was no use complaining about it.

As there was no use complaining that babies, like wheat and corn and even slime ponds, must be scheduled *just so*, the winter, labor-intensive crop of newborns timed to arrive *after* the harvest of the weather-dependent crops. Or about the cookie-cutter "parenting" largely outsourced to Marvin.

Only realism did nothing to ease the pain. He had seen the hurt again that morning in Rikki's eyes. The yearning, the ache, the need to bear her own child. *Their* child.

Weeks earlier, he had sought out Li to ask about it. In private, because Li was the last person with whom Rikki would share anything personal....

✳

"Bad idea," Li had told Blake.

"The gravity?" he had guessed.

"The gravity. It causes constant skeletal strain, wear and tear on the joints, and constriction of the blood vessels.

"Forty percent excess weight is nothing to sneeze it. That's for you and me. For Rikki it's almost four times the weight her body developed to handle. Even with nanites and meds, it's a struggle to keep her blood pressure controlled. Pregnancy would only exacerbate the problem."

"It would be uncomfortable?"

Li had shaken her head. "Quite possibly fatal."

"Jesus! What about the girls who'll be born here? When they're old enough?"

"I'm hopeful they'll be able to carry babies to term, but we'll have to wait and see. By then, maybe, I'll have a better handle on the situation, and better meds."

All the sacrifice, everything that the six of them had endured... it might *still* be all for naught? That was too horrifying to face, too cosmic. The personal tragedy was heartbreaking enough.

With a lump in his throat, he had asked, "What do I tell Rikki?"

"What I would tell her, if she'd been the one to consult me. The truth."

"I can't. It would destroy her."

Li had stood there, head tipped, lost in thought. "There is another possibility. We may need to go this way eventually, anyway."

"Tell me," he had demanded.

"IVF. In vitro fertilization. Afterward we transfer the embryo to one of the wombs for gestation."

"Then I'll say *that*."

"Okay." It had come out skeptically.

"Rikki wants a baby. *We* want a baby."

"Uh-huh."

Only Li had been right. When Blake broached the IVF option, Rikki had stormed from their home, slamming the door behind her.

✳

Suddenly glad for the engine's roar, Blake tried to lose himself in work.

Every selection of grain type, every depth of planting, every concentration of chemical fertilizer or chicken feces, was another experiment—performed with irreplaceable seeds. But trial and error was their only way to learn if and how fertilized silt would grow crops.

He told himself that Dark had neither weeds nor plant parasites. And, having once mentioned those advantages to Rikki, he brooded about her rejoinder: for now.

Evolution abhorred an ecological vacuum.

Late that morning Antonio arrived on the opposite bank of the nearby river channel, driving the colony's other tractor, to scatter diaspores from Carlos's latest batch of designer lichens. Even the most advanced terraforming lichen varieties *Endeavour* had brought, gene-tweaked to tolerate the ubiquitous arsenic, would not produce useful depths of true soil sooner than in decades. A glacial pace, for an all but glacial planet....

But Carlos and Antonio kept at it, as Blake and Rikki would on the silt plain, because the only large-scale food-producing alternative was the bacterial ponds. If nothing else, the lichens brought welcome splashes of color to the dreary countryside.

Blake hated farming, if he could so dignify their as yet futile toiling in the dirt, but he *loathed* working the slimy ponds. That festering blanket of scum. That fetid, pungent stench.

From the memory alone, he all but puked.

The tractor sputtered and stopped. From its seat, Rikki called, "I'm ready to switch places again."

"I'm ready for lunch," he countered, abusing the meanings of both *ready* and *lunch*.

Antonio had abandoned his tractor to handpick specimens from a nearby gravel deposit. He been gathering rocks, everywhere he went, since the onset of spring.

Blake had not asked why, lacking the energy for another of the esoteric circumlocutions that with Antonio too often passed for an explanation. An answer might start with the Big Bang.

"Join us for lunch?" Blake shouted, gesturing at the bobbing pontoon bridge that linked the delta to the shore.

Antonio looked up, not quite in Blake's direction. "No thanks. I've got things to do."

"What's with the rocks?" Rikki called.

"You'll be sorry you asked," Blake said sotto voce.

But all Antonio offered, with his attention already returned to his collecting, was, "I don't have postage stamps. Or...blueberries."

✳

Through the colony's array of safety cameras, Li watched the peasants traipsing home from their day's toil. She never called them peasants, not aloud, but how else did one describe those bound to the land to feed and serve their master?

She never called herself their master, either. It sufficed that at a subconscious level they knew. And anyway, she preferred Dark Empress. It had a certain cachet.

Above the two-tractor caravan, the sky had turned foreboding. Then the clouds opened up and rain spoiled her view. She had to imagine them wet, muddy, and miserable.

Well, the phosphate mines in the asteroid belt were dry enough.

She could almost envy Carlos and Dana. Li would kill for a change of scenery, not to mention a break from this oppressive gravity. Appearing indispensable had its price.

The caravan neared the edge of the settlement proper, the garage's overhead door creeping upward at a radioed command. That was Li's cue that someone, if not all three, would swing by soon to visit the children.

Li closed her office door behind her. Whoever came would find her, brow furrowed, shoulders slumped, expression sad, examining one of the babies.

28

Rikki lay bonelessly, eyes closed, head tipped back against the rim of the whirlpool tub, as the hot pulsing jets massaged away knots in her back, arms, and legs. Water and electricity, if little else, they had in abundance. She let the fizzing water buoy her, let it persuade her, that for a few minutes, anyway, gravity's cruel dominion had been overthrown.

After hard labor from dawn to dusk, it wasn't a bad way to end the day.

Blake said, "You look like you're only sleeping."

"Uh-huh."

"I'm going to get out now."

His voice rose in pitch, just a little, at the end of the announcement. Asking, without asking, "Unless you want to fool around?"

"I'll be along in a while," she said.

Eyes still closed, Rikki felt and heard the water slosh as he climbed from the sunken tub. Faint but brisk, she heard the whisper of fabric against skin as he toweled off, and the slap-slap of bare feet on the concrete floor as he padded from the bathroom.

Then she opened her eyes.

Part of her even wanted sex: for the closeness to Blake. To know he still found her desirable, no matter that this godforsaken rock had turned her into a muscle-bound Amazon. To exorcise some of her pent-up anger.

And that anger was why most of her didn't. Couldn't. Because what she *truly* craved, the ache more insistent with each passing day, was the feel of a child growing inside her.

A host of med nanites would not allow that to happen. And Li would not permit that to change. "For your own good," Rikki mimicked.

"What's that?" Blake called from the bedroom.

"Sorry. Talking to myself again."

"It's about time we head out for dinner," he said.

"Thanks." She permitted herself several seconds more buoyant relief. "Okay, I'm getting out."

He stuck his head through the doorway with a comically exaggerated leer.

"Maybe later," she said.

❋

Beneath diamond-bright stars, shivering in the evening chill, Rikki and Blake scurried down Main Street to the communal dining hall. Celestial sparkles and the nip in the air shared a cause. Dark's thin, dry air didn't block much inbound starlight; it didn't stop much of the day's heat from reradiating back into space, either.

She searched overhead for any hint of home. As always, the sky had nothing to offer her but alien constellations, many still unnamed, too large moons, and the soul-sucking, inchoate darkness that was the Coalsack.

"Make a wish," Blake said.

Turning toward him, studying the western horizon where he appeared to be looking, Rikki saw the meteor. Or a different meteor, because the sky was suddenly filled with faint streaks.

"Done," she said, trying to make her tone light. Alas, no mere wishing star would fix what ailed her.

The meteor shower ended in seconds, eminently forgettable. Planets glimmered overhead, too, the brightest of them so close that with binoculars you could clearly see its Saturn-like rings. Back home, Ayn Rand's orbit would not have encompassed the inner edge of the Asteroid Belt; the local version of a Belt was shoehorned in between the gas giant and Dark. Nearby asteroids meant nearby resources.

And though they had been fortunate so far, logically those rocks also made Dark a shooting gallery.

"I made a wish, too," Blake said, waggling an eyebrow at her.

She laughed. "It must be your lucky day."

"I'm not admitting anything, or it won't come true."

The dining hall smelled *wonderful*. Rikki couldn't place the aroma. Something different. Something she had not encountered in a long time. Carlos's muttering, from inside the kitchen, revealed nothing. It was his turn to prepare dinner, and that somehow always entailed guzzling the synthed swill that served as cooking sherry.

Wallpaper to her left and right showed an Earth forest; the wall straight ahead cycled through scenes of something from Marvin's media library. She didn't recognize the vid from its previews, and that didn't surprise her. For those who stayed after dinner, the communal movie was the cook's choice.

Behind Rikki, a door opened with a squeak. Li said, "I guess tonight's treat won't be a surprise. Wow, that smells good."

"Roast chicken?" Blake asked in wonder.

Because while they often had eggs, they had yet to eat meat. The priority remained expansion of the flock.

It pained Rikki to have learned the proper name for a bunch of chickens. And that tomorrow she would be up before dawn to collect eggs, scatter bucketfuls of feed pellets—dried, chopped bacterial mat—and muck out the coop.

Just as with cooking, they took turns caring for the chickens. Except Li. She refused to do anything so nonsterile lest one of the babies should need immediate care.

Logical…and *so* convenient.

"Some chickens got into a fight today," Li said. "Marvin alerted me. Before I could get to the coop, one chicken was severely pecked and clawed. I had to put the bird down, and saw no reason to let its meat go to waste."

"Fair enough," Blake said with enthusiasm.

Rikki sat at the dining-room table and Blake sat next to her. Li took the seat straight across from Blake.

Just to bug me, Rikki thought. And it works. Even after she had finally satisfied herself that while Blake respected Li, he did not much like her.

The door opened again, admitting the stragglers. "Sorry we're late," Antonio said. "Dana asked to look in on the children."

Did the little ones hate Dana, too? Did they avert their eyes, burst into tears, even back away, when Dana entered the nursery? Rikki was too ashamed of her failings ever to have asked.

"Not a problem," Li said. "But it's good that you're here."

"Do I smell *chicken*?" Dana asked.

Li beamed. "You do."

So Queen Li means to take credit for a melee among the chickens? Despising the woman, Rikki changed the subject. "How was everyone's day?"

Antonio shrugged. "Another day. Another few…calluses."

"About that chicken?" Dana prompted.

As Li started to explain, Carlos emerged from the kitchen pushing a serving cart. With the grand flourish of a magician, he raised the domed cover.

The roast chicken's skin was a crackly, golden brown. Clear juices oozed from punctures where he must have tested the bird's doneness with a fork.

Rikki's mouth started to water.

Nor did the feast end with the chicken. The greenhouse had contributed everything for a tossed salad: lettuce, tomatoes, peppers, onions, and cucumbers. There were baked potatoes, too, with synthed butter and dollops of faux sour cream. There were bowls of what looked like chocolate pudding.

When Carlos began carving the chicken, his hands were steady. If nothing else, the man could hold his liquor.

What were they celebrating, Rikki wondered, beyond Li's largesse with the bounty to which everyone *but* she contributed?

"It's a shame," Rikki began, sadness and sudden anger commingling.

Carlos stopped carving. Heads turned toward Rikki.

"Tonight feels like a Sunday family dinner. Only there's no family."

"*We're* family," Li said.

"Of course," Rikki said. "But I'm thinking bigger. I'm thinking of the children."

I'm thinking of bonding with them, or, rather, them bonding with us. Only Li doesn't see it. Li spends her days with the children, and they love *her* just fine.

Silence. Beneath the table, Blake gave Rikki's knee a pat. Maybe he meant it as comfort. It felt patronizing.

Forget your wish upon a star, fella.

Rikki plunged ahead. "We don't treat those kids—our kids— much different than the chickens in that egg factory down the street. We feed them and clean up after them like they're on some sort of production line. Apart from regular baths, they might as well *be* chickens."

"Except that we don't eat the children," Carlos said dryly, as he resumed carving.

Dana asked, "What do you have in mind, Rikki?"

"Dinner is the only time we're together," she answered. "We should eat with the kids. We should let them hear genuine conversation among adults, not abdicate to Marvin teaching them to speak." And so much else.

"That's seventy children." Li answered in the slow, calm, reasoned manner that drove Rikki up the wall, in the affected tone of voice that reminded: I'm the professional here. That reminded: they love *me*. "This year we'll add another sixty, more or less."

"And we want all of them to be civilized," Rikki said. "Or *they'll* be fighting like the chickens, too."

"Because during a sixteen-hour work day, on a short day, I would never think to speak to the children," Li said.

Spoken calmly and reasonably, damn the woman.

"We control the rate of births," Rikki said, "not the other way around. We shouldn't"—we mustn't!—"let an arbitrary decision shape how we bring up these kids."

"It's not arbitrary," Antonio said. "If *we* don't…raise the children while we're still alive, with firsthand knowledge of technology, culture, and civilization, they'll be savages. If that should happen, they…won't long outlive us."

Carlos again stopped carving to offer, "And we need genetic diversity."

More variety within your future harem, Carlos? Rikki bit her tongue. The children having children, no matter with whom, would not become an issue for years. She said, "They'll be savages if we don't slow down the pace, if we don't invest the effort to make them something better."

If we don't show them love.

"I agree with Rikki on this," Blake said.

On *this*? What hadn't made the cut?

"I've made a suggestion," Rikki said. "Let's discuss it."

"We have discussed it," Carlos said. "You've been told why it's impractical to—"

Dana cleared her throat. "Let's discuss options first. We could bring a few kids every evening. Rotate them through, making sure each child sees something like a normal family setting at least once a month. See how they fare in a social setting. Learn how *we* have to adapt."

Blake's pocket trilled; tonight was his turn on call. He took out the folded datasheet, glanced at it, and stood. "Sorry, people. Marvin needs hands in the nursery." He gazed with longing at the feast, not yet even on the table. "So very sorry."

Faster than Rikki could offer, Li said, "We'll save some dinner for you."

Rikki's thoughts—and her gut—churned. Hands. That's all we are to these children. What will they be like when they grow up?

Once again, Carlos returned his attention to the chicken. Blake set off toward the kitchen, perhaps for something he could eat while at the childcare center. Antonio, taking a serving bowl from the cart, managed to knock the salad tongs to the floor. He headed for the kitchen for, presumably, another set. Dana studied the forest scene.

The sudden silence was deafening.

It was as though Rikki had never spoken. As though she weren't even here. "We're running the universe's biggest, most impersonal orphanage," she said.

Leaning across the table, Li patted Rikki's hand. "This isn't about 'the children,' you know."

Rikki yanked away her hand. "Enlighten me. What *is* it about?"

"A particular child."

A nonexistent child. Though Rikki hated to admit it, even to herself, Li might be right.

There could be no denying the clanging of Rikki's biological clock, but she refused to accept that she was a slave to it. She leaned back in chair, trying to be objective, to separate motivations, to sort out her feelings. And ended up worried: do I crave pregnancy for a sense of worth?

Li was responsible for everyone's health, from day-to-day bumps and bruises to reversing the endless complications that cropped up in the wombs, from everyone's psychological wellbeing to assuring that their agricultural programs would satisfy the colony's long-term nutritional needs.

Dana had her ship to pilot, to keep them supplied with phosphates and metals and everything else not readily found or mined on the ground. Blake had the ship to keep flying, and a thousand other gadgets from tractors to chicken-feed dryers to design, build, and maintain. Carlos reprogrammed synth vats and nanites, built specialty medical gear for Li, and constructed and maintained the steadily growing number of artificial wombs.

Whereas Antonio and I are manual labor. Diaper changers and field hands.

Did Antonio ever feel insignificant, too? He shouldn't. But for him, they would never have escaped the GRB. His rock collection might serve no more purpose than his blueberry obsession, but at least he had interests.

I don't have laurels or interests to fall back on. Just survivor's guilt.

The colony would have much brighter prospects if Hawthorne had sent a farmer or miner in her stead. Of what use to *anyone* was a science historian? Of what earthly use....

"Are you all right, dear?" Li asked.

"We're bringing up the next generation like strays and foundlings. I don't like it."

Li's sad smile might have been intended to convey no more than, "What choice do we have?" but Rikki read it as, "Queen Li knows best."

I need *purpose*, Rikki decided. Something I can contribute. Something of my own. Something important.

In a flash of insight, she knew what that something would be.

29

The six of them had not discussed terraforming since before landing. Why would they? Dark *was* a terrestrial world.

But, Rikki decided, maybe they should.

Techniques that had been making Mars habitable could also make a difference on Dark. It was more than a matter of personal comfort: the crops that struggled here might thrive in a warmer climate. And she could *give* them that warmer climate: designer perfluorocarbons were incredibly effective as climate agents, some thousands of times more potent as greenhouse gases than carbon dioxide.

Nor would they need to pump much PFC into the atmosphere to begin altering the climate. Twentieth-century industries had, in a few short decades, without meaning to, almost destroyed Earth's ozone layer with chemically similar chlorofluorocarbons.

She began making order of magnitude estimates in her head—

And stopped. She was getting ahead of herself. The first rule of terraforming was, don't meddle with what you don't understand.

She didn't understand Dark. None of them did. They had experienced their share of *weather*, but four local years was too brief a time to reveal anything reliable about *climate*.

Continuous measurements covered only a few square klicks around the settlement. Their knowledge of anywhere else—spotty and haphazard, anecdotes rather than systemic data—was limited to whatever observations *Endeavour* had serendipitously made in the course of doing something else.

A remote-sensing satellite in synchronous orbit for the past few years would have told Rikki a great deal—but Dark had no synchronous orbits. Its moons soon destabilized the orbit of any artificial satellite placed at the proper distance.

Then there was the matter of oceans....

Oceans stored heat from sunlight, releasing that heat to moderate temperature swings both diurnal and seasonal. An ocean current like Earth's Gulf Stream could alter the climate of entire continents. Multiyear oceanic temperature cycles, like El Niño and La Niña, had global impact. Knowing what happened in Dark's ocean depths mattered.

The data that had been collected on this world's oceans and seas? Precisely zero.

She'd had the sense (or the lack of courage of her convictions?) to follow her instincts. She'd *not* spoken a word about any of this. Luckily so, because had anyone known how she'd been spending her time, she would only have looked useless. More useless. Marvin knew—she needed the AI's help with data retrieval, model building, and number crunching—but she had ordered it to keep her secret to itself.

Toiling in secrecy didn't help. By some miracle, the little ones had mostly slept the latest night she had spent at the childcare center. With a few minutes here and a few there, she had shoehorned in a couple hours of work. (For *them*, she told herself, guilt-ridden at not playing with everyone not asleep—and more guilt-ridden at the relief that came of sparing herself their rejection. For *their* future.) She got a bit more research accomplished when Blake spent the night in the nursery. Desperate for progress, feigning insomnia, on consecutive evenings she had squeezed in another few hours of work. But she couldn't keep up the pace. Without a decent night's sleep, and soon, she would keel over or run someone over with a tractor.

When the time came to commit serious astronomy, Rikki knew she had to enlist Antonio.

✱

Rikki threw off her side of the blankets. She got up and began dressing for outdoors.

"What?" Blake murmured sleepily.

"Insomnia," she told him. "Again. I'm going for a walk."

Blinking, he sat up. "Give me a minute. I'll walk with you."

"Wrong," she told him. "That I can't sleep doesn't mean you shouldn't."

"But I—"

"Gallantry noted. I'll be fine." This wasn't a campsite in some tropical jungle, surrounded by lions and hostile natives. The settlement's few buildings were surrounded by nothing and nobody. "Seriously, sleep."

"Stay close."

"I will." She gave him a quick kiss. "Sleep."

Antonio didn't put *all* his free time into his ever expanding rock collection, at least not at night. She found him where she had expected: using the ship's telescope. The main bridge display showed Ayn Rand, with two of its inner moons in transit. He seemed not to have noticed her arrival.

"Do you see something interesting?" she asked.

"I'm making a survey."

A nonanswer answer, she noted. Well, she had been on the taciturn side, too. He was in the pilot's acceleration couch, and she plopped into the copilot's seat. "I wondered if you could help me with something. Discreetly."

Because if she could harness his obsessive-compulsive focus, and his sometimes encyclopedic knowledge, he might do much to advance her research.

Finally, he turned away from the bridge console, if not to look directly at her. "If I can. Help, I mean."

"I'm trying to understand the climate here. Back home there were astronomical effects on climate."

Without leaving his seat Antonio seemed to strike a pose. Something in his voice changed. "You are remembering Milankovitch cycles."

Professorial mode. She wondered if he missed the academic life.

"The tilt of Earth's axis varies over…millennia. And like a wobbling toy top the Earth precesses about that axis, also over millennia. And because planetary orbits are ellipses, not circles, the axis of the entire orbit slowly revolves around the sun. In the case of Earth, that last cycle takes more than a hundred millennia. All three processes affect what sunlight strikes the planet, where, and at what angle. All three affect seasons and…climate."

As she had more or less remembered. "And those processes are independent, correct? Every so often, they peak together."

"Cycles peaking together have been implicated in triggering ice ages."

"And extrapolating to Dark? What does our long-range forecast look like?"

He studied his feet. "I don't know."

"What would it take to find out?"

"A lot of observing time. And modeling time, too." He gestured at the image on the big display. "Earth doesn't have a big neighbor planet like that to tug at it. Or three moons. The cyclic variations here are apt to be more complex."

Farming and childrearing didn't leave much time for, well, anything else. Maybe those were the only tasks she was good for.

Something she knew about the history of science had to be useful. Didn't it?

Maybe this was it.

✳

From the deep shadow alongside the reroofed phosphate storehouse, Carlos watched Rikki. Out in the middle of the night, slinking home from *Endeavour*. Having a bit of after-hours fun, are we?

But kudos for Antonio! Carlos would not have guessed the odd little guy had it in him. Or, more precisely, that he got it into Rikki.

After she slipped past, Carlos continued to his workshop. His extracurricular activities also demanded discretion.

Yawning, exhausted after a full day's work, he nonetheless toiled in high spirits. For months he had put his free nights into making things for Li. If what she wanted wasn't candy and flowers, nonetheless each new batch of the gadgets made her very appreciative.

He could appreciate that.

✳

Discovery set down on a broad plain, between soaring rock canyon walls.

"Touchdown," Blake announced. "The crowd goes wild."

They had landed on a pebbly shore along the Spencer River. A very damp shore, to judge by the steam that billowed around them, blocking Rikki's view from the cockpit. That fog would dissipate into the dry air long before the ground cooled enough for them to climb down.

"You do realize," she said, "that I've never seen a football game." Or cared to. Martians didn't do football: the playing field would have had to be ridiculously big.

"I know many things." He popped his helmet, unbuckled his safety harness, and twisted around to see her behind his headrest. "Such as that you've never asked to accompany me on a routine checkout flight. Not once. Today you announced you were coming *and* proposed a destination. What gives?"

"Nothing." Almost nothing, anyway: the vague memory of terrain glimpsed from a fast-moving shuttle, when the two of them had first flown over this region.

"Here in the canyon, we're out of radio contact. If you have secrets, this is the place to spill them."

His unhappy expression added, "Unless you're keeping secrets from *me*."

"No secrets," she dissembled. "I wanted to see these rock faces up close."

"Be that way." He turned forward.

"Really, that's why I came." And if she saw what she expected to see, she *would* explain. She just didn't want to look stupid.

The awkward, silent wait till he popped the canopy release seemed interminable.

Rikki hung a ladder over the cockpit's side, swung herself up and over, and clambered down the rungs. "I remember when doing that was hard."

"We're getting used to the place. Home sweet home."

Home, sweet or otherwise. That was why she had to get her head wrapped around the climate here. "I'm going to stroll along the river for a ways. Join me?"

"Sure."

The river's flow here was slow and placid. When she walked up to the shore and dipped in a fingertip, the water was icy. "No skinny-dipping," she told him preemptively.

"So what *is* this about?"

Slowly, she pivoted, taking in the panoramic view. "Isn't this enough?"

The flat plain stretched for at least a hundred meters behind them before rising to meet rugged cliffs. The river, gray with silt, hugged the canyon's other wall. Perhaps a half-klick downstream from where they stood, a small but spectacular cascade burst from the nearer rock face to crash into the waters far below. Rikki dubbed the torrent Beagle Falls.

How long ago had this valley silted up? Had the silt accumulated gradually, or had it settled out in the aftermath of some terrible flood? She didn't know, but an answer to that mystery could wait.

Craning her neck, peering up and up and up, Rikki studied the nearer canyon wall. Two hundred or so meters high. Sedimentary rock. Barren of life, of course, without even a hint of greenery. Great crags and brooding hollows carved as water and wind had patiently eroded the softest rock. Several dozen strata, of varying depths, in countless shades of gray. Subtle, subdued red tones here and there among the grays.

She took out her camera. With its laser rangefinder active to capture precise distances and scales, she started panning.

"Magnificent," Blake said. "It reminds me of the Grand Canyon."

"Then my suggestion was worthwhile?"

"You tell me."

She couldn't know without detailed analysis, but yes, she was sure. "The layering of the rock embodies sedimentation rates over time. Those reflect the climate." And cycles of the climate, over perhaps millions of years.

"And that's important?"

She couldn't know that yet, either. "It might be."

＊

The inevitable confrontation began after dinner, in an impassioned and arcane outpouring of verbiage from Rikki. Blake, Dana, and Antonio, looking on approvingly, were clearly in on it. And the four had waited till Carlos, Li's dependable ally (when sober, anyway), had left for his shift at the childcare center. Climate. Growing season. Terraform. Blah, blah, blah.

Rikki finally wound down.

"I don't know," Li told the assembled peasants.

The more candid answer would have been *I don't care.* Candor did not suit her purpose.

Nor did the topic matter. It mattered only that they found something over which to rebel. Something other than the manner of childrearing.

"It's *important*," Rikki insisted. She spoke too loud and stood too close. Her chin jutted out and she had crossed her arms across her chest.

Classic belligerence, Li thought. Excellent. "Maybe someday."

"Respectfully," Blake began, "I disagree. We shouldn't wait."

"Of course you disagree," Li said. Goading him by criticizing his woman. Because, as Li made a point of reinforcing from time to time, she was never subtle.

"Damn it, Li," Rikki said, "be reasonable. We need to understand the climate. Climate affects our food supply. You must care about that."

Li smiled condescendingly: another goad. "We settled almost inside the tropics. Can you find us someplace suitable anywhere warmer?"

"That's the point," Antonio said. "If the climate fails us…here, the colony is in trouble. Let's find out sooner rather *than* later. While maybe there's still the opportunity to change things."

Blake's turn. "Or we may find we've lucked out. This one set of observations, from this one canyon, suggests the trend might be to warmer weather. It would be nice to have an idea when and how far we can expand into higher latitudes."

Li said, "Planning for the long run."

"Exactly," Dana said.

In the long run, we're all dead. Li couldn't remember who, other than someone long dead, had first said that. The provenance didn't matter because she wasn't going to quote it. She *wanted* the four of them to prevail.

Convince me, people. Convince yourselves you convinced me.

"We need to eat," Rikki said. "The *children* need to eat."

They had an entire *world* to farm. How could they ever lack for food? But if she were wrong, if on occasion they wound up supplementing crops with a bit of bacterial sludge, so be it. What mattered was raising obedient, subservient children to do the colony's bidding.

To do *her* bidding.

And to that end, she needed the others too busy to interfere with her affairs.

Li permitted her shoulders to sag. She lowered her head, nibbled on her lower lip. Read: doubt. Read: you're winning me over. She said, "Can you fit in these studies without impact to our other work?"

"Well…," Dana conceded.

"Because," Li said, "I could take on longer shifts in the childcare center. If that would help."

"It *would* help," Antonio managed.

"Tell me again," Li said, "what will you do?"

Blake and Dana swapped glances. They'd caught her verb choice: *will*, not *would*.

"We need a more global data set," Rikki said. "There are other ancient canyons to read. Ice-core samples to collect from glaciers and the polar icecaps. Bore holes to drill in the sediments of lake and sea bottoms. All should tell us useful things about climate patterns and trends."

"It sounds major," Li said.

"It *is* major," Rikki said.

Li resumed chewing on her lip: sincere, accessible leader here, open to everyone's inputs. "Okay," she conceded. To grins all around, she added, "We'll have to figure out a revised work schedule first. We still have children to feed."

"Of course," Antonio said.

"Thanks, Li," Rikki said, at last letting her arms fall to her sides.

Li smiled. "You're welcome, and I thank you for bringing this matter to my attention."

Because while you're gadding about, the children will continue in my sole care. When you're here, you'll be crunching the data or laboring in the fields or in bed, exhausted, and the children will remain, under Marvin's watchful and carefully programmed eye.

Learning obedience. Discipline. Self-denial. Conformity. When (ever less frequently) the peasants questioned her methods, the analogy with which they struggled was an orphanage.

If any of her companions had read Dickens, they would still be on the wrong track.

Her true model—updated and improved, of course—was a Spartan barracks. The children would grow up to serve the State. The State *she* would define.

This, Mother, is how one wields power.

Before a single peasant ever suspected Li wanted them distracted by another project, it would be too late.

By then, all the children will be mine.

30

"Oh-two?" Dana asked.

"Two fresh tanks," Antonio answered.

"Oh-two pressure?"

"Nominal."

"Cee-oh-two?"

"Barely registering."

"Suit heater?"

Antonio had checked and rechecked everything on the long list, but he wouldn't dream of interrupting Dana's methodical run-through. Who better than he to respect obsessive behavior?

And she *was* being obsessive. Because she cared. She got him, not just better than anyone else alive—not a high hurdle—but better, almost, than anyone who had ever lived. As well, almost, as had Tabitha.

And knowing him, knowing how thoroughly he would have checked everything, Dana still made it her job to watch out for him.

After Tabitha died, he had never expected anyone to care again.

At last they left *Endeavour*, stepping from the forward air lock onto the sunbaked surface of Aristophanes. The terrain, what little could be seen before the freakishly close horizon, was less cratered than he expected.

A world at half-phase hung—loomed—overhead. Enormous. Thirty-five times the size of the Moon as seen from Earth. Icecaps and cloud tops sparkled, but could not overcome an overall gloominess.

Dark was aptly named.

"When you're done gawking," Dana said, with a hint of fond amusement in her voice.

They offloaded from cargo hold one the first of the remote-sensing stations. Though massive and bulky, here the unit weighed almost nothing. They set down the apparatus on a flat expanse and he stepped away. She would unfold the stabilizing legs, deploy the delicate solar panels, align the dish antennas, and run the final instrument calibrations. His job was to answer technical questions, should any arise, while keeping his ten left thumbs at a safe distance.

Duties that left him free to look around: the other, if unofficial, reason he was here. As often as he had championed exploration, the pursuit of knowledge for its own sake, something—typically farm chores and colicky babies—had always come first.

How much harder would Dana have it on this excursion for having *him* along, not Blake?

Antonio loved her all the more for bringing him, regardless.

The remote-sensing station was a kludge, the first among a whole constellation of kludges. Once Dana had it checked out, they would hop *Endeavour* a third of the way around this little moon and deploy a second station. Then take another hop, to deliver a third.

It wasn't bad enough that Aristophanes, orbiting so near Dark, precluded siting their sensor suites where above any rational planet they belonged: aboard synchronous satellites. Aristophanes also had an unhelpful rate of rotation; it didn't present a constant face to the world below, as the Moon presented to Earth. Only with *three* well separated stations would some *one* of them at all times have the planet under observation. Each station had to store its readings until Dark's rotation, the moon's rotation, and the moon's orbit combined to provide a line-of-site downlink opportunity to the settlement.

After finishing on Aristophanes they would get to reprise the triple deployment on Aeschylus and again on Euripides. And on occasion, parts of Dark would *still* go unmonitored.

Three fascinating little worlds, Antonio thought, sad that no one shared his fascination.

While Dana, with a multimeter in hand, fussed over some calibration, Antonio wandered about gathering rocks for his collection. As feeble as was Aristophanes' gravity, not even a klutz like him could trip off or leap free of it. He *could*, if he lost focus, bound high enough to spend a *long* while drifting back to the surface. And so he shuffled, sweeping aside ancient regolith with his boots, leaving sloppy troughs in his wake. His tracks shone paler than the undisturbed surface.

"Almost done here," Dana called. "How about you?"

Done scuffing up the surface? Done collecting rocks? "Ready when you are."

They remained suited up for the jaunt to their next landing site, sparing themselves another round of checkouts. Here they were on the moon's night side, with the planet half below the horizon. Antonio could still see clearly by—the word tickled him—Darklight.

He helped Dana carry their second station to an area clear of stony rubble. While she configured the unit, he resumed pebble collecting. Here, too, the ruts left by his plodding gait were paler than the undisturbed surface.

When, with an abrupt sneeze, Dana let fly the removable clasp of an access panel, he helped her search for it. When they gave up the fastener for lost, swallowed by the thick dust or hiding in the inky shadow of some boulder, he scavenged nuts and bolts for her from ship's stores. He found a spare thermocouple when an instrument failed diagnostics; without accurate temperature readings *here*, they could not calibrate long-range readings they made of Dark. Then, having bagged and labeled every interesting-looking pebble in the vicinity, he tried to entertain himself by tracing geometric shapes in the dust with his boot tip.

"Ready to move on?" Dana called.

"Sure."

Their third landing returned them to sunlight and gave them a line of sight to the settlement. Dana called down.

"How's it going, *Endeavour*?" Blake answered, yawning. He had gray bags beneath his bloodshot eyes, and his beard looked overdue for a trim. Maybe a shearing.

"Everything seems fine on this end," Dana said.

"With you, too, Antonio?"

"Indeed. Apart *from* the inefficiency of it all."

"Don't blame me. I didn't put the moons there." Arching an eyebrow, Blake leaned toward the camera. "What do you two crazy kids have planned, all unchaperoned?"

Dana and Antonio exchanged glances.

"Looking around a bit," he said. That sounded frivolous, even to him. "Survey the...area for useful minerals."

"Getting finished," Dana said firmly, "as fast as we can. Maybe a quick nap before the flight to Aeschylus."

"What is this nap thing of which you speak?" Blake yawned again. "Before you depart lovely Aristophanes, let's run an end-to-end system test of at least one station."

"Copy that," Dana said. "We're at station three. From my end, everything is a go."

"Power…check," Blake said. "Comm…ditto. Primary control… check. Moving on to the instruments. Radiometer…check. Scatterometer…check. High-res multispectral imager…looking good. Nice sharp image. Doppler radar…"

As the recitation droned on, as motes glinted in the furrows of his aimless shuffling, Antonio's thoughts wandered. Many instruments. Much data to come. And one Big Question.

Rock strata and ice cores: each sample told a tale, and no two stories ever quite agreed. Dark was a living world, on which storms and weathering, quakes and floods, volcanoes and even meteor strikes had all left their marks.

Read enough stories, though, and for all their idiosyncratic plot twists they confirmed what astrophysics predicted: that Dark experienced Milankovitch cycles. That the global climate had warmed and cooled, warmed and cooled, warmed and cooled, like clockwork, for as long—half a million years!—as the record could be reconstructed. That by its ancient rhythm, Dark was due, indeed, well into, a new warming era.

How pronounced were the historical climate swings? Antonio refused to guess. To infer anything about past average global temperatures from such paleogeological proxies as ice cores, he would first need to calibrate modern ice cores against years, at the least, of direct temperature measurements.

"Atmospheric sounder…check," Blake continued. "Wideband, ground-penetrating radar…"

Many, *many* instruments.

And yet Antonio had his doubts whether, even working together, the sensors they deployed could resolve the anomaly in the geological record of the past few centuries. That the sensors could explain why the climate had been steadily *cooling*. Or that sensors would answer the Big Question.

Just how frigid would Dark get?

31

At the soft scrape of approaching footsteps Carlos took a swig of vodka, then screwed shut the flask and stashed it inside a cabinet. He popped a breath mint into his mouth. The vodka was inferior, despite his best efforts. The mint tasted worse but smelled better.

He was in no mood to be lectured about his drinking. If and when he chose to, he'd stop.

Rikki loped through the lab door. Something about her (the berry-dark tan? the pouty lips? the long, high ponytail? the long legs in taut slacks?) reminded Carlos of a grad student he had had. And had and had and had. Very lithe and bendy, Helena was—and the more she fretted about her dissertation, the more imaginatively she strove to keep him happy. And so he, with a sigh or well-timed frown....

Blake followed his wife into the room, spoiling Carlos's fantasies. Then Antonio entered, more grizzled than ever. He and Dana were getting *old*.

Face it, Carlos told himself. We all are.

"Are you busy?" Blake asked.

Carlos sat in an arc of active displays, of nanite memory readouts, program listings, electron-microscope scans, and design documents. Props, all of them. He said nothing.

Blake grimaced. "Sorry, dumb question. Can you spare us a couple of minutes before we head to work?"

Carlos gestured at nearby stools. "What's up?"

Rikki said, "I think Li is up to something."

To the best of Carlos's knowledge, Li was *always* up to something. The challenge was ferreting out what and why. If he could accomplish either with any regularity, she would be in his power, not the other way around.

"Up to what?" Carlos asked.

"I don't know." Rikki frowned. "She's been too agreeable."

I wish, Carlos thought. The thrashing Li had given him on the ship had been no fluke. He had not required a third lesson.

He asked, "Agreeable about what?"

"About support for possible terraforming." Rikki finally dragged over a stool and sat. The other two stayed standing. "Yeah, I know how that sounds. The research program was my idea. But the weird thing, to me, anyway, is that Li hasn't tried to limit the effort."

"Here's a thought," Carlos said. "Ignore whatever contributions, if any, the off-world sensors make to our understanding of the climate. They've already improved our weather forecasting. That will help our crops, and that's something I'm sure Li cares about." *And because she let you plead for the deployment, you end up feeling indebted to her.*

And don't suppose for an instant she won't find a way to call in that debt.

"Could be." Blake pulled a scrap of thin wire from the jumble on a workbench, and began tying knots. "Or she imagines we'll rein ourselves in. Fatigue has a wonderful ability to clarify priorities."

Rikki gave her husband a dirty look.

Trouble in paradise? Carlos wondered. *Hubby isn't supportive enough of your science project?* "What does this have to do with me?"

"You know Li pretty well," Rikki said delicately.

You live together, she meant. *You side with Li on the issues. You must understand her.*

Carlos thought, *if you only knew.*

What he had with Li was a marriage of inconvenience. Hers was a cold beauty: look but don't touch. And yet he stayed. He was the last available man in the universe—and the last available woman couldn't care less. What did that say about him?

She had him by the pride as much as by the balls. When he got into her pants, all too seldom, it was because she wanted his backing.

Get inside Li's head? That had yet to happen.

"Do you plan on *ever* coming to the point?" Carlos asked.

Rikki grimaced. "We want to know what else Li isn't telling us."

Carlos countered, "Is she under some obligation to tell you what she's thinking?"

"No," Blake said, still torturing his piece of wire. "But also yes."

"Pretend you broke it already." Carlos plucked the much-knotted wire from Blake's hands. "Yes or no. Which is it?"

Rikki said, "As an individual, whatever Li thinks is her business. But in practice, she's our leader. We all defer to her."

I could be convinced to defer to you, Carlos thought. *Motivate me. Let's see how bendy you can be.*

He said, "On our trek, to survive, we needed one sort of expertise. We deferred to Dana and properly so. I doubt Dana shared everything she was thinking, and I'll bet we were happier for that. Rearing children and building a civilization? Those call for a different sort of expert. That's Li."

"That's Li," Blake agreed. "However…"

Antonio, who had been looking all around the lab, finally spoke. "I've been studying."

With Antonio's eclectic interests, those studies might involve *anything.* Carlos gestured to his workbench. "Guys, your couple minutes are more than up."

"Aristophanes I had heard of," Antonio said. "I didn't know who Aeschylus and Euripides were."

"I don't know if your interest is in moons or ancient Greek theater," Carlos said. "Either way it can wait till tonight at dinner." *When I also won't pay attention.* "Isn't there a crop somewhere that needs your attention?"

"I became interested in ancient Greece," Antonio went on. "And branched out from there. Are you familiar with…"

"At *dinner,*" Carlos repeated.

"Speaking of crops, why are you settled, all comfy, here in the lab?" Blake asked. "We could use a hand."

At transplanting a couple hundred potted apple, cherry, and pear seedlings from the greenhouse to the river delta. No thanks. "I'm doing something more critical."

"Figuring out how to mass-produce PFCs?" Rikki asked.

Right. As if what the climate might be like a hundred years hence was time sensitive.

"Nutrition related." Carlos pointed to a nearby cage, in which mice sniffed curiously. "They don't take up trace nutrients from diet as well as they should. I'm trying to tweak their nanites to compensate."

"Mouse nanites," Rikki said. "That sounds urgent. I vote you save those for a rainy day."

Had the short-term forecast shown rain, Carlos would have waited to tamper with the tissue samples he'd shown to Li that morning.

He half suspected from Li's sly smile that she knew. That by agreeing he should investigate his anomaly, she was doing him a favor. Throwing him a bone.

His other half guessed that she had planted the idea in the first place. That would explain the sly smile, too.

Pissing him off yet further. It was Li he was angry at, but Li wasn't here. And it was Li who had what he wanted.

"*Look*," Carlos said. "What affects the mice might well affect us. Or the children, or *their* children, some years hence. I propose to see what I can accomplish by tweaking nanites in the mice. Unless you prefer to make the children our guinea pigs."

Rikki flinched, as he had known she would.

By the time they *finally* left, Carlos needed another drink.

✳

Li's grandma used to claim that one caught more flies with honey than with vinegar.

Li eased herself out from under Carlos's out-flung arm *and* leg, thinking he was more spider than fly, and more octopus than spider. And she had no interest in catching any of them, far less this arrested-development adolescent.

With a snort Carlos flopped onto her side of the bed. The thick, coarse hair on his back disgusted her. *He* disgusted her.

She stood for a long time, her eyes closed, beneath the hot, pulsating spray of the shower. The water carried away Carlos's sweat and stench, but it couldn't touch her nausea. Sex with Carlos was for the greater good, and only for the greater good, because from time to time he proved useful.

As he had been today, bringing her a preview of the likely ambush that night at dinner.

You couldn't dignify the society here as an economy. They had no use for money. Whatever material goods they had were as readily produced for six people as for one. Carlos was too shallow and transparent to handle power, not that she would ever consider sharing power. The lone currency that remained was…favors.

She didn't feel dirty, exactly, nor degraded, but something. At an intellectual level, she even felt a touch of nobility, of self-sacrifice. Carlos had her body—when she permitted it—but never *her*. And he never would.

So what *was* it she felt? Out of joint. Out of sorts. Decoupled from reality.

How old would the girls need to be before they caught his eye?

✳

Long ago and far away, in a municipal campaign that had been Li's to lose—and she had—Li learned a hard lesson. Never let the other side choose the issue.

So: while the peasants still dug into synthed meatloaf with real mashed potatoes and mushroom gravy, or glanced sidelong at the strawberry shortcake that waited on the serving cart, *she* brought up childrearing. Indirectly, to be sure. She had guessed Antonio's digging into ancient Greece would lead him to Sparta and the education of its young, and Marvin had confirmed it. Antonio never bothered to conceal what he did with the AI.

Whereas the more…informative of her interactions with Marvin were as secure as possible. Not in any conventional sense, because access controls and personal firewalls would have screamed of something to hide, but subtly veiled. Too bad such computing legerdemain far exceeded her skills.

But not Carlos's. Li fought down a shudder.

The important thing was, she was prepared, if necessary, to discuss childrearing, and the relative virtues of Athens versus Sparta. She knew Antonio well enough, if it came to it, to sidetrack Antonio in a pointless meander through Thucydides' history of the Peloponnesian War.

She saw no reason to let matters come to that.

Li blotted her lips, folded and set down her napkin, and began. "With this spring's planting almost complete, in the comparative lull before we begin harvesting, I propose that we expand the childcare center."

"So that we can crank out *more* children?" Rikki blurted out.

"Interesting," Li said. "I was going to say that as the children get older we'll want separate dormitories for the boys and the girls. And I thought it would be nice to add an atrium, a little indoor park. But you're quite right, Rikki. The same expansion will allow us to raise more. Thank you."

Rikki blinked. She had not foreseen her sarcasm getting deflected into a proposal. "That's not what—"

"About that," Antonio interrupted.

Antonio wasn't the type to interrupt. Not unless he had something on his mind he was bound and determined to get out.

It seemed Carlos had earned his pre-dinner favor.

"If we could finish one topic before we move on to the next?" Li chided.

"Of course," Antonio said.

"Marvin, my sketch, please." Li slid back her chair to stand alongside the wall, which became a 3-D architectural rendering. "You see the enclosed area that I thought might serve as a garden or park. But maybe it's too large an expanse for that."

She studied the wall display, pensive, giving the peasants time to make the idea their own. And maybe to set aside their nitpicking, since she had just proposed this touchy-feely expansion of the facility.

"We could make a portion of that space an indoor playground," Rikki offered.

"Or maybe we should enclose only part of the area," Dana said. "At some point the children have to get used to the outdoors."

Li let them natter on, with each suggestion making the project more grandiose and labor-intensive. A screened-in solarium into which even the youngest children could be brought on nice days for fresh air. A rock garden. A flower garden. An ever more extensive playground.

The evening was unfolding better than Li had dared to hope.

While the peasants bulldoze and landscape and build with concrete, she thought, the children remained hers. As Rikki had observed—and as quickly let drop—the enlarged childcare center about which *they* now all waxed eloquent, would give *Li* the capacity to speed up decanting of the embryos. With, alas, some encouragement to Carlos to speed up womb production.

Li said, "Once the children have acclimated, they'll be closer to ready to meet the real world. Suppose we put up a fence, enclosed the area around the center and its neighboring buildings. If we put locks on the doors the oldest children could roam around." In answer to Rikki's raised eyebrow, Li explained, "I don't believe they're old enough to play among the explosives and chemical stocks."

The eyebrow went back down.

But as Blake and Dana grew giddy about the prospect of passing along the fine art of snowman construction, and with Antonio side-tracked into planning for a rock garden, Rikki's eyes narrowed with suspicion.

Too much, too fast, Li thought. The woman wasn't entirely gullible.

Li said, "I'm gratified by such enthusiasm, but we can't do *every-thing* at once. We also have a PFC factory, or refinery, or whatever I should call it, to build."

And Rikki relaxed.

Fool, Li thought.

32

In swooping arcs and soaring leaps, up and down through the clouds like a bucking bronco, *Endeavour* gyrated its way around the globe. The meandering course on its intricately constructed timeline did more than challenge Dana's reflexes. By the time she returned home, ship and the moons' observatories together would have compiled a thorough and precise global atmospheric survey, captured at more or less the same local time everywhere.

Too bad the prescribed local time was midnight, because she would have enjoyed the view. She wasn't enjoying the company.

Blake had accomplished the impossible: making Antonio look chatty. He was making the rocks from Antonio's collection look chatty.

Dana sighed. Antonio had asked to come along, looking *so* kicked-puppy disappointed when she'd said no. And though she hadn't lied about there being no time between collection points to gather southern-hemisphere rocks, and that this was fancy enough flying she should have a proficient copilot to spell her, neither had she been entirely honest with him.

On her console, a timer ticked down the seconds to the next atmospheric sampling. A real-time holo showed her displacement in three dimensions from the target collection point. As the high-altitude winds buffeted the ship, her hands danced over the controls to make endless course corrections.

A single moon above the horizon—everywhere—could have captured the data they sought. The moons did not cooperate like that, and so here she was. As for precision, computer-controlled navigation, forget it. Only all *three* moons in sight would have served to triangulate the ship's position. And so, as one moon or another sank below the horizon, as clouds turned her course into a game of peek-a-boo with the stars, as the buffeting of the jet stream befuddled the autopilot and played havoc with the short-range projections from inertial navigation, she fell back, time and again, upon the most basic navigational system of all: seat of the pants.

If the outing had been a summer evening's stroll through Kensington Gardens, she still would have left Antonio back in the settlement. She needed some one-on-one time with Blake.

"Collection on my mark," she announced. "Three. Two. One. Mark."

"Mark," Blake repeated. As he had for the past twenty or so collections.

"Throw me a bone," Dana said. "Are you satisfied? Dissatisfied? How does the data look so far?"

"Fine," Blake allowed.

"And the data is telling us...what?"

"Nighttime temperature and PFC trace concentration profiles—"

"By altitude on a grid of closely-spaced points surrounding the planet." Dana sighed again. "I *know* what we're collecting, and why. Is the data revealing anything useful? Is it what you expect?"

"I don't know. Rikki doubted the raw measurements themselves would reveal much; especially not point by point. It's all input to a global circulation model. Ask me after Antonio and Marvin have taken a crack at the full dataset, when we know how well the PFCs have dispersed."

The nav holo updated to show the way to the next collection point; Dana put her ship into another steep climb. "You're not very talkative these days."

"Well, you know."

"No!" Dana snapped, surprising herself. "I *don't* know, because you've locked me out. I thought we were friends."

"We are." After a *long* while, he said, "I'm not a deep thinker, you know."

Deeper than you credit yourself. "What's your point?"

"Except for Rikki, we're introverts, if not loners and misfits. Have you noticed that?"

"Uh-uh." Hawthorne had, though, in dossiers the existence of which Dana still kept to herself. More than once she had almost deleted the files. Other than the occasional piloting gig, her job was farming. She had no reason to keep the personnel data—and less inclination to share any of it with Li. "Not deep, you say?"

"I couldn't make a puddle jealous."

On Dana's console, a timer initialized and began counting down, showing when she should aim to reach the next collection point. She slowed the ship. "So, introverts and loners. What of it?"

Blake busied himself checking something on his console. With not answering. "My mom and dad were like oil and water. My sister, the raging extrovert, and I were more like oil and matches. The neighbors didn't offer many shining examples of stability, either. As for the broader community where I grew up, it was a mess. One-parent households were the norm. The schools sucked. To belong to something the choices were high-school sports, if you had talent, which I didn't, or the gangs."

"So you stuck to yourself."

"More like, I kept my head down. Then the oddest thing happened. I was either ten or eleven. Standard years, I mean. It was late summer, and I was getting the mandatory preschool physical from the family doctor. Doc Sullivan was this upbeat guy with a friendly, booming voice. Jovial, yet managing not to be obnoxious. He asked me some questions about school.

"Whatever he asked and I answered, he decided, and I couldn't tell you why, that I had potential. Then and there, he zapped two old college texts from his datasheet to my little-kid pocket comp. Both books were decades out of date and of no use to him, but I didn't know that."

"And that's why you became an engineer," Dana guessed. She had no idea what this had to do with, well, anything. "Nice."

Blake laughed. "Who gives a college text on biochemistry to a ten-year-old? It was Greek to me. No, less. At least I'd heard of Greece."

"And yet that *is* how I ended up an engineer. You'd like to believe it was because this engaging, successful professional saw potential in me. Did the gesture inspire me? Yeah, for the couple of weeks before the cops hauled Doc Sullivan away. My last, best hope of a role model had defrauded Federal Health Service of millions.

"So he set my career course, all right. He decided for me that, whatever I did when I grew up, it would involve machines, not people. Not that I understood engineering then, beyond that machines, maybe, could be fixed."

"I'm not buying you as a loner," Dana said, still at a loss where this might be going. "You can charm the pants off people."

"Off young women, anyway. That doesn't make me a people person. It makes—made—me a calculating, cynical, manipulative jerk. I want to believe I've grown since then."

The pieces fell into place. "So this is about Rikki."

"Of *course*"—his voice cracked—"it's about Rikki. Pretty much the first thing I knew about her, back on the cruise where we met, was how eager she was to get home. How much she had missed her family while she'd been away at grad school. It was real closeness, too, not part of some sitcom. And yet more amazing, soon enough they weren't *her* family, but *our* family.

"So here you and I are: loners. Carlos, it embarrasses me to admit, is much as I once was, if not as smooth. Antonio is, well, you know."

"I know," Dana said. And a dear, regardless, in his own way.

"Li, though…I can't read her."

"Me, either." At the end, Hawthorne had had only hours to round out the crew for this mission. Li's file, and Carlos's for that matter, was a short dump from the public record, little more than a résumé. "I'd bet that shrinks learn to mask their feelings." And politicians, too, only Li had never, to Dana's knowledge, volunteered to anyone here that facet of her past.

"Heads up." Blake's voice changed tone. "Radar shows a high mountain range."

"Yeah, I see it, but thanks. We'll have almost a klick of clearance. "You left out Rikki."

"She's not like you or me or any of the rest of us. She *is* a people person. I remember what happened back home. I do think occasionally about everyone we left behind. When it happens, I'm sad, but then I get over it.

"But Rikki? She *grieves*, still. For her family most of all."

"That she can't continue her family? And the rejection by the kids here? It's *killing* her, Dana."

At the catch in Blake's voice, Dana glanced away from the console. He was trembling.

In an anguished tone, not much above a whisper, he said, "I don't know how to fix this."

Dana didn't know how to fix *him*. "It's been years since you learned Rikki can't safely get pregnant. She still hasn't come to terms with it?"

"Worse." Blake hesitated. "If Li gave her blessing today, I think Rikki would be afraid to try. I think she's lost faith in herself as a parent."

"That's…ridiculous." Only Dana felt that inadequacy, too. More and more, whenever she swung by the childcare center. With sixty-four more children almost to term.

She hadn't admitted those feelings—failings—to anyone, either. She didn't know that she could.

For the remainder of the flight, she and Blake were both quiet.

❋

Wearing a big, welcoming smile, Dana closed the distance to the children's white picket fence. From afar you couldn't tell that the pickets were poured concrete, not fashioned from wood. From afar, you didn't see that the pickets stood two meters tall.

Drawing near, seeing the children through the pickets, the fence looked like a stockade.

"Kids grow," Li had said. "We don't want to rebuild the fence every couple years." It sounded reasonable. Most everything she said sounded reasonable.

The day was sunny and crisp. Perfect football weather Blake had declared it when they landed. But this being Dark, the few hints of fall colors came from inside the greenhouse and on saplings in clay planters glimpsed through the fence.

Dana flashed a hand signal. On a pole just inside the gate a camera bobbed: Marvin acknowledging that he had seen her. As she approached the gate, at which the handprint-reader lamp flashed READY, Li opened the gate from inside.

"Hi," Li said. "Did you have a good flight?"

"It had its ups and downs."

Dana slipped inside, the gate falling locked and shut behind her with a loud *click*. It must have rained while she and Blake were off flying, because the green carpet squished beneath her boots. Kids should play on grass, she thought sadly, although no one could spare the time to keep such a large expanse mowed, or to haul and spread the truckloads of river-delta silt a lawn would have required. Had there been time, no one would have permitted children around the quantities of fertilizer the lifeless silt would have needed applied several times each year.

Children clambered over the playground equipment. Younger kids with shovels and pails dug in sandboxes. Dark lacked soil, but it had *plenty* of sand. As she had sensed from the distance, several of the bigger kids were in the tiny garden plot. Picking tomatoes, apparently. All the boys and girls wore pants and sweaters, dressed alike except for color. Red for the oldest, blue for the cohort a year younger, green for those a year younger still.

Like uniforms. Why had she never noticed that?

The yard, for all the dozens of little ones, was quiet and orderly; the expressions on so many of the young faces seemed purposeful rather than playful. But on what basis could she form expectations? Only ancient memories of her own childhood.

Dana walked to the garden. She leaned forward, hand outstretched to tousle Eve's hair.

Eve scuttled away, circling behind a row of potted tomato plants, to shelter behind Li.

"Excuse me, Eve," Dana said. "I didn't mean to startle you."

"Tell Ms. Dana you're sorry," Li directed.

"No need," Dana said hastily. "Honey, how are you doing? Are you enjoying the nice weather?"

Eve buried her face in Li's back. "I'm sorry, Ms. Dana," she mumbled.

Her brothers (for lack of a more fitting term), had sidled close together.

"How are you big boys today?" Dana asked.

"Fine, Ms. Dana," Castor said. Pollux, his lower lip trembling, held out a tomato.

"Run along," Li told them. "Take inside what you've picked, and then see if Mr. Carlos could use your help."

Pails swinging at their sides, the three scampered toward the childcare center.

"What was *that* about?" Dana asked Li.

"What do you mean?"

Around the sandboxes most of the children had stopped their play. Several stared, wide-eyed, at Dana. She said, "Look at them."

"Kids watch adults. That's part of how they learn. They don't see you often, is all."

Only to Dana these children looked wary, not curious. "And Eve? I would swear she was afraid of me. Pollux, too."

Li sighed exasperatedly. "Shy. Eve was *shy*, Dana. Pollux, too. Kids sometimes are. Now look what he gave you, and what you did with it."

Dana looked. Her hand was wet and sticky. She had squeezed the tomato into goo; juice and pulp dribbled between her fingers.

"I guess I'm tense," she admitted. No, scared shitless that Rikki was right. That apart from Li, none of them knew what they were doing. "Maybe the kids picked up on that."

"They did," Li said flatly.

"Sorry about that." More sorry than you can imagine.

"Go home," Li said. "Take the afternoon off. There's something important I'll be bringing up after dinner."

✳

"We've reached a major milestone," Li said.

Around the dinner table, the peasants studied her with curiosity. Carlos wore a relaxed grin, from a beer or three too many rather than from foreknowledge.

"Every day is a new challenge," Li continued. "Every day has its chores. But look what we've accomplished. Wheat, corn, and barley crops ripening for the upcoming harvest, and enough freeze-dried bacterial mat to see us through bad weather. Remote-sensing instruments placed on the moons. Our very own climate-improvement program."

"And ever more thriving children," Carlos added. Giving Li credit, predictably. With hopes, no doubt, of…reward later.

"And thriving children," Li repeated.

She had set the dining-room walls to a peaceful seascape, a gentle froth of combers rushing up and swirling back down a sparkling white sand beach. In a cerulean sky, behind pink wisps of cloud, a tomato-red sun kissed the sea. Waves whispered, and tropical breezes sighed through palm trees, and sandpipers piped. Restful. Hopefully lulling. Even Carlos and Rikki, neither of whom had ever visited Earth or experienced such a sunset, must feel it.

The common experiences of thousands of generations embedded themselves in the genetic code. Not as simple as memory, genetic programming recorded the common heritage of the species. Genetic programming instilled fear of the dark, when predators hunted and proto-humans were wise to hide, and of predators yet unseen. Genetic programming suggested, too, what was *not* a threat and when—as in this case—it was safe to relax.

That basic neural hardwiring would not be denied. So be at peace, my peasants. Be at peace.

"Many accomplishments," Dana agreed. "But Li, what is this milestone you mentioned?"

"Specialization. I eat by the sweat of your brows. We stay healthy in large measure by Carlos's steady tweaking of our nanites. And if I may say so, the children continue to benefit from my attention."

"You may say so," Antonio said.

"The milestone," Li continued, "is this. That we're ready to recognize and make formal the patterns that are already working so well for us."

"What patterns?" Blake asked.

"Job specialization." Li counted silently to three. "Including those of us who will interact with the children."

Raw emotions scrabbled and jostled behind Rikki's eyes. For several long seconds Li thought relief would win, but guilt chased it away. Maternal instincts were hardwired, too.

Rikki swallowed hard. "We *all* help with the children."

"Perhaps that should change," Li said. "Not everyone is as... well-suited."

Not everyone is successful at it. The children don't recoil from everyone. You know who you are.

There was pain now in Rikki's eyes. In Dana's, too. Because Li was good at what she did. And when the two women conceded, their men would go along.

"Is it even possible?" Rikki asked. (Hoping for which answer? Li couldn't tell.) "Even with six of us, sometimes watching the children is draining. How could you alone handle it?"

"Yes, it's possible," Li asserted. "But it won't be just me. The children are comfortable around Carlos, too." And, you are free to infer, with no one else. "And Marvin, of course, who never sleeps. And Eve and the twins are old enough to help. They *want* to help."

"Children raising children," Blake said dubiously.

"You're a youngest child, correct?" Li said. It doesn't matter that you've never told me you're the baby of the family, because you're their freaking poster child: uncomplicated, attention-seeking, and transparently manipulative. "I can't believe your older—well, I'll say, sister—never baby-sat you."

Blake blinked. "Oh, Lynette did, and the experience does nothing to bolster your argument."

"Marvin," Li called, "how many diapers has Eve changed this evening since I left the center for dinner?"

"Six, Li."

"How many babies have Castor and Pollux fed?"

"Eighteen, so far. They gave bottles to fourteen and fed four directly."

"While you supervised. Thank you." To the peasants, Li added, "A dozen in the next cohort are eager to do like the big kids."

"And…us?" Antonio asked.

"You will contribute more in the ways you already do," Li said. "How much more progress will you make studying local geology"—you and your stupid rocks—"when you're not changing diapers every few nights? How much sooner, Rikki, will you understand the climate trends?"

How much more farming and chicken tending will you four get done? How many more cattle can you raise because you won't be with the children, and how many more cows can you milk? How much more mining of phosphates, and raising of barns, and a thousand other menial chores? But chores weren't selling points.

"And as…*the* colony…grows?"

Li said, "As children become old enough of course you'll teach them the many skills with which to maintain the colony." After I've made them dependably mine.

She could feel the others wavering. "Then we're in agreement?"

Dana's chair scraped back as she stood. "No."

"Excuse me?" Li said.

"No," Dana repeated. "No way. Uh-uh. Forget it. If I lack some skill, teach me. If I am a stranger to the children, I'll spend *more* time with them. The mission is to raise a family, a culture, a civilization—and I do not abandon my mission."

"No…nor I," Rikki squeaked. "Nor I," she repeated, the second time firmly.

Blake and Antonio nodded.

"We get *more* involved," Rikki said. "Once the harvest is in, we'll have more time. And any child old enough to baby-sit is old enough to start school. I'll help with that. I'd *like* that."

"Me, too," Antonio said.

"This is how you want it?" Li asked.

"Yes!" they chorused.

"Remember that I offered," Li said. Remember who made me do things the hard way.

33

"A needle in a haystack," Blake grumbled.

"I wish." Antonio didn't take his eyes off the sensor console. "Give me an electromagnet and I'll have your needle in no time."

"Heh," Blake said. "I bow to your superior physics."

"Don't forget it."

Blake shut his eyes. "Wake me when you find something."

He lolled bonelessly in the loose grasp of a seat harness. Deep inside the asteroid belt, sans Marvin, they wanted a human pilot on the bridge at all times. Dana was bunking in, which left him. Antonio, no matter the superiority of his physics, had terrible reflexes and a disturbing tendency to confuse left with right. At least the dumb-as-a-stump computer that remained aboard after moving Marvin in his servers into the bunker could spot incoming rocks on its own.

Rikki could have handled a shift. Especially after the arduous harvest, she would have welcomed a change of scenery. Not to mention the spells in zero gee, while Antonio surveyed all the nearby rocks.

But Rikki was suffering from, well, Li had yet to figure that out. Nothing serious, Li assured them. Whatever it was, Rikki wasn't keeping down much of what she ate. Might be some intestinal flora gone bad in a way her nanites had yet to learn to handle. Might be, though Li had insisted that the possibility was remote, a Dark-native bacterium that had jumped to humans. Might be food poisoning. Might be a nutritional deficiency. Ironic, that last scenario: that a need for some trace element might have kept Rikki from prospecting for a trace element.

"And we're back," Blake declared, opening his eyes. "Have you found any big nuggets?"

"Not yet." Antonio squirmed in his couch, readjusting the straps. "Vanadium isn't common, you know."

He knew—or, rather, Marvin had told them. A couple hundred parts per million in Earth's crust. Undetected to date anywhere in the Dark system. But in Sol system vanadium was common, comparatively speaking, in meteoroids and asteroids.

Why else would they be out here, probing rock after rock?

Blake studied his console. "Looks like another two are coming into range."

"Yes. Do you want...to do the honors?"

"Sure." Because it was something to do. Blake tagged the closer of the radar blips and dragged its trajectory data to the comm controls. (As he did, he checked for messages pending. Rikki hadn't answered his last few emails. He hoped that meant she was getting some sleep.) The long-range comm laser reached out, invisible, for empty space provided nothing to scatter the light. Within seconds, as the spectrometer examined the miniscule bit of glowing vapor boiled off the rock's surface, they would know a little about the rock's composition.

"No vanadium," Antonio said. And a minute later, after the laser hit the second target, he reported, "None there, either."

Logically speaking, they would end up surveying hundreds, maybe thousands, of rocks before encountering one with vanadium compounds on its surface. They would have flown around much of the belt to find it. That Li hadn't balked at four of them being gone, possibly, for *weeks* spoke volumes. Though slow to develop, this dietary deficiency must be serious.

Radar showed they had a while until more asteroids came within probing range. "Feel like a game of chess?" Blake asked.

"No thanks." Antonio waved vaguely at the datasheet draped across his lap. "Aristophanes data. This is fascinating. On the ground...I never had the time to look at it. The surface temperature readings..."

Evidently, definitions of fascination varied. "Do you see signs there of vanadium?"

"None. But—"

"Enjoy," Blake said. He began a new email to Rikki. *Wish you were here.*

✳

"Another shift," Blake announced, yawning. "Much nothing accomplished."

"I recommend a snack and sleep," Dana said. "For you, too, Antonio. Whatever there is to be seen will be in the comp when you come back."

"In a while," Antonio said absently. Scatter plots and bar charts cluttered his datasheet.

Much ado about asteroids.

Rikki had yet to answer emails, which Blake took to mean she'd gotten a decent night's sleep. Back at the settlement it was almost time for breakfast. He would rest easier once he heard how she was feeling.

Only as he dawdled in the galley over a sandwich and salad, no emails came to him.

He went back to the bridge. "Do we have contact with home?"

"Euripides is in position to relay," Antonio mumbled. "Before it sets in…an hour, Aeschylus will serve."

"You know moonrise and set times?" Blake asked.

The corners of Antonio's mouth, one at a time, twitched upward. "You don't?"

"More useful than old Paris subway schedules," Dana said. "But as for contact with home, here's a simpler demonstration. An email came in from Carlos a few minutes ago, inquiring about our progress."

Blake asked, "Anything in the message about Rikki?"

"No, sorry. But it was a short note. A one-liner."

No news means only no news, Blake told himself.

"This is very…interesting."

On Antonio's lap, the datasheet's graphics were denser than Blake remembered. Orbital parameters. Sizes. Rotation rates. One scatter plot bore the cryptic label ALBEDO VARIABILITY.

Blake asked, "What's albedo?"

"The fraction of the incident…light reflected."

Antonio had collected plenty of rocks on Dark. He'd collected rocks from Dark's moons when the opportunity had presented itself. It wasn't a big surprise that he would collect stats about these rocks now.

"And Li?" Blake asked. "What does she have to say?"

"No word," Dana said, "but that doesn't surprise me. We left them shorthanded."

"Especially if she's got a sick patient to deal with."

"Go," Dana said. "Sleep. I'll email Li and ask what's going on."

❋

"Rikki's fine," Dana greeted Blake on his reappearance eight hours later.

He saw she had the bridge to herself. On the radar display, the only nearby objects were receding. An aux display cycled through an album of kid holos.

"Freshly synthed." He had three drink bulbs of coffee; he handed her one. "And I'm glad to hear it, because Rikki has yet to answer me. What did Li say?"

"Not much. Rikki's better, and keeping down light meals. She's home, resting. Li and Carlos are busy with the kids, but one of them checks on Rikki every few hours."

"Any diagnosis yet?"

"Li's leaning toward a nutritional deficiency. Vanadium, in fact."

"Leaning."

"Here." Dana pulled up the message. "You now know what I know."

It wasn't much. Blake sent Li a reply asking her to have Rikki contact him.

Dana, reading over his shoulder, said, "You worry too much. And confident that you won't listen, here's my free advice. Let the poor woman sleep. And leave Li and Carlos alone."

"We'll see." Which they both knew meant "no."

"Between you and Antonio, I *will* go nuts."

Blake dropped into the copilot's seat, content to change the subject. "Asteroid albedo?"

"In part. They're too splotchy for his taste, and he wants to drop down and visit a few. Mostly he's worked up that too few asteroids dip within Dark's orbit."

Blake stiffened. "This isn't a science project. I hope you told him he can collect rocks where we find vanadium."

"I told him I loved him dearly, but that the absence of threatening asteroids is a good thing. I said the fewer rocks we landed on, the fewer we risked nudging the wrong way."

"Good answer."

"And after that rare vote of approval, I hand over the bridge to you. Vaporize wisely."

"Will do," Blake said. "Sleep tight. I'll wake you if I find anything."

She stopped in the hatchway. "Back home they're busier than we are. When they have news, they'll let us know."

"I'm sure you're right," Blake said.

That didn't keep him, as soon as Dana had vacated the bridge, from emailing Marvin for an update.

Blake was beginning to smell a rat.

34

The measure of just how lousy Rikki felt was that, lifting her head at the sudden tapping on her window, she felt relief at seeing Li.

"Door's open," Rikki croaked. She let her head flop back onto the sofa arm.

"I see you're better," Li chirped coming into the house. "I expected to find you in bed."

"I was going for some dry crackers. Halfway to the kitchen I re-considered." When I remembered they were made from sea slime.

Li set down her med kit. "I'd like to take a scan." Whatever Rikki's nanites had to report or the scanner found on its own must not have merited specific comment. "You'll live, though from the looks of you, at the moment that isn't a selling point."

The woman had no bedside manner.

"When will I be over this? Whatever this is?" Rikki hesitated—fearful, almost superstitiously so—of evoking a nightmare from an era before med nanites. "Am I *contagious*?"

"Don't know, don't know, and do you see me wearing a mask?"

Then came the repeat lecture about keeping hydrated and foods that might stay down, followed by megadoses of vitamins and anti-nausea meds. It all wore Rikki out. "What have you heard from *Endeavour*?" she asked as Li helped her back to bed.

"Only that they're still searching."

"And Blake?"

"He's busy. Now get some rest."

Fitfully, disappointed that Blake hadn't written, or even acknowledged any of her brief notes, Rikki drifted in and out of sleep.

✳

A few more seconds, Li told herself. And, don't look bored.

Finally, it stopped.

Wearing his customary smug and oblivious smile, Carlos rolled off her onto his side of the bed. He pulled up the sheet. His breathing slowed. In a minute or two, he would be snoring.

They needed to talk, and the best time for that was after sex. When he was relaxed. When even more than usual, the little head did most of his thinking.

Propping herself up on an elbow, resting her hand lightly on his chest, Li said, "You awake?"

"Mmm?"

"The sun's still high and there's just us. We can't sleep now."

"Watch me."

"I'm serious," Li said. "And this is important."

"Marvin is watching the kids."

"Eyes-open important. And sit *up*."

Carlos sat. Li spoke. And he, once she had finished, as she had known he must, had agreed to everything. She had Carlos well-conditioned. Like Pavlov's salivating dog. If only just saliva were involved....

On the verge of triumph, she felt pangs of disappointment. The grandeur of her vision was wasted on Carlos. The meticulous beauty of her planning—as much of it as she had shared—interested him only as it assured their success. All that he responded to was the expectation of future coupling.

She could live with that. She needed his help, and what mattered to *her* was the outcome.

As for the other four, she had given them their chance.

✹

Shuffling more often than walking, but feeling human for the first time in days, Rikki made her way down Main Street. She tried to forget the *uphill* trip that she faced to return home. As she passed the garage, its door began to rise. Carlos had hitched a trailer to the back of their dump truck; he sat on the backhoe-loader, revving the motor, evidently about to drive the contraption up the ramp onto the trailer.

Her voice was as feeble as a kitten's; he must not have heard her over the growl of the engine, asking what he was doing. Whatever, she could find out later. Or not: curiosity seemed too much like work. She waved, he waved back, and she shuffled on.

Between fence slats, Rikki watched children ramming around, climbing, swinging. Marvin had unlocked the gate at her approach, but she could hardly make it budge. "Marvin," she called. With a squeal of grit-clogged hinges, the gates swung inward.

Activity in the yard all but ceased.

Children fell silent, some staring, others sidling away. A few of the littlest took shelter behind Eve and the twins. Despite assurances that she wasn't contagious, Rikki was just as happy this one time that the kids were shy around her.

"Hi!" she called. "Who can tell me where I can find Ms. Li?"

It fell to Marvin to answer. "At her office in the childcare center."

Inside the center, Rikki paused at the glass wall that opened into the toddlers' room. All those little ones, unhugged. Untouched. Alone for most of the day, every day, apart from the insubstantial company of an AI. It broke her heart. She reached for the door, and hesitated.

"You're *not* contagious," Li said. "Go ahead."

Rikki jumped. "I didn't hear you coming."

"I heard you. I'm glad you're up and strong enough for an outing. As it happens, there was something I wanted to talk about with you. We can talk inside."

"Is it *Endeavour?*"

"Nothing like that." Li gestured at the door. "Inside."

At Rikki's entrance, several of the children froze. More shied away. Chubby-cheeked Carla (with the mass of black curls that *so* reminded Rikki of her sister Janna at that age) began to whimper.

"It's okay, sweetie," Rikki said, reaching to brush a tear from Carla's cheek.

Carla lurched, screaming, to cower behind a crib.

"Why do they *hate* me?" Rikki whispered. And why do they adore you?

"Let's go next door," Li said.

Next door meant the newborn unit. Li gestured Rikki ahead through this door, too. Empty cribs waited, row upon row, facing the one-way glass wall. In a few weeks, all the cribs would be occupied.

Li said, "You're a beautiful woman."

Well, I did wash my face and change into clothes without puke spatters. "Is that your big problem with me? That Blake finds me attractive?"

"Just an observation. You are more than welcome to Blake." Li changed tone. "Marvin, play kid-vid zero."

On the display integral with the low end panel of every crib, pastels morphed into the image of an old oak tree. From crib speakers came a soothing rustle of leaves. Let the vid play long enough, and it would cycle through clear skies, both sunny and starry, toddlers gleefully splashing in a wading pool, a time-lapse view of roses flowering, and other delights.

"I hadn't realized the vid had a name," Rikki said. "It's just what we play."

"It's what you and your friends play. There are others, vids that Marvin hasn't been at liberty to divulge."

"I don't understand," Rikki said.

"Perhaps a demonstration. Marvin, kid-vid one, please." The oak tree vanished, replaced by a close-up of Li's smiling face. The aural accompaniment was a deep rhythmic throb: the same heartbeat recording that pulsed in the artificial wombs. "Marvin is only permitted to play that at my direction, or when no adult is present."

Unctuous, smiling Li faces everywhere, and Rikki wanted to smash them—the flesh-and-blood face most of all. "You *programmed* the children to love you?"

Li smirked. "The proper term is imprinting. And yes, I did."

"No, the proper term is child abuse."

"You're such a drama queen. Marvin, show our guest kid-vid two."

The crib-panel displays went dark. The low, steady heartbeat became…something else. Primitive. Dissonant. On the crib-panel displays, lightning flashed. Beneath the music, thunder rumbled.

Rikki shivered. "What the hell is—"

"Watch," Li commanded. "Listen. Learn."

From the lightning-torn night sky slowly emerged…a face. *Rikki's* face. The music swelled, grew more urgent and…scarier.

"The Rite of Spring," Li said. "The children will never appreciate Stravinsky, I'm sad to say, but that's a sacrifice worth making."

And Rikki's face morphed into—

A hooded…*thing*. Coiled. Scaly. Black with, as it reared its head, a fish-white underbelly. Hissing, swaying. It studied her dispassionately through little beady eyes. A forked tongue flickered in and out, in and out between its jaws.

Rikki's skin crawled. She *felt* her eyes go round. On the back of her neck, hairs prickled. Before she could find her voice, the thing lunged. In full 3-D.

She yelped.

"The effect is even more impressive with the room night-dim," Li said. After a brief return to a stormy night sky, Blake's face began to emerge. "Stop vid."

This was…hateful. Psychological torture. Madness. Whether from shock or her lingering illness, Rikki's knees threatened to buckle. Groping behind her, she edged backward to lean against a wall.

"The vid goes on to Dana and Antonio, too, if you wondered."

"Why?" Rikki managed to get out.

"You can figure out *why*," Li said cheerily. "I doubt you can figure out *how*. Had you ever seen a king cobra?

"N-no."

"Nor have I. I've seen snakes, of course. On Earth. I don't recall ever seeing a snake on Mars. A good choice on someone's part, not to import any." Li laughed. "Or maybe Saint Patrick was involved.

"But I digress. King cobras are nasty things. Very poisonous. And without ever having seen one, at some level you knew to fear it. As the children do, instinctively.

"Dread and loathing of reptiles lives deep in our hindbrains. No one knows how early in mammalian evolution that wiring emerged. It could date to the twilight of the dinosaurs, when the reflex to flee reptiles would have served our earliest progenitors well. I merely associated your faces with that reflex. All in the children's first months, before they even began to speak. They can't conceptualize the fear, much less articulate it. They just *have* it. And when a child is loud or disobedient, a flashed image of a king cobra—or of *you*—sobers him up quickly."

Rikki shuddered. "You're a monster."

"Name-calling, really? That's the best you've got?" Li smiled. "Take comfort in knowing the children won't miss you."

"I don't understand," Rikki said.

"Perhaps this will make it clearer." Li reached behind her back, pulling something from her waistband. Something Rikki had not seen since helping to unload cargo from *Endeavour* soon after Landing Day.

A handgun.

35

"Something's wrong," Blake decided.

"Something often is," Dana agreed, eyes fixed on her nav console. "Might I trouble you to be more specific?"

"In a sec." The latest asteroid to be overtaken was almost within laser range. "Firing…now. Another dud. How many is that?"

"I leave the big numbers to Antonio. So tell me, what's wrong?"

"The latest one-line note from Rikki. They all *say* she's fine, but if she were she'd have more to say. Or she'd answer a question or two of mine. Or she'd record a vid, or at least a voice message."

"Or she's fine *and* very busy. As we are." Dana coaxed *Endeavour* onto a new course. "Call it fifteen minutes till the next rock comes into range."

"I'm not too busy to contact her."

"Well good for you. You're not the one dealing with more sick kids every day. I don't know what to tell you other than do your job. We need vanadium. We'll stay out here 'til we find it or Li says we're needed more back home. And just so you know, it would be a bit less creepy if you didn't spy on your wife through Marvin."

Blake wasn't proud of that, either. He had just wanted to *see* Rikki looking other than green around the gills. And when he saw her in the yard, keeping an eye on the healthy kids at play, he'd told Marvin he had all he needed.

Ignoring Dana's disapproving glance, Blake replayed the short vid clip. When it stopped, he left the final image open on an aux display.

They handled the next asteroid encounter with minimal words, and the all too familiar failure. And the asteroid after that. And the two co-orbiting rocks after that. Blake began counting the minutes until Antonio would relieve him.

"Will you please take down that vid?" Dana asked. "Rikki is fine. *You* have a problem."

"I can't put my finger on it, but I know. I'm certain. Something is wrong. We need to go back."

"When we have what we came—"

"An interesting thing," Antonio said from the hatchway. Blake hadn't heard him coming. "Did you—"

"Not now," Blake and Dana snapped in unison.

"Yes…now."

Something in Antonio's voice made Blake turn and look. Antonio was craning his neck, staring past Blake at the playground scene.

"See the…two moons?"

Two moons, daylight pale, glimmered above the childcare center. The larger body was at half phase; the smaller was only a crescent. By their sizes, Aristophanes and Aeschylus.

"Uh-huh," Blake said. "What about them?"

Antonio reached over Blake's shoulder, extending a fingertip into the holo. "The timestamp shows today's date. The positions and phases of the moons are from twelve days ago."

Before Rikki fell ill! Before they left! Blake said, "We have to head back. ASAP. Li and Carlos are lying."

"It could be an honest discrepancy," Dana said hesitantly.

Blake shook his head. "AIs don't make mistakes like that. Not on their own. Li or Carlos is using Marvin to hide something."

"I see another possibility." Dana took a deep breath. "Blake, you won't like this. Maybe the medical situation is more serious than they've admitted to us."

"And Rikki is…." Blake couldn't finish the thought aloud. "You think they're keeping it secret lest we come charging home without what they need."

"It's possible. Sorry, Blake."

"You think they'd lie, compel Marvin to lie, all because they don't trust us to do the right thing?"

Dana shrugged.

"They'd have told *you*, wouldn't they? Made sure *you* knew the urgency?" And to Antonio, who had jammed himself between pilot and copilot seats to poke at a console, Blake snarled, "Can't that *wait*?"

Dana said, "But they didn't. I'd have told you."

And she would have. Blake was certain. "Li and Carlos are hiding something."

"You don't know that."

"I can't *prove* it, but—"

"But *I* can," Antonio said. "Look."

The playground was gone, vanquished by a long-range surveillance image of Dark. On the shore of the Darwin Sea, the settlement was little more than a dot.

"From station beta on Aristophanes." Antonio reached into the holo to indicate a faint oval smudge, darkest around the settlement. "See that? It's most visible in infrared wavelengths."

Smoke? Precious little on Dark could burn, apart from the ethanol they produced. Blake banished insane notions of medieval plagues, of criers calling to bring out the dead, of mass funerary bonfires.

Dana must have had the same thoughts. "A dietary deficiency *can't* be contagious. What are they burning?"

Antonio shook his head. "That's not smoke. Area temperature readings *are* normal. We must be seeing dust. From major construction or...destruction."

"Amid a health crisis?" Blake said. "They *are* lying to us, and they're not letting Rikki communicate. Dana, we have to go back."

"You're right," she said. "Buckle up, guys."

They were deep within the local asteroid belt and almost a quarter of the way around the sun from Dark. Over the course of their search, they had built up considerable speed. Blake reached for his datasheet to do the math.

"Three and a half days," Antonio said. "More or less. That's with the DED running wide open."

Two gees all the way.

Blake said, "Let's get going."

36

As jails went, Rikki's accommodations weren't bad. She had windows (too small and high to wriggle through, even if she had had the strength), a padded bench on which to rest, a toilet and sink, even a shower. The room was clean. At night, the ceiling glow panel gave more than ample light. Prisoners in stories paced out the dimensions of their cells, so she had. Call it four meters by five.

When the nausea and vomiting returned she saw the silver lining to being locked inside a bathroom.

After the nausea passed and she could stop hugging the toilet, she attacked the exterior wall with a spoon, the only utensil provided with her—untouched—food tray. She scraped long enough to confirm she'd need geological time to dig through the concrete. The shallow scratch, if anyone asked, was to mark Day One. In stories, prisoners also kept calendars.

From afar, every so often, she heard engine roars, and rasping, and deep whooshing rumbles. She remembered Carlos on the backhoe-loader—could it have been only that morning?—and wondered how it could have *anything* to do with Li's…insurrection.

When Rikki called at a window (oddly dusty) for help, the children ran.

Damn that horrible video! Damn *Li*!

Do I instinctively fear snakes? Rikki wondered. Does everyone? Maybe I only learned the fear growing up. Grandma Betty had had a thing about snakes.

But none of that mattered. The morphing faces and jarring music were surely terrifying enough.

Just as the children's dread of her was clear enough.

Out of sight, around a corner of the childcare center, the sounds of play soon resumed. Every happy shriek was like a knife twisting in Rikki's gut.

There was nothing left to do but remember, and that was the most painful of all.

Her datasheet! Straight from her pocket, still folded, she whispered into it, "Marvin, unlock the bathroom door."

Silence.

She pushed on the door and it would not budge. Maybe the lock's wireless interface had been disabled. She tapped out an email warning to Blake. *Li's gone nuts. Come back at once!*

Rather than an acknowledgment when she tapped SEND, the pop-up read, *I'm sorry, Rikki. I'm afraid I can't do that.*

Nor, she found, could she access the safety cameras to monitor what transpired outside. It dawned on her: Marvin had been blocking her messages to Blake all along. Carlos's doing, she supposed. The man knew computers.

Weary, defeated, Rikki lay down and closed her eyes. And opened them almost at once, to banish the image of Li brandishing her gun.

If Rikki had even remembered *Endeavour* had weapons in its cargo, she'd have thought them packed away forever. Anachronisms. Useless. Not as much as a gnat existed on Dark to harm them. To take up arms after billions—whole worlds—had perished? It was more than horrendous, beyond obscene.

And *she* was hopelessly naïve. An end to violence would only come when human nature changed.

The lock clicked.

"Stand back," Li called. "I'm armed."

Rikki, who had been pacing, sat on the bench.

Li entered cautiously, looking around the room. With gun in hand, she indicated the food tray. "You should eat."

"You expect me to believe this meal isn't poisoned?"

"*That's* your theory?" Li laughed.

"You obviously poisoned me. To keep me behind as your hostage?"

"Not exactly. In fact, at first I was annoyed at how the timing worked out, that you'd be staying behind. Tying up loose ends would have been easier without you underfoot. But you know what? I'm glad you're here. You'll be more convincing when the others return."

"What do you mean, 'Not exactly?'"

"I did do something to you," Li said. "Someday, maybe you'll thank me. 'Til then I trust it will make you cautious."

"I'm your goddamned prisoner! I can't do a thing. So stop being coy and *tell* me. What did you do?"

"Carlos and me. Do you remember the immune-system booster shot at your last routine physical? That was actually software updates for your nanites." Li smiled. "All that's wrong with you is a major case of morning sickness."

"I'm…pregnant?"

✳

Pacing, sleeping, and staring out the window. It passed the time but provided no answers.

Nothing Li had done made sense. Why reveal having warped the children? Just to brag? Why hold Rikki as a prisoner? Did Li think she and her gun could hold everyone at bay once Blake, Dana, and Antonio returned? She had to sleep sometime!

And above all: why had Li enabled her to get pregnant?"

Staring out the window, Rikki screamed, at everyone and no one, "Are you *crazy?*"

Children scattered. In seconds they had abandoned all of the play area visible from her window.

Not once in two days had Rikki seen an adult in the yard to supervise the kids. Was that the shape of things to come?

✳

"Come," Li ordered. "And bring your coat. We're going outside."

Rikki didn't budge from her seat. "Why? Do you have more abuse to boast about?"

"I'm not the one yelling at the children." Holding open the bathroom door, Li backed into the corridor. Her other hand held a gun. "I assume you'd like to know what this is about. And before you try anything stupid, remember: you're pregnant."

"As an elaborate, especially cruel, slow-motion way to kill me?" Because you're that sick.

"Oh, never mind what I told your doting husband. 'Could be fatal' leaves a great deal of wiggle room. I'd give you four-to-one odds you'll be fine." Li gestured. "Out. I have things to show you. Things that, once you're free, you'll want to tell your friends."

Free? Without a hostage, how did Li expect—whatever she was up to—to outlast *Endeavour*'s return? She had to sleep sometime.

"You're adorable when you're confused. Come. Your questions will all be answered."

Seething, Rikki followed.

Just inside the open(!) gate at the north end of Main Street, she saw Carlos. And a bulldozer, parked. And a dozen or more of the older children with rakes and shovels. Only you *couldn't* dig in the rock-hard ground.

"What are they doing?" Rikki asked.

"All in good time."

Their first stop was the settlement's primary, deeply buried bunker. A tornado shelter, at Antonio's insistence, not that they had ever had a tornado. Li motioned Rikki away from the double steel doors to palm the handprint reader, then backed away.

"You first," Li said.

Rikki raised one of the heavy doors. It fell to the side with a crash. The late afternoon sun touched only the first few steps, and she tapped the light-switch sensor. Her heart pounding, she scanned their most precious possessions: the embryo banks, still almost full. Bags of seed. Marvin's servers. Everything appeared untouched—but she knew Marvin had been altered.

What else, unseen, had Li and Carlos…tainted?

"We don't have all day. Down."

"So you can shut me inside?"

Li sighed. "I could have locked you here in the first place, couldn't I? Just go down. Trust me, it'll be worth it."

Hugging the railing, Rikki started down the concrete stairs. A tall stepladder she had last seen in the greenhouse, where she had used it to replace a cracked roof panel, leaned against the opposite wall. Everything else in the bunker was as Rikki remembered it—even the sturdy steel hook of the chain hoist on which, as usual, she cracked her head.

She reached the bottom and had circled half the bunker floor before her captor descended the first few steps. Li said, "Look up. Higher."

Well beyond Rikki's reach, strapped to the two steel beams that braced the concrete ceiling, packages...blinked.

Li took something from her pocket. "The trigger."

Rikki did not want to believe. "Those are explosives?"

"More than enough to bring the roof of the bunker crashing down."

And thereby end...everything. As from a great distance, Rikki heard herself ask, "Why?"

"Here's some old Earth history you might never have learned. Two great-power archenemies. Each side had enough nukes to obliterate its rival many times over. And neither side ever launched its missiles. Neither side dared, knowing the other would retaliate. Even an overwhelming first strike without warning might leave intact enough weapons for a devastating counterstrike. Strategists called the policy MAD. Mutual assured destruction."

It was mad, all right. "What can you possibly hope to accomplish?"

"Our history lesson isn't quite done." Li poked at her remote. Overhead, alongside both blinking lamps, bright red numerals appeared. 25:14:06. A standard Dark day.

The counters began ticking down.

"I must reset the devices daily. That's my failsafe. If anything were to prevent me..."

Rikki shivered. "What if something comes up? What if you can't do the daily rest?"

"*Après moi, le déluge.*"

"What?"

Li sneered. "Didn't they teach history on Mars? You all deserve to be extinct. It's French. Louis XV. 'After me, the flood.' And, as prophecies go, close enough. His son lost his head."

"Meaning?" Rikki asked despairingly.

"Meaning you'd best see to it that nothing 'comes up' before I'm prepared to disarm. As to my purpose until then, you shouldn't be surprised. A free hand with raising the children. You and your friends wouldn't allow that when I offered you all the choice."

"Poisoning the children's minds against us didn't give you enough leverage?"

"Sadly, no."

"Then why *warp* them?"

"I'm molding them," Li said. "Dana's job was to find a refuge, a haven, like Dark. Now it's my turn. To mold the children. To mold a *civilization*. The rest of you don't have what that takes."

"Now that we know how important this is to—"

Li snickered. "Little Miss Sunday dinner? I'm supposed to believe you'll change your mind? Come back up. I have more to show you."

The heavy bunker door slipped from Rikki's grasp when she closed it, too. This time, aware of the explosives, she cringed.

Li gestured up Main Street with her handgun. "Good. They've finished."

Carlos was ushering children—their clothes, faces, and hands inexplicably filthy—away from the gate. One by one, they dropped gardening tools on a pile. Once the last child started down the street, Carlos did something with a gadget from his pocket.

Most of the children gave Rikki a wide berth. Some stared as they passed.

Rikki burst into tears. "I *love* you children."

If they heard her, if they cared, none showed it.

Behind Rikki, from one of the playground speakers, Marvin announced, "*Discovery's* radar shows *Endeavour* is inbound. It will be on the ground within ten minutes."

✳

Li motioned Rikki forward. "I'm almost impressed. They got suspicious faster than I expected."

The barren rock near the fence was…changed. Textured. Dug up, somehow, by the bulldozer? By the children, too, Rikki guessed from all those begrimed faces and hands.

Two paces closer and Rikki saw that something *covered* that strip of ground. A wavy gravel bed, all tiny hummocks, hollows, and shoeprints, extended about five meters inside the fence. The broad gravel band paralleled the fence until both, curving around buildings, were lost to sight.

"Stop!" Li picked up one of the rocks that little feet had kicked and dragged into the compound. "Do *not* approach the gate."

"Why not?"

Li lobbed her pebble toward the middle of the gravel strip, about ten meters to the left of the gate. Nothing happened.

"That was anticlimactic." Li took a rake from the tool pile. She tossed it after the pebble.

Blam!

Rikki ducked, hands clapped to her ears, as gravel rained down and something stung her cheek. Stones pinged off the fence and concrete chips flew from it. Children screamed. When the smoke and dust had cleared, a meter-wide crater remained. Of the rake itself, only scattered twisted shards could be seen.

"Pressure activated. That's why you should stay off the gravel."

Rikki wiped grit and tears from her face. "Why, Li?"

"The fence and gate suffice to keep the children in. The land mines are to keep you and your friends out. Except, of course, when I have need of you inside. The mines are radio controlled. I can turn them on and off."

"Six minutes," Marvin called.

"You see," Li went on, "we on the inside—and our numbers *will* grow—require food, water, and clothing. Every year or so we'll want a fresh bottle of deuterium. So rejoice. The four of you can still serve the new order."

"And if we aren't able to produce enough? If, say, the weather doesn't cooperate? You would blow the bunker?"

"You want to know, can you starve us out? You could try. But there is plenty of food and water in the pantry for just Carlos and me."

"You would take food from the mouths of *babies?*"

Li shrugged. "If you withhold food, what happens is on your heads. And when you come to your senses and resume deliveries, we can replace any children you starved."

Rikki just stared, dumbfounded.

"For lesser infractions, if you should be so foolish, I'm sure I can find other ways to get your attention. I might cut off power to your homes for a while. Have any other bright ideas?"

Did she?

Rikki pointed at the fence. "That encloses what, maybe a square klick? You can't mean to stay inside for long. You can't fit many more children inside."

"The secure compound is just about half that area, but you're correct. We won't stay forever. A few years will suffice. By then, hundreds of children, the cadre of a new civilization, will have been thoroughly shaped." Bright, fanatical eyes proclaimed, "They'll be thoroughly *mine*."

"How about this?" Rikki said desperately. "We construct a second settlement elsewhere. Far down the coast of Darwin Sea. Or on the coast of a different sea, if you prefer. You live there. You build your"— insane, twisted, tragic—"society there."

"Or *you* could move. Except no one will be going anywhere, because I need workers here to farm. Or I may find I need resources only *Endeavour* can fetch. And even if those weren't possibilities, I would still refuse. Know this: restored humanity will be a single society. One perfect society."

With Mad Queen Li to rule it.

The children, terrified by the explosion, had crowded around Carlos. Eve, taller than the rest, very blond, was unmistakable—and Carlos's hand rested on her shoulder.

Amid cosmic disaster: a tragedy of human scale.

Rikki said, "To feed so many, we'll need Carlos's help, too." Whether or not that was true, she couldn't bear the thought of leaving him inside the fence, with the little girls.

"Carlos outside?" Li hesitated. "No, I need him."

"Three minutes," Marvin advised.

Li took the controller from her pocket. "You have thirty seconds to cross the gravel."

"But I—"

"Twenty-five seconds. Twenty-four."

Rikki dashed, gravel scattering beneath her shoes. She didn't slow down until she was at least twenty meters outside the gate.

Li called, "Your friends will be on the ground soon. Tell them what you've seen. Tell them what I expect.

"And tell them the consequences if any of you fail to cooperate."

DEFIANCE

(Autumn, Year Ten)

37

With a throaty roar, straining against its massive load, the tractor lurched into motion. It crept from the granary and, with its motor protesting more than ever, negotiated the turn onto Main Street. Dana found herself leaning forward—as though by shifting her weight she could make the poor, overburdened vehicle and its trailer move faster. Maybe, she mocked herself, it will speed up if I make *vroom, vroom* noises.

On both sides of the street, a few potted trees provided hints of autumn color. Dry leaves skittered down the pavement. The twin greenhouses teemed with unseasonable green. In their respective enclosures, chickens clucked and cows lowed.

Blake *walked* past the lumbering tractor.

From Dana's perch on the tractor seat, she could see his shoulders tense as, passing through the open gate, he trod upon the strip of gravel. Nothing happened: the mines were switched off, as promised. As had been the case for countless deliveries.

Tribute, all of them, to Queen Li.

Carlos loitered inside the stockade, well back from the bright red-painted line that marked the inner edge of the minefield. Several of the oldest children were wrestling pipes embedded in concrete bases into position along the line: posts for the inside fence that must delimit the boundary once snow fell. The nip in the air suggested that wouldn't be long.

When three among the children on snow-fence duty looked Dana's way, she offered them a grandmotherly smile.

Boys? Girls? She couldn't tell. All the children had hair down to their shoulders or longer. If haircuts for hundreds weren't a massive enough undertaking, she still didn't suppose grooming ranked high on Li's list of priorities. Maybe unisex hair was part of the new order. Unisex garments definitely were, if only of practicality. Most of the hand-me-down pants, sweaters, and coats were too big or too small for their new owners; even the clothing that fit tended toward ragged and dirty.

The three watchful kids, whatever their genders, scowled back at Dana.

How many lies, and how vile, had these children been told over the years about the people who lived outside? She felt ill, just wondering.

"Stop!" Carlos shouted. "You know the drill."

Dana applied the brakes with the tractor still well outside the gate. Four tonnes of cargo took their sweet time responding. To the accompaniment of a squeal, she brought the tractor to a halt atop the inactivated minefield that Li—nowhere in sight, but doubtless watching—could reactivate in an instant. Or if Li did not like something she saw, she might merely take a potshot from hiding.

It was best not to raise suspicions.

Children were *everywhere*. Milling about. Walking, running, and climbing. Peeking from between, and out the windows of, buildings throughout the compound. Indoors, the choruses clashing, three groups recited their rote lessons. Little Eve (only she was a young woman, not little anymore) supervised toddlers on the playground.

So many kids, and yet, to Dana's knowledge, none had ever tried to escape. It would seem simple. Just run out when the gateway was opened for food. She thought of the children as hostages and prisoners. They must see themselves as besieged.

The kids were too active to make an accurate count, but she guessed a couple hundred and maybe a few dozen voices in the classrooms. The littlest kids would be in the childcare center. More of them all the time....

Three hundred in total, perhaps? That would be consistent with the quantities of food that Li so imperiously commanded to appear. In the few, low buildings, children would be sleeping cheek by jowl.

Carlos examined the underside of the tractor using a mirror mounted to a long carbon-fiber pole. "All right. Come forward two tractor lengths." That would bring the tractor inside the fence and put the grain-laden trailer onto the gravel.

"Must we go through this nonsense *every* time?" Blake burst out.

"Yes, as it happens," Carlos said. He eyeballed the bulging bags of wheat, then with his mirror began to inspect beneath the trailer.

Fooled you once, Dana thought, because even trivial successes came too seldom not to savor.

Not long after Li's coup, Blake had rigged a gadget beneath a trailer, hidden within a spare tire. His jury-rig scooped up a bunch of stones—together with what they had been going for: one of the land mines—and refilled the hole with fresh gravel. The mine itself went into a metal box, shielded against the rearm signal.

Far from the compound, inside a copper-screen-sheeted work-space, they had unsealed the box. Sneering at Carlos, Blake had opened the mine, traced its firing circuits, and defused it.

And failed ever after to find a way to remotely disable the re-mote-control circuits. The mines inside the stockade remained out of reach. Carlos, though he did not know it, had had the last laugh.

Soon thereafter, whether by coincidence or having noticed a sus-picious pattern in the gravel, under-vehicle inspections had begun.

What if, instead of trawling that day for a sample land mine to dissect, *Blake* had been under the trailer? If he had hidden within the compound till dark, sneaked into the bunker, disarmed the bombs....

Uh-huh. Suppose he *had* somehow evaded notice for hours and not gotten shot by Li. Then he would have had to disarm bombs he'd never before seen, using only the tools he'd been able to carry, while teetering atop a very tall stepladder. If anything had gone wrong, he'd have blown up himself and the last hopes of humanity.

Sending Blake in blind would have been a stupid, foolhardy stunt. It would have violated everything Dana had ever been taught about mission planning.

And through more sleepless nights than she would admit even to Antonio, she feared that by waiting to gather intel she had doomed them all.

"And that doesn't excuse treating us like..."

While Blake distracted Carlos, Dana surveilled. The concrete stockade pickets looked as untouched by weather on the inside as from without. The gravel bed remained pocked with countless dimples and bumps, masking unknown numbers of buried mines. Cameras atop tall poles continuously scanned the perimeter. All as always.

Nonetheless, she looked.

Even in darkest night, with the children asleep indoors, she couldn't bring *Endeavour* within the fence. It didn't matter that the DED made the ship silent; it was too big. In one or two spots a shuttle might fit—if she were insane enough to land on fusion drive within meters of the children. If the fusion drive's roar wouldn't be a dead giveaway from klicks away. If by magic she somehow swept away *all* those impediments, Marvin through his many cameras could hardly fail to see a spaceship on approach.

In short: there could be no swooping in for a rescue.

The answer never changed, because the compound never changed. Blake called her mindset the pilot's version of when all you have is a hammer, all problems look like nails.

Despite Blake's interruptions, Carlos finished his inspection. "All right, Marvin."

The AI's voice rang out from speakers across the compound, and children scattered.

"Pantry three," Carlos said.

"Thanks," Dana said. She put the tractor in gear. Once again, it crawled forward.

Blake was no less obstinate than she, in his case trying to *engineer* a solution. Since the day of Li's coup, he had tried to build autonomous robots. One model was to be small enough to squeeze between the pickets, light-weight enough not to set off any mines, and deft enough to disarm them. Another type was to be hidden in a grain bag, to sneak out of a pantry, somehow make its way into the locked bunker, and there defuse the bombs that gave Li her power.

Five years later, he still tinkered.

To be fair, it was not as though feeding the colony left any of them spare time. Or they had been left with synth vats in which to fabricate tiny, delicate parts. Or any of them had experience in robotics. Or access to Marvin's technical archives.

After five exhausting, futile years, Dana struggled to find the energy to be fair.

At the slowest creep the tractor could manage, lest any child dart out in front of her, she pulled the trailer into the compound. She did a three-point turn and backed up the trailer to the pantry. Then, panting with effort, shirt drenched with sweat despite the crisp autumn temperature, she helped Blake unload and stack twenty-kilo bags of wheat.

Leaning against a wall, sipping from a flask, wearing a coat, Carlos observed.

"Why don't you sit?" Blake suggested to Dana after they had off-loaded about half a tonne. He brushed dust and grain off his work gloves. "Carlos and I have some business to transact."

Dana perched on the tailgate of the trailer, more than ready to catch her breath.

"You brought it?" Carlos said.

"I said I would," Blake said. "And you?"

"You first."

Blake took a folded datasheet from his pocket and tossed it to Carlos. "Load us up."

"How dumb do you think I am? Or how drunk?" Carlos drawled, then tossed back the datasheet.

So much, yet again, for an engineered solution. Because if Carlos had accepted the datasheet, and not spotted its hidden Trojan, and been so careless as to net the comp, Blake would have obtained remote access to Marvin.

With a shrug, Blake repocketed the comp. He lobbed over the bulging bag that had been stowed in the trailer's toolbox.

Opening the bag, at his first whiff of fresh tobacco, Carlos smiled beatifically. "Smells *delightful*." He handed Blake a different folded datasheet. "A hundred vids. And because I'm a good guy, bunches of old books, too."

And then it was back to work.

"I need another break," Dana wheezed after a while. Maybe they had offloaded half the grain sacks. Even this task was getting to be too much for her. She'd been chosen to save humanity? If the stakes hadn't been so high, it would have been laughable.

"Take your time," Blake said. He went to sit on the tailgate of the trailer and she joined him.

She told herself not to give up. She told herself, this is what Li did: made them all feel helpless. Li was very good at what she did.

And mad as a hatter.

About the first thing Li had ever said to Dana aboard *Endeavour*—not even *Endeavour* yet—was, "Psychiatrists are nuttier than most people you'll meet."

"I should have listened," Dana muttered.

Blake leaned closer. "What's that?"

"Nothing," she said.

"It's getting late," Carlos prompted.

With a groan, Dana stood to resume the unloading. Champion of mankind, pilot extraordinaire, and third-rate pack mule.

"Bad p-people," George stuttered.

"It's all right," Eve told the little boy cowering behind her, clutching her leg.

"Why?"

Why were they here? Why were they bad? Why was their presence all right? An answer to any of those questions was complex. She tousled his hair. "They'll go away soon."

That seemed to satisfy him. He scampered off to line up for the slide.

Unlike most of the children, she remembered a time when the bad people had moved at will throughout the settlement. Before they became "the bad people," but were only Mr. Blake and Ms. Rikki, Mr. Antonio and Ms. Dana.

They were bad, though. Even then. Eve *knew* that. They frightened her, although she had never understood why.

And, blaspheming in her thoughts, she knew that not everyone bad lived outside.

"Eve?" Reese called, legs pumping as she worked a swing.

"I'm fine," Eve said. Except she wasn't: she had allowed her attention to wander. If Ms. Li or Mr. Carlos had noticed—

Eve shivered.

She separated Rhonda and Denise, who had begun squabbling. She helped Samir off the ground, shushed his sniffling, and inspected the scrape on his palm. It was nothing. She commanded Allan to stand in a corner and think about shoving.

"Why do the bad people come here?" Tanya whispered. And *she* was not one to accept, "Don't worry," or "They'll be gone soon," as an answer.

"To bring us food," Eve said.

"But they're bad and food is good. Why would they do something good for us?"

"It's complicated," Eve said. "Because of their many sins, God commands that they must work hard."

Happily, Tanya did not ask what sin was.

Not that Tanya had run out of questions. She never did. "Why are there bad people in the world at all?"

To disobey was sin, and Eve had been told to instruct the younger children on matters of faith. Even when she didn't understand herself. She began, "Once, in a place far away—"

"The other world."

"Right. Don't interrupt if you want an answer."

"Sorry," Tanya said, eyes downcast.

"The other world was filled with bad people. God told Ms. Li that He would destroy the world to end the evil." Eve wasn't clear who God was, either. Someone very powerful, a friend of Ms. Li's. Or what evil was, beyond not doing as God and His messenger decreed. "Ms. Li pleaded with God to spare the world, and He said He would if she could show Him ten good people. She could not find even ten, but God was so moved by her compassion—"

"Her what?" Tanya asked shyly.

"Her concern for all the others." One by one, as children heard Eve retelling the Great Story, they stopped their play and sidled closer to listen. Raising her voice so that everyone could hear, Eve continued. "God commanded Ms. Li to build a special ship called the ark to save herself, the five good people she had found, and all the unborn children."

"And you were the first to be born here."

Which meant the others looked to her for answers, whether or not she had any. Being the oldest didn't make her an adult! It didn't impart the wisdom of the other world.

I'm a child, too! Every day—every hour!—she wanted to scream the words but did not dare. She had duties, however unwelcome, and the children's trust, however undeserved. And a room of her own. A private room marked her as special, set her apart. She would *so* much rather sleep with the others, as she had when she was younger.

For *so* many reasons.

Tanya glanced to where the unloading continued. "But why are the bad people *here?*"

"I'm coming to that," Eve said. "Most people Ms. Li brought on her ark had tricked her by pretending to be good. They prepared to bring sin to this world. But Ms. Li had foreseen their evil plan. Mr. Carlos made the devices that protect us—"

"And you and the other oldest ones helped," one of the children interrupted.

"Right." Eve still did not understand *what* they hid in the gravel that day, but she would never forget the tooth-rattling *bang!* one made soon after they finished. And again when—

No. She could not bear to remember that.

But the things in the gravel, whatever they were, scared the bad people, too. They kept their distance except when bringing food.

"…is that, Eve?" little Jorge asked.

She had allowed her attention to wander again. "What?"

"Why doesn't God punish *these* bad people? Why do they get to have most of the world? Why did God allow them to steal the ark?"

The answer, when Eve had once made similar inquiries, involved rainbows, God's mysterious ways, and the promise Ms. Li would someday soon lead the children into a promised land.

"I guess it is God's will," Eve told the children, wishing once more that she understood. "Now go play."

From the corner of an eye, around the edge of a building, she resumed her study of Mr. Blake and Ms. Dana unloading the food.

Sometimes Eve watched Mr. Blake through the fence. He and a young girl, she about five and a half, would throw back and forth a striped ovoid ball, the girl as often as not dropping it or flinging it far beyond his reach. He called her Beth. She called him Daddy, and that Mr. Blake had a second name was yet another mystery to Eve.

She didn't understand the activity's purpose, or why Mr. Blake kept at it so patiently, ever calling out encouragement. She didn't understand why she never saw but the one child outside. She didn't understand why Mr. Blake prattled on about saints and bengals, cowboys and patriots, whatever those were, or the strange noises the girl sometimes broke into.

"Giggling," Marvin called the noise when Eve had asked.

"Is she injured?"

"No, Beth is fine," Marvin had said. "That is a happy sound."

"I don't understand," Eve had told it. She still didn't. Throwing and catching and shouting encouragement didn't seem like the things a bad person would do.

"You will have to ask an adult," Marvin had told her.

Eve knew better than that.

Had *she* ever giggled? Had she ever even played, like Tanya and Samir and the rest of her charges got to do? If so, it had happened so long ago that Eve no longer remembered.

Sometimes, watching man and child toss their ball, Eve had wondered if Mr. Blake slipped into the little girl's room at night. If Mr. Blake…touched things, and made Beth—

No. Eve refused to think about that.

As the bad people, gasping with effort, continued to unload the food—and as Mr. Carlos stood watching—Eve found herself trying to imagine something strange.

What would it be like to giggle and be happy?

38

Frowning in concentration, tongue peeking from a corner of her mouth, Beth colored feverishly. Rikki thought she had never seen anything so adorable—and, at the same time, if she allowed herself to ponder what sort of future her little girl could have, so terrifying.

"What do you have there?" Rikki asked.

Beth looked up, and coal-black bangs flopped into her beautiful, incredulous eyes. "That's *us*, Mommy."

Two big and one little person standing in front of a box with windows: that, Rikki hadn't needed help to decode. Six or more sketches like it adorned their kitchen at all times. It was the backdrop behind the house that puzzled her. Bunches of closely spaced vertical lines, with dots of color between.

Oh. The children of the settlement. Li's...puppets.

Rikki's heart sank. "Let's put your pretty picture up on the wall, hon."

"When can I play with other children?" Beth asked, reaching for a new sheet of paper.

"Someday." When Li couldn't stuff any more children into the settlement. Then the fences must come down, whether Rikki liked it or not. She had anticipated and dreaded that day since before Beth was born.

She and Blake had talked endlessly about a second child. But in standard years, she had already been almost forty-one when Beth was born. The pregnancy might have been hard even on Mars. Better her baby grow up an only child than without a mother.

No, the young ones inside were Beth's only hope for a normal life. Of companionship after her parents and Antonio and Dana had passed on.

But could anyone *be* normal, raised by lunatics inside a prison camp?

"Could you draw me another?"

"Sure, Mommy."

Rikki stood. Just stretching my legs, she told herself, knowing herself for a liar. Out her front window, across Main Street, through another window, she checked to see that Antonio still sat reading in his living room. With Blake and Dana away, Antonio had even offered to sleep on the sofa.

She would be damned if she'd let Beth see how terrified she was.

How could Antonio protect her anyway? How could anyone? Li had the guns, and the explosives, and the madness to use them.

What Rikki *really* ached to do was flee with her daughter into the hills, to hide within the maze of the caves. But she didn't dare to risk revealing that they had been stocking the caverns as an emergency shelter. Lugging supplies through the back entrance, flying *Endeavour* in from behind the ridge, below the hilltops, there was no way—in theory, anyway—that Li and Carlos could know. If they discovered that a significant food reserve had been set aside, Li would only speed up her baby factory.

Bedtime's approach brought new sadness. She couldn't read her daughter a simple bedtime story! Simple but impossible, even after Blake had returned from a recent food delivery with, among the many book files, a collection of classic children's stories.

Children's stories are about relating to…someone. A brother or sister. Classmates. Friends. Pets. Cute little animals as surrogate people. What did any of that have to do with Beth? How could it help to remind her baby that she was alone?

Beth was past old enough to learn to read. Only what could they give her to read?

"Mom! Look what you *did*."

"Oops." Rikki discovered she had Beth in a bear hug, arms pinned to her sides. In the process, she had caused Beth to scribble a big diagonal crayon streak across her paper. This drawing was shaping up as a close-up of the fence, and Rikki didn't want to think anymore about that. "It's time for your bath."

"Ten minutes."

They negotiated and settled on five. As Beth splashed in her tub, Rikki opened a novel on her datasheet. And sighed. And closed the file again. It seemed wrong until she found something to read to Beth.

At last she got the little imp into bed.

"Why didn't Daddy call tonight?"

Rikki gave her daughter a big kiss on the forehead. "He and Aunt Dana are very busy."

"Where did they go?"

"Exploring, hon. You know that. Looking for useful stuff before the snow starts."

Some things couldn't be explained to a child. Like a mother's stubborn insistence on understanding why five years of PFCs pumped into the atmosphere had yet to slow the globe's inexplicable cooling. That by drilling, by examining millennia of sediment samples, one peered into the past. That to Blake and Dana these expeditions had only been excuses, a cover for trips to sneak supplies into the caves.

That *she* fervently wished Blake and Dana had been correct.

Because the samples established, more with each expedition, that a terrible flood, or floods, had afflicted parts of Dark. The havoc in the physical record was extreme, such that even Antonio did not dare to date the catastrophe any more precisely than "within the past thousand years, give or take."

Geologically speaking, that wasn't as much as an eye-blink ago.

If a tsunami were to hit Darwin Sea, the wave would sweep away the farms, the bacterial basins, and even blast up the slope all the way to the settlement.

It would scour away—everything.

39

Children—shrieking, babbling, bickering, squealing with glee— were everywhere in the yard. Climbing, swinging, and sliding. Playing catch. Playing tag. Chasing snowflakes. Digging in sandboxes. Stomping in puddles. Jumping rope. Hopping. Skipping. Running races. Running aimlessly.

All that bedlam made Antonio, wandering up and down Main Street for fresh air and to clear his mind, very tired. That wasn't the hardest part. Having had the children in his life—and then lost them—made him very, *very* sad.

He couldn't watch, not directly. Try to watch and *he* would be running, screaming, from the area. So he kept track of things indirectly. From the corner of an eye. Listening.

And in that disarray, that spontaneity, the children zooming about like so many asteroids, he found a modicum of hope for the future. Li liked quiet and order.

Actually the local asteroids were far more orderly than these children.

For a few seconds Antonio took in a clear, cloudless sky. Today the sky seemed more blue than green, and the few hints of red dust hung close to the horizon. For most of his life, any glimpse of the sky had calmed him. Like numbers, the sky had been a refuge.

No longer.

He had feared asteroid bombardments since his first glimpses of this solar system. With both a gas giant and an asteroid belt close to Dark, bombardment was inevitable. Physics and math said so.

It drove him crazy how few incidents, even harmless, burn-up-in-the-atmosphere meteoroid encounters, the observatories on the moons reported. It drove him to suspect design flaws in the observatory instruments, only those weren't the problem. Many long nights with *Endeavour's* telescope, surveying the asteroid belt, had replaced one mystery with another. Dark, it seemed, was spared impacts because the nearby asteroid belt was…tidy. The orbits were all nicely circularized.

Neither math nor physics could explain that observation, either.

When the evidence mounted of recent widespread flooding—as unnerving as that was—at least the world made sense again. The law of averages had caught up.

Except that it hadn't.

If a big impact or impacts had unleashed the tsunamis, there would be signs. Granules of shocked quartz and natural glass, forged in the heat and pressure of impact, would be widespread. The asteroid strike that doomed the dinosaurs had left behind a worldwide scattering of iridium dust. Iridium was scarcer than gold—yet all around the Earth, a fine layer of iridium dust could be found at the geologic boundary between periods. That iridium had to have come from an asteroid. A big one. The kind of rock that, smacking into an ocean, unleashed a tsunami.

On Dark, across the past thousand years, ice cores, clay cores, and lakebed sediments alike showed only the disorder and the sudden salinity surges of floods. There was no layer of glass and shocked quartz. There were no elemental anomalies, such as Earth's iridium dusting at the boundary between the Cretaceous and Tertiary periods.

A distant chime sounded: Marvin signaling the end to recess. On the playground, chaos somehow transformed into lines. The cacophony settled down a notch to mere din. Boys and girls made their way into the childcare center.

Antonio continued his aimless shuffling, wishing that the confusion that afflicted *him* would resolve itself as easily.

✳

The hallway echoed with fussing toddlers, the murmurs of the children minding them, and the chiding of Marvin avatars. Childish shrieks and the squeaking of playground swings drifted in from outside. Wet flakes of an afternoon snow flurry spattered against the window.

Intent on statistics, Li hardly noticed any of it.

A fuzzy caterpillar of a holo hovered over her desk. In one compact graphic, it encoded everything useful to know about cohort six.

Dense thickets of colored lines radiated from the holo's primary axis. Each tint denoted a specific metric of social development, such as obedience, orthodoxy, and self-discipline. The length of each colored line segment encoded a child's performance in the corresponding metric. The length of each black segment, a weighted average, gave her one subject's overall socialization index. Concentric translucent gray cylinders provided the scale. Eighteen measurements multiplied by, for this cohort, seventy-two subjects: she had a significant dataset.

A few segments poked through the outermost translucent cylinder. She reached into the holo to zoom on a subject. 6/32/M/TODD the pop-up tag noted: from cohort six, hence not quite five years local; gestated in womb unit thirty-two; male. By random selection from Marvin's names database, named Todd.

Todd's metric for orthodoxy was two standard deviations from average. In the wrong direction. The rating had gotten worse in each of the last three monthly assessments.

"Okay, Todd," Li said to herself. "What's your problem?"

Because she couldn't read minds. Neither could Marvin, although it could analyze speech and categorize body language. It did a passable job, when the children confided, with dream interpretation. So what was going on with Todd?

It didn't take long to find recordings of the boy asking inappropriate questions at daily catechism. She had a skeptic on her hands.

Time, young Todd, for an intervention. Time to teach you and everyone else that, as her Grandmother Hideko used to put it, the nail that sticks up gets pounded down.

"Li? We should talk."

Intent on her work, Li had not heard Carlos approach. With a hand gesture she blanked her display. "If it's quick."

Not taking the hint he came into her office, closed the door, and sat. His hair and coat were damp, and snowmelt trickled down his face. He reeked of alcohol, even more than usual, even from across the room. So what had he been psyching himself up for?

Carlos said, "The ground is still too warm for anything to stick for long, but the snow is pretty heavy for this early in the season."

"Tell me you didn't interrupt my work to prattle about the weather."

"I've been in the yard, talking through the fence with Antonio." Picking up on her frown, at least, he added, "Relax. Without any kids in earshot."

"And?"

"It's not just this region experiencing an unseasonably cold fall. It's most of the northern hemisphere. It can't be an accident that the icecaps have grown every year."

"Per Antonio."

"Yes." Carlos took a while picking his next words. "It's not weather that concerns me, Li, but climate. The *climate* is getting colder. I've seen the downlinks from the moons and—"

"From observatories Antonio programmed."

"Yes, but—"

"Let me guess. Antonio wants you to give him access to Marvin, or the full data archives, or networked instruments, or all three."

"Well, yes."

How could Carlos not see? Was it the booze or willful obtuseness? "We retain control because we have Marvin and the others don't. Give Antonio access and how long do you suppose our control can last?"

"Let me rephrase. Antonio didn't ask for access to Marvin. Not directly—"

"Climate. Floods. If those don't convince us to lower our guard, they'll be back with dire warnings of blood, boils, and locusts."

Carlos sat forward, hands clasped, index fingers steepled. "Hear me out. *Endeavour* is just back from a trip collecting sediment cores.

"And how is that significant?"

Other than demonstrating that the peasants had too much free time on their hands. She must give them new assignments. Additional garments for the children, perhaps.

He said, "A fair proportion of sediment turns out to be diatoms. The pattern in those is scary."

Li rubbed her eyes. "Will you get to the *point*? Start with whatever a diatom is."

"A microscopic fossil. Some types of algae secrete silicate shells, and you can infer a great deal about climate trends from changes over the ages in the microfossils." He babbled on about isotope ratios and salinity clues, before finally concluding, "The data aren't good."

All parroting Antonio, of course. It proved nothing.

"Just how do *you* have this data? Have you already linked them to Marvin?"

Carlos shook his head. "No, but that *is* why Antonio brought me into the loop. He wants access to the data about cores collected before the settlement...split. And the use of some of my lab instruments, the better to analyze his new cores. And he wants access to the compute power of Marvin's servers."

Li stiffened. "How can you even consider—"

"Yell at me later," Carlos said. "This is serious. You know the recent Darwin Sea flooding that had Rikki worried? Antonio is coming to believe the tsunamis were global in extent."

"Damn it! You are *such* a gullible"—drunken—"fool. They've concocted a fable. Let them net in and I *guarantee* you they'll make the attempt to subvert Marvin."

"Suppose *I* went with them to collect new cores, picked the landing spots myself. I could vouch for the authenticity of the new samples."

Volunteering himself as a hostage! Oh, how she wished she could pitch him out—but if she did, who would synth meds and tweak nanites when she needed them? And if Marvin detected a hacking attack on itself, who could respond? With jaws clenched, she stared at him.

Carlos said, "What if Antonio didn't fake it? Suppose, just for a moment, that he's discovered something important. Suppose there is a danger of flooding."

Li laughed. "Do you imagine for a moment that if you share your toys all will be forgiven?"

"You really believe the others would make this up?"

"You really believe that they *wouldn't?*" she shot back.

"Okay," Carlos finally conceded, standing. "I'll tell Antonio, no."

✸

Li stared at the re-summoned data caterpillar. It stared back at her. She retrieved a recent image of 6/32/M/Todd. Rosy cheeks and big freckles. Twinkling eyes. Crooked smile with a couple of baby teeth missing. All in all, a mischievous little heretic. Back on Mars, he would doubtless have been the bane of his kindergarten teacher.

To hell with the little brat!

Li was on her feet, seething. At Carlos, for his credulity. At Antonio, for his transparent scheming. At outmoded bourgeois notions of family that had made it necessary for her to take charge. For the peasants' tiresome disapproval since she had.

A few more years, and nothing would shake the children's conditioning. A few more years and the oldest children could take on all the farming chores. A few more years, and she would have no need for *any* of the adults.

But that would be then. Her rage was *now*.

Storming into the yard, Li grabbed Todd by an arm. A deathly hush came over the playground. Children stared, round-eyed. Todd shook, his lower lip trembling.

"I understand you question your duty to God's plan," Li said.

"I...I don't understand," the boy said.

"Five days ago, did you not ask your friends why you should take shifts watching the little ones and changing diapers?"

His mouth fell open. The children had no idea that Marvin could eavesdrop across most of the compound.

"I didn't mean to—"

"And did you not question why you are not allowed outside the fence?"

"I ju-just asked—"

"And you make jokes. You mock rules." Li began dragging the brat toward the fence. "You belittle. Such behavior is not acceptable. Perhaps you should see the nature of life *without* God's grace."

"I'm s-so sorry." Todd began to sob, great tears rolling down his cheeks, mucus bubbling over his lips and down his chin. Though he dug his heels into the outdoor carpet, he had to yield to her adult strength. "I w-won't ask *anything*."

A few at first, then more and more, children on the playground burst into tears. Slowly, fearfully, keeping their distance, they trailed after Li and the boy.

Let this be a lesson for all *of you.*

Carlos burst from his lab. He whispered urgently into Li's ear, "He's just a kid."

She ignored him.

She ignored the boy, too, until she had dragged him almost to the snow fence. "I have no use for troublemakers," Li said. "Marvin, open the gate."

"What are you doing?" Carlos hissed.

Through eyes narrowed to slits she stared him down.

As the gate swung open, Todd pissed his pants.

"Go." She shoved the boy forward. His abject terror had slaked her rage, but she would not be seen backing down.

"Li!" Carlos shouted. "The mines."

"Very well." Li took the controller from her pocket and switched off the minefield. She gave the boy a shove. "Go, now. Live among the bad people. Live among your own evil kind."

He stood stock-still, paralyzed with fear.

Li unholstered her handgun and fired a round into the air. Children scattered, screaming. "Marvin, shut the gate." As the gate slowed, then reversed its swing, she pointed her weapon at Todd. "If you are still inside when the gate closes…"

The boy ran.

Eve pressed through the children toward Li. "*I* question the teachings. I must leave, too."

Li shoved the girl at Carlos. "You have duties here."

40

"Did you hear that?" Beth asked.

Over the squawking of the chickens. Antonio might have heard…something. Not the haphazard chattering and shrieking of the children, of course; he had learned to listen past that. A popping sound? Maybe, but thunder and snow showers tended not to mix. A sonic boom, then. "I think your parents"—and Dana—"are coming *home*…early."

The question was: why?

The three were away in *Endeavour*, ostensibly to collect ice-core samples. The big glacier was far to the south, sufficiently remote to cover for another delivery of emergency supplies. More of the undeclared surplus from this year's harvest. Spare tools and clothing. Additional ethanol for the emergency generator. Meds. Extra water filters. Way too much stuff to have already offloaded and hauled into the caves.

"Maybe we can play in the snow," Beth said. "Before it all melts."

"Maybe." Antonio emptied his bucket and returned to the feed bin for more pellets. "Before we play, we need to finish our chores."

They fed and cleaned up after the chickens, gathered eggs, and moved on to the barn to feed the cows. Squawking and clucking gave way to lowing. No one came looking for them, nor did any messages come into his datasheet. After a while, Antonio said, "I guess that... noise we heard wasn't the...ship."

Beth stomped a foot. "Then just you and I will play."

"When we're done." In his pocket, the datasheet trilled. "Wait. Maybe they will *be* back soon."

The message, relayed through observatory gamma on Aeschylus, was from Carlos!

Don't bother trying to answer, because Li vetoed giving you access. She's certain you're lying. By the time you read this I'll have removed the tunnel through the firewall.

Did you make up a story for me? Then it won't matter that I analyzed both the old cores in the archives and the data I accessed on *your* servers. Laugh if you want.

And if your data are real? Then I hope to hell you can make sense of this.

The annotated globe holo attached to the message stopped Antonio cold.

And when he and Beth finally completed their chores and left the barn, the wailing, sticky-faced child—thumb in his mouth, seated amid the snowmelt puddles in the center of Main Street—was an even bigger surprise.

✺

"Come to bed," Dana called.

Aristophanes hung overhead, at almost full phase, mocking Antonio. "In a minute."

Dana came out of the house to stand with him. "I know all about your minutes."

He smiled. *At*, not near her. Not to the side of her. Not at her slippers. That he could—without effort, even—said something about them both. "And yet you joined me?"

"Sigh." And she did. "What's so interesting out here tonight?"

"The wind in the trees? The Broadway marquees?"

She laughed. "Okay. So there aren't many options. What is it about Aristophanes, besides that it's not an asteroid?"

"All three of them."

"All three moons?"

"Right. And though they're not asteroids, they still perplex me."

"Do you want to talk about it?"

Astronomical puzzles went above and beyond spousal duty. Even on a normal day, and today had been far from that. "It's on the esoteric side."

Dana hugged herself against the cold. "If it will get you inside faster, tell me."

"You silver-tongued smoothie," he said. And proceeded to dump on her everything that had been driving him crazy.

Beginning with that none of Dark's moons was tidally locked to Dark. The Moon showed one face to Earth. Phobos and Deimos were locked in the same manner to Mars. Eight inner moons of Jupiter were tidally locked. Fifteen of Saturn's. Five of Uranus's—

"What of the other planets in *this* system?" she interrupted his inventory. "Are their moons tidally locked?"

"Most of them are locked. As they should be." He tipped back his head, staring in frustration at the world overhead. "Why not these?"

"I have no idea."

Finally noticing that Dana was in pajamas and a thin robe, he removed his sweater and slipped it around her shoulders. Her attention kept wandering across the street to where Rikki and Blake still tried, and failed, to calm that poor, terrified little boy.

With a shiver, Dana turned back toward Antonio. "Sorry. That's hard to listen to. About the moons, though. Could this be a young planetary system? Maybe it's too early for everything to have tidally locked."

"There's no single time for locking to happen. It depends on the orbit and the original rate of rotation. But that said, we're talking at most a few million…years."

"Dark can't be that young, can it?"

He shook his head. "I've radiometrically dated rock samples from asteroids. The oldest rocks go back four billion years. So this solar system is that old."

Across the street, the uneven, heartrending weeping became a loud wail.

Dana looked ready to cry. She shook it off. "This system is that old? Then I don't get it."

"If you think *that's* strange, here is another. The coastal-erosion rates in the geological record changed within the last millennium. Until then, the erosion was way too little for the tides we observe."

"Changing when? About the time of the floods?"

"I think so."

"I give up," Dana said. "I can't imagine any explanation."

"I can." But the answer he had found had left him stunned. "I believe that Dark's three moons are...*new*. I think it was their arrival that triggered the tsunamis worldwide."

❋

Blake stopped pacing his living room long enough to ask, "You're serious?"

Eyes kept shifting from Antonio to the wall common with Beth's bedroom. He found that odd. Usually *he* was the one to look away from people.

"Maybe one of us should sit with them," Rikki said, perching on the edge of the sofa. She had yet to examine the datasheet spread across the low table in front of her.

"We all must be in on this discussion," Antonio insisted. "The kids will call if they need anything." Except that Todd wouldn't. Apart for Beth, everyone outside the fence terrified him. "I can't explain why, but I don't believe this *can* wait."

"So," Blake said. "New moons. Rocks four hundred or so klicks across. Seriously?"

From the other room: the synthesized tones of music played on a datasheet. Rikki relaxed a bit without leaning back.

Simple, direct sentences. "It's surprising. I know."

"One such would be surprising," Blake said. "But three? Do you know how implausible that sounds?"

"Nevertheless." Because, of course, *he* would never work with numbers. "It would explain a lot. Moons shifting orbits could tip Dark's axis, could alter the Milankovitch cycles."

"Uh-huh," Blake said. "And do you have any idea how much energy tipping the *planet* takes?"

Rikki had finally taken notice of the annotated globe—and she shuddered.

"What?" Blake asked.

Rikki said, "If Carlos's reconstruction is right, these waves were *huge*. Now ask yourself this. If the moons did this once, however that happened, what's to say it can't happen again?"

✳

"I must have access to Marvin," Antonio insisted, as Rikki vigorously nodded. "I can't model the situation with just data sheets. And we'll need to see Carlos's full analysis, see what that tells us."

Dana and Blake exchanged a long-suffering look. Or maybe it was a he'll-never-get-it look. Blake said, "We can bring the matter up with Li, tell her what we think we found, but you know she'll never go along. Carlos's message has already told you as much."

"But I wouldn't know...how to invent such complex data...sets. Not in a way that hangs together."

Rikki smiled sadly. "Convincing someone that you *don't* know something will be hard."

"With Marvin's help, and...Carlos's, maybe I...could. But without?"

Dana patted his knee. "We'll have to find another way."

What other way *was* there? Antonio tried to think deviously. "Carlos went behind Li's back to contact me. I think I can get through the firewall and threaten to expose him. Threaten to tell Li what he did if he doesn't help us."

Blake and Dana exchanged another look—this time, incredulous.

"An assertion you can't prove and that Carlos will deny," Dana said. "How about you cut out the middleman? If you can do it, hack directly into Marvin."

41

"**F**ool!" The word erupted before Carlos could stop himself.
Antonio or Blake? Either knew enough to try hacking into the settlement's network. Neither was half the programmer Carlos was.

And so: giant crimson letters— INTRUSION ALERT—pulsed over his open datasheet, even as an audible alarm echoed and reechoed in his lab.

After Li's meltdown the day before with Todd, Carlos hated to imagine how she would react. "Alert acknowledged," he called out, and the electronic wail faded. "Marvin, I'll review the security logs. Don't interrupt Li until we know if that was a false alarm."

"She has already been informed," Marvin said.

Then she would be here any minute. Carlos had scarcely fortified himself with Scotch from the flask in his desk when Li arrived, letting in a blast of cold night air. Her fists were clenched and her face livid. It was hard to remember that he had once found her attractive. Beautiful enough, in fact, to have ruined his life—to have ruined *many* lives—over.

Some lives more even than Todd's. If he adjusted, Todd would be better off outside. *He* had made it past the fence in one piece. Unlike little Zoltán, the summer before, guilty only of being a rambunctious five-year-old. Minefields were unforgiving.

Li's opinion be damned, Carlos downed another long swig. He had allowed himself to be conditioned like some kind of lab rat. Why not lose himself in booze?

Because at the margins, on occasion, he could sometimes alleviate bits of the mess he had made possible. He set down his flask.

"Whenever you're ready," Li said. "I imagine you know why I'm here."

Never, in the years since Li's coup, had the four outside attempted to penetrate the net—till now. Scarcely a day after *he* had surreptitiously passed along his own analysis. Antonio's floods must be real.

Carlos said, "Let me check it out." Give me a few minutes to erase the evidence, and get word to Antonio and Blake not *ever* to try that again. "If this is anything more than a glitch, I'll let you know."

"Marvin, was there an intrusion?"

"Yes, Li," the AI said.

"What do you know about it?"

"The probing originates from a datasheet beyond the perimeter. I have triangulated the origin to the residence occupied by Antonio and Dana."

"*Damn* them!" Li shouted. "They won't get away with this. I'll teach them."

"They feed us," Carlos reminded her.

"Indeed." Li smiled wickedly. "Then let them huddle for warmth with the cows in the barn, like the peasants that they are."

✳

As Rikki brushed Beth's hair for the night, the child's bedroom went dark. No, the *house* went dark. Only glimmers of moonlight penetrated the heavy curtain.

In the bathroom, Todd screamed.

"Todd! Stay where you are!" Rikki shouted back.

She pulled aside the curtain, then made her way by memory and moonlight across Beth's room and down the hallway to the closed bathroom door. "It's all right. Something went wrong with the lights. Blake will look into it."

Only the problem wasn't limited to the lights. She wouldn't have heard the house fan over the boy's screaming, but the fan, too, must have stopped working. Not even the slightest breeze came from the wall register.

"Todd!" she shouted again. "Stay in the tub. I'll be right back with a flashlight."

Blake showed up first with his own flashlight. He had been at Antonio's. How had he known?

"Coming in," Blake called. He lifted the hysterical child from the tub and wrapped him in a towel. He rocked the boy until the screaming stopped.

By then, Beth had found a flashlight.

Rikki asked, "How did you know our lights were out?"

Blake grimaced. "It's not just this house. Li cut off all the power for the night."

✳

"I'm bad," Todd moaned. "We're all bad."

Though the boy shied away from Rikki as they fled together up Main Street, he clutched Beth's hand as though for dear life. Rikki didn't mind having one hand free to hold a flashlight, but Todd's rejection cut her like a knife.

"None of us is bad," she told the boy. It didn't interrupt his litany.

The latest forecast showed the overnight temperature dropping below freezing. They could not stay in their home. Nor in Antonio and Dana's home, also without power. This side of the fence, lights shone only from the cow barn, the chicken coop, and the greenhouses. Lights indicated power, and power meant heat.

Within the fence, as though to mock them, bright light streamed from every building.

From behind Rikki, Antonio said, "It's just one night. We'll be fine."

One night if Li doesn't change her mind, Rikki thought. The woman has gone insane. More insane.

"I vote for a greenhouse," Blake said. "Any building that still has heat will reek of manure, but at least a greenhouse should be quiet."

"What about the caves?" Rikki asked.

"My opinion?" Blake said. "That's too far to hike in the dark with kids." They had come to an end of Main Street and stopped. "Maybe in the morning, if the power still hasn't come back."

"*Endeavour* is closer than the caves," Dana said, "offering all the power you could want. With all the comforts of home."

Because, for so long, it *had* been home. Rikki felt a rush of nostalgia—and an inconsolable sense of loss. They had built so much on this world. What if they had just lost it?

She said, "Lead on."

Todd kept moaning as, by moonlight and flashlight, the six of them crept up the shadowy, rubble-strewn slope to the landing field. Picking up on the boy's fear, Beth began whimpering, too. As they approached the landing field, Dana signaled the ship from her data-sheet and its running lights came on.

"The ark!" Todd sobbed. "The stolen ark. This is bad." But when they reached the ship, the cold had bested his fear and with little urging he followed Beth up a cargo-hold ramp.

"I'll get the children settled in the crew quarters," Rikki said.

"Cargo hold one is empty," Dana said. "We'll talk there."

The little ones were exhausted, from the trek and emotionally. Rikki got both children settled in hammocks. After dimming the galley ceiling lamp to night-light levels, she headed for the cargo hold. The last thing she heard from crew quarters came from Todd, something about having been cast out.

As she entered the hold, Antonio was saying, "But we have to know more about the moons."

"No one's arguing," Dana said. "The question is how. Look where hacking got us."

Standing in the hatchway, Rikki cleared her throat. "If I could interrupt."

"All ideas cheerfully accepted," Blake said. "We've got nothing."

"Not this idea," Rikki said. "And I'll start by admitting I'm no Biblical scholar."

She knew a few of the old stories—didn't everyone?—but she had grown up knowing God as just Someone invoked to add zest to cursing. Learning that the Church made Galileo recant what he had seen with his own eyes hadn't given her religion, either. But Dana sometimes seemed to respect the old tradition, and Rikki would not offend her friend for anything.

Rikki continued, "Still, listening to Todd scares the crap out of me. Li has that poor child—and so, I assume, all the children—believing she is God's messenger. Li has made herself into Noah and Lot and Moses and I-don't-know-who-else all rolled into one. Casting us out of the settlement, commanding us to feed everyone else by the sweat of our brow, she's like God banishing Adam and Eve for original sin. To contradict Li is more than wrong, it's heresy."

Antonio nodded. "To the children we're the bad people."

"It's horrible, I know," Dana said. "But the flooding, the moons—"

"Are parts of a bigger problem," Rikki interrupted. "We have to be *one* colony again. The problem is bigger than getting at the lab instruments, bigger than access to Marvin."

"Bigger than…drowning like rats?"

Rikki slammed the bulkhead with a fist. "Yes, damn it. Bigger than that. Li was right, years back, about one thing. Our survival was never about us. It's about who and what comes after us. Despite every warning, despite Li's evident fascination with every manner of authoritarian and utopian society, we allowed her to take charge. We continue to do her bidding. We've stood by as she brainwashed more and more children. Is *that* the legacy we plan to leave behind?"

Stony silence—and then the other three began speaking at once.

"She's got us over a barrel," Antonio said. "Without endangering the children we…we can't…"

"There's no way past the land mines," Dana said. "If I could get *over* the mines, silently, then maybe…"

"There has to be a way to disable them," Blake said. "I keep racking my brains for something new. I admit Marvin or Carlos can be as good with software as us, or Antonio and my hack wouldn't have gotten caught. But maybe if I can…"

"Just *stop* it!" Deep inside Rikki, something had snapped. "All of you. I've heard it too many times. Pilot our way in. Invent our way in. And tonight's failure, hacking our way in, the transgression for which Li would freeze us back into submission. I am *so* sick of the delusions!

"To rescue those children and redeem ourselves, we need to start working *together*."

42

B ulging, rippling—and threatening, with each errant draft, to tear itself apart against the rough stone walls of the sink-hole—the hot-air balloon strained against its tethers. Its eth-anol-burning heater roared.

"Eighteenth-century tech," Dana said, shaking her head. "Your wife."

"You asked to pilot your way in," Blake said. In the night-dark sinkhole shaft, he was a shadow: face smeared with grease; flight suit, gloves, and boots all matte black. She was made up the same. "Be careful what you wish for."

Was it piloting when you couldn't steer the damned thing? Well, they wouldn't be in the balloon long. One way or another.

"Uh-huh." She glanced at her wrist. "Time to go."

With little time to spare. They would have a bare forty minutes tonight without a single moon in the sky. In duration of darkness, several other nights would have been better, but the prevailing wind had not cooperated. Tomorrow offered a longer window—and the forecast of snow. Snow and reduced visibility were complications they didn't need. The later into the season it got, damned near every night might bring snow, even a howling blizzard.

"Saddle up," he agreed.

She pretended not to have heard the quaver in his voice.

Dana clipped them together, chest pressed against his back. She wore a bulky black backpack; he a black satchel strapped over his stomach. Pockets in their flight suits bulged with tools and supplies. More gadgets—holstered or bagged lest they clink together or reflect any light—dangled from their tool belts. Stealthy, they might hope to be. Agile, they were not. Groping behind her, she backed them onto the seat, little more than a child's swing, that dangled from the bal-loon. They slipped on smart specs. He grabbed hold of the seat's ropes.

She throttled down the burner to its pilot-light setting and switched off the dimmed flashlight that hung from her belt. The seconds she gave her eyes to adjust to the dark—while, within the balloon, the air would already be cooling—seemed interminable. The only sounds were a slow, echoing drip from deep within the cave, the faint hiss of the burner's blue flame, and the creak of tether ropes. She wondered how much more tension stalactites could take before they snapped.

The better question might be how much more tension *she* could take. Search and Rescue was a young person's game.

"Godspeed," she wished them both, then armed and triggered the tether release.

They fell up through the sinkhole into a starry sky.

✻

She could only guess at where the ground was. A hundred meters beneath her toes, at the least, the distance growing by the second as the balloon wafted upward and the slope tipped down toward Darwin Sea. A portable radar unit would have been nice—and its pulses might have given them away.

"Are we having fun yet?" Blake asked.

"Ask me in a few minutes."

With so much gear to gather and, more often, to cobble together—without doing anything to arouse the suspicions of those inside the compound—they had managed only a single test run. A hemisphere away, where it was late spring. In full daylight. With winter almost upon them *here*, determined to act *now*, there had not been time for a second rehearsal under more realistic conditions. Mostly Dana had practiced in a flight simulator, also improvised. How good could that be?

"Trust me," Antonio had said of his improvised trainer. "It's only physics."

Quit griping, Dana chided herself. Had the harvest not been complete, she'd have had to prepare with nothing but simulation. And scolded herself again: stay focused on the here and now.

On her specs, a red disk represented her target, the settlement's puddle of illumination digitally replaced to protect her night vision.

Even by starlight she could sense where the sea must meet the sky. If she saw horizon, so did her specs. As camera and processor identified individual buildings and interpreted their foreshortened appearance, the specs overlaid in dim red: contour lines, distance and bearing, altitude and ground speed.

Antonio had called retrofitting nav mode into the specs simple physics, too.

Borne along by the wind, the air seemed still. But this was late autumn, and the ground had long since surrendered the day's scant warmth to a cloudless sky and back into space. Dana, shivering, cranked up the current to the heating elements of her flight suit.

"Um, Dana?" Blake said.

"I know." The higher they rose, the farther the wind pushed them off course. But she needed altitude. "Trust the pilot."

"With my life. Every time we launch."

They had yet to reach the altitude she wanted, but the range to the target kept changing and not for the better. She muttered, "Close enough for government work."

"What's that?"

"It's time," she translated. She armed and smacked the seat release. Freed of their weight, the balloon bounded away.

Plummeting to the ground, Dana declared, "*Now* we're having fun."

✳

Sooner than her specs advised, trusting her instincts, Dana yanked the ripcord.

Nylon fabric whipped from her backpack, grabbed by the air stream, heard and felt more than seen. The paraglider, like the balloon they had just jettisoned, like their flight suits, was all black.

Air rammed into the glider's cells. With a brutal yank the inflated wing braked their fall—and knocked the breath right out of her. Her specs went flying into the darkness. Grabbing the risers, she flattened their angle of attack. Shifting her weight, she started them on a slow, banking curve toward the island of light below.

"I need your specs," she told Blake.

"I lost mine, too," he said. "Damned inferior straps. You should fire your engineer."

"Not a problem," she assured him.

That we don't know what we'll find once we're down? That this is my first night jump, ever? That apart from the one practice run, I haven't paraglided since college? More than fifty standard *years* ago! In a sane universe, I'd be taking up knitting.

Those were problems.

❋

No one's looking, Blake kept reminding himself. If someone were, this is the dark of night. We're all in black. They'd never expect us to arrive *this* way. And anyway, we'll be on the ground soon.

As buildings loomed out of the darkness—as he and Dana fell out of the freaking sky!—that became *too* soon.

"Get ready," Dana whispered into his ear. "Legs together. Knees bent."

Turning into the wind, their boots all but grazing the top of the stockade, they swooped toward the open end of the playground. He felt a jerk as Dana flared the wing. They were coming in fast! Maybe a meter off the ground, she hit the brakes again. Hard.

She hissed, "Hit the deck running."

He did, and somehow their feet tangled. They tumbled to the ground, Blake on the bottom with the wind knocked out of him. He heard the paraglider flapping.

Dana unclipped them. Faster than he could climb to his feet, she had off her backpack. He helped her squeeze air from the paraglider cells, wincing at every wheeze and faint whistle. Together, they crammed the flapping, deflated wing into her pack. She shrugged the pack back on.

"My turn," he mouthed.

"Li? Is that you?"

Carlos's voice! He wasn't in sight—yet.

They sprinted across the playground, Dana hanging onto his arm and limping. She had injured herself, doubtless his fault from his clumsy landing. They flattened themselves against the childcare center, between windows.

She took out her air gun. Blake, lacking her training, not trusting himself with a lethal weapon, left his air gun in its holster. He went for his improvised shock device, of use only up close.

Carlos emerged from behind the childcare center, cigar in hand, its tip aglow, to peer into the playground. "Li? Is that you?"

Blake tased him.

Carlos folded, spasming.

They had rehearsed takedowns. In the instant after Blake cut the circuit, Dana had her knee in Carlos's back and his arm twisted behind his back. Blake slapped tape over Carlos's mouth, then offered Dana one of their improvised plasticuffs. She bound Carlos's wrists together behind him.

Blake pocketed his weapon's spent cartridge and reloaded before he and Dana hauled Carlos to his feet. With current no longer flowing, Carlos was already recovering. His eyes round, his gaze darting from one captor to the other, Carlos followed meekly where they led.

Toward the bunker.

Now it was Blake's turn.

✳

The bunker door sensor flashed green at Carlos's handprint, lifted weeks earlier from a datasheet. Who could have guessed they would end up in possession of Carlos's actual hand?

"I thought that would come in handy," Blake whispered. His own handprint might still have been in the system. And it might have triggered an alarm.

Dana did a slit-her-own-throat gesture. As in: shut up.

He had never doubted he could bypass the lock—security on the bunker was to keep out children, not bank robbers—but happily matters hadn't come to that. The handprint was quicker.

Blake doused the door hinges with lubricant spray. A test tug gave off a faint squeak, so he lowered the door and sprayed more. On his second try, the door opened silently.

Apart from the wind, the compound was deathly still.

In the bunker, only the glimmer of scattered LEDs broke inky darkness.

Dana crept down the stairs, clutching the handrail. Still not putting much weight on her left leg, he noticed, before she disappeared into shadow. Again, Blake cursed his big, dumb feet.

At Blake's shove, Carlos followed her down.

When Blake lowered the massive door from inside, Dana was ready with her flashlight. Not trusting an old gasket to be light-tight, he taped over the gap between the two doors. Only then did he pat the top-of-the-stairs wall sensor and activate the bunker's ceiling lamps.

Two blinking packages, just as Rikki had described, were bound to support beams high overhead. The timers showed almost twenty hours remaining till a reset would be needed.

One way or another, matters would be resolved before then.

"Safe to talk?" he whispered.

"Should be," Dana said. "You know, having Carlos here changes things. Li didn't build these bombs."

Doubtless Carlos had built the devices. Under other circumstances, he might have been the right person to disarm them. Not at gunpoint, shaking as he was. Not with his nostrils flared wide, his eyes round, and a tic. No *way* would Blake risk that man messing with detonators.

"If I have questions, he's here," Blake said. "But Carlos is no more an explosives expert than I am. The controls he devised will be simple, like in the land mine I took apart. We agreed upfront to that."

But had that agreement reflected sound logic, or only shared wishful thinking? Believing anything else, they could never have dared this raid.

"It's your call," Dana said. "Let's get him out of the way."

"I'll handle it. And I'm sorry about your foot."

"Sprained ankle, I think. I'll live."

Blake pushed Carlos toward a mound of seed sacks. "Sit. Do *not* make a sound."

Carlos nodded. Hands still bound behind him, he dropped to his knees. From there he swiveled, toppled awkwardly, and squirmed into a sitting position, his back against a couple of sacks.

The day of Li's coup, Rikki had seen a folded stepladder leaning against a bunker wall. Too bad the ladder wasn't still here. Blake found the chain hoist's remote control and lowered the steel hook.

Too small to accommodate his foot, alas. Catching the hook in a link of the sturdy chain, he fashioned a simple loop. When the bunker was new, he had moved cargo far heavier than himself using this hoist.

With the loop positioned in the notch between the heel and sole of a boot, the chain snug in the crook of an arm, Blake told Dana, "I'm ready. Raise me up."

43

I'm going to die.

It scared Carlos, just a bit, how little that prospect scared him.

Death could come in many ways. Blake might blow up the three of them, together with the future of mankind. Or Li could happen upon them and—by accident or in a rage—do the same. Or someone might slit his throat while he sat trussed up, helpless.

While Blake examined the bombs up close and Dana's attention was on him, Carlos began inching bound hands to his side.

The left-hand pant pocket was where he kept his cigar-trimming penknife.

✻

Li had no idea what, but something was off.

She raised her head from the pillow, listening. Fussing newborns, to the extent noise cancellation failed to negate their babbling. The children on duty, crooning and shushing. Outside the window, the wail of the wind.

None of that would have awakened her.

Quickly, quietly, she dressed. She buckled on her holster, tucked the remote detonator in a pocket, and went outside.

✻

"What is *taking* so long?" Rikki asked.

Antonio, his face a featureless, pale oval, might have shrugged. In the unlit garage, it was hard to know. He said, "No news is…no news."

True but not helpful, she thought.

Outside the garage, by the glow of newly risen Euripides, the compound appeared normal. For all she knew, Blake and Dana hadn't even managed to make the attempt. She could only wait and worry. About them. About two young children left home unsupervised.

About all the children, most as yet unborn, their futures hanging in the balance tonight.

✽

Slowly, straining to reach, and entirely by feel, Carlos worked the penknife from his pocket. The way he slumped against a seed bag, his captors couldn't see. He froze whenever Dana started to turn.

On the hoist, muttering to himself, Blake must have bypassed the circuits on one bomb. Its counter had gone dark without blowing them all to pieces. Blake had been right, of course. The circuits were as simple as Carlos knew how, as straightforward as he and Marvin together could devise, the better not to blow himself up.

Tearing one fingernail after another, trying to pry out the blade of the penknife—without crying out, wincing at the pain, or in *any* way attracting attention—Carlos tried to imagine how the others had gotten their hands on a land mine.

The blade, finally, had pivoted enough for him to grasp between finger and thumb. Muffled by his body and the seed sacks, he barely heard soft click as the blade snapped into its locked-open position. His captors were across the bunker and otherwise distracted. They couldn't have heard—but he watched and waited anyway before moving.

Then, with slow, precise motions, Carlos began sawing at his restraint.

✽

The digital display on the second bomb went dark, with Blake still alive to notice. None too soon, he thought, his left leg trembling with the strain. He could no longer feel that foot, mashed through his boot by his weight pressing on the chain.

"Got it," he announced with relief.

"Never doubted it," Dana answered.

Blake worked the metal hook of a bungee cord beneath the strap fastening one of the inert bombs to its support beam. Wrapping the bungee cord around the bomb, he hooked both ends together. He added two more bungee cords before snipping the strap. Just as carefully, he unstrapped the second bomb.

Then, one by one, to Carlos's goggle-eyed stare, Blake tossed the bombs down to Dana.

✳

Something had awakened Li, but she couldn't figure it out. She circled the main corridor of the childcare center. Nothing out of place. She circled the building from outside. Still nothing out of the ordinary.

Until, by moonlight, she encountered one of Carlos's precious, hand-rolled cigars. All but unsmoked. Lying on the ground. Flattened at one end as though by a broad shoe.

Li whirled about, searching around her for intruders.

✳

Long after Eve was finally alone, she stayed in bed. Shivering. Degraded. Ashamed.

"Serve your elders and serve God," she had been taught.

If God was good, why did serving make her feel so...sinful?

Eve threw off the tangled top sheet. She gargled and brushed and spat, over and over. She showered under scalding hot water, then toweled herself roughly until her skin felt raw.

Still, she felt dirty.

She hated herself—again—for not using the knife she had long hidden under the mattress. Once more she thought about turning the blade on herself. But if she succeeded, the ordeal would only shift to Denise, or Leah, or another girl she had helped to raise. Another friend.

This had to end.

She dressed, sliding the knife into her waistband, her untucked shirt hiding the haft.

✳

The disarmed bombs lashed together and sealed inside a black bag, the balloon rig ready to inflate, Blake dared to believe: *we're actually going to pull this off.* "Ready when you are," he said.

Hobbling up the bunker stairs, he had limped worse than Dana. Neither of them wanted to unlace his boot to see how badly he had injured the foot.

While Dana shone her flashlight up at him he flicked off the overhead lamps. By the beam of her flashlight he switched on his own, turned its beam as dim as it would go, and hung the flashlight from his belt. He peeled off the tape between the doors.

"This is it," he whispered. He turned off his flashlight altogether. Slowly, silently, he opened one of the heavy doors, then stepped outside. He retrieved the balloon rig from where he had set it on the top step, attached the bag with the two disarmed bombs, and took hold of the rig by its hydrogen tank—

Failing dismally in his vow *not* to remember the Hindenburg. To fill even a small balloon with hot air would have taken time they might not have, even if they had been willing to risk the flame giving them away. Helium would have been ideal—if they had had any. What they had was hydrogen, easily split from water.

Quit stalling.

By the ambient light of the compound, he opened the gas valve.

Caught by the wind, the balloon floated off toward the Darwin Sea. In the darkness, he soon lost sight of the balloon.

✳

Handgun at the ready, Li prowled the compound looking for intruders. Since the crushed cigar, she had found nothing. If the ground gave any trace of strangers, she couldn't tell their footprints apart from hers and Carlos's. Carlos himself was nowhere to be found.

A *hiss!*

She spun toward the unexpected noise. Almost at once, the noise stopped.

From behind the childcare center, *something* large, round, and dark soared into the night sky.

She began firing.

✳

Blam! Bla-blam!

"Something's gone wrong!" Rikki hissed. "We've got to help!"

She grabbed her knapsack and jumped onto the bulldozer, priming its engine. Antonio hopped up onto the running board behind her seat. To save seconds, they had left the overhead door open. As she turned from the garage onto Main Street, the shooting continued.

Those weren't air guns!

With the bulldozer's blade hoisted as a shield, Rikki couldn't see straight ahead. Her gaze sweeping from side to side, she struggled to keep the vehicle on the roadway. Crescent Euripides, just rising, seemed to cast more shadows than light. At no more than a walking pace, afraid she would tip them into the ditch and snap a tread—or a neck—the dozer lumbered toward the fence.

"Now," Antonio yelled into her ear, and she shoved the transmission into idle.

They leapt free just before the bulldozer, coasting forward, rammed the concrete gate. Scrambling to her feet, gritting her teeth, hands pressed to her ears, she dashed from the minefield about to receive the bulldozer's weight.

But the blast that flung her to the ground came from overhead.

44

The airburst sent Blake tumbling down the bunker stairs and crashing into Dana. Though his ears rang, he sensed a cascade of smaller blasts had followed that huge first one.

Around the floor of the bunker, status lights shone a healthy green. The explosions had been distant enough. The embryo banks and Marvin's servers remained okay!

Helping Dana to her feet, Blake said, "We have to take out Li." He couldn't hear himself speak, but she nodded. Shutting Carlos in the bunker to deal with later, they went looking.

Just within the fence stood the twisted remains of a bulldozer. In silhouette before the dancing flames, holding a gun, stood a woman.

✸

Eve clapped her hands to her ears, shrieking in terror. In the childcare center, hundreds of voices joined hers.

She remembered the loud noise when Ms. Rikki was cast out. Liberation Day, Ms. Li called it. But *Eve* had not been liberated. Quite the contrary.

By the flames at the open gate, she saw Li. And near the bunker, their faces in shadow, two people. Two *elders*. Neither was tall enough to be Mr. Carlos. Then the strangers began slinking toward Ms. Li.

What horrible thing had the bad people done?

Creeping closer, Eve found something on the ground outside the bunker. Something that did not belong. It went into her waistband, beneath her shirttails, next to the knife.

✸

Carlos had all but cut through his restraints when a bone-rattling explosion smashed him into the hard floor. His reflexive spasm snapped the plasticuffs.

He guessed that Blake and Dana had accidentally triggered the bombs. And that the concussion set off…some of the land mines?… as a rat-a-tat of lesser explosions shook the bunker. He wondered about the dazzling blue flash through the crack between the bunker doors the instant before the huge blast had struck.

On the slight chance Blake and Dana had survived, Carlos counted to a hundred before creeping from the bunker.

✸

Roaring flames. Wailing children, in the childcare center and, more and more, spilling out onto the grounds. From speakers across the compound, Marvin's vain exhortations for calm and quiet. Beyond the fence Antonio and Rikki paced, stymied by the fire that engulfed the twisted remains of a bulldozer.

Dazed, bloodied, Li stood and gaped.

"It's *over*," Rikki shouted through the fence.

In answer, Li shot at her. Chips flew from a concrete fence picket, and Rikki and Antonio dived for the ground.

Nothing is over till *I* say it's over, Li thought. But it might have been. What the *hell* was that stealthy object she had destroyed? What the *hell* had the peasants tried? To fight bombs with bombs?

Fuck 'em. *Après moi, le déluge.*

Li took the remote from her pocket. She armed it and the lamp changed from red to green. She flipped up the safety cover, tapped in the security code. The green light started to blink. She pressed the detonator button.

Nothing.

Again and again she jabbed the button. Not a damned thing happened. In a rage, she flung the worthless remote to the ground.

Gun in hand, Li ran deeper into the compound. *Someone* would pay for this outrage.

✸

"Damn," Dana whispered. She had yet to get close enough to risk taking a shot. And between her sprained ankle and Blake's maimed foot, neither of them could keep up.

Not that she wanted to shoot the last medical doctor in the world—however bat-shit crazy Li had gone. That wasn't why Dana hesitated. She *saved* people, damn it!

But exiling Li and Carlos to some cave far, far away? Letting them break their own backs for a change to feed themselves? Dealing with them only if and when some dire emergency should require their technical skills? *That* would be just fine.

If only she could get close enough to tase the bitch....

Blake said, "Is this a bad time to mention I seem to have lost my air gun somewhere?"

Not that he could have hit anything at this range, anyway. "It's been that kind of day," Dana told him.

"So what now?"

"We hobble after Li," Dana said.

✸

A bunker door was open!

Li tapped on the bunker's overhead lamps, went down several steps, and looked up into the rafters. No bombs!

Après moi, le déluge.

Gun in hand, she considered how best to spend her ammo. Servers and embryo banks alike had been designed with massive redundancy. Even a clip emptied at close range was no guarantee of revenge.

Maybe there was another way.

✳

Rikki aimed a fire extinguisher at the bulldozer's tortured, twisted remains and the flaming puddle of ethanol beneath it. When the foam spray sputtered, she switched to a second extinguisher. Then a third.

Burning wreckage was strewn across a large area downwind. Antonio ran to douse those fires, lest a shifting wind carry flaming debris into the settlement.

The last flame around the bulldozer succumbed to the foam. The creaks and pings of cooling metal slowed. The smoke cleared. Antonio had returned.

"Good enough," she decided.

She slipped on insulated gloves. Antonio donned his own pair. One by one, they scrambled up onto the steaming wreckage—

From which they leapt past the edge of the minefield, to run into the compound.

To help Blake and Dana.

✳

Her ankle about to give way, struggling not to pant with exhaustion, not to *collapse* with exhaustion, not to give them away by crunching on the broken glass strewn *everywhere*, falling farther and farther behind, Dana limped after their quarry. Li popped into the open bunker (Huh! Hadn't they left the doors closed?), only to emerge after a few seconds with her face twisted into a feral snarl.

Leaving Carlos on the floor, bound and gagged? Not plausible. Li would want help. He must have escaped on his own, leaving the door open in his haste to find her.

The op is falling apart, and so am I.

Li strode into the structure that housed their backup, etha-nol-burning generator. This time she didn't come right out.

"Idiot." Blake swore under his breath. "I missed a scenario."

"What's that?"

"Power to the embryo freezers. The emergency fuel cells in the bunker will last only for a few hours. If Li manages, even for a day, to cut off power to the bunker…"

✳

Just for a moment, reflected in a window—one of the few panes she had seen intact—Li had glimpsed two figures, all in black, limping after her. The enemy.

She dashed into the backup power plant, ran through the build-ing, to come out the backdoor. *Behind* her pursuers.

"That's far enough." For emphasis, she fired a round into the air. "Turn around."

Beneath the face grease, she scarcely recognized Blake and Dana.

"It's about time you got here," Li said as Carlos emerged from the darkness. "Take their guns."

Approaching from behind, he gingerly relieved Dana of two kludged-looking weapons and Blake of a third. Two guns went into his pockets and one into his belt.

"Go. Keep an eye out for the others," Li ordered. Carlos nodded and faded away.

"As for the two of you," Li said, never allowing her aim to waver, "it's time you learn how badly you blew it tonight."

✳

Eve lurked in the shadows.

Mr. Blake and Ms. Dana were on their knees, hands raised be-hind their heads, fingers interlaced. Throughout the compound, aban-doned, children moaned and whimpered and wailed.

And Ms. Li…gloated.

The two forced to kneel before her were irredeemably bad, blas-phemers, heretics, fallen from God's grace. So Eve had been taught. So she felt, so she knew, at a visceral level.

But she didn't *understand*.

Why did Mr. Blake play with that little girl, Beth, always so patient? Why did he and the girl keep inviting poor, blasphemous, terrified Todd to join their games?

Why did Mr. Blake not *seem* bad?

Unless good could extend beyond the wall, just as evil had reached within....

While doubts roiled her mind, while Euripides climbed over the fence to spill its wan light down Main Street, the adults prattled on.

✳

Li's voice!

Rikki peeked around a corner to find Dana and Blake at gunpoint. A cluster of children, wide-eyed, peered back from the shadows. "We've got to stop Li," she whispered to Antonio.

She took out her air gun. Antonio took out his.

"On three," she whispered. "One. Two."

The gun rammed into her back preempted "three."

"Hands up," Carlos said.

He took her weapon. From the corner of an eye she saw him disarm Antonio.

"I've got them," Carlos called loudly, herding them forward, "and their guns."

✳

Adult conversation often bewildered Eve, but this was the worst ever. Not just the words but entire concepts were without meaning to her. Milankovitch cycles? Tsunami? Social justice? Utopia? Extinction? What was phosphorus, and why would they always need more of it? What were the proletariat, totalitarianism, and sociopath loons?

Still, Eve made sense of snippets. Something about the bunker. Embryos, she knew, was the adult term for all the children waiting to be born. Electricity and power (were they the same thing?) made light and heat and refrigerated food. Mr. Carlos had once told Eve that electricity was a wonderful thing and that, if she would study very hard, someday she could understand it.

Power, apparently, also kept the embryos cold enough not to spoil.

Why would Ms. Li threaten to take power from the unborn babies?

And why was it the four who knelt on the ground, the supposed bad ones, who pleaded for the defenseless?

Stepping from the shadows, Eve said, "No one will harm the babies. I will not allow it."

Ms. Li motioned her over. "Come here, little one."

Her skin crawling, Eve repeated, "No one."

"I'll explain later," Li said, still beckoning. Her gun hand never wavered from those on their knees before her. "Child, know that evil speaks cunningly to confuse you."

Am I confused? Eve wondered. Or for the first time, am I seeing and hearing clearly?

She took from beneath her shirttails the weapon she had found. Finger on its trigger, mimicking how Ms. Li held her gun, Eve swept the barrel back and forth. Tears ran down her cheeks. "No one harms the babies."

From Mr. Blake, a sharp intake of breath.

"*This* is your brave new world, Li?" Ms. Rikki asked. "Children driven to kill, to save other children?"

"Eve, bring me that," Mr. Carlos said, a vein twitching in his neck.

"No!" Eve sobbed. "I need this to save the babies. I *must* save the babies. Somebody *help* me."

"Come to me," Ms. Li ordered. "Now! You will do as I say!"

Eve held her ground. She knew that tone of voice all too well.

"I don't want you to get hurt, Eve," Mr. Carlos said.

Sobbing, Eve raised her weapon. It did not matter, least of all to her, if she got hurt. She must save the babies. She must spare the other children—especially the girls—from evil.

From bad, bad, evil Ms. Li.

"Carlos," Ms. Li growled, "It's time that you put an end to this foolishness."

"I agree," he said.

He pivoted, and the gun in his hand sputtered: *pfft, pfft, pfft.*

On Ms. Li's pale shirt, dark splotches blossomed. She toppled face first to the ground.

Mr. Carlos handed Ms. Dana his gun. "It's over," he said. "Above all, it's over for that poor abused child. For what it's worth, whether or not you believe me, I never touched these kids."

Dropping her weapon, sobbing with relief, Eve crumpled to the ground.

EPILOGUE

(Spring, Year Eleven)

"This isn't a race," Blake called out.

Castor, revving the engine, showing off for his friends, didn't hear. At least he pretended not to hear. Four boys and three girls, waiting their turns on the tractor, cheered him on.

Eve, who already had had her turn—and squashed three plastic traffic cones, a personal best—gazed up at Castor with round, adoring eyes. He revved the engine even louder.

"Slow *down!*" Blake shouted. What had he been thinking, assigning those two kids to the same group? "And take it easy on that curve!"

With an innocent expression, letting up on the accelerator, Castor made it around the curve at the north end of the driving course without tipping over. But two more traffic cones went down.

They needed more tractor drivers to put additional fields, distant fields, under cultivation as insurance against future floods. And so: driving lessons on the barricaded-off end of the landing field. None of the kids had acquired the finesse to drive on a slope or over uneven, boulder-strewn terrain, much less on the shifting-beneath-your-treads surface of a silt plain, much less to till or sow. If they *had* mastered driving, it remained too early in the season to farm. Snow mounds still dotted the landscape, and a final wintry blast remained possible.

Blake hoped not. On Main Street, two potted cherry trees had already bloomed.

"Time's up," he called. "Andrew, you're up next."

Castor used the brakes as overenthusiastically as he had the accelerator. The tractor jerked to a stop, rocking the boy in his seat.

"Take it *easy!*" Blake yelled. "Set the parking brake. Turn off the engine."

"Yessir," Castor mumbled abashedly, before climbing down from the tractor.

Into the transitory, blessed quiet drifted the sounds of the settlement. Laughter from Main Street, where Dana lectured a group of kids, their daily milking chores done, on basic cultivation. Happy chatter from the greenhouses, where Rikki had yet more kids—Beth and her inseparable friend Todd among them—hard at work. Clanging and banging from inside the garage, where Carlos assembled more tractors. From the playground, where Antonio supervised the little ones, hollers and squeals of glee. And from the classrooms of the childcare center, led by Marvin (who also kept watch over the toddlers and babies), the competing drones of several group reading lessons.

Andrew climbed up onto the tractor. With much gnashing of teeth, both Blake's and within the gearbox, the boy got the vehicle into motion.

When Blake dared to glance away, down toward the Darwin Sea, he noted with satisfaction the rainbow-spanning palette of lichens and the flowering (however spindly the trees) of the orchards. Even the stubble of last year's corn crop introduced a touch of color—*pale browns*—into the vista.

As the sun climbed and, on occasion, the wind died down, it was positively *nice* outside.

Maybe this weather would last. Observatories on all the moons agreed: the cooling trend had flattened out. PFC levels continued to climb. Someday soon, maybe they would even find the time to check out the moons more thoroughly. Antonio wouldn't stop asking to go back.

"Andrew," Blake called. "Good job. Come to a smooth stop. Denise, you're next."

And the tractor accelerated.

"*Brakes!*" Blake yelled. "The *left* pedal."

"Sorry," Andrew said. The tractor slowed.

"Having fun yet?"

Blake whirled around.

Rikki grinned. "What, you didn't hear my dainty footsteps over the sound of your own screaming?"

"Try teaching ten- and eleven-year-olds to drive. See how calm *you* are." And to eager-beaver, beaver-toothed Denise, already groping for the brake release, Blake called, "Not yet! Fasten your seatbelt!"

Rikki said, "Only in Dark years. In standard years, they're teenagers."

"And that's somehow better?" he said, in mock despair.

"You do realize," Rikki said, "in a few years our daughter will be a teenager, too."

"And that's somehow better?" he repeated.

She laughed, pointing.

At the back of his cluster of trainees, Castor and Eve held hands.

The sun warm on his face, Blake considered: a young man's fancy lightly turning to thoughts of love. And: aren't those two cute?

And, with the gentle breeze riffling Rikki's hair, her cheeks aglow in the morning light, her eyes sparkling, Blake decided: I'm not so old, yet, after all.

This world still guarded her secrets, but of two things he was certain.

They had made a home here.

And, on many levels, spring was coming to Dark.

✳

After consecutive cycles of anomalous sensor readings, low-level automation roused the Supervisor.

Something had gone awry. Something that mere automation could not undo.

Something the Supervisor itself did not understand.

For years it had labored. To remove excess carbon dioxide. To wring the excess moisture from the atmosphere and deposit the water, as snow and ice, at the poles. To cool and dry a world.

And it had.

All according to plan.

Until now.

While the Supervisor, its preparations complete, had lain dormant, global temperature had ceased its decline. And an exotic gas, nowhere to be found in the Supervisor's databanks, had appeared, had accumulated, had begun to *warm* the climate. Nothing in the Supervisor's programming could explain the changes.

It ran simulations. Fine-tuned hundreds of parameters in its planetary-engineering model. Assessed its options. Simulated anew. Reassessed. Reached a conclusion.

From its perch on the planet's innermost moon, the Supervisor radioed orders.

A hundred asteroids turned mottled, or striped, or entirely changed shade. And those surfaces continued to change:

—Morphing and shifting in real time as the rocky bodies spun and tumbled.

—Attentive to the distant sun.

—Mindful of the feeble pressure of light itself.

—Delicately harnessing the slightest of differences in pressure between light striking pale and dark surfaces.

All but imperceptibly, orbits began to shift.

Soon after arriving in this solar system, and on a grand scale, by similar means it had redirected asteroids to *avoid* this planet. The Supervisor's purpose now was quite different.

A few years hence, the dust hurled into the atmosphere by asteroid impacts would quickly cool things down—

This world had been entrusted to the Supervisor's care. It *would* be ready, on schedule, for the arrival of Those Who Come....

✳●✳

Afterword and Acknowledgments

D id a gamma-ray burst bring on the Ordovician Extinction: the sudden obliteration of more than half the world's marine species? Not surprisingly, the jury remains out. The evidence is indirect and the events beyond ancient.

Might a modern-day GRB scour Earth's continents clean of life (including the lives of certain curious primates) and even bring the slaughter far into the oceanic deeps?

Yes. Before that happens, let's hope humanity has starships.

If we do, will the mechanism be a Dark Energy Drive? That's harder to know. Dark Energy is less an explanation than a label of convenience for our present state of ignorance. Still, *something* pushes apart galaxies, causes the accelerating expansion of the universe. Scientists will, someday, learn to understand that something. Who is to say they won't learn to harness it?

And on, and on, it goes. From cosmic strings to terraforming, from alternative biochemical schemes for life to moving asteroids by applying sunlight pressure, my aim with *Dark Secret* was to hew to scientific research and foreseeable technology.

Even, in a speculative sense, Those Who Come.

New extrasolar planets are discovered, seemingly, every day. A few of those planets (like Dark) have been Earth-like in size. A few (like Dark) orbit within their sun's Goldilocks zone, wherein water can remain liquid on a planet's surface.

Are any of those worlds home to life? Not to anyone's knowledge. But *might* there be living worlds Out There? It's difficult for me to believe otherwise, given how Earthly life fills every conceivable niche—and niches that were once thought inconceivable. High in the stratosphere. Deep in oceanic trenches. In the highly radioactive cooling ponds of nuclear power plants. In arsenic-tainted lakes. Inside rock, deep within the earth's crust.

None of which is to claim expertise in these (and other) disciplines upon which the novel draws, although I know more now than when I began work on the book. I won't bore anyone with a list of reference materials. The people who were generous with their expertise—and patient with my many questions—are another matter. Them, I would like to acknowledge.

For many topics astrophysical, I thank Andreas Albrecht, Ph.D. (University of California, Davis) and Neil Cornish, Ph.D. (University of Montana).[1]

Regarding matters of geology, planetary engineering, and orbital mechanics, I thank science journalist—and fellow science-fiction author—Richard A. Lovett, Ph.D.

For feedback on psychological aspects, I thank Jeffrey Barth, Ph.D. (University of Virginia).

Where the novel gets the details right, thank the experts. As always, responsibility for extrapolations, errors, simplifications, and fictional license lies with the author.

Last but certainly not least, I thank my first and favorite reader: my wife, Ruth.

— *Edward M. Lerner*

---

[1] The possibility that the speed of light is faster near a cosmic string than elsewhere came courtesy of astrophysicist João Magueijo, Ph.D., Imperial College, London, from his engaging book, *Faster Than The Speed of Light: The Story of a Scientific Speculation*.

About the Author

Hugo Award-nominated author Edward M. Lerner worked in high tech and aerospace for thirty years, as everything from engineer to senior vice president, for much of that time writing science fiction as a hobby. Since 2004 he has written full-time.

His novels range from near-future technothrillers, like *Small Miracles* and *Energized*, to traditional SF, like his InterstellarNet series, to (collaborating with Larry Niven) the space-opera epic Fleet of Worlds series of *Ringworld* companion novels. Lerner's most recent novel, *InterstellarNet: Enigma*, won the inaugural Canopus Award for "works that contribute to the excitement, knowledge, and understanding of interstellar space exploration and travel."

His short fiction has appeared in anthologies, collections, and many of the usual SF magazines. He also writes the occasional non-fiction technology article.

Lerner lives in Virginia with his wife, Ruth.

His website is *www.edwardmlerner.com*.

Printed in Great Britain
by Amazon